FIVE BRAND-NEW WORLDS ... FOR THE PRICE OF BECOMING MERCENARIES

Corwin felt himself tense involuntarily as the Troft walked into the Council room and announced in its high-pitched catertalk: "I am Speaker One of the Tlos'khin'fahi demesne of the Trof'te Assemblage."

The Trofts had been the Cobra Worlds' trading partner for nearly 14 years now, but Corwin still remembered the undercurrent of fear that he'd grown up with: the Troft occupation of the Dominion worlds Silvern and Adirondack had been the impetus for the original Cobra project. It was no accident that most of the people who now dealt with the Troft traders were in their early twenties. Only the younger Aventinians could face the aliens without wincing.

The Troft fingered something on his abdomen sash and Corwin's display lit up with a map showing the near half of the Troft Assemblage. On one edge three stars began blinking red. "The Cobra Worlds," the alien said. A quarter of the way around the bulge a single star, also outside Troft territory, flashed green. "The world named Qasama by its natives. They are described by the Baliu'ckha'spmi demesne-lord as an alien race of great potential danger to the Assemblage. Here—" a vague-edged sphere appeared at the near side of the flashing green star— "somewhere, is a tight cluster of five worlds capable of suporting human life. We will give you their location and a pledge of human possession if your Cobras will undertake to eliminate the threat of Qasama. I await your decision."

TIMOTHY ZAHN

COBRA STRIKE

BAEN BOOKS

COBRA STRIKE

Copyright © 1986 by Timothy Zahn

A Baen Books Original

Baen Publishing Enterprises
260 Fifth Avenue
New York, N.Y. 10001

First printing, February 1986
  Second printing, November 1987

ISBN: 0-671-65551-5

Cover art by Vincent Di Fate

Printed in the United States of America

Distributed by
SIMON & SCHUSTER
1230 Avenue of the Americas
New York, N.Y. 10020

Chapter 1

The whine of Troft thrusters drifted in through the window on the late-summer breezes, jarring Jonny Moreau awake. For one heart-wrenching moment he was back in the midst of the Adirondack war; but as he tipped his recliner back to vertical the abrupt stab of pain in elbows and knees snapped him back to the present. For a minute he just sat there, gazing out the window at the Capitalia skyline and trying to bring his brain and body back on-line. Then, reaching carefully to his desk, he jabbed at the intercom button on his phone. "Yes, Governor?" Theron Yutu said.

Jonny leaned back in his chair again, snagging a bottle of pain pills from the desktop as he did so. "Is Corwin back from the Council meeting yet?"

The image jumped to another desk and Jonny's 27-year-old son. "Haven't gone yet, Dad," he said. "The meeting's still an hour away."

"Oh?" Jonny squinted at his watch. He'd have *sworn* the meeting was scheduled for two . . . sure enough, it was just a few minutes past one. "Felt like I'd slept longer," he muttered. "Well. You all set to go?"

"Pretty much, unless there's something new you want me to bring up. Hang on—I'll come in there and we can talk."

The screen went blank. Flexing his elbows experimentally, Jonny eyed the pain pills. *Later*, he decided firmly. His arthritis would ease some as he started moving around again, and the drugs invariably left his brain fuzzier than he liked.

The door opened and Corwin Jame Moreau strode into the room, the inevitable comboard tucked under his arm. The boy—the *man*, Jonny reminded himself— had taken to the world of politics with a zest the older Moreau had never been able to generate. More and more Corwin reminded Jonny of his own brother Jame, working up through the ranks of the Dominion of Man's highest political power. Fourteen years ago Jame had been a trusted aide to a member of the Central Committee itself. What was he now, Jonny often wondered—aide, designated successor, a Committé himself?

Jonny would never know. It was one of the few results of the Troft Corridor closing that he was still able to wholeheartedly regret.

Setting his comboard on a corner of Jonny's desk, Corwin pulled up a chair. "Okay, let's see. The main points you wanted me to present were the exclusivity clause of the new trade agreement with the Hoibe'-ryi'sarai—" the Troft demesne-name flowed smoothly from Corwin's tongue— "the need for more Cobras to be shifted to spine leopard duty in the outer districts, and the whole question of whether Caelian is really worth hanging onto."

Jonny nodded, feeling a twinge of guilt for once again skipping the Council duties a governor emeritus was supposed to perform or at least put up with. "Lean on the latter two especially—I don't know how the spine leopards figure out their numbers are down, but their breeding rate sure shows that they know *somehow*. Make sure even the densest syndics understand that we can't take on a full-scale spine leopard resurgence *and* also make any headway on Caelian without lowering the standards at the Cobra factory."

A frown flickered across Corwin's face. "Speaking of the academy. . . ." He stopped, looking uncomfortable.

Jonny closed his eyes briefly. "Justin. Right?"

"Well . . . yes. Mom wanted me to try and get you to change your mind about using your Council veto on his application."

"To what end?" Jonny sighed. "Justin is smart, exceptionally stable emotionally, adaptable, and with a strong desire to serve his world this way. You'll forgive a father's pride, I trust."

"I know all that—"

"More to the point," Jonny inturrupted, "he's 22 years old and has been wanting to be a Cobra since he was 16. A period, you'll notice, in which he's had ample opportunity to mull over exactly what a few decades of Cobra gear does to a man." He raised his hands slightly as if offering his body for inspection. "If that hasn't dampened his resolve—and the tests show it hasn't—then I'm not about to veto his admission. He's exactly the kind of man we need in the Cobras."

Corwin waved a hand in a gesture of defeat. "I almost wish I could argue with you, for Mom's sake. But I'm afraid I have to agree."

Jonny looked out the window. "Your mother's had a lot of this kind of pain in her life. I wish I knew how to make it up to her."

For a long moment the room was silent. Then Corwin stirred, reaching for his comboard. "Spine leopards and Caelian it is, then," he said, standing up. "You going to be here or the therapy room when the meeting's over?"

Jonny looked back at his eldest son, grimacing. "You *had* to bring that up, didn't you? Oh, all right; I'll go make the torturers happy. What's left of me will be back here by the time you're through."

Corwin nodded. "Okay. But be nice to them—they're just trying to do their jobs."

"Sure. See you later." Jonny waited until the other had closed the door behind him and then snorted. "Their jobs, indeed," he muttered under his breath. "Bunch of experimentalists poking around with human white-rats." All in hope that they could come up with a therapy that would someday be able to help the rising generations of Cobras.

One of whom was going to be his own son.

Sighing, Jonny gripped the arms of his chair and got carefully to his feet. He would get outside to his car on his own, and without his pills, even if it killed him. The old man, as he was fond of saying, wasn't helpless *yet*.

Even with traffic in the Cobra Worlds' capital as dense as it was these days, it would be only a ten-minute drive to the Dominion Building for the Council meeting. Corwin nevertheless gathered together his magcards and other paraphernalia as quickly as possible, hoping to get there early enough for some cloakroom soundboarding with the other Council members. His father had left for his therapy session, and Corwin was about ready to leave himself, when his mother came in.

"Hello, Theron," she smiled at Yutu. "Corwin, is your father still here?"

"He just left." Corwin felt his muscles tense in anticipation of the confrontation he knew was ahead. "He'll be coming back after his physical therapy."

"What did he say?"

Corwin consciously unclenched his jaw. "Sorry, Mom. He's not going to block it."

The age lines framing her features seemed to deepen. "You'll be casting the vote," she said, her meaning clear.

"Let me restate it, then: *We* are not going to block it."

"So that's it, is it?" she said coldly. "You're just going to let them condemn your brother to—"

"Mother." Corwin stood up, gesturing to his chair. "Sit down, will you."

She hesitated, then complied. Corwin pulled up a guest chair to face her, noting peripherally that Yutu had apparently just discovered something that needed to be done in Jonny's office. Sitting down, Corwin took a moment to look—*really* look—at his mother.

Chrys Moreau had been beautiful when she was younger, he knew from old pictures and tapes, and even with the assorted physical changes of middle age she was still strikingly attractive. But there were other changes, not all of them explained by simple maturation of viewpoint or even a response to her husband's long illness. She seemed to smile less these days, and to move with the restricted motions of one deathly afraid of knocking something over. This business with Justin was part of it, that much Corwin knew ... but there was more, and so far he hadn't found the right words to open up that section of his mother's thoughts.

Nor was this time going to be any different. "If you're going to give me the old arguments why Justin should be a Cobra, please don't bother," Chrys began. "I know them all, I still don't have any logical counters for them, and I'll even admit that if he weren't my son I'd probably agree with them. But he *is* my son, and irrational as it may seem, I don't think it fair that I should lose *him* to the Cobras, too."

Corwin let her finish, though her words represented no new ground either. "Have you asked Joshua to talk with him?" he asked.

Chrys shook her head minutely. "He won't. *You* should know that better than anyone else."

Despite the seriousness of the moment Corwin felt a brief smile touch his lips at the memories evoked. Five years older than the twins, he had nevertheless been successfully ganged up on more times than he cared to remember. Their unshakable loyalty to each

other even in the face of parental punishments had
made for equally unshakable alibis. "Than I'm afraid
it's out of our hands," he told his mother gently.
"Legally—not to mention ethically—Justin has a perfect right to choose his life's work. Besides, the political fallout of such a nepotistic veto would be awfully
messy to clean up."

"Politics." Chyrs turned her head to stare out the
window. "I'd hoped your father would be finished
with it when he retired from the governorship. I
should have realized they wouldn't let him escape
that easily."

"We need his wisdom and experience, Mom."
Corwin glanced at his watch. "And speaking of that,
I'm afraid I'm going to have to go give the Council its
monthly dose now."

A shadow briefly crossed Chrys's face, but she nodded and stood up. "I understand. Will you be coming
by for dinner tonight? The twins have said they'll be
able to make it."

And it would be the last time until Justin's Cobra
training was over that they'd all have a chance to be
together. "Sure," Corwin said, walking her toward
the door. "I'll be talking to Dad after the meeting, so
I'll just come with him when we're finished."

"All right. Around six?"

"Fine. See you then."

He walked her to her car and watched as she drove
off. Then, with a sigh, he went to his own car and
headed for the Dominion Building. Why, he wondered, did the internal problems of his own family
always seem more insurmountable than those facing
three entire worlds? *Probably,* he thought flippantly,
*because there isn't anything the Council can do any-
more to surprise me.*

He would afterward recall that thought and its
unfortunate timing . . . and wince.

Chapter 2

The Council of Syndics—its official title—had in the early days of the colony been just that: a grouping somewhat low-key of the planet's syndics and governor-general which met at irregular intervals to discuss any problems and map out the general direction they hoped the colony would grow in. As the population increased and beachheads were established on two other worlds, the Council grew in both size and political weight, following the basic pattern of the distant Dominion of Man. But unlike the Dominion, this outpost of humanity numbered nearly three thousand Cobras among its half-million people. The resulting inevitable diffusion of political power had had a definite impact on the Council's makeup. The rank of governor had been added between the syndic and governor-general levels, blunting the pinnacle of power just a bit; and at *all* levels of government the Cobras with their double vote were well represented.

Corwin didn't really question the political philosophy which had produced this modification of Dominion structure; but from a purely utilitarian point of view he often found the sheer size of the 75-member Council unwieldy.

Today, though, at least for the first hour, things went smoothly. Most of the discussion—including the points Corwin raised—focused on older issues which had already had the initial polemics thoroughly wrung out of them. A handful were officially given resolution, the rest returned to the members for more analysis, consideration, or simple foot-dragging; and as the agenda wound down it began to look as if the meeting might actually let out early.

And then Governor-General Brom Stiggur dropped a pocket planet-wrecker into the room.

It began with an old issue. "You'll remember the report of two years ago," he said, looking around the room, "in which the Farsearch team concluded that, aside from our three present worlds, no planets exist within at least a 20-light-year radius of Aventine that we could expand to in the future. It was agreed at the time that our current state of population and development hardly required an immediate resolution of this long-term problem."

Corwin sat a bit straighter in his seat, sensing similar reactions around him. Stiggur's words were neutral enough, but something explosive seemed to be hiding beneath the carefully controlled inflections of his voice.

"However," the other continued, "in the past few days something new has come to light, something which I felt should be presented immediately to this body, before even any follow-up studies were initiated." Glancing at the Cobra guard standing by the door, Stiggur nodded. The man nodded in turn and opened the panel . . . and a single Troft walked in.

A faint murmur of surprise rippled its way around the room, and Corwin felt himself tense involuntarily as the alien made its way to Stiggur's side. The Trofts had been the Worlds' trading partner for nearly 14 years now, but Corwin still remembered vividly the undercurrent of fear that he'd grown up with. Most of the Council had even stronger memories than that: the Troft occupation of the Dominion worlds Silvern and Adirondack had occurred only 43 years ago, ultimately becoming the impetus for the original Cobra project. It was no accident that most of the people who now dealt physically with the Troft traders were in their early twenties. Only the younger Aventinians could face the aliens without wincing.

The Troft paused at the edge of the table, waiting as the Council members dug out translator-link earphones and inserted them. One or two of the younger syndics didn't bother, and Corwin felt a flicker of jealousy as he adjusted his own earphone to low volume. He'd taken the same number of courses in catertalk as they had, but it was obvious that foreign language comprehension wasn't even close to being his forté.

"Men and women of the Cobra Worlds Council," the earphone murmured to him. "I am Speaker One of the Tlos'khin'fahi demesne of the Trof'te Assemblage." The alien's high-pitched catertalk continued for a second beyond the translation; both races had early on decided that the first three parasyllables of Troft demesne titles were more than adequate for human use, and that a literal transcription of the aliens' proper names was a waste of effort. "The Tlos'khin'fahi demesne-lord has sent your own demesne-lord's request for data to the other parts of the Assemblage, and the result has been a triad offer from the Pua'lanek'zia and Baliu'ckha'spmi demesnes."

Corwin grimaced. He'd never liked deals involving two or more Troft demesnes, both because of the delicate political balance the Worlds often had to strike and because the humans never heard much about the Troft-Troft arm of such bargains. That arm *had* to exist—the individual demesnes seldom if ever gave anything away to each other.

The same line of thought appeared to have tracked its way elsewhere through the room. "You speak of a triad, instead of a quad offer," Governor Dylan Fairleigh spoke up. "What part does the Tlos'khin'fahi demesne expect to play?"

"My demense-lord chooses the role of catalyst," was the prompt reply. "No fee will be forthcoming for our role." The Troft fingered something on his abdomen sash and Corwin's display lit up with a map showing the near half of the Troft Assemblage. Off on one edge three stars began blinking red. "The Cobra Worlds," the alien unnecessarily identified them. A quarter of the way around the bulge a single star, also outside Troft territory, flashed green. "The world named Qasama by its natives. They are described by the Baliu'ckha'spmi demesne-lord as an alien race of great potential danger to the Assemblage. Here—" a vague-edged sphere appeared at the near side of the flashing green star— "somewhere, is a tight cluster of five worlds capable of supporting human life. The Pua'lanek'zia demesne-lord will give you their location and an Assemblage pledge of human possession if your Cobras will undertake to eliminate the threat of Qasama. I will await your decision."

The Troft turned and left . . . and only slowly did Corwin realize he was holding his breath. Five brand-new worlds . . . for the price of becoming mercenaries.

He wondered if the Troft had any idea of the size snakepit he'd just opened.

If the alien didn't, the Council certainly did. For the better part of a minute the room was silent as an isolation tank as each member apparently tried to track through the tangle of implications. Finally, Stiggur cleared his throat. "While we of course have no intention of replying to this offer today, or even to fully discuss its relative merits, I would nevertheless appreciate hearing whatever initial reactions you might have."

"I, for one, would like a little more information before we listen to any hard-wired-reflex comments," Governor Lizabet Telek said. Her perennially gravelly voice gave no clue to her own reaction. "Something about these new aliens would be nice for starters—bio specs, tech level, specifics of their alleged threat; that sort of thing."

Stiggur shook his head. "Speaker One either doesn't have any more data or won't give it away free—I've already pressed him on that. I suspect the former, personally; there's no particular need for the Tlos demesne to buy what would be little more than abstract knowledge to them. Same goes for information on these five alleged worlds the Pua demesne's offering, before anyone asks."

"In other words, we're being asked to sign an essentially blank agreement?" one of the newer syndics asked.

"Not really." Governor Jor Hemner shook his head, the movement looking risky on one so frail. "There are lots of intermediate possibilities, including buying the Baliu's data or sending our own survey team out to take a look. Standard Troft trade procedure assumes we'll come up with these suggestions ourselves. What *I'm* worried about is whether setting a precedent of this kind is a good idea."

"Why not?" someone else spoke up from Corwin's side of the room. "It's the fear of the Cobras that keeps the Trofts friendly, isn't it? How better to show them that kind of caution is good policy?"

"And if we lose?" Hemner asked stiffly.

"The Cobras haven't lost anything yet."

Corwin glanced at Governor Howie Vartanson of Caelian, wondering if he'd comment. But the other merely curled his lip slightly and kept silent. Politicans from Caelian tended to adopt that low-profile position when they came to Aventine, Corwin had noticed; but the point, he felt, ought to be made. Subtly, if possible. . . . "I'd like to point out," he spoke up, "that one or more new planets would enable us to solve the problem of Caelian without depriving the 19,000 people there of the right to their 'own' world."

"Only if they'd be willing to leave," Stiggur said;

but the mention of Caelian, as Cowrin had planned, seemed to bring the members' thoughts to the current stalemate between the Cobras and that strange world's hostile ecology. "Fluid genetic adaptation," the official reports elegantly called. it. The Caelians' own term was considerably cruder: *Hell's Blender*. Every species on the planet, from the simplest lichen to the largest predator, seemed mindlessly determined to hold onto his ecological and territorial niche against all efforts to dislodge it. Clear some land and soak it with vegebarrier, and within days there would be a dozen new plant variants attempting to reclaim it. Build a house where a thicket had been, and before long the local fungi would be growing on the walls. Create a city, or even a small town, and the displaced animals would find their way in somehow ... and not only the small ones. A world under perpetual siege, Corwin had once heard Jonny call it. Only the Caelians themselves knew how—or why—they put up with it.

For another long moment the room was again silent. Stiggur looked around, nodded at what he saw. "Well. I think we can safely agree with Governor Telek that considerably more information is needed before we can even consider acting. For the moment, then, you're to keep this proposal a secret from the general populace while you work out the various pros and cons for yourselves. Now, then—one final item and we'll be adjourned. I have a list of Cobra applicants awaiting final Council approval." The twelve names—an unusually high number—appeared on Corwin's screen, along with their home towns and districts. All the names were familiar ones; the Cobra Academy screeners had sent in their test results nearly a month ago. Justin Moreau was the seventh one listed.

"Do I hear any votes against these citizens becoming Cobras, either individually or as a group?" Stiggur asked the standard question. A couple of nearby heads turned in Corwin's direction; clamping his jaw tightly, he kept his eyes on the governor-general and his hands in his lap. "No? Then this Council affirms the decision of the Cobra Academy officials, and hereby directs them to begin the irreversible stages of the Cobra process." Stiggur pushed a button and the room's screens blanked. "This Council session is adjourned."

Irreversible stages. Corwin had heard those words at least twenty times before at these meetings, but somehow they'd never sounded so final. But then, he'd never heard them applied to his own younger brother before, either.

Justin Moreau let the car roll to a stop in front of the house, feeling the tension in his shoulders translate along his arms to a brief white-knuckled squeeze on the wheel. The word had come by phone only an hour ago that the Council had given final approval to his application. Tomorrow the surgery would begin that would finally and firmly set him down in his father's footsteps ... but tonight he would have to face his mother's pain.

"You ready?" Joshua asked from the seat next to him.

"As ready as I'll ever be." Opening the door, Justin got out and headed toward the house, his brother falling into step beside him.

Corwin answered Joshua's knock, and despite his tension Justin found himself enjoying the inevitable half-second it took their older brother to figure out which was which. Even among identical twins Joshua and Justin were unusually hard to tell apart, a fact that had caused untold confusion throughout their lives. Family and close friends were generally able to manage the trick, but even with them a secret swap of tunics could sometimes go undetected for hours. They'd pulled such stunts innumerable times when they were younger, a game they'd given up only after their father threatened to color-code them with liberal applications of paint.

"Joshua; Justin," Corwin nodded, looking at each in turn as if to prove he'd gotten them straight. "Abandon all hope of light conversation, you who enter here. The Moreau War Council is in session tonight."

Oh, great, Justin groaned inwardly. But Corwin had stepped aside, and Joshua was already heading in, and it was too late to back out now. Squaring his shoulders, Justin followed.

His parents were already seated together on the living room couch, and from long habit Justin gave his father a quick once-over. A little weaker-looking, perhaps, than the last time he'd seen him, but not much. Of more significance was the slight flicker of pain that crossed Jonny's eyes as he gave the twins an abbreviated wave in greeting. The pain pills for his arthritis really didn't affect his mental facilities all *that* much; if he'd opted to do without them there was some high-powered thought going on in here indeed. A glance at his mother's grim face confirmed it, and for a long minute Justin wondered if he'd drastically underestimated the level of family opposition to his Cobra ambitions.

But that assumption didn't last long. "Dinner'll be ready in about half an hour," Jonny told the twins as they chose chairs and sat down. "Until then, I want to feel you out on a proposal Stiggur dropped on the Council session today. Corwin?"

Corwin took a seat where he could see all the others' faces. "This is all to be kept secret, of course," he said . . . and then launched into the damnedest story Justin had ever heard.

Jonny let a few seconds pass after his eldest had finished and then cocked an eyebrow at the twins. "Well? Reactions?"

"I don't trust them," Joshua said promptly. "Especially the Tlos demesne. Why shoud they offer their set-up services for nothing?"

"That much is obvious," Jonny told him. "This is what's known as a free sample—and running both ways. If we take the job and the Baliu demesne likes our work, the Tlossies will undoubtedly offer themselves as our agents to any other interested demesnes."

"And if *we* like the deal, they'll offer us their services in finding new jobs," Corwin nodded. "They pulled the same type of inducement scheme when we were first opening up trade with the Trofts generally, which is one reason they now handle so much of it."

"All right," Joshua shrugged. "Assume the offer's legitimate. Are five planets of dubious value worth fighting a war for? An unprovoked war, yet?"

"Flip that over, though," Corwin said. "Suppose this new alien *is* a genuine and imminent threat. Do we dare simply ignore it and hope it won't find us? Maybe it *would* be better to take it out now while it can be done relatively easily."

"And what does 'relatively easily' mean?" Joshua countered.

Justin glanced at his mother's tight-lipped expression. The pattern was now a familiar one: Corwin usually took the devil's advocate position in these round tables, which implied Jonny was leaning toward the nay side on the issue. His reasons would be interesting to hear, but he was unlikely to voice them until the twins had had their say. But Chrys might not be so reticent. "Mom, *you* haven't said anything yet. How do *you* feel?"

She looked at him, a tired smile touching the corners of her mouth. "With you about to become a Cobra? Of course I don't want to risk your life for worlds we won't even need for another millennium. But aside from that emotional reaction, my logic center can't help but wonder *why* the Trofts want *us* to do this. They have a war machine the equal of the Dominion's—if they can't handle this alien threat, what do they expect *us* to do?"

Justin looked at Joshua, saw his own sudden thoughtfulness only hinted at in his brother's face. Understandable; Justin knew much more about both

Cobra capabilities *and* limitations than Joshua did. He turned to his father, who seemed in turn to be watching him. "Odd," he said.

"Indeed," Jonny agreed. "The only advantage Cobras have over combat-suited troops is the fact that our weapons are concealed. It's hard to imagine a normal, non-guerrilla war where that's a deciding factor."

"Of course, the nearest known combat suits are way over in the Dominion—" Corwin began.

"But if they can hire *us* they can just as easily hire *them*," Justin finished for him. "Right?"

Corwin nodded. "Which leads me, at least, to only one answer for Mom's question."

There was a brief pause. "A test," Joshua said at last. "They want another crack at seeing just how powerful Cobras really are."

Jonny nodded. "I can't see any other explanation. Especially since the demesnes at this end of the Assemblage probably didn't have any direct contact with human forces during the war. All they've got are the farside demesnes' reports, and they may think those are exaggerated."

"So ... what do we do?" Joshua asked. "Play it safe and say we're above mercenary work?"

"That would be my recommendation," his father sighed. "Unfortunately—well, you tell them, Corwin."

"I took a quick sample of Council opinion right after the meeting," Corwin said. "The eight syndics and two governors I talked to who'd followed this same line of reasoning were split straight down the middle on whether backing down would be a dangerous signal of weakness."

"If we try it and fail, what kind of a signal is *that*?" Joshua snorted.

Justin looked at Corwin. "What about the other Cobras on the Council?" he asked. "Did you talk to them?"

"One of them, yes. He was more interested in discussing the various modifications that would be needed to bring the Cobras back to full war footing."

"Actually, it wouldn't take much more than a replacement of the optical enhancement system," Jonny said. "The ones we've got now don't have the multiple targeting lock we'd need in combat. We'd have to change the academic and some of the practical content of the training, too, but aside from that a changeover would be easy. The nanocomputers still carry all the combat reflex programming, certainly."

Justin's tongue swiped briefly at his lips. *Combat reflexes.* The Cobra information packets were never quite that blunt; but that *was*, after all, what the Instant Defense Capabilities really were. *Combat reflexes.* What had sounded perfectly reasonable for a one-on-one confrontation with a spine leopard didn't seem nearly as reliable for the confusion of full warfare.

Still ... one of those same little computers had helped keep his father alive through three years of guerrilla war against the Trofts; his father and Cally Halloran and hundreds of others. The computer, and the bone-strengthening laminae, and the servo motor network, and the lasers, and the sonics. . . . He found his eyes ranging over his father's form as he catalogued the weaponry and equipment implanted there ... the equipment that the surgeons at the Cobra Academy would start putting into his own body tomorrow ...

Someone was calling his name. Snapping out of his reverie, Justin focused on his older brother. "Sorry," he said. "Thoughts were elsewhere. What did you say?"

"I was asking what you thought of the idea of being a mercenary, if that's what it ultimately boils down to," Corwin said. "Ethically, I mean."

Justin shrugged uncomfortably, avoiding his mother's eyes. "Actually, it doesn't look to me like we *can* be pure mercenaries on this one. We *may* be defending the Worlds against an alien threat; we *will* be making a statement to the whole Troft Assemblage as to what kind of defensive capabilities we have here. Either way, we're ultimately serving our own people ... which is what Cobras are supposed to do."

"In other words, you wouldn't mind going off to fight?" Chrys asked quietly.

Justin winced at her tone, but kept his voice steady. "I don't mind fighting if it's necessary. But I don't think we should hand that decision to the Trofts, either. The Council should get all the data on these aliens that we can and then make their decision without regard to these five planets being dangled in front of us."

In the kitchen a soft tone sounded. "Dinner time," Jonny announced, levering himself carefully out of the couch. "And with the food comes an end to political talk. Thank you for your feedback—it's nice to know we have a family consensus on this. Now hop to the kitchen and give your mother a hand. Table needs setting, vegetables a final rinse, and I believe it's your turn, Corwin, to carve the roast."

Corwin nodded and headed for the kitchen, Joshua hard on his heels. Chrys stayed at Jonny's side; and Justin lingered long enough to see his father fumble out his vials of pain pills. *The political talk is indeed over*, he told himself.

Leaving his parents to themselves, he hurried toward the kitchen to assist his brothers.

Chapter 3

Sometime in the past year or two one of Aventine's violent springtime thunderstorms had swept this part of the Trappers Forest, and the region's highest hill had taken a real beating. At least one tree had been blown to kindling by the lightning; six others had been knocked flat by either lightning or wind. The result was a hilltop which, despite its lousy footing, provided a clear line of sight for thirty meters in every direction. An unnecessary luxury for the average Cobra command post ... but then, the average Cobra mission didn't have civilian observers to watch out for, either.

Audio enhancers at full power, Almo Pyre sent his gaze slowly around the edges of the informal clearing, acutely conscious of the middle-aged woman standing at his side. A civilian was bad enough; but to have one of Aventine's three *governors* out here was the sort of unnecessary—not to say damnfool—risk no Cobra leader in his right mind would take. *I should have left her behind*, Pyre though irritably. *The official mayhem would've been nothing to what'll happen if she gets killed*.

A soft hum—three brief notes—sounded from the receiver in his right ear: Winward had spotted one of their target spine leopards. Pyre hummed an acknowledgement into the wire-mike curving along his cheek, adding an alert to the others. Limited and sometimes awkward to use, the humming code had the advantage that it wasn't loud enough to kick in the cutoffs in the listener's audio enhancers.

"Hmm?" Governor Lizabet Telek hummed. The sound was louder than another Cobra would've used, but at least she knew enough not to ask her questions out loud.

Pyre notched back the audio, automatically shifting more attention to his visual scan as he did so. "Michael's found one," he explained quietly. "The others will be sweeping in with a net pattern, watching for cubs and other adults."

"Cubs." Telek's voice was even, but there was more than a touch of dissatisfaction beneath it.

Pyre shrugged fractionally. Had he seen a flicker of movement in the shadow between two trees? "This year's cubs will be next year's breeders," he reminded her. "If you biology people can come up with a way—"

A *swoosh* of branches came from his right, and he spun to see a large feline body shooting down at them from the trees.

The leap would be short—that much was instantly obvious—but Pyre knew the predator would hit the ground running. His hands were already in firing position—little fingers pointed toward the spine leopard, thumbs resting against ring fingers' nails—and as the animal stretched its hind legs downward for a landing he squeezed.

The lasers in his little fingers spat needles of light into the spine leopard's face, burning fur and bone and brain tissue. But Pyre's intended target, its eyes, escaped destruction, and the creature's more decentralized nervous system shrugged off the brain damage as if not noticing it. The spine leopard landed, feet stumbling slightly on the branch-littered surface—

Pyre had twisted and was swinging his left leg to bear when Telek gasped. "Behind you!" she snapped.

A glimpse over his shoulder was all Pyre could get from his angle, but it was enough. The flicker he'd seen in the forest had become a second spine leopard, charging them like a furry missile.

And spinning the direction he was, Pyre was out of position to do anything about it. "Down!" he barked at Telek, hoping desperately he could attract the spine leopard's attack to himself. His programmed reflexes gave him a fighting chance, but they had no provision for defending bystanders, as well. . . . An instant later his left leg reached firing position, and from the heel of his boot the brilliant spear of his antiarmor laser lanced out.

There was no time to assess the damage—he would just have to assume the first spine leopard was at least temporarily stopped. Continuing his spin, he dropped his left leg back to the ground and brought up his right—

In time to catch the second spine leopard full in the face with his foot.

There was no way Pyre's precarious balance could absorb the full impact of the predator's charge—and even as the animal's teeth scrambled for a grip on his boot he felt himself falling sideways. Letting his left leg buckle beneath him, he drew his right back from the fangs . . . and as spine leopard sailed over him he straightened the leg sharply to send a servo-augmented kick hard into the creature's belly.

It shrieked, and even through the blur of motion Pyre saw its foreleg spines snap outward into defense position. It knew it was hurt . . . though perhaps not that it was doomed. For whatever incidental damage Pyre's kick had caused, it had also pushed the creature higher into the air—and the extra half second it took the spine leopard to reach the ground was all the time Pyre needed to again bring his left leg to bear. The antiarmor laser flashed twice, and the predator landed in a smoking heap.

Pyre scrambled to his feet, eyes automatically

searching out the unmoving figure of the first spine
leopard. Only then did he turn back to see what had
happened to Telek.

The governor was on hands and knees in the small
hollow between two fallen tree limbs, the small pel-
let pistol she'd been carrying clutched in one hand.
"Is it safe to come out yet?" she asked, only a slight
quaver in her voice.

Pyre gave the edge of the forest a careful scan. "I
think so," he said, stepping forward to help her up.
"Thanks for the warning."

"No problem." She waved off his assistance, brushing off dead leaves as she got to her feet. "I'd heard
reports from other areas that the spine leopards were
occasionally hunting in pairs these days, but I didn't
think it'd started here yet. Survival pressure's supposed to be lighter in the major forests."

"It's strong enough," Pyre told her grimly. "And as
I was saying, unless you biologists can come up with
a way to counteract it, these hunts are going to have
to continue."

"I'm hardly on the forefront of biological research
these days—"

She broke off as Pyre held up his hand. "Report,"
he said quietly into his wire-mike. ". . . yes. Need any
help? . . . all right. Return here when you're done."

Telek was watching him. "They found the den site,"
he told her. "Ten cubs in it."

Her mouth compressed into a tight line. "Ten.
Twenty years ago a spine leopard litter never ex-
ceeded two or three. Never."

Pyre shrugged uncomfortably, running a hand
through his thinning hair. *Forty-seven years old, and
chasing through the forests like a newly-commissioned
kid.* He might have been bitter if the duty wasn't so
vital. "We've cleared out too many of their territories,"
he said with a shake of his head. "However it is they
sense these things, they *know* there's room on Aventine
for a whole lot more spine leopards. Theoretically."

Telek snorted gently. "Theoretically, indeed. Spine leopards in the streets of Capitalia." She shook her head in turn. "If you only knew, Pyre, how often biologists have yearned for a truly self-healing planetary ecology. And now we've got two . . . and they're a damn bloody nuisance."

" 'Nuisance' is hardly a word I'd apply to Caelian, Governor," Pyre murmured.

"True." Something in her tone made him glance over, and he found her gazing tight-lipped into the forest. "Well . . . maybe there's something we can do about it."

"About all we could do about Caelian is abandon it," he retorted.

"That's exactly what I had in mind," she nodded. "Tell me, would you be available for some consultation before the Council meeting the day after tomorrow? I need some expert advice from an experienced Cobra team leader."

"I suppose so," he said reluctantly. "But only if we're finished completely out here."

"Fine," she agreed. "I think you'll find my proposal very interesting."

I doubt it, he told himself morosely, turning his attention back to the forest. *Another political mind with another political solution. Once—just once—I'd like to hear something else. Anything else.* Unbidden, the face of Tors Challinor rose before him: Challinor, who had tried years ago to take military control of Aventine. *Well, all right*, he told the memory with a shudder. *I'd like* almost *anything else.*

Chapter 4

"This meeting is officially come to order," Governor-General Stiggur announced, bringing his hand down in a dramatic gesture to start the sealed recorder.

Somehow, Corwin thought, the whole thing lost a lot of effect when translated to a room the size of a large office and an audience of six. "I've called you here," Stiggur continued, "to discuss the issue raised at the Council meeting two weeks ago: namely, whether to undertake the job the Tlos demesne has offered us."

Corwin glanced surreptitiously around the table at the five governors, feeling as he never had at Council meetings the sheer *weight* of political authority assembled around him. An oppressive, almost suffocating presence—

Until Governor Lizabet Telek spoke up and broke the bubble. "I realize, Brom, that you're speaking for posterity here," she said to Stiggur, "but can we try to do without the heavy historical phrasings?"

Stiggur tried to glare at her, but his heart clearly wasn't in it. None of them had come to Aventine all those years ago with any political aspirations, and while they'd stepped into these positions with reasonable success, they were all still non-politicians beneath the trappings. "All right—point taken,"

Stiggur sighed. "Fine. So who's got anything to report?"

"I'd like to know first of all where Governor Emeritus Moreau is," Caelian's Governor Howie Vartanson spoke up. "It seems to me this issue should take priority over therapy sessions or whatever."

"My father's in the hospital at the moment," Corwin said, resisting the urge to say something nasty about the other's unthinking callousness. He *knew* Jonny was a first-generation Cobra, after all. "Immune system trouble, the doctors think."

"How serious is it?" Stiggur asked, frowning.

"Apparently not very. It came on rather suddenly last night, though."

"You should have let someone know," Jor Hemner said, one frail hand playing restlessly with his wispy beard. "We could have postponed this meeting."

"Not if we want to have a recommendation for the full Council meeting this afternoon," Corwin said, glancing at Hemner before returning his gaze to Stiggur. "I know my father's thoughts on this matter, sir, and have his authority to act for him. I presume you'll accept my council proxy in this session?"

"Well, the strict legality—"

"Oh, for heaven's sake, Brom, let him sit in and be done with it," Telek put in. "We've got a lot of ground to cover this morning, and I want to get to it."

"Fine." Stiggur raised his eyebrows at the others. "Any objections? All right. Anyone managed to find out anything from the Trofts about this Qasama?"

Olor Roi of Palatine cleared his throat. "I tried playing the old independent-planets routine on Speaker One, but I think it's starting to wear thin. They're finally tumbling to the fact that we're a political unit even though we can all make our own trade agreements. Still, I think he was being honest when he said he'd already given us all he had."

"Maybe he was just holding out in hopes we'd outbid you," suggested Dylan Fairleigh, the third

Aventine governor. It was a rather naive comment, Corwin thought, betraying the lack of experience with Troft trade that almost automatically came with the other's Far West Region jurisdiction.

Vartanson, predictably, didn't bother to take that into account. "Don't be ridiculous," he snorted. "Trofts don't *hold out* without making it known that they *have* something for sale. Where've you been the past 14 years, anyway?"

Fairleigh's forehead darkened, but before he could speak Telek cut in. "Okay—so it's established the Tlossies haven't got anything. Next step is obviously to get to someone who *does*. I see two choices: the Baliu demesne or Qasama itself."

"Just a second," Corwin spoke up. "Isn't the next step to see whether we're going to *need* this information?"

Telek frowned at him. "Of *course* we need it. How else can we make a rational decision?"

"The most rational decision would be to give the Tlossies a simple no sale right now," Corwin answered. "If we do—"

"Since when is hiding from reality a rational decision?" Telek interrupted tartly.

"Saying no now is a statement of principle," Corwin told her, feeling sweat break out on his forehead. Jonny had warned him this view was unlikely to be well received, but Corwin hadn't been prepared for so strong a negative reaction. "It says we're not interested in becoming mercenaries for—"

"What about our own interests?" Vartanson put in. "If Qasama is a threat to the Trofts it's probably a threat to us, too."

"Yes, but . . ." Corwin stopped as words and logic suddenly tangled into a knotted mess. *Relax*, he ordered himself. *No one here's anyone to be afraid of*.

But even as he fought his sudden shyness Stiggur came to his rescue. "I think the point Corwin's trying to make is that we can still send expeditions to

Qasama or wherever once we've turned down the Baliu demesne's deal," he said. "At that point we're not constrained by what the Trofts want done, but are free to take action as *we* see fit."

"Sounds very noble," Telek nodded. "Unfortunately, it runs very quickly into one important practical detail. Namely, who pays for this if the Trofts don't?"

Fairleigh shifted in his seat. "I was under the impression the Trofts were offering only those five planets, not payment of costs too."

"No deal's been officially struck—we could demand costs as part of the package," Roi pointed out thoughtfully. "But it would still take a lot of Cobras out of circulation for up to several years. How fast can the academy replace them?"

"Surgery and training together take three months," Corwin spoke up, feeling better on balance. "Candidate screening adds another two weeks."

"But the whole process can be shrunk to less than seven weeks," Telek said, brandishing a magcard for a moment before dropping it into her reader. "In the past few days I've spoken with two authorities on Cobra matters: Cally Halloran, who was Jonny's old teammate in the Troft War; and Almo Pyre, currently head of Cobra operations in Syzra District. Together they've provided the data necessary for a cost analysis of both the initial scouting expedition and the three most likely types of military operation."

Corwin stared at the figures that appeared on his display, the two names she'd dropped so casually into the discussion bouncing like unexploded grenades around his numbed brain. *Cally Halloran*—one of his father's oldest and most trusted friends; and *Almo Pyre*—a Moreau family friend for as long as Corwin could remember. Sneaking a glance over his screen, he found Telek's calm eyes on him ... and suddenly he realized what she was trying to do.

By choosing Jonny's friends as her experts, she hoped to stifle any disagreement the only Cobra in

this inner circle might have had with her numbers
... and as he began studying those numbers he saw
the conclusion they inevitably led to.

For even the smallest of the projected military actions the costs were simply staggering. Halloran and
Pyre had estimated a minimum of nine hundred
Cobras—a full third of the three Worlds' current
contingent—on or near Qasama for six to twelve
months. Equipment, transport, supply, replacement
of casualties—it was far more than the Worlds could
hope to scrape together from their modest econo-
mies. The abrupt loss of that many Cobras alone
would bring to a dead halt all territorial expansion
on Aventine and Palatine; on Caelian it could easily
precipitate the final destruction or abandonment of
that beleaguered colony.

Fairleigh broke the silence first. "We'd better hope
the Qasamans aren't *too* immediate a threat," he
muttered. "Nine hundred to three *thousand* Cobras.
How long would it take to replace—? Oh, there it is."

Corwin found the line on his own display. "That
assumes an unlimited supply of qualified candidates,"
he said.

"Well, if that pool doesn't exist—or can't be generated—we're in serious trouble already," Roi growled.
"Our safety from the Trofts themselves depends on a
healthy respect for Cobra fighting skills. If they thought
our paltry twenty-eight hundred were all they'd ever
have to deal with . . ." He shook his head.

"All the more reason to show them how easily
expandable the Cobra program is," Telek argued.
"We *can* do it—especially with the Trofts paying for
the demonstration."

The discussion raged on for a half hour more, but
Corwin could see the battle was lost. Of the six others in the room, only Hemner and Roi seemed at all
willing to consider Jonny's position. If neither of them
switched sides, Corwin's double vote would deadlock
the issue at four to four, which would mean throwing

it to the full Council without any official recommendation. The Council's handling of matters even with a recommendation was chancy enough; without one, the results were impossible for anyone to predict.

And as the probability of victory slipped ever closer to zero, Corwin realized that, for the first time since obtaining his father's proxy, he was going to have to make a deal on his own initiative. A deal he wasn't at all certain Jonny would approve of. . . .

He waited until the last minute, hoping against the odds; but as the governor-general called for a vote he raised his hand. "I'd like to ask for a short break before we go any further," he said. "It seems to me some private thought or discussion might be useful before we commit our votes to the record."

Stiggur's eyebrows lifted slightly, but he nodded without hesitation. "All right. We'll meet back here in 20 minutes."

The general exodus was quiet—apparently the others felt in need of a break, as well—and a minute or two later Corwin was sitting in his father's Dominion Building office. For a long moment he stared at the phone on the desk, wondering if he should discuss this with anyone before he went ahead and did it. But his father would still be in the depths of biochemical surgery, and he could guess what his mother would say. Theron Yutu, across town in Jonny's main office? No. The twins—he ought to discuss it with them. But Justin was incommunicado in the surgery wing of the Cobra Academy, and to tell only Joshua would be unfair . . . and Corwin realized he was stalling. Taking a deep breath, he got up from his father's chair and headed down the hall to Governor Telek's office.

If she was surprised to see him, it didn't show. "Corwin," she nodded, closing the door behind him and ushering him to a seat. "Nice dilemma we have here, isn't it? What can I do for you?"

Corwin waited until she was seated again at her

desk before speaking. "How do you see the vote?" he asked bluntly.

Again, she showed no surprise. "Myself, Brom, Dylan, and Howie for; you, Jor, and Olor against. Deadlock. You come here to try and change my mind?"

He shook his head. "You knew my father would be against the whole thing, didn't you? That's why you dragged Cally and Almo into it."

"Your father was one of the strongest opponents of the Cobra Academy when it was set up some twenty-five years ago," she reminded him. "It wasn't hard to guess he'd be against any proposal that would increase the number of Cobras."

Which made Jonny's philosophical objections to Cobras-for-hire sound like nothing more than camouflage for an old habitual reflex. Corwin swallowed hard against the rebuttal that wanted to come out. Now was not the time to defend his father's stand. "So what exactly do *you* want?" he asked instead. "A contractual commitment to handle whatever this threat is that Qasama poses?"

"Of course not," she snorted. "No one in their right mind would give a Troft a carte blanche like that. All I want is to commit us to a survey mission—at Troft expense."

"Won't that commit us to carrying out the rest of it, too?"

"Not if the agreement's drawn up carefully enough." She pursed her lips. "You're about to bring up the image question if we look Qasama over and then back out. I don't really have any better answer to that than the one I gave fifteen minutes ago. The risks of *not* knowing what kind of threat Qasama is are greater than the risks of looking weak to the Trofts."

Corwin took a deep breath. "Then I presume you'd like to have that as the official recommendation to the Council in a few hours?"

"I'd like that very much," she said cautiously. "What's it going to cost me?"

Corwin gestured toward the conference room down the hall. "Your proposed survey mission would include a maximum of twelve people plus ship's crew, as I recall. I want two of those twelve to be my father's choice."

"With his skeptic's attitude to keep the mission honest?" She smiled wryly. "As a matter of fact, that's probably a good idea . . . but giving a governor emeritus sixteen percent of the package isn't likely to fly very smoothly."

"I can sweeten the deal considerably. How would you like to send an *undetectable* Cobra on the mission?"

He had the satisfaction of seeing her eyes widen with surprise. "I thought a careful deep-body scan would pick up even Cobra gear."

"It will," Corwin nodded. "But a scan of that type takes almost fifteen minutes to complete. How many times is a host likely to subject visiting dignitaries to that sort of thing?"

She frowned at him for several heartbeats. "My immediate reaction is that you're being anthropomorphic in the extreme. Suppose their deep-body stuff is more sensitive or just faster than ours, for example? But assuming you're right, then what? —cram a Cobra surgery team into the *Dewdrop* for some fast work?"

"Not at all. I propose sending a Cobra and a non-Cobra who are virtually indistinguishable from each other. My twin brothers Joshua and Justin."

Telek's breath came out in a thoughtful hiss. "Cute. Very cute. So the Cobra stays aboard ship until the aliens have done all their studies on the landing party, and then they switch places? Interesting proposal. But suppose the Qasamans use something besides sight for identification? Sound or scent, for instance?"

Corwin shrugged, trying to make the gesture look casual. "Then we're out of luck. But most land predators we know of—including those on Troft and Dominion worlds—rely heavily on sight. I think it's a fair gamble, and if it doesn't work we haven't really lost anything."

"Except two places in the mission that could have gone to other people." Telek leaned back in her chair, her eyes focused somewhere behind Corwin's head. He waited, forcing himself to breathe normally . . . and abruptly her eyes returned to him and she nodded. "All right, it's a deal . . . on one further condition. You—or, rather, your father—must support *my* bid to go on the mission."

"You?" Corwin blurted. "But that's—"

"Ridiculous? Hardly. The mission's going to need both scientific and political experts aboard, and I'm the only governor who qualifies in both fields and is healthy enough to make the trip."

"Your biological degree is a long way behind you."

"I've kept up with the field. And we need *someone* of governor rank in case some major policy decision comes up. Unless you know any syndics you'd trust with that task."

But can I trust you *with it*? He pursed his lips tightly, unsure of what he should do.

"You've got time to think," she said calmly as the silence began to stretch. Glancing at her watch, she stood up. "The mission team's not likely to be determined for at least a week or two. Talk it over with Jonny, work through the logic—I think you'll agree I should be aboard. But it's time to go back in there and get a recommendation for the Council to chew on."

Corwin stood up, too. "All right . . . but if I vote with you now, I want you to support my getting Justin and Joshua aboard—whether my father ultimately backs your own bid or not."

She smiled wryly. "Realized you were giving away too much, did you? Well, that's how you learn. Sure, I'll support your brothers. It's a good idea . . . and to be perfectly honest, I don't expect I'll need Jonny's vote to get on the mission, anyway."

The vote was four to two in favor of Telek's proposal when it came to Corwin's turn. He avoided Hemner's and Roi's eyes as he made it six to two, but he could feel their astonished gazes on him as Stiggur recorded the vote into the record.

Three hours later, the full Council made it official.

Lying propped up in his hopital bed, Jonny listened silently to Corwin's report of the governors' session, the Council meeting, and the private deal he'd made. *I should be angry*, Jonny thought, peripherally aware of the IV tubes feeding clear fluids into his arms. *Some calming factor in the antibiotic voodoo mixture? Or did I really know all along my plan wouldn't make it?*

Corwin stopped speaking and waited, the tension lines visible in his face. "Have you spoken to Justin or Joshua about this?" Jonny asked. "Or your mother?"

Corwin actually winced. "No, to both questions. I came up with the basic idea last week, but I hoped I wouldn't have to suggest it to anyone. At least, not without talking to you first. I think they'd be willing, though."

"Oh, they'll be willing, all right—that's not the problem." Jonny turned his head to gaze out the window. Capitalia's streetlights were visible below, the cityscape superimposed on the reflection of the hospital room around him. "You boys have always been very precious to your mother, you know," he said. "You provided the extra family warmth that I often wasn't able to give her. Too often wasn't able to. As a Cobra ... then a syndic ... then a governor ... it takes a lot of time to serve people, Corwin. Time taken away from your family. You came to work with me here, and Justin's becoming a Cobra ... and now Joshua's going to be taken from her, too." He realized abruptly he was rambling and brought his eyes back to Corwin.

The other was looking pretty miserable. "I'm sorry.

Maybe I shouldn't have done it. They *can* still back down."

Jonny shook his head. "No, you did the right thing, all the way down the line. Putting the twins aboard could give us a key tactical advantage, and the full council probably wouldn't have gone for my proposal any more than Brom and company did. Especially with the cost estimates Cally and Almo provided." He shook his head. "Pity Cally's too old to go along—a Cobra with military experience would be awfully nice to have on the scene. . . ." He trailed off thoughtfully as an idea suddenly occurred to him.

"You're not planning to go yourself, are you?" Corwin asked suspiciously into his train of thought.

"Hm? Oh, no. Not really. I was just trying to think of a way to make this all up to your mother." Taking a deep breath, he let it out in a controlled sigh. "Well. I'll be out of here in the mornng, or so they say—soon enough for us to break this to her. Why don't you talk to Joshua tonight, get his reaction. If possible, I think we should all be together when we tell Chrys."

"All except Justin," Corwin reminded him. "He'll be in surgical isolation for another week."

"I know that," Jonny said, a touch of asperity making it through the emotional damper around him. "But the three of us should be there."

"Right," Corwin nodded, standing up. "I'll let you get back to resting now and see you in the morning. I can check on my way out when you'll be released and be here to drive you home."

"Fine. Oh, and while you're checking that, would you ask the doctor to drop by when he's got some time? There are some things I want to discuss with him."

"Sure," Corwin said. He held his father's eye another second, then turned and left.

Shifting to a more comfortable position, Jonny closed his eyes and let all tensions melt away. Had there been another touch of suspicion in Corwin's face as he left? Jonny wasn't sure. But it didn't really matter. Unlike his son, he had several other governors besides Telek with whom he could cut a deal . . . and by the time Corwin found out about it, it would all be arranged.

And the other would surely approve, anyway. Eventually.

Chapter 5

The room they'd taken him to was the first surprise—
Justin had had the impression that the new trainees
would be kept together for their first postoperative
orientation session. A quick glance around the office
as his escort left him alone was a second shock: no
Cobra training instructor could possibly have an office this ornate. The desk—had he seen its carved
cyprene wood in the Cobra lecture tapes he'd studied
before applying? If so, this was the private office of
Coordinator Sun himself. Whatever was going on,
this was *not* part of the published schedule.

Behind the desk, a private door opened. Justin
tensed; and as a man stepped into the room, he felt a
relieved grin spread over his face. "Almo! I thought
you were still out in Syzra District hunting down
spine leopards."

"Hello, Justin—no, please stay seated." Pyre sat
down behind the desk.

And Justin suddenly realized the other hadn't even
smiled in greeting. "What's up, Almo?" he asked, his
pleased surprise evaporating. "Is something wrong?
Good Lord—is it Dad?"

"No, no, your family's fine," Pyre hastened to reas-
sure him. "Although in a couple of months—" He

broke off. "Let's start over. How much do you know about the Qasama thing?"

Justin hesitated. Admitting to Pyre that his father had given the family confidential information was no big deal in and of itself ... but under *these* circumstances.... "Just the basics of the Troft offer," he said. "My father wanted to discuss the ethical aspects with us."

"Fine," Pyre nodded. "Then I won't need to go over that with you. In the past three weeks there've been some twists added—by the Council and, believe it or not, your own brother."

Justin listened in silence as Pyre explained the Council's expeditionary plan and Corwin's suggestion, his emotions turmoiling between shock and excitement with very little room left amid it all for rational thought. "The Council's voted to put you two aboard *if* you're both willing to go," Pyre concluded. "Any immediate reactions?"

Justin took a moment to find his tongue. "It sounds ... interesting. Very interesting. What's Joshua had to say about it, and where do you fit in?"

"Joshua you can ask yourself—I'll send him in when I'm done. As for me—" Pyre's lip twitched in something between a smile and a grimace. "I'm going to be head of the shipboard Cobra contingent—four of us in all. And if you choose one of those slots, I'll be handling all your Cobra training for the next few weeks."

Justin was suddenly aware of the neckwrap computer nestling around his throat—the programmable training computer that would be replaced by the implanted Cobra nanocomputer if and when he graduated. "Specialized training, I gather? Stuff you don't need to fight spine leopards?"

"And special-function programmed reflexes that are built into the standard nanocomputer but never needed in forest work," Pyre nodded. "Ceiling flips, backspins; that sort of thing."

"Won't your other Cobras need that, too?"

"They'll be joining us once your basics are out of the way, three to four weeks from now." Pyre leaned his elbows on the desk, steepling his fingertips in front of him. "Look, Justin, I've got to be honest with you. I can tell you're seeing this as a big fat adventure, but you have to realize the chances are fair we'll all wind up dying on Qasama."

"Aw, come on, Almo," Justin grinned. "*You'll* be there, too, and you're too lucky to be killed."

"Stop that!" Pyre snapped. "Luck is statistical chance, with a weak coupling to skill and experience. Nothing more. I've got a little of both—you'll have practically none of either. If anyone dies, it's likely to be you."

Justin shrank into his chair, taken aback by Pyre's outburst. The older man had been one of Justin's most admired role models when he was younger, the one who—as much as his father—had catalyzed his decision to become a Cobra himself. To be chewed out by that role model was more of a shock than he'd ever dreamed such a thing could be.

His expression must have mirrored his feelings; but Pyre nevertheless continued to glare for several more seconds before finally letting his eyes soften. "I know that hurt," he said softly, "but it didn't hurt nearly as much as a laser would. Get it into your head right now that this is a probe into *enemy* territory. Your father will tell you that fighting spine leopards is a picnic in comparison."

Justin licked his lips. "You don't want me along, do you?"

For the first time Pyre's gaze slipped away from Justin's face. "What I want personally is irrelevant. The Council made a decision, all the old war veterans concurred that it made good tactical sense, and Governor Telek persuaded them I was the man to lead the Cobra contingent. My job's been defined for me, and it's now up to me to carry it out. Period."

"And you're afraid I won't be able to handle it?" Justin asked, the first stirrings of anger starting to seep through the numbness.

"I'm afraid *none* of us will be able to," Pyre replied tartly. "And if the whole thing goes up, I don't like the fact that my attention will be split between the mission's safety and yours."

"Why should it be?" Justin retorted. "Because you've known me since I was in diapers? Because you've been Dad's friend even longer? I'm 22, Almo, old enough to take care of myself now—and if you want logic, how about the fact that I won't have to *un*learn all the little tricks of fighting spine leopards that the rest of you will? You have any complaints about my youth, save them for after the training, all right? Then maybe we'll have some actual specifics to discuss."

Pyre's eyes were again locked with his and unconsciously Justin braced for a second outburst. But it didn't come. "Okay," Pyre said softly. "I just wanted to make sure you knew what you were getting into. Believe it or not, I *do* understand how you feel ... though you'll find that others may not." He stood up, and a hint of the old Almo Pyre peeked through for an instant. "I'll let Joshua come and talk to you now. I'll be in the office across the hall; just come on over when you're finished. Take your time, but try not to make this one of those wide-ranging starvation sessions you two are famous for." With a glimmer of a smile he left the room.

Justin let out a shuddering sigh of relief. His heartbeat was heading back toward normal when his twin arrived a minute later. "Almo told me to keep this talk under six months," Joshua said, seating himself in the recently vacated desk chair. "Do we *really* talk that much?"

"Only together," Justin said.

"Probably true," the other conceded, running a critical eye over his brother. "So. How do you feel?"

"From the surgery, fine. From Almo's little talk, like someone just threw an oversized gantua at me. Accurately."

Joshua nodded his commiseration. "I know how you feel. So . . . what do you think?"

"Sounds like something I'd really like to do—or it did before Almo went into an amazingly deep discourage mode. I gather you also have reservations?"

Joshua frowned. "Not especially, aside from the obvious aversions to getting myself killed. Who said I did?"

"Almo implied someone was having problems with the plan."

Joshua's frown became a pained grimace. "Probably referring to Mom."

"Mom." Justin ground his left fist hard into his right palm with chagrin at having forgotten all about her in the excitement—and an instant later the stab of pain from both knuckles and palm reminded him that, even with the limitations imposed on it by the neckwrap computer, his new strength-enhancing servo network wasn't something he could afford to ignore. Fortunately, the skeletal laminae had made his bones virtually unbreakable, which meant that this time he'd get away with only bruises. On his pride, as well as on his skin. "Grumfick it, I didn't even think of what this would do to her," he admitted to Joshua. "She been told yet?"

"Oh, yeah—and believe me, you were having lots more fun in surgery." Joshua shook his head. "I don't know. Maybe we ought to pass this up."

"What did she say?"

"About what you'd expect," the other sighed. "Dead set against it emotionally, only marginally more for it intellectually, and feeling generally betrayed that Corwin would even suggest such a thing. We tried to convince her that you were getting off easier than if you'd been assigned to Caelian, or even to the spine leopard extermination squads, but I don't think she believed us."

"Almo doesn't believe that," Justin pointed out dryly. "Why should she?"

Joshua waved a hand in futility. "I didn't invent the art of wishful thinking; I just market it locally."

"Yeah." Justin found a vacant corner to stare at for a moment, then returned his gaze to this brother. "So you really think we should pass this up?"

"To be brutally honest, no." Joshua began ticking off fingers. "Corwin's basic idea sounds good, and it's obvious we're the only two in the Worlds who could pull it off. We're likely to also be the only ones aboard who share Dad's view that hiring ourselves out is a dangerous precedent. And finally—" He grinned suddenly, shyly. "Heck, Justin, you felt it in school, too. We're *Moreaus*—sons of the Cobra, Troft War veteran, governor emeritus, original Aventinian pioneer Jonny Moreau himself. People *expect* something great from us."

"That's a pretty blithering reason to do something."

"By itself, sure. But combined with reason number two, it means our report and recommendations will carry a hefty bit of inertia when we get back from Qasama ... and given the current Council leaning, Dad may need that extra bit of weight to keep them from doing anything stupid."

And on the other hand, Justin thought grimly, *is what it'll do to Mom. Your basic no-win situation*. But Joshua was right ... and if there was one thing they'd learned from *both* parents, it was that personal comfort and preference were never to stand in the way of service to the whole. "All right," he said at last. "If you're game, so am I. 'Gantuas, hell: charge!' and all that."

"Okay." Joshua stood up. "Well, then, we'd better get to it. Almo's got some serious sweat waiting for you, I don't doubt, and I've got a couple of surgeons down the hall warming up an operating table for me."

"Surgeons?" Justin frowned, getting—carefully—to his feet. "What do they want *you* for?"

Joshua winked slyly. "You'll find out. For now, suffice it to say that it's something that'll let you be the best me possible when we get to Qasama."

"The best *what*? Come on, Joshua—"

"See you in a couple of months," Joshua grinned and slipped out the door.

You and your stupid guessing games, Justin thought after him, and for a moment considered chasing him down and badgering whatever this was out of him. But Almo was waiting across the hall; *and we're not 16 years old anymore*, he reminded himself. Squaring his shoulders, he headed out to confront his new tutor.

Telephone screens had never in their long history come anywhere near the fine-detail resolution even the simplest computer displays required. It was a failing deliberately built in, Jonny had once heard, not for financial reasons but psychosocial ones. Wrinkles, worry lines, minor emotional perturbations—all were edited out, to the point that if the picture on the screen was happy, sad, or angry, it could be safely assumed the person himself was deep into the corresponding state.

It was a shock, therefore, to see how utterly *tired* Corwin appeared.

"As of ten minutes ago we were back to deadlock, Dad," his eldest son told him, shaking his head. "Of course, the Tlossies are really bargaining for the Baliu demesne, and Speaker One has only limited flexibility to work with. Expecially on the survey mission budget. Every time we try to add something he has to take something else away. Or so he claims."

Jonny glanced over the screen. Chrys, seated at the

dining room table, was pretending to be engrossed in the collection of electronics parts she'd spread out there, but he knew she was listening to the conversation. "Maybe I'd better come back down there, then," he told Corwin. "See if I can help."

"Not worth it," the other shook his head. "Governor Telek's bargaining at least as hard as you could, and everyone's keeping out of each other's way for a change. Besides, the temp's dropped ten degrees since sundown."

Jonny grimaced; but it was just one more environmental factor he'd had to learn to live with. Capitalia was in the middle of the first cold snap of autumn, and moving in and out of heated buildings was more than his arthritic joints could stand. The only alternatives to hiding indoors were heated suits or extra pain medication, neither of which expecially appealed to him. "All right," he told his son. "But if you guys don't break for the evening soon, call me back and I'll relieve you. You look beat."

"I'll be all right. The main reason I called was to check a couple of things on this parallel survey mission request you put in. How much of that are you willing for the Worlds to finance?"

"Not a single quarter," Jonny told him flatly. "At the bottom line this is a trade deal, Corwin, and *no* one trades for merchandise he hasn't even seen, let alone inspected. Of course, since it's the Pua demesne that's actually offering the five planets, you can probably insist the Speaker charge *them* the survey costs. All that'll ultimately do is throw the issue back to Pua and Baliu to work out between themselves, but at least it should get it out of *our* hair."

"Yeah." Corwin shook his head in bemusement. "Hard to believe this collection of business cutthroats actually got together long enough to fight a war."

"They did. Believe me, they did. And there's nothing that says they couldn't do it again."

"Point taken. Well . . . are you willing for us to use

the *Menssana* for the survey mission if the Trofts—whichever Trofts—pay all the other expenses?"

Jonny bit at his lip. "I'd rather they provide the ship, too. But okay—if you have to fall back to that position, go ahead and do so. They pay for the fuel, though."

"Okay. Actually, I'll probably wind up holding that option against something the Qasama mission needs. Talk to you later."

They signed off, and for a moment Jonny gazed at the screen as he tried to visualize all the various lines the negotiations could move along. But it was too much like an oversized game of trisec chess, with just too many possibilities to hang onto simultaneously. Getting to his feet—an easy enough operation in the overheated room—he went over to the table and sat down next to Chrys. "How's it coming?" he asked, eyeing the mass of wires, microcomponents, and centipeds set into her circuit board.

"Slow," she said, fiddling with the controls on her diagnostic display. "I'm beginning to see why everyone prefers buying finished Troft electronics to just getting the components and building things themselves. These centipeds in particular have a lot of odd and not entirely obvious response characteristics outside their quote normal unquote usage range."

"You'll figure it all out," Jonny assured her. "You were once the best electronics tech in—"

"In Ariel?" She snorted. "Thanks a spangle. There were only two of us there—I *had* to be best or runner-up."

"Best, definitely," Jonny said firmly. A touch of the old Chrys, the sense of humor that had been so muted lately . . . perhaps she was finally getting a grip on the turmoil of the past few weeks.

Or perhaps she was simply retreating into her own past. It had been years since she'd done anything serious with her electronics training.

"You realize, of course," she cut quietly into his

thoughts, "that if you let the *Menssana* go on this survey mission, there'll be no backup ship available if the *Dewdrop* gets in trouble on Qasama."

Jonny shook his head. "We weren't going to use the *Menssana* for that anyway. There'll be one or more Troft warships hanging back from Qasama in case some extra muscle is needed."

"I thought the Trofts didn't want to fight the Qasamans."

"If the mission has any trouble, they'll damn well have to," Jonny said grimly. "But they shouldn't have any real qualms—a local commando-type strike is hardly the same as committing to a full-scale war."

"Besides which, they'll want to protect their investment?"

"*Now* you're thinking like a Troft." Reaching over, he put an arm around her shoulders. "Just remember, Chrys," he added more seriously, "that the Baliuies had to have gotten at least one diplomatic team into and out of Qasama safely to have anything like the data we know they have. The third-level translator program they'll be giving us shows *that* much. Joshua and Justin will be all right. Really."

"I'd like to believe that," Chrys sighed. "But you know it's a mother's prerogative to worry."

"I seem to remember that being a *wife's* prerogative thirty years ago."

"Things change." Chrys toyed with a hex-shaped centiped. "Always do."

"Yes," Jonny agreed. "And not always for the better. I seem to also remember a time when the two of us went on trips together—*just* the two of us, with no kids along. What would you say to seeing if we can bring back those days?"

Chrys snorted faintly. "You think the Council could function without you that long?"

He winced at the implied criticism. "Sure they can," he said, choosing to take the question at face value. "Corwin knows the ropes well enough, and nothing important's likely to happen while the Qasama mission's gone, anyway. Perfect time for a vacation."

"Wait a second." She turned a frown his direction. "Are you talking about a vacation while your sons are out there in who knows *what* kind of danger?"

"Why not?" he asked. "Seriously. There's not a single thing we can do for them from here, even if we knew something had gone wrong, which we won't— sending shuttles back and forth has already been rejected as too possibly provocative. Giving your mind something besides worry to occupy it would be good for you."

She gestured minutely at the electronics in front of her. "If *this* can't keep my mind busy, I doubt a vacation will."

"That's only because you don't know the kind of vacation I have in mind," he told her, mentally crossing his fingers. If he presented this right she might just go for it . . . and he knew with a solid conviction that it was something they both needed. "I was thinking of a leisurely cruise sort of thing, with stops at various points for relaxing strolls through forests and grasslands, or maybe a swim through warm waters. Companionship with others when we want it, privacy when we want *that*, and all the comforts of home. How's it sound?"

Chrys smiled. "Like the coastline cruises they used to advertise when I was a child. Don't tell me some enterprising soul's bought a deep-sea liner from the Trofts?"

"Ah—not exactly. Would it help if I told you the cruise itinerary includes five planets?"

"Five pl— Jonny!" Chrys's eyes widened with shock. "You don't mean—the *survey mission*?"

"Sure—and why not?"

"What do you mean, why not? That's a scientific expedition, not a vacation service for the middle-aged."

"Ah, but I'm a governor emeritus, remember? If

Liz Telek can talk her way aboard the Qasama trip on the grounds someone with authority should be present, I can certainly borrow her argument."

A muscle in Chrys's jaw twitched. "You've already arranged this, haven't you?" she asked suspiciously.

"Yes—but I'm going only if you do. I didn't misrepresent any of this, Chrys—I'll be there strictly to observe, make a policy decision should one come up, and otherwise just stay out of everyone else's way. It really *will* be just like an out-of-the-way vacation for the two of us."

Chrys dropped her eyes to the table. "It'd be dangerous, though, wouldn't it?"

Jonny shrugged. "So was life in Ariel when we were first married. You didn't seem to mind it so much."

"I was a lot younger then."

"So? Why should Justin and Joshua have all the fun?"

He'd hoped to spark a reaction of some kind, but was completely unprepared for the burst of laughter that escaped Chrys's lips. Genuine laughter, with genuine amusement behind it. "You're impossible," she accused, swiveling in her seat to give him a mock glare. "Didn't I just tell you I planned to be worried about them? What're we going to do—make this a Christmas exchange of worries?"

"Or we can deputize Corwin to do the worrying for all of us," Jonny suggested with a straight face. "Brothers in the morning, parents in the afternoon, and he can worry about the Council for me in the evenings. Come on, Chrys—it'll probably be our only chance to see the place our great-great-grandchildren may someday live." *At least our only chance together*, he added to himself, *in the three or four years I have left*.

Her face showed no hint of having followed that train of thought: but a minute later she sighed and nodded. "All right. Yes—let's do it."

"Thanks, Hon," he said quietly. It wouldn't, he

knew, quite make up for losing her sons to the universe at large . . . but perhaps having a husband back for a while would be at least partial compensation.

He hoped so. Despite his assurances, it was quite possible two of those sons would soon be swallowed up by that same universe, never to return.

Chapter 6

The Council—along with an ever-expanding ring of agents/confidants—kept the secret of the Troft proposal remarkably well for nearly four weeks longer; but at that point Stiggur decided to release the news to the general population. From Corwin's point of view the timing couldn't have been worse. Still in the midst of detailed financial negotiations with the Trofts, he was abruptly thrust into the position of being answer man for what seemed sometimes to be all three hundred eighty thousand of Aventine's people. Theron Yutu and the rest of the staff were able to handle a lot of it on their own, but there were a fair number of policy-type questions that only he and Jonny could answer; and because of his private commitment to keeping his father's workload as light as possible, Corwin wound up spending an amazing amount of time on the phone and the public information net.

Fortunately, the reaction was generally positive. Most of the objections raised were along the ethical lines the Moreau family had discussed together in their own first pass by the issue, and even among those dissenters support for the Council ran high. Virtually no one raised the point Corwin had been most worried about: namely, why the Council had waited nearly two months before soliciting public feedback. That one he would have found hard to answer.

But all the public relations work took his attention away from the mission details being hammered out— took enough of it, in fact, that he completely missed the important part of the proposed survey mission team until the list was made public ... and even then Joshua had to call and tell him about it.

"I wondered why you were taking it so calmly," Jonny said when Corwin confronted him a few minutes later. "I suppose I should have mentioned it to you."

"Mentioned, my left eye," Corwin growled. "You should have at least *discussed* it with the rest of us before you went ahead and signed yourselves up."

"Why?" Jonny countered. "What your mother and I do with our lives is our business— we *are* old enough to make these decisions for ourselves. We decided we wanted a change of scenery, and this seemed a good way to get it." He cocked an eyebrow. "Or are you going to suggest neither of us would know how to handle an alien environment?"

Corwin clamped his teeth together. "You're a lot older than you were when you came to Aventine. You could die out there."

"Your brothers could die on Qasama," Jonny reminded him softly. "Should we all sit here in safety while they're out risking their lives? This way we're at least in a sense sharing their danger."

A cold shiver rippled up Corwin's back. "Only in the most far-fetched sense," he said. "Your danger won't diminish theirs."

"I know." Jonny's smile was wry but clear, without any trace of self-delusion in it. "That's one of the most fascinating things about the human psyche—a deep subconscious feeling can be very strong without making any logical sense whatsoever." He sobered. "I don't ask you to approve, Corwin; but grant that I know enough about myself and my wife to know what I'm doing on this."

Corwin sighed and waved a hand in defeat. "All right. But you'd both darn well better come back safely. I can't run the Council all by myself, you know."

Jonny chuckled. "We'll do our best." Reaching over to his phone, he tapped up something on the display. "Let's see ... ah, good—Council's discussing Cobra contingent this afternoon. That one we can safely skip. How would you like to see some of your father's practical politics in action?"

"Sure," Corwin said, wondering what the other was talking about.

"Good." Jonny tapped a few more keys. "This is Jonny Moreau. Is the special aircar I ordered ready yet? ... Good. Inform the pilot we'll be lifting in about twenty minutes: myself and two other passengers."

Signing off, he got to his feet and stepped over to the rack where his heated suit was hanging. "Go get your coat," he told Corwin. "We're about to give a customer the Aventine equivalent of a free sample ... which, with any luck, won't turn out to be *exactly* free."

The third passenger turned out to be Speaker One.

Corwin watched the Troft in a sort of surreptitious fascination as they flew high above the Aventinian landscape. He'd seen plenty of Trofts in his life, but never one so close and for so long a time. The back-jointed legs and splaytoed feet; the vaguely insectoid torso and abdomen; the arms with their flexible radiator membranes; the oversized head with its double throat bladder and strangely chicken-like face—all the gross anatomical features were as familiar to him as those of human beings or even spine leopards. But there were fine details which Corwin realized he'd never so much as noticed. The faint sheen of the

alien's skin, for example, was a more muted version
of the same shimmer shown by its leotard-like outfit.
Even at a meter's distance he could see the tiny lines
crisscrossing its skin and the slender hairs growing
out of each intersection. Seated on its specially designed couch, the Troft moved only occasionally during the flight, but whenever it did Corwin caught a
glimpse of wiry muscles working beneath the skin
and—sometimes—a hint of its skeletal structure as
well. The large main eyes were a different color than
the three tiny compound eyes grouped around each
one. The main eyes, he'd once read, were for good
binocular vision; the compound eyes permitted both
night vision and the detection of polarized sunlight
for cloudy-day solar navigation. The alien's short beak
remained closed during the trip, which Corwin re-
gretted: he'd have liked to have seen what Troft tri-
cuspid teeth really looked like.

Jonny said virtually nothing during the 20-minute
flight, beyond giving the pilot their destination. Apparently he and Speaker One had worked this out in
advance and neither felt the need to discuss anything
further. Corwin considered pressing his father for
information, but decided reluctantly that Jonny's silence was a cue to be followed. Splitting his attention between the Troft and the view out the window,
he cultivated what patience he could muster.

They landed at last near a large, squarish building
nestled inexplicably out in the snowy forest far from
any village Corwin was familiar with. A two-man
escort was waiting as Jonny led the way out of the
aircar . . . and it was only then that Corwin began to
get an inkling of what his father had in mind.

High on each man's chest was a patch with the
words "Training Center"; beneath it was the stylized
hooded-snake emblem of the Cobra Academy.

"Governor," one of them nodded at Jonny. "You
and your guests are cleared for monitor room access.
If you'll all follow me. . . ."

Together they headed through an armored door and down an exceptionally drab and anonymous corridor, footsteps echoing oddly against the metallic walls. Their guide led them into an elevator; thirty seconds later they exited into a large, unevenly lit room and a scene of muted tension. In the darker areas along the wall at least thirty people sat before banks of small display screens, working away at keyboards and joysticks, while in the center a large semicircular console with larger displays was the focus of attention for a half-dozen men in the red and black diamond-patterned tunics of the Cobras. One of them headed over to meet the newcomers, and as he approached Corwin recognized him as Cobra Coordinator Sun himself. *The royal treatment, indeed,* he thought.

"Governor," Sun said, inclining his head briefly to Jonny as he neared the group. "Speaker One; Mr. Moreau," he added with similar nods to the Troft and Corwin. "If you'll step this way, the team has just penetrated the outer perimeter section."

"Is there an attack taking place?" Speaker One asked as they followed Sun back toward the crescent-shaped console.

"In a manner of speaking," Sun told it. "The Cobra team who'll be going to Qasama is practicing their building assault techniques. Let's see how they're doing."

The displays showed various degrees of activity, and Corwin scanned them quickly in an effort to make sense of it all. Despite the multiple camera angles shown, it was soon apparent that there were actually only a total of four Cobras involved: Almo Pyre, Justin, and two more Corwin knew only from pictures and Council reports, Michael Winward and Dorjay Link. The latter two were moving stealthily down a corridor, while Pyre and Justin huddled before a formidable-looking door.

"Those two," Sun explained, pointing at Pyre and Justin, "are blocked by a blast door with an elec-

tronic lock. They could probably force it open with
their antiarmor lasers, but at this point there's been
no general alarm and it's worth the time to see if
they can get through more quietly. Looks like one of
the Qasamans is about to surprise them, though." He
tapped a display whose rolling image showed the
gait of a mechanical remote—

The camera turned a corner and stopped, the blast
door and Justin framed in its view. *Justin alone?*
Corwin thought. *But Almo was there, too.*

The screen flared abruptly and went black. Corwin
shifted his gaze to the fixed-camera monitors just in
time to see Pyre drop from the ceiling to land in a
crouch beside the disabled remote, hands curled into
fingertip laser ready position. He checked around the
corner, then lifted the remote and carried it back to
the door. "All clear," he whispered to Justin.

"Just about ready here," Justin whispered back.

"Inside," Sun said, "is a key missile control tracking station." He leaned over to touch a switch, and a
vacant display came to life with an overhead schematic of the entire test area. Corwin quickly located
the dots representing his brother and Pyre ... and
with a stomach-wrenching shock saw that the room
they were about to enter was far from unoccupied.
"You'll note," Sun continued in the same emotion-
less voice, "that there are eight Qasamans on duty in
there. All are armed, but the Cobras ought to have
the advantage of surprise. Let's see. . . ."

Justin stood up and pulled on the door ... and an
instant before it began its swing the tense silence
was shattered by the blare of alarm bells.

Corwin would later learn that Winward and Link
had accidentally triggered the alarm, but for that
first instant it seemed horribly obvious that Justin
and Pyre had walked into a trap. The two Cobras
seemed to believe that as well and, rather than charging through the open door, they hit the wall on either
side. Beside him, Corwin heard Jonny mutter some-

thing vicious . . . but by the time it seemed to dawn
on the Cobras that they'd make a mistake it was too
late. The remotes in the tracking room were on guard,
and when Pyre risked a glance around the door jamb
he nearly caught a laser blast for his trouble.

Corwin's jaw was clenched hard enough to hurt;
but the figures on the monitor wasted no time in
recriminations. Pyre sent Justin a half dozen quick
hand signals, got an acknowledging nod, and seemed
to brace himself. Both men took a second to fire apparently random fingertip laser shots through the doorway . . . and then, gripping the jamb for leverage,
Pyre hurled himself into the room.

Into *and* up. The tracking room monitors caught a
perfect view of him arcing spinning into the air like an
oddly shaped gyroscope coming off a jump board,
the antiarmor laser in his left leg carving out a
traveling cone of destruction. He'd just reached the
peak of his jump when Justin came in behind him,
the younger Cobra's flat dive and somersault landing
him on his back in a sort of spinning fetal position
. . . and his antiarmor laser, too, began its deadly
sweep.

It was a classic high-low maneuver Corwin recognized from his father's stories of the war. Between
Pyre's sensor-guided air attack and Justin's lower
horizontal spray, effective cover simply ceased to exist, and in the space of maybe a second and a half all
eight of the remotes' displays went dark.

Corwin suddenly realized he was holding his breath
and risked a quick look to see what Winward and
Link were up to. They'd split up since he'd last seen
them, with Link at what was obviously an open outside door and Winward standing guard with fingertip lasers ready at the intersection of two hallways.
Between them, the overhead schematic showed an
impressive number of disabled remotes.

A flash and thunderclap jerked Corwin's attention
back to the other displays, and he was just in time to

watch as Justin aimed his right fingertip laser at one of the control panels in the tracking room and triggered his arcthrower. Corwin's hands curled into tight fists as the second flash and crash came; he had been burned once by a faulty electrical outlet as a child, and the arcthrower with its high-amperage current flowing along an ionized laser path made his skin crawl in a way the far more powerful antiarmor laser never did. But he forced himself to watch as Pyre and Justin worked methodically around the room, destroying every scrap of electronic equipment in sight. Pyre paused once before a large shielded display, and a low hum abruptly filled the room. "Sonic disruptor," Sun murmured, presumably for the Troft's benefit. A few seconds later Corwin thought he detected a muffled *crack*, and the hum disappeared as Pyre moved on.

Their escape from the room, two arcthrower blasts later, was so straightforward as to be anticlimactic. Link and Winward, it now became clear, had spent most of their time clearing the exit route, and Pyre had to take out only two more remotes. Winward joined them as they passed his crossroads guard post, and by the time all four headed into the woods through Link's door Corwin's heartbeat was almost back to normal.

"And that," Sun said, "is that. All remotes, shut down; signal the team to return."

Corwin glanced beyond the central console as, in the darkened areas around the room, displays went uniformly black and the remote operators began to stretch and stand up. Beside him, Corwin felt his father's hand grip his shoulder. "I'd forgotten what it was like to see Cobras in genuine combat situations," Jonny said, his voice showing lingering traces of his tension.

"Amazing how much adrenaline the human body can put out," another familiar voice said. Corwin looked past his father in surprise. So engrossed had

he been in the displays that he'd never even noticed
Jonny's old teammate Cally Halloran was among the
group Sun had assembled. Halloran nodded a greeting in Corwin's direction and then shifted his attention to the Troft standing silently beside him. "I
understand the Baliu'ckha'spmi demesne feels the
cost of this initial expedition is too high, Speaker
One," he said. "Having now seen Cobras in action, do
you agree?"

Speaker One stirred, its arm membranes stretch-
ing out like bat wings for a moment before resettling
against its upper arms. "The Tlos'khin'fahi demesne
has always been aware of *koubrah*-warrior fighting
skill," it said.

Which wasn't exactly an answer, Corwin realized.
His father wasn't fooled by the evasion, either. "But
not sufficiently impressed, I gather, to absorb the
extra costs the Baliu demesne isn't willing to pay?"
the elder Moreau suggested. "Perhaps your demesne-
lord would like to see a tape of this exercise."

"It would be likely to interest him," the Troft agreed.
"Presuming the price is reasonable."

"Quite reasonable," Jonny nodded. "Especially as
you'll be able to recover some of the cost by selling a
copy to the Baliu'ckha'spmi demesne. I think perhaps your two demesne-lords will be able to come to
a new agreement afterwards on how much each is
willing to spend to have our services."

"Yes," Speaker One said, and Corwin imagined he
could hear a note of thoughtfulness in the flat translator voice. "Yes, I think that likely."

The prediction proved correct, and within two weeks
the financial quibbles from the Troft side of the nego-
tiation table suddenly ceased. It made little difference to the actual planning groups, which had already
committed themselves to the twin goals of not scrimp-
ing on vital equipment while simultaneously keeping
costs to a bare minimum. But emotionally, the tacit

carte blanche was a big boost to all concerned; and
politically Corwin found in the action a not-so-subtle
enhancement of the Cobra Worlds' general reputation. A good thing, to a point ... but he still had
vivid memories of the days when the Trofts considered the Worlds a threat. The closing of their connection with the Dominion of Man had ended the Troft's
fears in that direction, but it was easy to see how a
rumor of power could wind up being as disquieting
to the aliens as the real thing. For the first time he
began to understand that part of his father's twin-
edged reluctance to demonstrate the Cobras' true
war-making capabilities. But it was far too late to
back out now.

Three weeks later—barely eleven since the Council's approval of the project—the Cobra Worlds' two
long-range spacecraft headed out from Aventine. On
the *Dewdrop*, bound for Qasama, were Justin and
Joshua Moreau; aboard the *Menssana*, destinations
as yet not officially named, rode Jonny and Chrys
Moreau.

Corwin watched the ships leave, and was left to
wonder how a planet with nearly four hundred thousand people could suddenly feel so lonely.

Chapter 7

The *Dewdrop* had been Aventine's only interstellar craft in the days when the planet was first colonized, and since its sole purpose then had been to reconnoiter nearby systems for possible future habitation it made little sense to the Dominion planners to tie up anything larger than a long-range scout ship. With the normal complement of five crewers and four observers the *Dewdrop* had probably seemed adequately roomy; with a current load exactly twice that, it was pretty damned crowded.

Pyre didn't find it excruciatingly uncomfortable; but then, he'd grown up under conditions that were in their own way equally claustrophobic. The small village of Thanksgiving, ringed by spine leopard-infested forests, had by reasons of physical space been a very cozy place, and though Pyre had experienced both the greater anonymity of larger cities and the wide-open spaces of Aventine's frontier regions since then, he'd never lost his ability to create mental privacy where physical privacy didn't exist.

To varying degrees, most of the other ten passengers also seemed to adapt reasonably well. Justin and Joshua, of course, had shared a room for most of their lives, and even in a cramped stateroom got along together better than most other sets of brothers Pyre had known. The other two Cobras, Link and Winward, had survived both the academy's barracks arrangement and the intense training of the past few weeks, and Winward commented at least once that shipboard life was almost a vacation by comparison. The contact team members—who, besides Joshua, consisted of Yuri Cerenkov, Marck Rynstadt, and former Dominion Marine Decker York—had been screened for anything vaguely resembling a neurosis, and Pyre doubted much of *anything* would bother them, at least noticeably. And the two chief scientists, Drs. Bilman Christopher and Hersh Nnamdi, were so busy testing equipment, programs, and contingency branch schemes that it was unlikely they even noticed the lack of breathing space.

Which left Governor Telek.

To Pyre it was still a mystery why she was aboard this mission. Arguments about high Council representation notwithstanding, it seemed to him incredible that Governor-General Stiggur should allow a woman on what was looking more and more like a military mission. Pyre's attitudes were as healthy as anyone else's, and he had no qualms whatsoever about female doctors or engineers; but warfare *was* different, and Stigger with his roots back in the Dominion should feel that even more strongly than Pyre did. Which led immediately to the conclusion that the decision had been purely political ... which led even faster to the question of why *he*, Pyre, was aboard.

And *that* was the really troublesome one. Pyre hadn't had as much access to closed-door information lately as he'd had when he'd been living near the Moreaus, but even so it was pretty obvious that Stiggur wouldn't have let Telek come unless he expected her report and recommendations on Qasama to fall more or less in line with his own expectations. Pyre was a good friend of Jonny Moreau, who had both as governor and governor emeritus locked horns regularly with Telek ... and yet it was *Pyre's* team she'd asked to

observe in the field back on Aventine; and it was *Pyre*
whose cost/manpower estimates she'd solicited for
presentation to the governors; and it was *Pyre* she'd
sponsored to be Cobra team leader on this mission.

Why? Did she expect to flatter him into support for
her more aggressive stance on the Qasama issue? To
offer him one last chance at real Cobra action before
the implant-related diseases began their slow but
inevitable crippling of his body, in the hope that, in
gratitude, he'd become a political ally when he retired to advisory positions on the sidelines? Or had
she simply concluded he was the best man for the job
and to hell just this once with politics?

He didn't know the answer ... and it quickly became clear he wasn't going to figure it out en route.
Telek's field biology background had left her little
prepared for the *Dewdrop*'s overcrowded zoo, and
though she gamely tried to maintain both minimal
sociability and her responsibilities as official head of
the mission, it was obvious there weren't going to be
any opportunities to sound her out properly on her
thoughts and motivations. Perhaps when they reached
Qasama and the contact team disembarked there'd
be time for that. Assuming there was time for anything at all.

So he spent his time working out contingency plans
with his team, renewing his friendship with the Moreau twins, and listening to the dull background drone
of the *Dewdrop*'s engines as he tried to think of anything he'd forgotten. The nightmares of sudden, over-
whelming disaster he did his best to ignore.

Taken at low-power, high-efficiency speeds, the forty-
five light-years to Qasama would have run them a
shade over a month; at the *Dewdrop*'s top speed, with
frequent refueling stops at Troft systems, they could
have made it in six days. Captain Reson F'ahl chose a
reasonably conservative middle course, both out of
fears for the *Dewdrop*'s aging systems and also—Pyre

suspected—out of an old, lingering distrust of the
Trofts.

So for fifteen days they were cooped up in the
blackness of hyperspace, with only the deep-space refueling stops every five days to break the viewport's
monotony . . . and on the sixteenth day they arrived
at Qasama.

Purists had claimed for centuries that no photo-
graphic emulsion, holographic trace-record, or computerized visual reproduction ever made had quite
the same range and power as the human eye. Intellectually, Joshua tended to agree; but on a more
visceral level he discovered it for the first time in
gazing out his stateroom viewport.

The poets were indeed right: there were few sights
more majestic than that of an entire world spinning
slowly and serenely beneath you.

Standing with his face practically welded to the
small triple-plate plastic oval, he didn't even notice
anyone had come into the room behind him until
Justin said, "You going to build a nest there?"

He didn't bother to turn around. "Go find your
own viewport. I've got land-use rights on this one."

"Come on—move," Justin said, tugging with token
force on his arm. "Aren't you supposed to be with
Yuri and the others anyway?"

Joshua waved a hand in the general direction of
the intercom display. "There's no room up there for
anyone bigger than a hamster—oh, all *right*." Snort-
ing feigned exasperation, he stepped aside. Justin
took his place at the viewport . . . and Joshua waited
for the other's first awe-filled whistle before turning
toward the intercom.

The display showed the room euphemistically called
the lounge—and "crowded" was far too mild a term
for it. Packed in among the various displays and
equipment monitors were Yuri Cerenkov, the scientists Christopher and Nnamdi, and Governor Telek.
Back near the viewport, almost out of the intercom

camera's range, Pyre and Decker York stood together, occasionally sharing inaudible comments. Joshua turned the volume up a bit, just in time to catch Nnamdi's thoughtful snort. "I'm sorry, but I simply don't see what in blazes the Trofts are so worried about," he said, apparently to the room at large. "How can a village-level society be a threat to anyone outside its own atmosphere?"

"Let's show a little patience, shall we?" Telek said, not looking up from her own bank of displays. "We haven't even finished a complete orbit yet. All the high-tech cities may be on the other side."

"It's not just the matter of technology, Governor," Nnamdi countered. "The population density is too low to be consistent with an advanced society."

"That's anthropomorphic thinking," Telek shook her head. "If their birth rate's low enough and they like lots of room around them they could still be high-tech. Bil, what're you getting?"

Christopher sat in silence another moment before answering. "Nothing conclusive one way or the other yet. I can see roads between some of the villages, but the tree cover's too thick to tell how extensive the network is. No satellite communications systems, though, and no broadcasts I can detect."

Joshua touched the intercom's talk switch. "Excuse me, but is there any way to see how much of the ground around the villages is being cultivated? That might be a clue."

Telek looked over at the intercom camera. "So far that's not conclusive, either," she said. "There are some good-sized candidates for crop fields, but the terrain and vegetation color scheme make real measurement iffy."

"Besides which," Christopher put in, "whether a given village is growing crops for local use or for export is something else we can't tell from up here."

"So let's go on down," Justin muttered from his place at the viewport.

Joshua looked back at his brother. Justin's face was thoughtful as he gazed at the planet below ... but nowhere in expression or stance could Joshua detect the same hard knot that had taken up residence in his own stomach. "Let's be a little less anxious to throw the landing party outside, shall we?" he said tartly.

Justin blinked at him. "Sorry—did I sound callous?"

"You sounded overconfident, and that's worse. Your tendency toward optimism could be downright dangerous down there."

"Tiptoing around up here like we've got some guilty secret to hide will be better?"

Joshua grimaced. Alike as two electrons, they'd often been called ... but when the crunch came it was really very easy to tell them apart. Deep down, Justin had a strangely potent variety of fatalistic optimism that refused to let him believe the universe would really hurt him. A totally unrealistic philosophy, to Joshua's way of thinking—and all the more incomprehensible because Justin *wasn't* simply incapable of recognizing potential danger. He was as good at looking ahead and weighing odds as anyone else in the family; he just acted as if those odds didn't apply to him. It was this attitude, more than anything else, that had fueled Joshua's private reservations about Justin's Cobra amibitions ... and had nearly persuaded him to back them out of this mission entirely.

"Aha!" Cerenkov's satisfied exclamation came from the intercom speaker into Joshua's musings. "There we go. You wanted a city, Hersh?—well, there it is."

"I'll be damned," Nnamdi murmured, fingertips skating across his display controls. "That's a city, all right. Let's see ... electric power for sure ... still no radio broadcasts detectable ... looks like the tallest buildings are in the ten- to twenty-story range. Bil, can you find anything that looks like a power plant?"

"Hang on," Christopher said. "Got some odd neutrino emissions here—trying to get a spectrum analysis. . . ."

"Another city showing now—south and a little west of the first," Cerenkov reported.

Joshua let a breath hiss slowly between his teeth, caught between the desire to rush down to the lounge and see the cities for himself and the fear of missing something important en route. "I think I can see them," Justin said behind him. "Come take a look."

Joshua joined him at the viewport, glad to have found a compromise. The cities were just barely visible. "Your telescopic vision show anything interesting?" he asked his brother.

"At this range? Don't be silly. Wait a second, though—I've got an idea."

Stepping back to the intercom, Justin busied himself with the keyboard. A moment later the crowded lounge was replaced by a slightly fuzzy still picture. "Got the ultra-high-resolution-camera feed," he told Joshua with satisfaction.

Joshua craned his neck to look. The city seemed normal enough: buildings, streets, park-like areas . . . "Odd angle for a street pattern, isn't it?" he remarked. "I'd think it simpler to run their streets north-south and east-west instead of whatever angle that is."

He hadn't realized the voice link with the lounge was still open until Telek's voice came in reply. "The angle, in case you're interested, is twenty-four degrees, rotated counterclockwise from true north. And the southeast-northwest streets are considerably broader than the perpendicular set. Speculations as to why? Anyone?"

"Second city's the same way," Cerenkov grunted. "The streets are only skewed twenty-three point eight degrees, but the same wide/narrow pattern's there."

"Doesn't look like they're ringed, either, the way the villages are." Justin spoke up, leafing through the ultra-camera's other shots.

There was a short pause from the other end. "What do you mean, 'ringed'?" Nnamdi asked.

"There's a dark ring around each of the villages," Justin told him, backtracking a few photos. "I assumed it was shadow from the surrounding trees, but now I'm not so sure."

"Interesting," Telek grunted. "What's the number on that photo?"

"While you're doing that," Christopher put in, "we've got the neutrino spectrum indentified now. Looks like they're using a tandem fission/fusion reactor system for their power supply."

Someone in the lounge gave a low whistle. "That's pretty advanced, isn't it?" another voice—Marck Rynstadt's, Joshua tentatively identified it—came in on the intercom hook-up.

"Yes and no," Christopher said. "They obviously haven't got anything as reliable as our fusion plant design or they wouldn't be fiddling with a tandem system. On the other hand, fission alone ought to be hundreds of years beyond a village society's capabilities."

"Dual cultures, then?" Joshua hazarded. "Cities and villages on separate development tracks?"

"More likely the cities are run by invading aliens," Nnamdi said bluntly, "while the villages are home to the original natives. I concede the technology issue—and it therefore becomes rather clear what the Trofts are worried about."

"That Qasama is the leading edge of someone else moving toward Troft territory," Telek said grimly. "Moreau—whichever of you asked—we've got an ID on those ring shadows now. They're walls, about a meter thick and two to three meters high."

The twins exchanged glances. "Primitive defenses," Justin said.

"Looks that way," Cerenkov said. "Governor, I think we'd do well to cut this part of the run to one or at most two more orbits. They're almost certainly aware

by now that we're up here, and the longer we wait
before landing, the less forthright and honest we look.
Remember that we aren't going to be able to pretend
we didn't know Qasama was here."

"At least not if we intend to use the Troft translator," Telek agreed—reluctantly, Joshua thought. Steal-
ing a glance back at the intercom screen, he studied
her face . . . but if she were feeling any fear at order-
ing them down into the snake pit, it wasn't visible.
Two of them, he thought morosely, turning back to
his brother and the viewport. —*Or else it's me who's
the odd one. Maybe I'm just overcautious . . . or even
an out-and-out coward.*

Oddly enough, the possibility carried no sense of
shame along with it. Justin and Telek, after all,
wouldn't be leaving the relative safety of the *Dewdrop*
the minute they landed; Joshua and the rest of the
contact team would. An extra helping of native caution would likely be more an asset than a liability
out there.

They came down on the next orbit over what
Nnamdi had dubbed the "city belt," aiming for a set
of runways at the north end of the northernmost of the
five cities in the chain. There had been some excitement when the runways had first been noticed,
Nnamdi pouncing on them as evidence that Qasama
was indeed the forward base of a star-going people.
Christopher, though, had suggested their width and
length were more suitable for aircraft than robot
glide-shuttles, and for a while a tension-sharpened
argument had raged in the lounge. It was Decker York
who eventually pointed out that the runway directions
seemed oriented more along prevailing wind directions than along the most likely orbital launch/land
vectors. Further study had failed to come up with
anything else that could possibly be a starfield, and
Telek had elected to use the airport as the next best
site.

For Pyre, it was the most unnerving part of the mission thus far. Strapped into an emergency crash chair near the main exit hatchway, far from any viewports or intercom displays, he felt more helpless than a Cobra had any business feeling. If the Qasamans had any interest in shooting the *Dewdrop* down, the approach glide would be the ideal time to do so. More so than the aliens might think, in fact; they presumably had no way of knowing that the *Dewdrop* was a gravity-lift, VTOL craft and that her crew had little experience with the emergency runway landing procedure Telek had insisted they use.

But no one opened fire, and with only the mildest of lurches the ship touched down. Heaving an unabashed sigh of relief, Pyre nevertheless kept one eye firmly on the hatch's inner door as he unstrapped and got once more to his feet. The plan was to wait a few minutes and then send Cerenkov outside to wait for whatever reception committee the Qasamans might send. Through all of that Pyre and one of his Cobras would be the *Dewdrop*'s only real defense.

His auditory enhancers, still set on high power from the landing, picked up Nnamdi's gasp from down the hall in the lounge. "My God, Governor. Look! It's—oh, my *God*!"

"Almo!" Cerenkov's voice boomed from the other direction an instant later. "Get up here!"

Pyre was already moving, his hands automatically curving into fingertip laser firing position as he sprinted for the bridge, where Cerenkov had been for the landing.

The small gray-tone room was alive with color when he arrived, as virtually every screen displayed views of the city and surrounding forest outside the ship. Pyre hadn't realized before then just how colorful the city itself actually was, its buildings painted with the same wide range of shades as the forest, as if in deliberate mimicry. But for the moment the

Qasamans' decorative sense was the last thing on his mind. "What's up?" he snapped.

Cerenkov, standing behind F'ahl's command chair, pointed a none too steady finger at a telescopic view of the nearest buildings a couple of hundred meters away. "The Qasamans," he said simply.

Pyre stared at the screen. Six figures were indeed heading in the *Dewdrop*'s direction, each with the bulge of a sidearm at one side and something that seemed to be a small bird perched on the opposite shoulder. Six figures—

As human as anyone aboard the *Dewdrop*.

Chapter 8

For a long minute Pyre just stood there, brain struggling mightily to reconcile what his eyes showed him with the sheer impossibility of it all. Humans *here?*—over a hundred and fifty light-years from the nearest world of the Dominion of Man? And past the Troft Assemblage, to boot?

Back in the lounge, someone cleared his throat, a raspy sound in the bridge intercom speaker. "So you say we've all been thinking too anthropomorphically, Governor?" Nnamdi said with exaggerated casualness.

For once, it seemed, Telek was at a loss for words. A moment later Nnamdi continued, "At least now we know for sure the Baliu demesne didn't have much to do with the Troft-Dominion War. They could hardly have failed to mention that the Qasamans were the same species as we were."

"This is impossible," York growled. "Humans can't be here. They just *can't*."

"All right, they can't," Christopher spoke up. "Shall we go out and tell them that?"

"Maybe they're an illusion of some kind," Joshua suggested from the twins' room. "Controlled psychic hallucination or something."

"I don't believe in *that* sort of thing, either," York snapped.

70

"Besides," F'ahl added, touching some controls, "if they're an illusion they're a mighty substantial one. Short-radar's picking them up with no trouble and confirms shape."

"Maybe they're the slaves of the real Qasamans," Cerenkov suggested. "Descendents of people kidnapped from Earth centuries ago. Regardless, Governor, we've got to go out there and meet them."

Telek hissed between her teeth, finally seeming to find her voice. "Captain, what's the analyzer showing?"

"Nothing inimical so far," F'ahl reported, running a finger down one of the few displays not showing an outside view. "Oxygen, nitrogen, carbon dioxide, and other trace gasses in acceptable amounts. Uh ... no evidence of unusual radioactive or heavy-metal contamination. Bacteria analysis has barely gotten started, but so far no problems—computer shows similar DNA and protein structures in the ones it's analyzed, but doesn't show any health hazards from them."

"Hmmm. Well, I'll want to check that data over myself later, but if the Aventine pattern holds here microbes probably won't be a big problem. All right, Yuri, I guess you can go out. But you'd better wear a filter bubble, to be on the safe side. The number two should be adequate unless Qasanan viruses come a *lot* smaller than ours."

"Right." Cerenkov hesitated. "Governor, as long as we've got a reception committee on its way, I'd like to take my whole team out with me."

The six Qasamans were almost to the ship now. Pyre watched the magnified view, his eyes shifting from the details of the faces to the silver-blue birds perched on each person's left shoulder to the pistols belted on each hip. "Governor, I'd recommend we let Yuri go alone first," he said.

"No, he's right—we ought to show good faith," Telek said with a sigh.

Cerenkov didn't wait any longer. "Marck, Decker, Joshua—meet me at the dock with full gear." He got three acknowledgments and hurried out of the bridge.

"Almo?" Telek called as Pyre turned to follow. "I want you back here for this."

Pyre grimaced, but there wasn't time to argue the order now. "Michael, Dorjay—back up positions by the hatch," he called into the intercom. The two Cobras acknowledged and Pyre once again headed aft.

He passed the furious activity near the hatch without actually colliding with anyone; and by the time he skidded to a stop beside Telek, the lounge displays showed Cerenkov just emerging from the airlock.

If the Qasamans had been a shock to the *Dewdrop's* passengers, the reverse was equally true. The welcoming committee jerked raggedly to a stop, and Pyre saw astonishment and disbelief sweep across their faces. He tensed; but the guns stayed firmly in their holsters. One of the birds squawked and flapped its wings, settling down only when its owner reached up to gently stroke its throat.

Pyre was aware of Telek leaning closer to him. "Do you buy Hersh's theory about the Baliuies?" she murmured.

"That ignorance was bliss?" he muttered back. "Not for a minute. The Baliuies knew we were the same species, all right—and if we were supposed to free human slaves from the Qasamans they sure as hell would have told us."

Telek grunted. Nnamdi and Christopher, Pyre noted, seemed to have missed the by-play. Shifting his own attention fully to the displays, the Cobra waited for the Qasamans to speak, wishing he knew what sort of game the Baliuies were playing.

The Qasaman delegation had shown a remarkably quick recovery to the contact team's appearance, a fact Cerenkov took to be a good sign. Whether the humans were slaves or masters, it was clear they weren't in the ignorant savage category. Which meant . . . what? Cerenkov wasn't sure, but he knew it was a good sign anyway.

The delegation had come to a halt now a couple of meters in front of the contact team. Cerenkov half-raised his right hand, freezing midway through the motion as one of the birds abruptly ruffled its wings and emitted a harsh caw. He waited until its owner had calmed it, then brought his hand chest high, palm outward. "I greet you in the name of the people of Aventine," he said. "We come to visit with peaceful intent. I am Yuri Cerenkov; my companions are Marck Rynstadt, Decker York, and Joshua Moreau. Whom do I have the honor of addressing?"

For another few seconds the translator pendant around his neck continued to talk, and Cerenkov sent a quick prayer skyward that the Trofts had indeed put together a decent translation program. All they would need now would be for him to have dropped an unintentional insult into his greeting. . . .

But if the translator had glitched it wasn't obvious. One of the Qasamans stepped a half pace forward, raising his hand in imitation of Cerenkov's gesture, and began speaking. "We greet you in turn," Cerenkov's earphone murmured seconds later. "I am Moff; I welcome you in the name of Mayor Kimmeron of Sollas and the people of Qasama. Your interpreter speaks our language well. Why does he rest aboard your craft?"

"Our translator is a machine," Cerenkov told him carefully, wishing he knew just how technologically advanced these people were. Would they understand the word *computer*, or relegate the whole process to black magic? "Each word I speak is sent to it from this microphone, where it compares the word to those it knows of your language—"

"I understand translation devices," Moff interrupted him. "Other visitors here used such things, though

we have no need of them on Qasama. Your machine
uses many of the same inflections theirs did."

The hidden question was obvious, and Cerenkov
had a split-second decision to make as to how to
answer it. Honesty seemed the safest approach. "If
you speak of the Trofts of the Baliu'ckha'spmi demesne, we did indeed purchase our translator from
them. That's also how we knew you were here, though
they failed to mention that we are of the same race.
How did you arrive here, so far away from other
human worlds, if I may ask?"

Moff ran his eyes over the *Dewdrop* for a moment
before turning back to Cerenkov. "A large craft, though
much smaller than the one of legends," he commented.
"How many people does it usually carry?"

In other words, Cerenkov thought, *how many are still
aboard*? Again, honesty would be best ... honesty
tempered with the fact that Justin Moreau was to be
treated as nonexistent. "There are seven crewmen
and six members of the diplomatic mission still
aboard," he told Moff. "For various reasons they will
remain there."

"During which time you four intend to do what?"

The question caught Cerenkov off guard. He'd expected to hold talks with the leadership and to be
given a grand tour of the area—but he hadn't expected to have to make such requests out here beside
the ship. "We'd like to visit with your people," he
said. "Share information of mutual interest, perhaps
open trade negotiations. We *do* share a common heritage, after all."

Moff's eyes bored into his. "*Our* heritage is one of
struggle against both men and nature," he said bluntly.
"Tell me, where is this world Aventine you come
from?"

"It's about forty-five light-years from here," Cerenkov said, resisting the urge to point dramatically
toward the sky. "I'm not sure of the actual direction
or whether our sun is even visible at this distance."

"I see. What is your relationship with the Lords of *Rajan Putra* and the Agra Dynasty?"

Cerenkov felt his heartbeat pick up. At last, a clue of sorts as to when the Qasamans had left the Dominion of Man. He himself had only the vaguest idea when the Dynasties had existed—and no recollection at all of any *Rajan Putra*—but Nnamdi's sociologist training ought to cover at least some history as well.

But that wouldn't tell him what the Qasamans' own feelings toward the Dynasties had been . . . and if he didn't come up with a safely neutral answer the whole expedition could be shifted into the "enemies" column without any further warning. "I'm afraid that question doesn't mean anything to me," he told Moff. "We left the main group of human worlds ourselves some time ago, and at that time there wasn't any government calling itself a dynasty, at least not that I know of."

A slight frown creased Moff's forehead. "The Agra Dynasty claimed it was eternal."

Cerenkov remained silent, and after a moment Moff shrugged. "Perhaps a search through your records will show us what happened after we left," he said. "So. You wish to visit our world. For how long?"

Cerenkov shrugged. "That's entirely up to you—we wouldn't want to impose overmuch on your hospitality. We can also bring our own supplies if you'd like."

Moff's eyes seemed to focus on the clear bubble around Cerenkov's head. "You will have trouble eating like that, won't you? Or would you want to return to your craft for every meal?"

"That shouldn't be necessary," Cerenkov shook his head. "By the time we're likely to get hungry, our analysis of your air should be complete. I'm expecting it to show nothing dangerous, but we need to be cautious."

"Of course." Moff glanced to both sides, as if waiting for a protest from one of his party. But they remained silent. "Very well, Cerenkov, you and your companions may come with me into the city. But you must agree to obey my commands without question, for your own safety. Even in Sollas the many dangers of Qasama are not wholly absent."

"Very well, I agree," Cerenkov said with only the slightest hesitation. "We're well aware of how dangerous a planet can be for visitors."

"Good. Then my first order is for you to leave all weapons with your craft."

Beside Cerenkov, York stirred slightly. "Yet you just said Qasama could be dangerous," Cerenkov said, choosing his words carefully. He'd half expected this, but had no intention of giving in without at least trying to talk Moff out of it. "If you're afraid we might use our weapons against your citizens, let me assure you—"

"Our citizens have nothing to fear from your weapons," Moff interrupted. "It's *you* who would be in danger. The mojos—" he gestured to the bird resting on his shoulder— "are trained to attack when weapons are drawn or used, except for hunting or self-defense purposes."

Frowning, Cerenkov studied the bird. Silver-blue in color, built rather like a compact hawk, it returned his gaze with what seemed to be preternatural alertness. The talons clinging to the oversized epaulet were long and sharp, the feet themselves disproportionately large. A hunting bird, if he'd ever seen one . . . and he'd heard enough stories of professional falconers to have plenty of respect for such creatures. "All right," he said. "We'll—"

"By my instructions, and one at a time," Moff said, his hand curving up to stroke his mojo's throat again. "You first, Cerenkov. Rest your hand on your weapon, say 'clear,' and then draw it . . . slowly."

Cerenkov's laser was holstered across his belt, only its grip visible beneath his loose jacket. Reaching for it, he thumbed off the holster's safety strap. "Clear," he said, waiting for the translation before drawing it free.

The mojos' reaction was immediate. Practically in unison all six birds gave a single, harsh caw and snapped their wings out into flight position. Two of the birds even left their owners' shoulders, tracing a tight circle half a meter above Cerenkov's head before settling back onto their perches. Beside him, York spat something and dropped to a crouch; Cerenkov himself bit down hard on his tongue in an effort to remain absolutely motionless.

And as quickly as it had begun, the flurry of activity was over. The mojos, wings still poised at the ready, became living statues on the Qasamans' shoulders. Moving with infinite care, Cerenkov walked back to the *Dewdrop*'s hatchway and laid his laser in the airlock. As if on cue, the mojos relaxed again, and Cerenkov returned to the line. "Marck?" he said, striving to keep his voice steady. "Your turn."

"Right." Rynstadt cleared his throat. "Clear."

The mojos reacted a bit more calmly this time around; and their responses eased even further for York and Joshua. Clearly, they'd picked up rather quickly on the fact that hostilities were not being initiated. Just as clearly, they weren't taking chances, either.

"Thank you," Moff said when all four lasers were in the airlock. He raised both hands over his head, and Cerenkov's peripheral vision caught movement at the edge of the colorful city. A large vehicle was approaching, an open car type of thing with two Qasamans in it. Both figures had bulging left shoulders; Cerenkov didn't have to see any more clearly to know the lumps would turn out to be mojos. "Mayor Kimmeron is waiting to meet you," Moff continued. "We'll be taken to his chambers now."

"Thank you," Cerenkov managed. "We're looking forward to meeting him.

He took a deep breath and tried not to stare at the mojos.

*   *   *

There were cultures in the Dominion of Man, Justin knew from his studies, that went in heavily for artistic expression on their buildings, and his first thought had been that the Qasamans were a branch of such a society. But as the contact team was driven slowly through the streets, he gradually began to question that assumption. There were no murals anywhere that he could see, nor were there any recognizable human or animal drawings, either realistic or stylized. The splashes of color seemed to have been thrown up more or less randomly, though in ways the Cobra found aesthetically pleasing enough. He wondered if Nnamdi would be able to find anything significant in the whole thing.

Cerenkov cleared his throat, and it was quickly obvious the contact leader had other things than the Qasamans' artistry on his mind. "Looks like a lot of your people have mojos with them," he commented. "Mojos *and* guns. Are conditions in Sollas *that* dangerous?"

"The weapons aren't often used, but when they are it's a matter of survival," Moff told him.

"I would think the mojos would be enough protection," York put in.

"From some things, yes, but not from everything. Perhaps while you're here you'll have the chance to see a bololin herd or even a hunting krisjaw enter the city."

"Well, if that happens, don't forget we're unarmed," Cerekov said. "Unless you plan to issue us weapons and mojos later on."

It was clear from his tone he wasn't exactly thrilled by that option, but Moff laid any such fears to rest. "As strangers I don't think the mayor would allow you to carry weapons," he said. "And the mojos seem too uncomfortable in your presence to serve as your protectors."

"Um," Cerenkov said and fell silent. Justin shifted

his attention from the buildings to the people walking along the sidewalks. Sure enough, all of them had the ubiquitous mojos on their shoulders. A light breeze came up, ruffling human hair and mojo feathers and whistling gently in his ears. *Odd*, he thought, *to be able to* hear *the wind but not to feel it.*

Somehow, on a gut level, that seemed stranger even than the fact that he was possibly the first man in history to be almost literally walking in his brother's shoes.

From somewhere behind him a new voice spoke up. "Is that just an excuse?" Pyre asked.

"I don't think so," Telek's voice replied. "The nearest mojos *do* look a bit more nervous than those further away. I'd guess it has to do with the fact that we smell slightly different than the Qasamans."

Pyre grunted. "Genetic drift?"

"More likely dietary differences. Something, Hersh?"

"I think I've got their departure time bracketed," Nnamdi said. "The Agra Dynasty was the government that ruled Reginine from central Asia on Earth. It began in 2097 and ended when the Dominion of Man formally took over in 2180."

"What about the, uh, the Lords of *Rajan Putra*?" Telek asked.

"We'll have to check the full history records back on Aventine for that. But I know there was a major migration from Reginine when it was opened to general colonization, and I *think* the emigres founded the world Rajput."

"Hmmm. Ethnic separatists, basically?"

"No idea. My guess, though, is that the Qasamans were either one ship of that group or a separate emigration, in either case overshooting their target rather badly."

"Badly and a half," Telek snorted. "Where were the Trofts while they were wandering through Assemblage territory?"

"Probably never saw them coming," Christopher

spoke up. "Really. The Dominion's early stardrives were nasty unstable things, and when they went supercritical they hit about ten times the speed we can get nowadays."

"Sounds rather handy, actually," Pyre said.

"Only if you didn't need to stop," Christopher said dryly. "Coming out of hyperspace in that condition would fry the drive and most other electronics on the ship. There are literally dozens of colony ships— *colony* ships, mind you, not just probes or scouts— that are listed as simply having disappeared. I guess Qasama was one of the lucky ones."

"Or else they were the *un*lucky ones who were kidnapped and brought here," Nnamdi put in. "You'll recall we haven't scrapped that possibility yet."

"We'll keep it in mind if we see any sign of another race," Telek assured him. "But it's hard to imagine slaves being allowed to carry guns."

Via the direct feed from Joshua's implanted optical sensors to his own, Justin saw that the car carrying the contact team had turned onto one of the broad streets they'd noted from orbit, and he waited for Cerenkov to ask about it. But the contact leader had apparently decided to hold off pumping the Qasamans for more information, at least for the moment. Probably just as well, Justin thought, since the lull enabled him to continue splitting his attention between the cityscape and the conversation in the lounge around him.

"Any indication in the translator program as to what bololins or krisjaws are?" Pyre asked.

Justin could almost see Telek's shrug. "Local fauna, I gather," she said. "Obviously pretty nasty—those guns of theirs don't look like target pistols."

"Agreed. So why didn't they put up a wall around the city, like they did around the villages?"

There was a short pause. "No idea. Hersh?"

"Maybe the village walls aren't there to keep the animals out," he suggested, not sounding particulary convinced. "Maybe both species fly or jump too high for walls to be effective."

"So why do the villages have them?" Pyre persisted.

"*I* don't know," Nnamdi snapped.

"All right, take it easy," Telek put in. "Finding out all of these things is Yuri's job. Let's just relax and leave it to him, okay?"

There was another pause. Back in Sollas Joshua turned his head to follow the passage of a particularly attractive woman. Justin admired the view himself, wondering whether it was her appearance or the fact that her mojo rode her *right* shoulder which had caught his brother's attention. He tried to see if her pistol was also strapped to the opposite side, but Joshua turned back to face forward before he could do so. *Left-handed*? he speculated, making a mental note to watch for others.

From the other reality Christopher spoke up. "Hersh, have you got anything like a population estimate for Qasama yet? Given that they're human, I mean, and that human personal space requirements are pretty well known."

"Oh, I'd guess somewhere between fifty and three hundred million," Nnamdi said. "That requires them to have bred like hamsters over the past three centuries, but you can get rates that high on new worlds. Why?"

"Would it be likely that you could keep track of that many people on a single-name basis?"

"Like *Moff*, for instance? Not hardly. Especially since they originally came from a multi-name background."

"Which means Moff wasn't giving his full name," Christopher said. "Which means in turn that the mojos aren't the only ones that are nervous about us."

"Yeah," Nnamdi said heavily. "Well . . . suspicion toward strangers is part of the heritage of lots of human cultures."

"Or else the Trofts who came here earlier started a

new tradition," Telek growled. "I wish to hell we had a record of their visit. Either way, I suppose we ought to remind the team that they need to walk on eggs."

There was a faint click and Telek delivered a short message to the contact team along the translator carrier—a message that, for Justin, had a built-it echo as bone conduction carried part of the sound from Joshua's earphone to his implanted auditory pickups. The car seemed to be slowing now, and Justin scanned the buildings within view, wondering which one housed the mayor's office. Fortunately, the rest of the conversation in the lounge had ceased as the scientists returned to watching the same view on their more prosaic displays, so there was no risk of his missing anything while his primary attention was locked into Joshua's implants. There was a lot about this setup that annoyed him, but he had to admit it was doing its job well. Whenever he wound up replacing Joshua out there, he would have the same memories of Qasama that his brother did ... and those memories could easily spell the difference between success and failure for such an impersonation.

The car had come to a halt by the curb. Resisting the urge to run his own muscles through the proper motions, Justin lay quietly on his couch as Joshua followed Cerenkov and the others up the three outside steps and into the building.

Decker York had been a Marine for twenty years before leaving the Dominion for Aventine eighteen years ago. During his hitch he'd served on eight different worlds and had seen literally dozens of officials, ranging in pomp and power from village councilor to full Dominion Committé. From all of it he'd developed a mental image of what human leaders and their surroundings should be like.

By those standards, Mayor Kimmeron of Sollas was a severe shock.

The room Moff led them to was hardly an office, for starters. The sounds of music reached them even before the liveried guards flanking the door pulled the heavy panels open, and the tendrils of smoke that drifted past as the group started in were evidence of either incense or drug use inside. York's nose wrinkled at the thought, but fortunately the filter bubble enclosing his head seemed to be keeping most or all of the smoke out. Inside, the room's lighting was muted and leaned to reds and oranges. The room itself seemed large, but free-hanging curtains all around gave it the feel of an elegant and soft-walled maze. Moff led them through two right angles to the room's center—

And a scene straight out of mankind's distant past. On a cushion-like throne lounged a large man who, while not fat, clearly hadn't seen strenuous exercise in quite some time. Facing him was a group of dancers, both male and female, in exotic dress; behind them was the semicircle of musicians—*live* musicians— who were providing the music. Seated on other cushions scattered around the room were a handful of other men and women, all seemingly splitting their attention between the dancers and low work tables set before them. York sent a studiously casual glance at one table as Moff led them toward the central throne, noting especially what seemed to be a portable computer or computer terminal among the papers there. Qasaman technology, it seemed, extended at least somewhat beyond guns and cars.

Everyone in the room, except the dancers, was accompanied by a mojo.

Moff stopped them a few meters to the side of the throne—and if its occupant was surprised by their appearance he didn't show it. He said something cheerful sounding, his voice clearly audible over the music; "Ah—welcome," York's earphone translated it. The big Qasaman raised a hand, bringing the musicians and dancers to an orderly halt a few notes later. "I am Mayor Kimmeron of the city of Sollas; I welcome you to Qasama. Please, sit down."

Moff indicated a group of cushions—four of them, York noted—placed in a row in front of the mayor. Cerenkov nodded and sat down, the others following suit. Moff and the rest of their escort remained standing.

"Now," Kimmeron said, rubbing his hands together in a curious gesture. "Your names are Cerenkov, Rynstadt, York, and Moreau, and you come from a world called Aventine. So. What exactly—exactly, mind you—do you wish from us?"

It seemed to take Cerenkov a moment to find his tongue. "You seem to know a great deal about us," he said at last. "You surely also know, then, that we're here to reopen communication with brothers we didn't know we had, and to explore ways of making such contact mutually profitable."

Kimmeron had a sly smile on his face even before the translator finished its version of the speech. "Yes, that is indeed what you have claimed. But why would you, who retain space flight, believe we would have anything worth your time?"

Careful, boy, York warned in Cerenkov's direction. *Primitive doesn't necessarily imply naive.* His eyes flicked to Moff and the rest of the escort, wishing he knew how to read this culture's body language.

But Cerenkov was on balance again and his answer was a masterpiece of pseudo-sincerity. "As anyone who's opened up a new world must surely know, sir, each planet is unique in its plants and animals, and to a lesser extent its minerals. Surely your foodstuffs and pharmaceuticals will be markedly different from ours, for a start." He gestured toward the musicians and dance troupe. "And for any people who respect artistic expression as much as you clearly do, there are the less tangible but equally rewarding possibilities of cultural exchange."

Kimmeron nodded, the half-smile still playing

around his face. "Of course. But what if we came to Qasama for the express purpose of *avoiding* cultural contamination? Then what?"

"Then, Mr. Mayor," Cerenkov said quietly, "we would apologize for the intrusion and ask your permission to leave."

Kimmeron regarded him thoughtfully, and for a long moment the room rang with a brittle silence. Again York glanced toward Moff, his hand itching with the desire to have a weapon in it . . . and at last Kimmeron shifted on his cushion throne, breaking the spell. "Yes," he said, waving a hand casually. "Well, fortunately, I suppose, we're not quite that strict here on Qasama. Though some of us perhaps would prefer otherwise." In response to his gesture a new group of five men had moved forward from the edges of the room to stand behind the visitors, a group Moff now stepped over to join. "Moff, escort our guests to their quarters. if you would," the mayor addressed him. "See that their needs are taken care of and arrange a general tour for tomorrow. If you have no objections—" this to Cerenkov— "we'd like to run a general medical study of you this afternoon as well. For your protection as well as ours."

"No objections at all," Cerenkov replied. "Though if you're worried, our experience on Aventine indicates most disease organisms from one planet don't seem to bother much with creatures from another."

"That has been our experience, as well," Kimmeron said, nodding. "Still, it never hurts to be cautious. Until tomorrow, then."

Cerenkov got to his feet, York and the others following suit. "We look forward to seeing you again," Cerenkov said with a small bow to the mayor. Turning, they fell into step behind Moff and headed from the room.

And now straight to the hospital, York thought grimly as they emerged once more onto the sunlit street and were steered toward their car. The physical exam itself didn't particularly worry him; but he would bet goulash to garnets there'd be the Qasaman version of military ordnance experts assisting the doctors. And if they somehow managed to figure out exactly how his calculator watch, pen, and star sapphire ring fit together . . . and what they became in such a configuration. . . .

Cerenkov and Rynstadt were in the car, and it was his turn to get in. Trying not to grimace, he did so, telling himself there was no need for worry. The Marine palm-mate, after all, had been deliberately designed to be undetectable.

But he worried anyway as the crowded vehicle set off between the color-spattered buildings. Contingency worrying was part of a soldier's job.

The room Joshua and Rynstadt had been assigned to had been dark and quiet for nearly half an hour by the time Justin finally unhooked himself from the direct feed apparatus and rolled stiffly to a sitting position on his couch. The *Dewdrop*'s lounge, too, was quiet, its only other occupant a dozing Pyre. Justin moved carefully, working the kinks out of his muscles as he walked toward the door.

"There's food by the corner terminal if you're hungry."

Justin looked back to see Pyre stretch his arms out with a sigh and straighten up in his chair. "Didn't mean to wake you," he apologized, changing direction toward the tray the other had mentioned.

"S'okay. I'm not actually on duty, anyway—I just wanted to wait till you were up, make sure you were doing okay."

"I'm fine." Justin sat down beside the other Cobra, balancing the tray on his knees as he attacked the food. "So . . . what do you think?"

"Oh, hell, I don't know," Pyre sighed. "I'm not sure we can take anything they say or do at face value. That mayor, for instance. Is he *really* some throwback to the old despot tradition, or was all of that set up to confuse us? Or is that really the way they conduct business here?"

"Oh, come on," Justin growled around a mouthful of fried balis. "Who could concentrate in a din like that?"

"It was only a din because you're not used to it," Pyre said. "The music *could* actually have a calming effect on the brain's emotional activity, allowing the people in there to think more logically."

Justin replayed the scene in his mind. Possible, he decided—those hunched over the low tables had been doing *something*. And the smoke—? "Supplemented by tranquilizing drugs, maybe?"

"Could be. I wish we'd had some sampling equipment in there to run a quick analysis on the air." He snorted. "Though a lot of good it would have done."

Justin grimaced. Every bit of the contact team's recording and analysis equipment had been politely but firmly confiscated during their hospital examination. The best Cerenkov's protests had done was to elicit Moff's promise that the gear would be returned when they left. "I was locked into Joshua's sensors at the time, but I have the impression Governor Telek was pretty mad about that."

"That's putting it mildly. She was on the edge of a full-fledged tantrum." Pyre shook his head slowly. "But I think maybe she was right, that this is looking less and less like it's going to work. Yuri can't find out anything the Qasamans want to keep hidden, not with Moff steering them around like tame porongs and his equipment buried in some back room somewhere. And *we* sure can't do anything ourselves stuck out here."

Justin eyed him suspiciously. "Are you leading up to the suggestion that someone take a little midnight stroll in a day or two?"

"I don't know how else to find out their true threat potential," Pyre shrugged.

"And if we're caught at it?"

"Trouble, of course. Which is why the operation would have to be handled by someone who knew what he was doing."

"In other words, one of the Cobras or Decker. And since we're in plain view and Decker is both watched *and* unarmed, not getting caught starts sounding a bit unlikely."

Pyre shrugged. "At the moment, you're right. But maybe something will change." He gave Justin a long look. "And in that event . . . you weren't supposed to know this, but Decker *isn't* unarmed. He's carrying a breakapart palm-mate dart gun with him."

"He's *what*? Almo, they said *no weapons*. If they catch him with that—"

"He'll be in serious trouble," Pyre finished for him. "I know. But Decker didn't want the party completely helpless, and the gun *did* make it through the big inspection okay."

"As far as you know."

"He's still got it."

Justin sighed. "Great. I hope the Marines taught him patience as well as marksmanship."

"I'm sure they did," Pyre grunted, pushing himself to his feet with an ease that was probably due solely to his implanted servos. "I'm going to crash for a few hours—if you're smart you'll do likewise after your exercises."

"Yeah," Justin said with a yawn. "Before you do, though, has the governor said when she's going to call Joshua back in for our switch?"

Pyre paused halfway to the door, a look of chagrin flicking across his face. "Actually . . . her current plan is to go ahead and leave Joshua out there for the foreseeable future."

"What?" Justin stared at him. "That's not what we planned."

"I know," Pyre shrugged helplessly. "I pointed that out to her—rather strongly, in fact. But the situation seems pretty stable at the moment and. . . ."

"And she likes having Joshua's visual transmission too much to give it up. Is that it?"

Pyre sighed. "You can hardly blame her. She'd wanted the whole contact team implanted with those optical sensors, I understand, and been turned down on grounds of cost—split-frequency transmitters that small are expensive to make. And now with all our other eyes taken away, Joshua's all we've got left if we want to see what's going on." He held up a hand soothingly. "Look, I know how you feel, but try not to worry about him. The Qasamans are hardly going to attack them now without a good reason."

"I suppose you're right." Justin thought for a moment, but there didn't seem anything else to be said. "Well . . . good night."

" 'Night."

Pyre left, and Justin flexed his arms experimentally. Thirteen hours in the couch had indeed left the muscles stiff, but he hardly noticed the twinges as his thoughts latched onto Pyre's last comment. *Without a good reason* . . . but what would constitute such a reason in the Qasamans' minds? An aggressive act or comment on Cerenkov's part? Discovery that the ostensibly voice-only radio link to the ship also had a split-freq channel that was carrying the visual images they'd obviously tried to suppress? Violent use of York's illegal gun?

Or perhaps even the outside reconnaissance Pyre had clearly already decided on?

Eyes on the darkened display, Justin settled into his exercises, pushing his body harder than he'd originally intended to.

Chapter 9

With less need for immediate debarkation—and more comfort and room aboard ship in which to wait—the *Menssana*'s passengers didn't bother with filter helmets, but simply stayed inside until the atmospheric analyzers confirmed the air of Planet Chata was indeed safe for human use.

Long tradition gave Jonny, as senior official aboard, the honor of being the first human being to step out on the new world's surface; but Jonny had long since learned to put discretion before pomp, and the honor was claimed by one of the six Cobras who went out to set up a sensor/defense perimeter about the ship. Once again the passengers waited; but when an hour of Cobra work failed to entice any predators out of the nearby woods—or to flush out anything obviously dangerous within the perimeter itself—Team Leader Rey Banyon declared the *Menssana*'s immediate area to be safe enough for the civilians.

Jonny and Chrys were near the end of the general exodus of scientists through the *Menssana*'s main hatch. For Jonny it was a step into his own distant past. Chata looked nothing at all like Aventine, really; certainly not after even a cursory examination of plant life and landscape. Yet the simple fact of Chata's strangeness relative to Aventine's by-now familiarity gave the two experiences an identity. A new world, untouched by man—

"Brings back memories, doesn't it?" Chrys murmured at his side.

Jonny took a deep breath, savoring the almost spicy aromas wafting in along the light breeze. "Like Aventine when I first arrived," he said, shaking his head slowly. "A kid of twenty-five, just about overwhelmed by the sheer scope of what we were trying to do there. I'd forgotten how it all felt . . . forgotten what all of us have really accomplished in the past forty years."

"It'll be harder to do it again," Chrys said. Dropping to one knee, she gently fingered the mat of interlaced vine-like plants that seemed to be the local version of grass. "Chata may only be thirty light-years from Aventine, but we don't have anything like the Dominion's transport capability. It hardly makes sense to spend our resources this direction with so much of Aventine and Palatine still uninhabited. Especially—" She broke off abruptly.

"Especially when this whole group is only ten to fifteen light-years from Qasama?" Jonny finished for her.

She got to her feet with a sigh, brushing bits of greenery off her fingers as she did so. "I've heard all the arguments about buffer zones and two-front wars," she said, "but I don't have to like it. And I keep coming back to the fact that the *only* reason we consider Qasama a threat is because the Trofts say we should."

The beep of his phone preempted Jonny's reply. "Moreau," he said, lifting the device to his lips.

"Banyon, Governor," the Cobra team leader's voice came. "Got something off our satellite I think you should look at."

Chrys's presence beside him was a silent reminder of his promise to play passenger on this trip. "Can't you and Captain Shepherd handle it?" he said.

"Well . . . I suppose so, yes. I just thought that your advice would be helpful on this."

"Unless you're talking emergency—" Jonny broke off as a fluttering hand waved between him and the phone.

"What are you doing?" Chrys stage-whispered fiercely. "Let's go see what they've got."

If I live to be a thousand, the old line flashed through Jonny's head. "Never mind," he told Banyon. "I'll be right there."

They found Banyon and Shepherd on the *Menssana's* bridge, their attention on a set of three displays. "It wasn't something that registered right off the blocks," Banyon began without preamble, indicating a dark mass now centered in the largest display. "Then we found out it was moving."

Jonny leaned close to the screen. The mass seemed to consist of hundreds or thousands of individual dots. "Enhancement all the way up on this?"

Shepherd nodded. "There's a lot of upper atmosphere turbulence over us at the moment, and that's limiting drastically what the computer has to work with."

"I'd say it's a herd or flock of some sort," Jonny said. "I gather it's headed this way?"

"Hard to tell—they're still a hundred kilometers away—but it looks right now like the flank will sweep across us," Shepherd said. He touched a switch and the infrared picture on one of the other screens was replaced by a schematic. The various extrapolation regions were done in different colors; and, sure enough, the edge of the red "90% probable" wedge just touched the *Menssana's* indicated position. The mass's average distance and speed were also given: 106 km, 8.1 km/hr.

"So we've got thirteen hours till they get here," Jonny murmured. "Well . . . we can break camp in one if necessary, but the scientists won't like all their *in situ* stuff being moved. I suppose the logical thing

would be to send a squad of Cobras to check out this
herd and see if they can be stopped or deflected."

"Yes, sir, that's what we thought." Banyon hesitated, and Jonny saw on his face the same expression
that, on his sons, had usually signaled a favor request was coming. "Uh, Governor . . . would you be
willing to fly out with the team? We'd all feel better
with someone of your experience along."

Jonny looked back at Chrys, raised his eyebrows.
She was still studying the displays, though, and when
she finally met his gaze she seemed surprised he was
even asking. "Of course," she said. "Just be careful."

If I live to be ten *thousand.* . . . Turning back to Banyon, he nodded. "All right, then. Let's get cracking."

It was indeed a herd—a *big* herd—and to Jonny,
who'd seen such things only on tape, the sight of so
many wild animals together at once was both awe-
some and a little bit frightening. Even just jogging
along, the mass of brown-furred quadrupeds made a
thunder audible inside a sealed aircar two hundred
meters overhead, and their wide hooves raised a
dust cloud despite the damping effect of the webgrass
underfoot.

"I think," Banyon commented as they all took in
the sight, "we're going to have to rethink our basic
plan."

One of the other Cobras snorted, and someone else
let loose with a rather strained chuckle. Jonny let the
tension-easing noises ripple around the crowded aircar
and then gestured out the window. "Let's get a few
kilometers ahead of them and see if we can come up
with a way to shift them off their course."

Banyon nodded and turned the vehicle around, but
as the roar faded behind them Jonny studied the
landscape below with decreasing hope. The Cobras
had already established that there weren't any natural obstacles between the herd and the *Menssana*,
and now that he knew what they were up against it

seemed very unlikely they could do *anything* to the terrain that would make any difference whatsoever. Something more drastic was likely to be necessary. Drastic *and* dangerous.

Banyon had apparently reached the same conclusion. "We're going to have to scare them, I'm afraid," he murmured, just loudly enough for Jonny to hear.

"There used to be herds this size all over parts of Earth and Blue Haven," Jonny said. "I wish I knew how they'd been hunted. Well. We don't have anything like real explosives aboard, and we don't yet know what this species' predators even look like. I suppose that leaves close-in work with lasers and sonics."

"Laser range isn't *that* short—oh. Right. If they don't *see* us, there's no guarantee they'll figure out which way to run."

"Or even notice they're being killed off." Jonny thought for a minute, but nothing else obvious came to mind. "Well . . . let's try buzzing them with the car first. Maybe that'll do the trick."

But the animals apparently had no enemies that were airborne. Completely oblivious to the darting craft above them, they continued stolidly on their way. "We do it the hard way now?" one of the others asked.

Banyon nodded. "Afraid so. But hopefully not *too* hard. Saving the biologists some work isn't worth anyone getting killed over."

"Or even hurt," Jonny put in. "We'll just—"

A ping from the car's phone interrupted him. "Governor, we've got something here that may or may not mean anything," Captain Shepherd said, his attention somewhere off-camera. "The satellite's been completing its large-scale geosurvey . . . and it looks very much like that herd is running along one of the planet's magnetic field lines."

Banyon looked at Jonny, eyebrows raised. "I thought

the only things that used geomagnetic navigation were birds, insects, and tweenies."

"So did all the *Menssana*'s biologists," Shepherd returned dryly. "But they admit there's no reason something larger couldn't make use of the mechanism."

"If we assume they're indeed paralleling the field lines, is the camp still in danger?" Jonny asked.

"Yes. The probability actually goes up a couple of points."

Jonny looked questioningly at Banyon. "Worth a try," the other grunted. "Captain, is there anything aboard the ship that can generate a strong magnetic field?"

"Sure—the drive modulators. All we'll need to do is pull off some of the shielding and we'll get enough field leakage to overwhelm their direction finders. *If* that's what's really happening."

"It's worth trying," Banyon repeated. "How fast can you get that shielding off?"

"It's already being done. Say another hour at the most."

The gently rolling terrain could not by any stretch of the imagination be called hilly; but even so the flatfoot herd was audible long before it could be seen. Standing a few meters back from the main line of Cobras, Jonny wiped the perspiration off his palms as the thunder steadily grew, hoping this was going to work. In theory, the Cobra's antiarmor lasers should be able to make fungus feed out of the herd if something went wrong ... but Jonny couldn't help remembering how hard the equally herbiverous gantuas of Aventine were to kill.

"Get ready," his phone said. He glanced up to see the car as it hovered above and ahead of the Cobras. "You'll see them any minute now. Wait for the captain's signal. . . ."

And the leading edge of the herd came over a low rise, like a dark tsunami clearing a breakwater.

They weren't heading directly toward the Cobras, and in actual size were quite a bit smaller than gantuas, but the sheer numbers and ground-level view more than made up for it. Jonny clenched his jaw firmly, fighting hard against the urge to turn and run for cover . . . and as the wave poured over the rise a new voice on the phone barked, "*Now!*"

The answer was a volley of Cobra antiarmor lasers—directed not at the flatfoots, but at the clusters of boulders the Cobras had wrestled into position fifty meters closer to the herd. Very special boulders . . . and if the *Menssana*'s geologists had been right about that particular formation—

They had. The mix of high- and low-expansion minerals in each boulder could survive for only a second or less under a laser's glare before disintegrating with a crack that was audible even over the herd's rumble. Like a string of firecrackers the boulders blew up as the Cobras continued their sweep . . . and like firecrackers, they actually produced little more than noise. But it was enough; and as the herd's headlong rush faltered in sudden confusion, Jonny could almost see them lose their internal sense of direction. An instant later the hesitation was gone and the herd had doubled its speed to a flat-out run . . . but in the slightly altered direction the *Menssana*'s additional magnetic field was defining for them from the ship's new position some ten kilometers away. The flank of the herd would now miss the line of Cobras; and when the *Menssana* lifted in an hour or so and the flatfoots resumed their original direction their path would be shifted at least a kilometer out of the way of the human encampment.

Theoretically. But there would be time to make sure.

The aircar was dropping toward the ground and the Cobras were beginning to converge on it. "Good job,"

Banyon's voice came from Jonny's phone. "Let's head back."

The last few clouds had cleared shortly before sunset, and the night sky was alive with stars. Walking hand in hand just inside the perimeter, Jonny and Chrys took turns naming the recognizable constellations and trying to match the more distorted ones with their Aventinian counterparts. Eventually, they ran out, and for a time they just walked in silence, enjoying the night air. Jonny, his audio enhancers activated, heard the faint roar before Chrys did; and by the time she took notice the steady volume level showed their plan had succeeded.

"The flatfoot herd?" she asked, peering off into the darkness.

"Right," he nodded. "And they're not getting any closer. At least a kilometer away—maybe two."

She shook her head. "Strange. I remember some biology class in school where the instructor took it upon himself to 'prove' that no land animal larger than a condorine could ever evolve with a magnetic sense unless there was some ridiculously high local field present. I wish he was here to see this."

Jonny chuckled. "*I* remember reading about the old theory that all the native plants and animals on the various Dominion worlds were mutated descendents of spores or bacteria that had ultimately been blown there by solar winds from Earth. The argument was still going strong when the Trofts and Minthisti were found, I understand, and I have no idea *what* its proponents made of Aventine. If there are still any of them around. I guess the possibility of making a public fool of yourself is just one of those risks scientists have to face."

"You know, that universal genetic code thing has always bothered me, too," Chrys mused. "Why *should* all the life we find show the same DNA and protein forms? It doesn't seem reasonable."

"Even if that turns out to be the only workable structure?"

"I've never liked that theory. It seems arrogant, somehow."

Jonny shrugged. "I don't especially care for it either. I've heard the Troft theory is that some major disaster three or four billion years ago nearly sterilized this whole region of space, taking with it an early starfaring people. The algae and bacteria that survived on each world were therefore all from one common stock, though they've since evolved independently."

"That must've been one gantua of a disaster."

"I think it was supposed to be either a chain of supernovas or the final collapse of the galaxy's central black hole."

"Uh-*huh*. Almost simpler to believe God set it up this way deliberately."

"Certainly makes a colonist's life easier to be able to digest the local flora and fauna," Jonny agreed.

"Though the vice versa is occasionally a problem."

Jonny tensed; but Chrys's tone hadn't been one of accusation. "I appreciate your letting me go with the others today," he said, as long as they were now on the topic. "I know I promised to stay out of things on this trip—"

"You could hardly hold out when you were needed," she put in. "And it wasn't like you were in serious danger out there. Were you?"

"No, not with the aircar and *Menssana* as backup. Still, I'll try to behave myself the rest of the trip."

She chuckled and gave his hand a squeeze. "It's all right, Jonny. Really. I wouldn't want you to just sit on your hands when you're needed. Just be careful."

"Always," he assured her, wondering at her abrupt attitude change. This was the old Chrys back again, the one who'd been so supportive of his service when they were first married. What had happened to change her? Was she simply reacting to the new environment, slipping into old thought patterns with the reminder of their past struggles on Aventine?

He didn't know. But he liked the change . . . and he had the rest of the trip to figure out how to keep her this way when they returned home.

Chapter 10

The clearance to remove their filter helmets had come from the *Dewdrop* just before the evening's medical exam, and in the hours between then and bedtime Joshua thought his nose had become thoroughly accustomed to the exotic scents of Qasama's air. But the group hadn't taken more than three steps outside their guest house in the morning before Joshua realized that belief had been a little premature.

The new odor seemed to be a mixture of baking aromas with some not-quite-aromatic smoke with something he couldn't begin to identify.

He apparently wasn't the only one. "What *is* that I smell?" Cerenkov asked Moff, sniffing the breeze.

Moff inhaled thoughtfully. "I smell the bakery one street down, the boron refinery, and the exhaust of vehicles. Nothing more."

"A boron refinery?" Rynstadt spoke up. "In the middle of the city?"

"Yes. Why not?" Moff asked.

"Well ..." Rynstadt floundered a bit. "I would assume it would be safer to put industries like that away from populated centers. In case of an accident or something."

Moff shook his head. "We have no accidents of any

100

consequence. And the equipment itself is safest right where it is."

"Interesting," Cerenkov murmured. "Could we see this refinery?"

Moff hesitated a second, then nodded. "I suppose that would be permissible. This way."

Bypassing the car waiting for them at the curb, he set off, the four Aventinians and five other Qasamans following. The refinery turned out to be less than a block away, located in an unremarkable building midway between two of Sollas's extra-wide avenues.

Joshua had never seen this kind of light industrial plant before, and the masses of tanks, pipes, and bustling Qasamans gave him more of a feeling of confusion than of productivity. But Rynstadt—and to a lesser extent York—seemed fascinated by the place. "Very nice setup," Rynstadt commented, gazing around the main room. "I've never heard of a boron extraction method using cold bubbled gas. What gas *is* that, if I may ask?"

"I'm really not sure," Moff said. "Some sort of catalyst, I expect. You are an expert in this sort of chemistry?"

"No, not really," Rynstadt shook his head. "I dabble in a lot of fields—my job as an educator requires me to know bits and pieces of almost every subject."

"A general scientific expert, then. I see."

There was something about the way Moff said that that Joshua didn't care for, as if Rynstadt's supposed expertise had added a point against the mission's peaceful image. "Would something like this method be marketable on Aventine, Marck, do you think?" he spoke up, hoping Rynstadt would pick up the cue.

He did. "Almost certainly," the other nodded at once. "Boron plays a major part in at least a dozen different industries, and while our methods aren't expensive something cheaper would always be welcome. Perhaps we can discuss this in more detail later, Moff, either with Mayor Kimmeron or someone in planetary authority."

"I'll pass on your request," Moff said. His tone was neutral, but to Joshua's eye he seemed to relax just a bit. *Like tiptoeing through a mine field with these people*, he thought.

"Well, I think we might as well move on, then," Cerenkov said briskly. "I'd still like to see the art gallery you mentioned yesterday, and perhaps one of your marketplaces."

"Of course," Moff agreed. "Back to the car, then, and we'll be off."

"Well?" Telek asked.

Christopher straightened up from his terminal. "I don't find any reference to this kind of boron refinement method," he said. "Again, these records are by no means complete—"

"Sure, sure. So have they got a new technique or were they lying about what that plant was doing?"

The intercom beeped and Pyre leaned toward it, tuning out the conversation beside him. "Yes?"

It was Captain F'ahl. "Just come up with a correlation that you people might like to know about," he said. "Those extra-wide streets in Sollas and the other cities? Well, it turns out that in each instance they run exactly parallel to Qasama's geomagnetic field."

The intricacies of boron refinement were abruptly forgotten. "Say again?" Christopher asked, turning toward the intercom.

F'ahl repeated his statement. "Any reason you can think of for that, Captain?" Telek asked.

"Nothing that makes sense," F'ahl replied. "You don't have to skew your whole city to use the field for navigation, and the field strength is far too weak to produce any effect on power lines or the like."

"Unless it periodically surges," Christopher mused. "No, even then the design doesn't make any sense."

"Maybe it has to do with their long-range communication system," Telek suggested. "Sending modulations along the lines of force or something."

From a corner of the lounge Nnamdi looked up in irritation. "I wish you'd all get off this idea that the Qasamans *have* to have broadcast communications," he growled. "We've already seen that Sollas is wired for both power and data transmission—that's really all they need."

"With nothing between the cities?—not to mention all those little villages out there?" Telek retorted. "Come on, Hersh—the isolated city-state concept may appeal to your sense of the exotic, but as a practicing politician I tell you it isn't stable. These people have calculators or even computers, as well as cars, machined weapons, and presumably something to use the runway we're sitting on. They can*not* simply have forgotten the basics of electromagnetic waves or unified government."

"Oh? Then how do you explain the village walls?"

"How do *you* explain the cities' lack of them?" Telek shook her head irritably. "We can't assume the villages are primitive and fight among themselves and at the same time say the cities are advanced and don't."

"We can if there's no communication between city and village," Nnamdi said doggedly. "Or if the villagers are a different species altogether. I notice neither Moff nor Kimmeron has mentioned the villages at all."

Pyre caught Telek's eye. "It *might* be good to clear up that point."

She sighed. "Oh, all right." Picking up the translator-link mike, she dictated a short message to the contact team. Pyre switched his attention back to the displays and waited for Cerenkov to raise the subject with Moff.

The wait wasn't long. The car was approaching one of the narrower cross streets, and as they reached the corner Joshua's implanted cameras showed the street was lined on both sides by permanent-looking booths, each displaying the seller's goods on a waist-high ledge beneath an open window. Dozens of people were already milling about, inspecting the merchandise or engaged in animated conversation with the sellers. "This is the main marketplace for this part of Sollas," Moff said as the car pulled up behind others parked along the wide avenue. "There are eight others like it elsewhere in the city."

"Seems an inefficient way of marketing," Rynstadt commented as they left the car and walked toward the bazaar. "Not to mention uncomfortable in the winter or on rainy days."

"The street can be sealed in bad weather," Moff said, pointing upwards. Joshua looked, and Pyre saw that at the third-floor level on the flanking buildings were two long roof sections, folded drawbridge-fashion against the walls. "As to inefficiency, we prefer to think of it as an expression of individual liberty and freedom. Lack of those qualities was the reason our ancestors came here originally. You've not said why *your* ancestors left the rule of the dynasties."

"Oh, hell," Telek growled, grabbing for the microphone. "Keep it non-political, Yuri," she instructed him. "Sense of adventure or something."

"We went to Aventine for various reasons," Cerenkov told the Qasaman. "The desire for adventure or to see a new world, dissatisfaction with our lives—that sort of thing."

"Not political pressure?"

"Perhaps some came for that reason, but if so I'm not aware of it," Cerenkov answered cautiously.

"Tell that to the First Cobras," Pyre murmured.

"Quiet," Telek shushed him.

The contact team and its Qasaman escort was walking among the other shoppers now. A mojo on one of the buyers squawked, causing Rynstadt to jerk to the side. Pyre jumped in sympathetic response; he'd almost stopped noticing the ubiquitous damn birds.

"Are all your goods from Sollas and the immediate area?" Cerenkov asked Moff as they passed a stand featuring neatly packaged loaves of bread.

"No, our commerce extends to the other cities and villages as well," the other told him. "Most of the fresh fruit and meat comes from the villages east of here."

"Ah," Cerenkov nodded, and continued walking.

"Satisfied?" Christopher asked Nnamdi.

The other glowered back. "Still doesn't prove the villagers are human," he pointed out stiffly. "Or are on an equal plane with the cities—"

"Almo?"

Pyre turned to the couch where Justin was lying. "What is it?"

"I . . . hear something . . . low rumble . . . from Joshua." The boy stopped, strain evident on his face as he fought to split enough of his attention from Joshua's sensors to speak. "Getting closer . . . I think."

Christopher was already at the controls, trying to find the sound Justin's Cobra enhancers had already gleaned form Joshua's signal. "Captain, we may have aircraft approaching," Pyre snapped toward the intercom.

"I'm on it," F'ahl replied calmly. "No sign of anything yet."

An instant later Pyre nearly went through the lounge's ceiling as a bellow erupted from the display speakers. "Yolp!" Christopher exclaimed, grabbing the volume control he'd just turned up. The roar subsided to a hooting sound . . . and as he looked at the screen, Pyre saw the Qasamans had abandoned their shopping and were beginning to move toward the wide avenues at each end of the bazaar. "What's going on?" Cerenkov asked Moff as the escort, too, joined the general flow. A second set of rumbles added to the first, and Pyre got a glimpse of cars being hurriedly moved off the avenue, presumably to the narrower cross streets.

"A bololin herd has entered Sollas," Moff told Cerenkov briefly. "Stay back—you're not armed."

Telek grabbed the mike. "Never mind that. Joshua—move up at least close enough to see what's going on. Decker, better go with him."

The two men began to move in Moff's wake. None of the Qasamans seemed particularly disturbed by whatever was about to happen . . . but as Pyre looked closer, he realized the same wasn't true of the mojos. Every bird in sight was fluffing its feathers, half opening its wings, and generally showing signs of agitation.

The rumble was clearly audible now as Joshua and York squeezed their way to the third rank of watchers. "Clear," a voice came faintly over Joshua's sensors, and someone off to the right in the front row drew his pistol, holding it muzzle upward in a ready position. A dozen more calls and the entire front row had followed suit. Across the avenue, Pyre could just see that another group of people waited in the street there, weapons similarly drawn. "Crossfire situation, Decker," he called toward the mike Telek was still holding, drowning out whatever instructions she was giving the team. "Watch for trouble with that."

The rumble became a roar . . . and the animals appeared.

To Pyre it was instantly obvious why the Qasamans considered it worthwhile to walk around armed. The fact that there was an entire herd of beasts stampeding through their city was bad enough; but even *one* of these would have been cause for serious alarm. Each a good two meters long, the bololins were heavily muscled, with sets of hooves that looked as if they could break rock by running impact alone. A pair of wicked-looking horns sprouted from the massive heads, and running down the back was a dorsal strip of thirty-centimeter quills that even an Aventinian spine leopard would have been proud to possess. There were at least a hundred of the creatures in sight already, running shoulder to shoulder and head to tail, with more pouring in behind them ... and as Pyre tensed in automatic combat reaction, the Qasamans opened fire.

Christopher spat something startled sounding, and even Pyre—who'd had an idea what to expect—jerked at the sound. The Dominion had given up simple explosive firearms long ago in favor of lasers and more sophisticated rocket cartridges, but such progress had apparently passed Qasama by. The guns ahead of Joshua roared like miniature grenades going off ... and some of the bololins in the herd abruptly faltered and fell.

Pyre happened to be looking directly at one of the quadrupeds as it was hit; and he was thus the first one in the lounge to see the tan-colored bird that shot upward from the carcass.

It was at least half again as large as a mojo, that quick glance showed him as the bird arrowed off the screen, but seemed built along the same predacious lines. Its hiding place, as near as he could tell, had been the bololin's dorsal quill forest ... an instant later Joshua reacted and the view shifted upward, and Pyre saw more of the birds already in the air, presumably having similarly deserted dying bololins.

Closing rapidly on them was a flock of mojos.

"They're crazy," Christopher said, barely audible over the gunfire. "Those birds are bigger than they are—"

"And *they* seem to be predators, too," Telek growled. "Something's wrong here—predators don't usually pick on other predators. Joshua!—keep tracking the birds."

The display steadied, and Pyre watched in morbid fascination as a mojo came in from above and behind one of the larger birds, swooping down with talons ready. It hit—got a grip—and for half a dozen heartbeats it clung there in piggyback position. The larger bird twisted violently, to no avail, leveled out once more—

And the mojo spread its wings and dropped off and back. Making no attempt to pursue, it turned in a lazy circle and headed back to the crowd of Qasamans.

"What the blooming *hell*?" Telek muttered.

Pyre couldn't have put it better himself.

Joshua's gaze returned to the street now. The herd was out of sight, and through the settling dust about twenty carcasses were visible, mangled to various degrees. One of the Qasamans—Moff, Pyre saw—stepped out into the avenue and looked carefully in both directions. Holstering his pistol, he stepped back; and as if on signal, the other guns likewise vanished and the crowds began to break up.

Telek squeezed the mike hard. "Yuri—everybody—find out everything you can about what just happened. Especially the thing with the birds."

Silently, Pyre seconded the order. Though he doubted the contact team really needed that prompting.

Joshua certainly hadn't needed Telek to state the obvious—bursting with curiosity, he could barely wait until Moff had pushed his way through the dispersing crowd to fire off his first question. "How did those animals get into the city so easily?" he asked.

Moff frowned, throwing a glance at York as well. "I told you to stay back."

"Sorry. What were those—bololins, you called them? —what were they doing here?"

Cerenkov and Rynstadt had joined the group now, as had most of Moff's associates. "The bololins migrate periodically," he said, almost reluctantly. "A herd like that always forms for a run, and you'll agree something like that would be almost impossible to stop. So we've built the city to pass them through with as little damage as possible."

York glanced at the carcasses in the avenue. "As little damage to *you*, anyway."

"Crews will be along momentarily to take them to

a processing area," Moff said. "Both meat and hides will be saved."

"You'd do better to split a few off from the herd and stop them before you shoot," York persisted. "Letting them get trampled like that doesn't do hide *or* meat any good."

"What was all that with the mojos and those other birds?" Joshua asked as Moff started to reply. "Do mojos hunt like that even when they don't intend to eat?"

"To—? Oh, I see." Moff reached up to stroke his mojo's throat. "Tarbines aren't a food animal. Mojos seek them for reproduction. Cerenkov," he said, turning away from Joshua, "we will need to cut short our visit to the marketplace if we intend to reach the art gallery during the time it will be cleared for us. If you wish, we can return here another time."

"All right." Cerenkov sent a long look toward the bololin carcasses as Moff steered them down the avenue to the cross street where their car had been moved. "Does this sort of thing happen very often?"

"Occasionally. Perhaps more often in the next few days—there is a major migration underway. But there's no need for concern. The probability you will be near the affected streets is small, and even if you are the rooftop alarms always give adequate warning. Come now; we must hurry."

Conversation ceased. As they walked, Joshua nudged York and slowed his pace a bit. York matched his speed; and as Moff and the others pulled a few paces ahead, Joshua reached up to put his thumb over the microphone on his translator pendant. "You've lived on a lot of worlds," he murmured to the other. "You ever seen a male and female of the same species that look that different?"

York shrugged minutely, his hand similarly on his translator. "I've seen or heard of some that are even more mismatched than that . . . but I've never heard of a mating that looks that much like an out-and-out attack. Almost like—well, hell, I'll say it: like a rape."

Joshua felt a shiver run up his back. "It did, didn't it? The mojos were hitting them like condorines swooping down on rabbits."

"And the tarbines were trying like crazy to get away. Something really weird's happening here, Joshua."

Ahead, Moff glanced back. Casually, Joshua dropped his arm back to his side and increased his speed, York doing the same beside him. They'd have to find some private way to clue Cerenkov in on this and get him to start probing, Joshua knew, already trying to figure out a way to do that. He hoped the other's silver tongue would be up to the challenge . . . because if the mojo's mating behavior was evidence of some significant biological principle here, it could be vital to root such information out.

And it was sure as hell that the support team, stuck inside the *Dewdrop*, wouldn't be able to do anything in that direction.

"No," Telek shook her head. "Absolutely not. It's insane."

"It's *not* insane," Pyre retorted. "It's feasible, practical, and there's no other way to get hard data." He glanced at the displayed map of Sollas and the red mass that was the computer's estimate of the bololin herd's position. "And we've got maybe fifteen minutes to take advantage of that herd."

"You'll be outside—alone—in unknown and presumably hostile country," Telek growled, ticking off fingers with quick, almost vicious motions. "You'll have limited communication with us and none at all with the locals, should you stumble on any. And you probably wouldn't have a chance of sneaking back in unnoticed—which means that if you got hurt you'd be forcing me to choose between your life and anything further for the mission."

"And if I don't go you may never find out why male mojos rape their females," Pyre said quietly. "Not to mention why the tarbines ride bololins. Or for that matter, why the bololins are so hard to keep out of cities."

Telek looked at Christopher and Nnamdi. "Well?" she demanded. "Say something, you two. Tell him he's crazy."

The two scientists exchanged glances and Christopher shrugged uncomfortably. "Governor, we're here to learn everything we can about this place," he said, his eyes not meeting either Telek's or Pyre's. "I agree it's dangerous . . . but Almo's right about the bololins probably not getting this close again."

"And he *is* a Cobra," Nnamdi put in.

"A Cobra." Telek almost spat the word. "And so he's invulnerable to accidents and snake bites?" She dropped her eyes to the city display.

For a moment there was silence. "We have survival packs already made up," Pyre said quietly. "One would suffice for a week; I can take two. There are laser comm setups I could use to keep in touch from the woods without the Qasamans catching on. I've seen biological field analyzers being used; I'm sure I can set one up for you or even run it a little myself if necessary. And I could take a couple of small freeze boxes if you wanted a whole tarbine to study later."

She shook her head, eyes still on the screen. "You're Cobra team leader. Do what you like."

Which was not exactly enthusiastic support, but Pyre would have to take what he could get. The bololins were barely minutes away. "Michael, Dorjay—two survival packs and laser comm to the port cargo hatch; stat," he said into the intercom. The two Cobras acknowledged and Pyre left the lounge at a fast jog, heading for his stateroom for a quick change into more suitable clothing. There was a boxed bio field analyzer down in the cargo hold; he could grab it on his way out. The hatch itself, facing away from the city, should let him out into the ship's shadow unseen. At that point he would just have to hope the bololins were indeed running deliberately along magnetic field lines ... and that the runways were as dusty as they looked.

He was in the cargo hold three minutes later. A minute after that, laden like a pack cart, he was crouching outside, hugging the *Dewdrop*'s hull as he moved toward the bow. The rumble of the bololins was audible without his enhancers now, and a quick glance under the *Dewdrop*'s nose showed they were indeed on the projected path, one that would take the herd's flank within fifty meters of the ship. Behind the first few ranks the dust was already beginning to obscure the city beyond, and it was getting thicker. Taking a deep breath, Pyre gave the edge of the forest a quick scan and got ready to run.

The leading edge of the herd thundered by. Pyre let the next few ranks pass as well; and then he was off, running bent over to present as low a profile as possible. Equipment banging against back and thighs with each step, he traced a curved path that ended with him pacing the snuffling herd barely a meter from its flank.

It was instantly obvious the nearest bololins didn't care for his presence. One or two veered at him as they ran, horns hooking toward his side; but even without his programmed reflexes he was more maneuverable than the massive beasts and evaded them without trouble. More troublesome—and unexpected— were the two-meter-long whiplash tails no one had noticed. If the first such blow hadn't landed across his backpack it would undoubtedly have left a painful welt or even torn muscle. As it was, his nanocomputer had to take over servo control briefly to restore his balance.

But it was only a few more seconds to the edge of the forest, and as the herd passed the first few trees Pyre parted company with them, angling off to the side and coming to a stop only when a glance behind showed nothing but greenery.

For a long moment he just stood there, turning slowly around as his auditory and optical enhancers probed as much of the surroundings as possible. Gradually the sound of the bololins faded into the distance, to be replaced by the chirps, clicks, and whistles of birds, insects, and God alone knew what else. Small animals moved in trees and undergrowth, and once he thought he heard something much heavier on the prowl.

It was just barely possible that this *hadn't* been the smartest idea he'd ever had.

But there was nothing for it now but to go ahead and do the job he'd promised Telek he would. Setting his equipment at the base of a tree, he made sure his auditory enhancers were on full and got to work.

Chapter 11

"If ever there was a world designed for colonization," Captain Shepherd said with satisfaction, "this is definitely it."

Gazing around the gray-brown landscape, Jonny had to agree. Whatever the mechanism that had scoured this region of space down to nucleic acids, it was clear Kubha had suffered more than most. Nothing but the most primitive life existed here: one-celled plants and animals, and perhaps a few hundred species of only slightly more complex organisms. A virtual blank slate, ready to accept whatever ecological pattern any future colony chose to set up on it.

Any pattern, that is, that could stand the heat.

A young biologist trudged up the knoll where Jonny and Shepherd were standing, a full rack of sample tubes held carefully to his chest. "Captain; Governor," he nodded, blowing a drop of sweat from the tip of his nose. "Thought you might be interested in seeing the preliminary compatibility test results before I file them."

Jonny hid a smile as he and Shepherd stooped to peer into the tubes at the various mixes of native and Aventinian cells. At Chata, at Fuson, and now at Kubha, the scientists had never ceased their efforts to persuade Shepherd to grant them more time for sample taking and general study, and getting him interested in the results was just one of the more subtle approaches. It wouldn't work, of course; the Council had made it very clear that this was to be a whirlwind tour, and Shepherd took his orders very seriously.

"Interesting," the captain nodded, straightening up from his brief examination. "Better get them to the freeze chamber, though, if you want time to gather any more. We're lifting in about two hours."

A hint of chagrin crossed the biologist's face before it could be suppressed. "Yes, sir," he said, and headed toward the *Menssana*.

"You're a cold-blooded taskmaster without a drop of scientific curiosity; did you know that?" Jonny asked blandly.

Shepherd's lip quirked. "So I've been told. But the Council said a fast prelim study, and that's exactly what they're going to get. Besides, I want to be back when the *Dewdrop* arrives, just in case—"

"Hi, Chrys," Jonny interrupted, turning as his wife came up to join them. His enhanced hearing had picked up the sound of her footsteps, and the last thing he wanted to remind her of was the *Dewdrop* sitting on alien soil with two of her sons aboard. "What do you think?" he added, waving a hand at the landscape.

"Too empty for my tastes," she said, shaking her head. "Seems spooky, somehow. *And* I'm not crazy about pan-frying my brain out here." She gave Jonny a careful look. "How are *you* feeling?"

"Fine," he told her, and meant it. "The heat's not only helping my arthritis, but also seems to be pushing my heart rate and circulation up enough to compensate a bit for my anemia."

"Which means you're going to trade anemia for a heart attack?" Shepherd grunted. "Great. Maybe you'd better get back inside until we're ready to lift, Governor."

"My heart's in no danger," Jonny protested. "It'll probably live two years longer than I do."

"Sure it will." Shepherd hooked a thumb in the *Menssana*'s direction. "Go on, Governor. Call it an order."

For a moment Jonny was tempted to unilaterally take himself out of the chain of command. He found it refreshing to be out in the open air—especially where there was no danger of anything sticking teeth, claws, mandibles, or stings into him—and very much wanted to enjoy the last hours he'd have here. But there *was* that promise to Chrys. . . . "Oh, all right," he grumbled. "But under protest."

Together, he and Chrys trotted down the knoll. "The Council sure named this one right," Chrys remarked as they reached level ground and slowed to a more sedate walk.

"Named what right? Kubha?"

"Uh-huh. You know—the five stars of the Southern Cross constellation of Asgard—"

"I know how the planets were code-named, yes," Jonny interrupted her.

"Well, it happens that Kubha's the hottest of those stars; and *this* Kubha's the hottest of these planets, at least so far. Must be an omen."

Jonny snorted. "Let's not give either the Council *or* the universe that much credit."

Chrys smiled. "Hey, cheer up," she said, taking his arm. "Everything's really going pretty well. The Jonny Moreau luck seems to hold up even when you're only along for the ride."

"Um. Aside from little things like snakele venom in the nucleic acid analyzer—"

"Fixed," she said. "We got it working again about ten minutes ago. Which was why I'd been released from my desk and could come out to drag you kicking and screaming back inside."

He shook his head in mock exasperation. "I swear,

Chrys, you do a poorer imitation of a loafing passenger than *I* do."

"And you're delighted. Go on, admit it."

"Why? You're going to send me to my room anyway, aren't you?" he said, putting a well-remembered five-year-old's whine into his voice. "You always *want* me to play outside on nice days."

She poked him in the ribs. "Stop that—I had my fill of tantrums years ago."

He captured her attacking hand and wrapped the arm around his waist, and for a moment they walked like that in silence. "It *would* be an ideal planet for colonization, wouldn't it," she said quietly. "And that's going to make it all the harder to say no."

"No to the Trofts?"

She nodded. "The Council's going to want this world, and probably the others as well. And to get them they'll take on the Qasamans . . . whether that's the smart thing to do or not."

Jonny grimaced. The same thought had been lurking in the back of his own mind for at least two planets now. "We'll just have to hope the *Dewdrop's* report is solid enough that it relegates ours to footnote status as far as that decision is concerned."

"With Lizabet Telek in charge of writing it?" Chrys snorted. "She wants these worlds so badly she can taste it. She'll make sure the Qasamans sound like crippled porongs as far as fighting ability is concerned."

"I don't know if she's *that* underhanded," Jonny demurred cautiously. "And with Almo, Justin, and Joshua aboard she'd have a hard time slanting things too far."

Still, he thought as they passed the Cobra guard at the *Menssana's* airlock and stepped through to the cool shock of the ship's climate control, *it might not hurt to tone down our report a shade or two. Emphasize Chata's flatfoot herds, perhaps, and Fuson's spit-*

ting *snakeles. Every world's got its drawbacks—all we
have to do is find them and make them visible.*

*And hope the Council doesn't take them too seri-
ously.* Already the ship's cooler air was affecting his
arthritic joints, reminding him with each twinge that
he'd been a bit lax with his medication schedule. He
would hate to see a world like Kubha slip through
mankind's fingers for no real reason.

Whether it was worth a war . . . well, that decision
didn't yet need to be made.

Chapter 12

The complete tour of Sollas and its environs took six days; and for Cerenkov the most amazing part was how the Qasamans could keep them so busy while showing them so little.

So little of real importance, anyway. They spent a great many hours touring art galleries, cultural museums, and parks, while evenings were usually filled with dance and musical performances at their guest house and long discussions with Mayor Kimmeron or other high-ranking officials. At no time, despite Cerenkov's carefully phrased requests, was the contact team taken to anything resembling a communications or computing center; nor were they shown any of the city's industrial or manufacturing capability.

And yet such capability obviously existed. The glimpses they got of intercity roads and the relatively sparse traffic on them showed Sollas's goods weren't simply being shipped in from somewhere else.

"It's got to be underground," Rynstadt commented that evening as the four men relaxed in the lounge that connected their two sleeping rooms. "All of it: refining, manufacturing, waste processing—maybe there's even a tunnel network for product distribution."

"Except for smaller operations like the boron plant

we saw the first day?" Cerenkov shrugged. "Possibly. Probably, even. Sure seems to be the hard way to do it, though."

"Depends on what they were after," Joshua put in. "Aesthetically, this is a clean, beautiful city, a good place to spend your leisure time even if you have to work underground all day."

"Or else," York said quietly, "they were simply worried about having everything out in the open."

Cerenkov felt his jaw tense up, forced it to relax. The unspoken assumption was that the Qasamans were eavesdropping on these conversations, and to go anywhere near military concepts made him nervous. But on the other hand, ignoring such a normal aspect of human societies was likely to look even more suspicious. As long as York didn't let his professional interests run away with him— "What do you mean? They built underground to protect their manufacturing base from attack?"

"Or from detection," York replied. "Remember our assumed starting point: émigrés—or exiles—from perceived repression, having gone way farther than they intended and now stuck on Qasama with a useless stardrive."

"Do you suppose they ran into some Troft ships on the way here?" Joshua suggested. "The Dominion probably hadn't met either them or the Minthisti when the Qasamans left. If *I'd* just seen a Troft for the first time, I think I'd probably have kept going until my tanks ran dry."

Nodding, York said, "I suspect that's exactly what they did. The distance seems right for a colony ship's full dry-tank range." He looked back at Cerenkov. "I'd guess they had their whole city underground to begin with, moving up only as they started to outgrow the space and no one showed up to stomp them."

"And they came up smack in the middle of the bololin migration pattern," Cerenkov sighed, shaking his head. "Definitely poor planning on someone's part."

"That doesn't explain where the villages came from," Rynstadt mused. "Though maybe we can get some of their history tomorrow. Assuming the trip is still on."

Cerenkov shrugged. "As far as I know Moff and company are driving us out there first thing tomorrow morning." He broke off as a familiar hooting sounded faintly in the distance.

York grimaced. "More bololins. I think I'd have stayed underground until I found a way to keep the damn things out."

At least, Cerenkov thought, *the streets ought to be pretty empty by now. I wonder how many people those things kill every year*? "I assume they had their reason. Maybe Moff will loosen up some day and talk about it."

First time in a week I'm close enough to make a grab, Pyre groused silently to himself, *and the damn herd decides to be nocturnal*.

From Pyre's end, of course, it wasn't all that bad. Locking in the light amplification capability of his optical enhancers gave him as good a view as he would have had on an overcast afternoon, and with magnification also on he'd be able to target any likely tarbines as soon as they emerged from the obscuring buildings. And once he had targeting lock established he could follow his chosen bird into the woods, where he could shoot it without anyone seeing the flash.

The problem was that with most good Qasamans tucked away in their beds there weren't likely to be many bololins running into bullets out there, and correspondingly few impregnated tarbines for him to hunt. Muttering under his breath, he mentally crossed his fingers and waited for the herd to appear.

It did; and his pleadings were answered from an entirely unexpected direction. Across the landing area—about half a kilometer away and somewhat northeast of his current position—a door suddenly opened in a tall building the *Dewdrop*'s crew had tentatively labeled the control tower, spilling light and people out onto the pavement. Flickers of fire erupted from outstretched hands, and even as their mojos took to the air the sound of gunfire reached Pyre's ears. Shifting his attention back to the herd, he waited. Within seconds the tarbines began to appear.

The multitarget capability hadn't been a part of Cobra optical enhancers since Jonny Moreau's war, but Pyre's team had trained with them prior to the Qasama mission and he'd developed a healthy respect for both their advantages and their dangers. Once he target-locked one or more tarbines, his nanocomputer and servos would make sure his next laser shots would be in that direction—whether or not he suddenly found a predator he needed to deal with first. He'd run into at least twenty such creatures since leaving the *Dewdrop*—dog- or monkey-sized, most of them, but none he'd care to give a free shot at his back regardless. But it was a chance he'd have to take. Keeping an ear cocked for suspicious sounds, he activated his multitarget lock and waited.

The wait wasn't long. As before, the mojos attacked swiftly, swooping in through the tarbines' attempts at evasion. With the larger birds' head start, though, most made it into the cover of the nearest trees before their mojos could disengage. Pyre targeted two of the tarbines just before they entered the forest and, on slightly reckless impulse, locked onto one of the riding mojos as well. The birds swept through the branches, disengaged . . . and, raising his hands, Pyre squeezed off three fingertip laser shots.

The birds dropped with a crunch of dead leaves into the undergrowth. Pyre sprinted over, scooped them up, and hastily got out of the way as the main herd caught up. Keeping well to the side, he paced them another hundred meters into the woods. Then, spinning on his right foot, he swung his left leg up and fired his antiarmor laser.

The trees flashed with reflected light as the targeted bololin crumpled to the ground. Its tarbine took off for the sky; it got maybe ten meters before Pyre's fingertip laser brought it down.

And as the rest of the herd continued on their way, silence returned. Retrieving his last tarbine, Pyre took his prizes to the bush where he'd cached his freeze boxes and stuffed them inside. Then, crouching with his back to a large tree within sight of the dead bololin, he settled down to wait.

It was an hour before the sounds of the Qasaman collection team faded from the area between forest and city. During that time Pyre had also heard someone else poking around the edges of the wood, whistling occasionally as he apparently searched for the mojo Pyre had killed. But he and the others clearly knew better than to go too deep into the forest at night, and no one came anywhere near Pyre's position.

Finally they were gone, and Pyre could address the task of moving the bololin carcass closer to the *Dewdrop*. With his servos the creature's weight wasn't a significant problem, but it took him four tries to find a grip that was reasonably balanced. Finding a wide enough path through the trees and bushes was another problem, and more than once he found himself wondering how in hell the beasts managed it on their own.

Eventually, though, he made it. Dumping the carcass beside his camouflaged laser comm, he activated the latter and slipped on the headphone. "Pyre to *Dewdrop*," he muttered. "Anyone home?"

"Lieutenant Collins," a voice came back promptly. "I believe Governor Telek and her people are still in the lounge, sir; let me switch you."

"Fine," Pyre said. A moment later Telek came on the circuit.

"Everything all right, Almo?" she said.

"Far as I can tell. Listen, I've got a bololin carcass for you and two freeze boxes' worth of tarbines and mojos. You want to warm up your equipment or wait until I can deliver them in person?"

"You got a tarbine? Wonderful! Impregnated or not?"

"Both types—which is why I've got a spare bololin."

"Uh-*huh*. I understand. Well . . . I suppose I ought to do the bololin first, before any scavengers get to it. Can you hook up the field analyzer to the laser comm for me?"

"Sure."

It took only a few minutes to set up the field analyzer and plug its control line into the laser comm's telemetry port, and by the time he'd finished Telek had the necessary control/display console hooked up at her end. "Okay," she said. "Now stand clear."

The analyzer remote, looking for all the world like a large double starfish with gripper treads, crawled up the bololin's flank to where the heart would be on most earthstock animals. A scalpel extended from one arm to slice a neat incision in the dark hide. Pyre paused long enough to make sure the analyzer's camera units were firmly mounted to nearby trees and then headed out to walk a sentry circle around the area. They couldn't afford to have either scavengers or Qasamans stumble onto the post-mortem now . . . and besides, it wasn't really something he wanted to watch.

It was three hours before the remote's return to the ground signaled the operation was at an end—and the bololin was no longer recognizable as such. Averting his eyes, Pyre again put on the headset. "Pyre."

"Ah, you're back." If Telek was at all tired, it wasn't evident from her voice. "You want to open up the freeze boxes and get me one of the tarbines? Better start with the unimpregnated one."

"You sure you want to do it out here?" he asked doubtfully.

"I've got as much sensitivity with the remote as I do with my hands," Telek assured him, "and I'd just as soon start getting some answers before we have to leave. Or at least have the questions I'll want Yuri to ask."

"You're the boss." Finding the proper box, Pyre opened it and set the chilly tarbine down on a patch of bare ground. The remote skittered over to it and Pyre resumed his walk.

He returned twice more, replacing the mess first with an impregnated tarbine and then with the mojo, wondering each time how long Telek could continue to handle delicate surgery without sleep. But she kept at it, and the eastern sky was starting to glow when the remote's operating light finally flicked out. "Well?" he asked into the headset as he started collecting the gear together.

"I'm not sure," Telek said slowly. "The data *seem* clear enough . . . but I'm not really sure if I believe it. Mojos and tarbines appear to be entirely different species . . . and the mojos don't seem to *impregnate* the tarbines as much as they *inoculate* them."

"They *what*?"

"Well . . . the mojo's only external sex organ is designed like an organic hypodermic needle. What it does is inject a seminal fluid that contains virus-like nuclei instead of more complete sperm cells. The nuclei . . . well, this is still preliminary, but it *looks* like they invade some of the cells in the tarbine's back and turn them into embryo mojos."

Pyre stared down at the mutilated mojo on the ground, already beginning to crawl with insects in the growing light. "That's—*weird*."

"That's what *I* said," Telek agreed with a sigh. "But the more I think about it the more sense it makes. This way the mojo relegates both the nourishment and protection of its young to another individual—an entirely different *species*, in fact—and therefore doesn't have to make that sacrifice itself."

"But what incentive does the tarbine have to live until the embryo kills it?" Pyre objected. "*And* what about the training most young have to receive from their parents?"

Christopher's voice came on the circuit. "You're thinking of the usual insectean pattern where one species lays eggs in the body of another, which becomes the larvae's food when they hatch. But the young mojo doesn't *have* to kill its host. If you look closely at the way the skin and muscle are arranged in the tarbine's back, it looks very much like the critical area could be split open and resealed with a minimum of damage and no real loss of flight capability."

"Assuming the mojo doesn't exceed a maximum size," Telek added. "And as to post-natal instruction, the mojo's brain seems to have a larger proportion of the high-neural-density 'primary programming' structure than earthstock or Aventinian animals I've studied. That's an assumption, of course; Qasaman biochemistry doesn't *have* to be strictly analogous to ours—"

"And you fried part of the brain shooting the thing down—" Christopher put in.

"Shut up, Bil. Anyway, it looks very possibly like the mojo young can simply poke through the tarbine's skin, fly its separate way and take up housekeeping in the forest."

"Or on somebody's shoulder." Pyre frowned as a sudden thought struck him. "On somebody's shoulder . . . the same way the tarbines ride bololins?"

"So you noticed the similarity, did you?" Christopher commented. "What makes it even more intriguing is that the tarbines have the same organic hypo organ the mojos do."

"As do the bololins themselves," Telek added, "though God only knows what species *they* use as embryo-hosts. Maybe each other; the top of the size chain has to do *some*thing different."

" 'Big fleas have little fleas upon their backs to bite 'em,' " Pyre quoted the old saying.

" '—and little fleas have lesser fleas, and so ad infinitum,' " Telek finished for him. "You're the third person who's brought that up tonight. Starting with me."

"Um. Well ... the contact team still going sight-seeing tomorrow?"

"Yes. I think I'll clue them in on all this as soon as they wake up—maybe Yuri will be able to worm out some more information from Moff." Telek paused and Pyre could hear, faintly, the sound of a jaw-cracking yawn. "You'd better get under cover and get some sleep, Almo," she said. "I think under the circumstances you can skip that riverside fauna survey we talked about yesterday—I've got enough data to keep me busy for quite a while."

"No argument," Pyre agreed. "I'll call in when I wake up."

"Just be careful you're not seen. Good night—or morning."

"Same to you." Shutting down the laser comm, Pyre spent a few moments rearranging its camouflage and hiding his other equipment. A dozen meters away was his shelter tree; tall and thick, its lowest branches a good five meters above the ground. A servo-powered jump took him the necessary height, and a few branches higher he reached his "shelter," a waterproof one-man hammock bag slung under a particularly strong branch and surrounded by a glued-stick cage sort of arrangement. It made Pyre feel a little strange to sleep inside such a barrier, but it was the simplest way to make sure no carnivore could sneak up on him, no matter how quiet it was or how deeply asleep *he* was.

Entering, he sealed the cage and worked himself into the hammock with a sigh. For a minute he considered setting his alarm, ultimately decided against it. If anything came up, the *Dewdrop* had one-way communication with him via his emergency earphone, and if they were careful how they focused the beam, it was unlikely even a snooper set in the airport control tower could pick it up.

The control tower. His drift toward sleep slowed as he remembered the men who'd charged out of that dark and supposedly deserted building for bololin target practice. Certainly their presence didn't mesh with the building's assumed main function—no aircraft had so much as shown its nose since the *Dewdrop*'s arrival. But if they weren't in there to handle planes, then what *were* they doing there? Monitoring the visitors' ship? Probably. Still, as long as they were just watching they weren't likely to bother anyone.

Closing his eyes, Pyre put the image of silent watchers out of his mind and slid into oblivion.

Chapter 13

For the drive to the outer villages Moff exchanged their usual open-air car for a small enclosed bus. The reason wasn't hard to figure out; barely a kilometer out of Sollas the road began passing in and out of the patches of forest that had been visible from orbit. "Just a normal precaution," Moff explained about their vehicle at one point. "Cars are rarely attacked, even by krisjaws, but it does happen occasionally." Joshua shuddered a bit at the thought, wondering for the hundredth time what had possessed Pyre to go out into the forest alone—and what had possessed Telek to *let* him go. The *Dewdrop* had been maddeningly uninformative on everything dealing with Pyre's mission; and Joshua, for one, found it uncomfortably suspicious. He and Justin had discussed in some length the mystery behind Pyre's presence here during the trip from Aventine, though without finding any good answers. The possibility that Telek might have brought Pyre along solely because his political view made him expendable wasn't one that had occurred to Joshua before; but it was occurring to him now, and he didn't care for it at all.

But for the moment, at least, it was a low-priority worry. Pyre had demonstrated his ability to survive the Qasaman wilderness . . . and, besides, the biological breakthrough he and Telek had made last night was just too fascinating to ignore. Joshua's schooling had included only a bare minimum of the life sciences, but even he could see how radically different the Qasaman ecology was from anything known either in the Worlds or the Dominion and could guess at some of the implications. The contact team hadn't had a safe chance to discuss it among themselves yet, of course—as far as their hosts knew, they should have no inkling of any of this. But Joshua could see the same thoughts and speculations in their eyes. Watching the brightly colored folliage outside the bus, he waited impatiently for Cerenkov to start the gentle probing Telek had suggested.

Cerenkov's grip on his curiosity was apparently stronger than Joshua's, however, and he waited until the fifty-kilometer trip was nearly over before nudging the conversation in that direction. "I've noticed a fair sprinkling of smaller birds flying among the trees," he said, gesturing toward the window beside him, "but nothing that seems to be the size of the mojo or its female form of tarbine. Do they nest in trees in the wild, or do they raise their young in those quill forests on the bololins' backs?"

"There is no need of nests or the raising of young," Moff told him. "A mojo's young are born with all the necessary survival skills already present."

"Really? Doesn't the tarbine at least have to nest long enough to hatch the eggs?"

"There are no eggs—mojo young are born live. In this sense most of the bird-like Qasaman creatures are not true birds, by the old standards."

"Ah." Joshua could almost see Cerenkov casting about for a question that wouldn't reveal that he knew Moff was being deliberately misleading. "I'm also interested in the relationship between the tarbines and bololins. Is the tarbine merely a parasite, getting a free ride but not contributing anything?"

"No, the relationship is more equal than that. The

tarbines often help defend their bololins against predator attack, and it's thought that they also help locate good grazing sites from the air."

"I thought the bololins liked to travel along magnetic field lines," Rynstadt put in. "Can they just get
off that path any time they want to go foraging?"

Moff gave him an odd look. "Of course. They only
use the magnetic lines as a guide to and from the
northern breeding areas. How did you deduce the
mechanism?"

"The layout of Sollas was the major clue," Cerenkov
replied before Rynstadt could do so. "Those wide
avenues all point along the field lines, with no real
provision for bololin herds going any other direction.
I think Marck's question refers to the fact that when
the herd we saw was coming through the city the
people stood just barely inside the cross streets, as if
they knew the bololins wouldn't stray even slightly
off their path. One of those still aboard the ship had
wondered whether they were actually constrained to
follow their individual lines pretty closely."

"No, of course not." Moff's quizzical look was edg-
ing toward suspicion. "Otherwise many would crash
into buildings instead of finding their way into the
streets. But how did your companion know where
the people were standing?"

Joshua's heart skipped a beat. The Qasamans hadn't
shown the slightest indication that they knew about
his implanted sensors, but he still abruptly felt as if
every eye in the bus had turned in his direction. It
jump-kicked him back to childhood, to all the times
his mother had easily penetrated his innocent expression to find the guilt bubbling up beneath it—

But Cerenkov was already well on top of things.
"We told them about it, of course," he said, his tone
one of genuine puzzlement. "We described the whole
scene while you were up there shooting. They were
interested in the odd mojo mating pattern, too—at
least what I was able to tell them about it seemed

odd to them. Was there some kind of ritual dance or pattern that I missed?"

"You seem excessively interested in the mojos," Moff said, his dark eyes boring into Cerenkov's.

Cerenkov shrugged. "Why not? You must admit your relationship with them is unique in human history. I know of no other culture where people have had such universal protection—*defensive* protection, I mean, not just a widespread carrying of weapons. It's bound to have reduced every form of aggression, from simple assault all the way to general warfare."

Joshua frowned as that fact suddenly hit him. So busy had he been observing the details and minutiae of Qasaman life that he'd missed the larger patterns. But Cerenkov obviously hadn't ... and if he was right, perhaps the Trofts had cause to worry after all. A human culture that had had the will power to break the pattern of strong preying on weak would be long on cooperation and short on competition ... and a potential threat to its neighbors no matter what its technological level.

Moff was speaking again. "And you think our little mojos deserve the credit?" he asked, stroking his bird's throat. "You give no credit to our peole and philosophy?"

"Of course we do," Rynstadt said. "But there've been countless cultures throughout history who've paid great lip service to the concepts of justice and freedom from fear without doing anything concrete for their citizens. You—and in particular the generation which first began taming the mojos—have proved humanity is capable of truly practical idealism. That achievement alone would make contact between our worlds worthwhile, certainly from our point of view."

"Your world has difficulties with war, then?" Moff's gaze shifted to Rynstadt.

"So far we've avoided that particular problem," Rynstadt answered cautiously. "But we have our share of normal human aggressions, and that occasionally causes trouble."

"I see." For a moment they rode in silence, and then Moff shrugged. "Well, you'll see that we aren't completely without aggression. The difference is that we've learned to direct our attention outward, toward the dangers of the wild, instead of inward toward each other."

Dangerous indeed, Joshua thought; and even Cerenkov's eyes seemed troubled as conversation in the bus drifted into silence.

A few minutes later, they reached the village of Huriseem.

Joshua could remember arguments aboard ship as to whether the rings around the villages were actually walls; but at ground level there was no doubt whatsoever. Made of huge stone or concrete blocks, painted a dead black, Huriseem's wall was a stark throwback to ancient Earth history and the continual regional warfare of those days. It seemed gratingly out of place here, especially after the discussion of only a few minutes earlier.

Beside him, York cleared his throat. "Only about three meters high," he muttered, "and no crenels or fire ports."

Moff apparently heard him. "As I said, there is no war here," he said—a bit tartly, Joshua thought. "The wall is to keep out bololins and the more deadly predators of the forests."

"Why not build along the same open lines as Sollas?" Cerenkov asked. "That works well enough for the bololins, and I didn't see any predators getting in there."

"Predators are rare in Sollas because there are many people and there is a wide gap between city and forest. Here such an approach would clearly not work."

So clear back the forest, Joshua thought. But perhaps that was more trouble than a single village was worth.

The bus followed the encircling road to the southwest side of the village, where they found a black
gate set into the wall. Clearly they were both expected and observed; the gate was already opening
as they came within sight of it. The bus turned in,
and Joshua glanced back to see it close behind them.

The wall and the forest setting had somehow led
Joshua's subconscious to expect a relatively primitive, thatched-hut scene, and he was vaguely disap-
pointed as he left the bus to find the buildings, streets,
and people as modern as those they'd seen in Sollas.
Three men waited off to the side, and as the last of
the Qasaman escorts left the bus they stepped forward.

"Mayor Ingliss," Moff nodded in greeting, "may I
present to you the visitors from Aventine: Cerenkov,
Rynstadt, York, and Moreau."

Where Mayor Kimmeron of Sollas had been almost
cheerful, Ingliss was gravely polite. "I welcome you
to Huriseem," he said with a nod. "I understand you
seek to learn about village life on Qasama. To what
end, may I inquire?"

So Qasaman suspicion isn't limited to the big cities.
Somehow, Joshua found that more of a disappoint-
ment than the lack of thatched huts.

Cerenkov went into his by-now familiar spiel about
trade and cultural exchange, and Joshua allowed his
gaze to drift around the area. Huriseem seemed to
have none of the taller six-story-plus buildings of
Sollas, and the colorful abstract wall paintings were
also absent, but otherwise the village could have
been a transplanted chunk of the larger city. Even
the wall's presence was not intrusive, and it took him
a moment to realize the structure's inside surface
was painted with effectively camouflaging pictures
of buildings and forest scenes. *So why is the outside
painted black*? he wondered—and with a flash of inspiration it hit him. *Black—the same color as the tree
trunks. A charging bololin must see the village as a
giant tree and therefore goes around it.* And that meant—

Reaching to his neck, he covered the pendant's translator mike. "I've got it," he murmured. "The Sollas street paintings make the place look sort of like a clump of forest—same colors and everything. Keeps the bololins from shying away."

There was a long enough pause that he began to wonder if no one on the *Dewdrop* was monitoring the circuit. Then Nnamdi's voice came in over the earphone. "Interesting. Weird, but entirely possible. Depends partly on how good the bololins' eyesight is, I suppose. Governor Telek's still asleep, but I'll suggest this to her when she wakes up, see if she got any data on that last night."

"Fine," Joshua said, "but in the meantime can *you* find any sociological rationale for wanting those herds to come trampling through Sollas?"

"That *does* put into doubt Moff's assertion that they simply can't keep the bololins out, doesn't it?" Nnamdi agreed thoughtfully. "I'll work on it, but nothing comes immediately to mind. Wait a second— face left a bit, will you?"

Joshua obediently turned his head a few degrees in the requested direction. "What is it?"

"That red-bordered sign near the gate—haven't seen anything like it anywhere in Sollas. Let me get the visual translator going. . . ."

Joshua held his head steady for a moment to give the tape a good image, then turned back to face the others. "Okay," Nnamdi said after a moment. "It says, 'Krisjaw hunts this month: the 8th and 22nd at 10.' Today's the eighth, I think, if the numbers we've seen elsewhere are accurate. Wonder why they bother to post a sign with the other comm lines they have."

"Maybe a village this small doesn't have the same wiring as Sollas does," Joshua suggested. It looked like Cerenkov and the Qasamans had about finished the preliminaries; Mayor Ingliss was gesturing toward an open car of the sort they'd used in Sollas all week.

"I'll try to find out," he added and let his hand fall to his side.

Its mike open again, the translator came back on-line. "—will be able to visit the farming areas later," Ingliss was saying. "At the moment many of the workers are out hunting, so there would be little to see."

"Is that the krisjaw hunt?" Joshua spoke up.

Ingliss focused on him. "Yes, of course. Only krisjaws and bololins are worthy of mass hunts, and you would have heard a warning siren if a bololin herd were approaching."

"Yes, Moff has mentioned krisjaws once or twice," Cerenkov said. "I get the impression they're dangerous, but we don't know anything more."

"Dangerous?" Ingliss barked a laugh. "Immensely so. Two meters or more in length, half that from paws to shoulder, with wavy teeth that can shred a man in seconds. Savage hunters, they threaten both our people and our livestock."

"Sounds a little like our spine leopards," Rynstadt commented grimly. "Native Aventinian predators that we've been fighting ever since we landed."

"It wasn't always that way here," Ingliss said, shaking his head. "The old legends say that krisjaws used to be relatively peaceful, avoiding our first settlements and willing to share the bololin herds with us. It was only later, perhaps as they realized we intended to stay, that they began to turn on us."

"Or as they found out humans were good to eat," York suggested. "Did this happen all at once or gradually?"

Ingliss exchanged glances with Moff, who shrugged. "I don't know," the latter said. "Records of those early years are spotty—the malfunction that stranded us here ruined much of our electronic recording equipment, and interim historical records did not always survive."

Nnamdi's voice clicked in on the circuit. "Pursue

this point, Yuri; everyone," he said. "If the krisjaws are really showing signs of intelligence we need to know that."

"The reason I asked," Cerenkov said, "was that if they really did 'realize' you were settling here, they might be a sentient species."

"Our own biologists have studied that question," Moff said, "and they think that unlikely."

"They don't show any great ability to learn, for example," Ingliss offered. "All the villages—and some of the cities, too—hold periodic hunts in which often as many as fifty villagers and visitors participate. Yet the krisjaws haven't learned to stay away from civilized areas."

The light dawned. "Ah—so *that's* why you post a krisjaw hunt notice by the gate," Joshua said. "So anyone passing through will know about it, as well as just the local population."

Ingliss nodded. "Yes. It's an opportunity to practice the human predator's own hunting skill, and all who wish to come are welcome. Krisjaw hides are also very prestigious, and many people find the meat superior to that of bololins. If you'd arrived an hour sooner—but, no, you haven't got mojos, of course. Nor weapons, I see."

"Sounds like you should be close to wiping the things out by now," York grunted.

"Actually, we are," Ingliss nodded, "at least in the inhabited regions of Qasama. I speak of them as dangerous and numerous, but in fact a 50-man hunting group is fortunate to return with one or two trophies. In the days when Huriseem was first built a man could stand atop the wall and shoot one each hour."

"You're lucky any of you survived," York said.

Ingliss shrugged, a more deliberate gesture than the Aventinian version. "As I said, we were fairly well established before they began threatening us in earnest. And by then our adoption of the mojos as bodyguards was also well underway. Ironically enough, that program was stimulated in large part by concerns over the krisjaws."

"But that's enough about ancient history," Moff put in. "We have a limited amount of time; if you wish to observe the village we'll need to begin at once."

For just a second Joshua thought he saw something odd in Moff's face. But then the Qasaman had turned away toward the open car pulled up behind Ingliss and his companions, and Joshua decided he'd imagined the whole thing.

Looking around curiously, he followed the others to the car.

It had been literally decades since Telek had pulled the kind of all-night lab work she'd done the previous night—and *never* had she done it via the waldoes of a remote analyzer. Clumping into the *Dewdrop*'s lounge around noon, she felt like a good computer simulation of death. "What's happening?" she asked Nnamdi, heading immediately for the cahve dispenser in the corner.

"What're *you* doing here?" he frowned up from the displays at her. "You're supposed to be in bed doing some REMs."

"I'm *supposed* to be running a mission," she growled back, bringing her steaming mug over and dropping into the seat beside his. "I can sleep *next* year. Bil still down?"

"Yes. Left a call with the bridge for four o'clock."

And Christopher had done little except watch and make occasional suggestions. *Amazing how tiring it can be to kibitz*, she thought acidly, then put him from her mind. "Is this the village Moff promised us?"

"Yes; Huriseem. The stately fellow screen left is Ingliss, the mayor. This seems to be their version of the marketplace we saw in Sollas. Minus the bololins."

"Then the place *is* walled?"

"Solidly. And Joshua brought up an interesting point about Sollas's wild color scheme a while ago."

Telek listened with half an ear as Nnamdi described Joshua's idea about the cities seeming like clumps of forest to the bololins, the remainder of her attention on the scent and taste of her cahve and on the organized chaos on the displays. With the smaller marketplace of the village, she realized for the first time that services as well as goods were on display. One booth seemed to be manned by a builder, with wood and brick samples on a back table and what looked like a floor plan on a computer display screen set on the front counter. *So why don't they do the whole thing via computer*? she wondered. *They like the personal contact? Could be.*

Nnamdi finished his recitation and she shrugged. "Could very well be. I'll check later and see if the computer can make an estimate of the bololins' visual resolution. Sure seems stupid to help the bololins stampede your city, though."

"That's almost exactly what Joshua said," Nnamdi nodded. "Could there be something we're missing here? About the bololins and people, I mean?"

"I don't think we've got the whole society figured out after a week here, no," she said dryly. "What exactly did you have in mind?"

"Well ..." He waved a hand vaguely. "I don't know. Some symbiotic relationship, like the people have with the mojos."

"I'd call the mojos more pets than symbionts, myself, but given the bololin-tarbine arrangement the point is well taken." Telek frowned into space, trying to remember all the forms of symbiosis that existed on the Worlds. "About the only possibility I can think of is that banging away at the bololins helps drain off the city-dwellers' aggressions. Keeps them peaceful."

"Oh, their aggressions aren't drained off, just rerouted," Nnamdi snorted, gesturing toward the display. "You missed the bargaining session at a jewelry store half a block back. These guys would put Troft businessmen to shame."

"Hmm. Probably a logical avenue to channel it into, given the mojo ban on fighting. That and politics, maybe. . . ."

She trailed off. "Something wrong?" Nnamdi asked.

"I'm not sure," she said, picking up the mike. "Joshua, do a slow three-sixty, would you?"

The scenery shifted as Joshua complied, pausing occasionally as he pretended to look at some booth or other . . . and by the time he'd completed his circle Telek's odd feeling had become a cold certainty. "Moff is missing," she told Nnamdi quietly.

"What?" He frowned, hunching his chair closer to the display as if that would do him any good. "Come on, now—Moff doesn't even go to the bathroom unless the contact team's off in some corner where they won't get into anything."

"I know. Yuri; everyone—Moff's gone. Anyone know where he went or notice him leave?"

There was a short pause. Then, at the edge of the display, Telek saw Cerenkov raise a hand to his pendant. "I hadn't even noticed, Governor," he said. "There're so many people around us here—"

"Which may be precisely why he picked this place," Telek cut him off with a grunt. "Has he said or done anything unusual this morning? Anyone?"

There were four quick negatives. "All right. Everyone keep an eye out for him, without being too conspicuous about it, and try to notice his expression when he shows up."

She turned off the mike and sat glaring for a moment at the noisy market scene. "What do you think it means?" Nnamdi broke into her thoughts.

"Maybe nothing. I hope nothing. But I think I'm going to replay this morning's tapes, see if I can spot anything in Moff's behavior myself. Keep an eye on things; let me know if anything happens." Picking up her cahve, she stepped to an unused display in the corner and keyed for the proper records.

"Should we alert Almo and the bridge?" Nnamdi asked.

"The bridge, yes—but don't make too big a deal of it." She hesitated. "And Almo . . . no, let's not bother him yet. There'll be plenty of time to talk to him when we've figured out what if anything is going on."

"Right."

Telek turned to her display. The semidarkness there was interrupted by a flickering light, the Qasamans' version of a wake-up alarm. Shifting one way and then the other, the picture changed as Joshua rolled over and then sat up. "Rise and glow, Marck," he said to Rynstadt in the other bed. "Busy day coming up."

"So what's new about that?" the other returned in a sleepy voice.

Groping blindly for her cahve mug, Telek settled down to watch.

Chapter 14

The blue skies of Tacta were just a shade redder than those of Chata and Fuson had been, Jonny thought idly as he paused from his contemplation of the bush forest that edged to within fifteen meters of the *Menssana*'s perimeter. More dust in the upper atmosphere, the experts had decided, probably spewed there by the dozens of active volcanos their pre-landing analysis had located. A potentially dangerous place to live, though that could probably be minimized by judicious choice of homestead. The weather and climate could be subject to rapid change, though, regardless of where one settled. All in all, he decided, a distinct fourth on their five-planet survey.

Or in other words, Junca would be keeping its dead-last spot.

Returning his gaze to the bushes, he found a large bird sitting on one of the thicker branches looking back at him.

His first thought was disbelief that neither his enhanced vision nor hearing had detected its approach; but hard on the heels of that came the realization that the bird had probably been sitting there quietly for as long as Jonny had been standing there, its protective coloring and motionlessness serving to hide it.

"You're in luck," Jonny murmured in its direction. "I'm not in charge of collecting fauna samples."

A footstep behind him made him turn. It was Chrys, a vaguely sour look on her face. "Feel like being a politician again?" she asked without preamble.

Jonny flicked a look past her at the bustling activity in the protected area between them and the ship. "What's up?" he asked, focusing on her again.

She waved a hand in disgust. "The same fight they've been having since we hot-tailed it off Junca. The scientists want to take the time we didn't use there to go back for an additional look at Kubha or Fuson."

"And Shepherd wants to just drop the two days we saved out of the schedule and head back home as soon as we're done here," Jonny finished for her with an exasperated sigh. He was roundly sick of the whole issue, especially when Shepherd's first refusal should have settled things long ago. "So what do you want me to do?"

"*I* don't want you to do anything," she returned. "But Rey seems to think you might be able to inject a few well-chosen words into the debate."

Put another way, Banyon wanted him to thunder the scientists back into their labs. Jonny had no doubts which side of the issue the Cobras supported—having been saddled with both the defense of the expedition *and* its hardest work, they were quite ready to head home as soon as possible. The four who were still in sickbay with injuries from the mad scramble off Junca probably held triple batches of that opinion.

And it would certainly be the easiest way to settle the debate. Jonny Moreau the Cobra, Governor Emeritus, had more physical and legal authority than anyone else aboard, including Shepherd himself. He was opening his mouth to give in when he took a good look at Chrys's expression.

It was angry. She was trying to hide the emotion, but Jonny knew her too well to be fooled. The tension lines around her eyes, the slight pinch to her mouth, the tight muscles in cheeks and neck—anger, for sure. Anger and a smattering of frustration.

It was the same expression he'd seen on her far too often these past few years.

And with that sudden connection came the *truly* proper response to the *Messana*'s intramural squabbles. "Well, Rey and the others can just forget it," he told her. "If Shepherd's too polite to chew the scientists' ears off he can just put up with their yammering. I'm on vacation out here."

Chrys's eyes widened momentarily; but even as a faint smile flickered across her lips the tension was leaving her face and body. "I'll quote you exactly," he said.

"Do that. But first take a look here," he added as she started to turn back toward the encampment. "It looks like we're starting to attract the local sightseers."

The bird was indeed still sitting quietly on its branch. "Odd," Chrys said, studying it through a pair of folding binoculars. "That beak looks more suited to a predator than to a seed or insect eater. The feet, too."

Jonny bumped his optical enhancers up a notch. They *did* rather look like condorine talons, now that she mentioned it. "What's odd about it? We've catalogued birds and rodentoids here small enough for it to prey on."

"I know . . . but why is it just *sitting* there? Why isn't it out hunting or something?"

Jonny frowned. Sitting motionlessly amid the low bushes . . . as if afraid of losing what little cover its position provided. "Maybe it's hurt," he suggested slowly. "Or hiding from a larger predator."

They looked at each other, and he saw in her eyes that she was following the same train of logic and reaching the same conclusion. And liking it no better than he did. "Like . . . us?" she eventually voiced the common thought.

"I don't see anything else it could be afraid of," he admitted, giving the sky a quick sweep.

"A ground animal—? No. Anything the size of a cat could get it in those low bushes." Chrys's eyes shifted to the bird. "But . . . how could it know—?"

"It's intelligent." Jonny didn't realize until he'd said the words just how strongly he was starting to believe them. "It recognizes we're tool-makers and aliens and is being properly cautious. Or is waiting for us to communicate."

"How?"

"Well . . . maybe I should go over to it."

Chrys's grip on his arm was surprisingly strong. "You think that'd be safe?"

"I *am* a Cobra—remember?" he growled with tension of his own. Contact with the unknown . . . his old combat training came surging back. *Rule One: Have a backup.* Carefully, keeping the movements fluid, he pulled his field phone from his belt. "Dr. Hanford?" he said, naming the only zoologist he knew to be close by, the only one he remembered seeing near the ship when Chrys came up a few minutes ago.

"Hanford."

"Jonny Moreau. I'm at the southeast part of the perimeter. Get over here, quietly. And bring any Cobras nearby with you."

"Got it."

Jonny replaced the phone and waited. The bird waited too, but seemed to be getting a little restless. Though perhaps that was his imagination.

Hanford arrived a couple of minutes later, running with an awkward-looking waddle that made for a fair compromise between speed and stealth. Banyon and a Cobra named Porris were with him. "What is it?" the zoologist stage-whispered, coming to a stop at Jonny's side.

Jonny nodded toward the bird. "Tell me what you make of that."

"You mean the bushes—?"

"No, the bird there," Chrys said, pointing it out.

"The—? Ah." Hanford got his own binoculars out. "Ah. Yes, we've seen others of the species. Always at a distance, though—I don't think anyone's ever gotten this close to one before."

"They're rather skittish, then?" Jonny prompted. "Normally, that is?"

"Um," Hanford grunted thoughtfully. "Yes. He *does* seem unusually brave, doesn't he?"

"Maybe he's staying put *because* he's afraid of us," Banyon said.

"If he's afraid then he should take off," Hanford shook his head.

"No, sir. We're too close to him for that." Banyon pointed. "The instant he leaves that bush he'll be silhouetted against the sky—*and* he'll be in motion. Either one would be more than enough for most predators. He's in lousy position where he is, but it's the best option he's got."

"Except that he's a bird and we're obviously not," Hanford said. "Once he's aloft he shouldn't have anything to fear from us."

"Unless," Jonny suggested quietly, "he understands what weapons are."

There was a short silence. "No," Hanford said at last. "No, I can't believe that. Look at that cranium size, for starters—there's just not enough room in there for a massive brain."

"Size isn't all-important—" Porris began.

"But cell number is," Hanford shot back. "And Tactan cell sizes and biochemistry are close enough to ours to make the comparison valid. No, he's not a sentient lifeform—he's just frozen with fear and doesn't realize he can escape any time he wants to."

" 'Ladybird, ladybird, fly away home,' " Chrys murmured.

"Yes, well, he's missed his chance now," Hanford said briskly. "Porris, you know where the flash nets are stored?" He half-turned toward the *Menssana*—

And the bird shot off its perch.

Chrys gasped with the suddenness of it, as beside her Banyon reflexively snapped his hands into firing position. "Hold it!" Jonny barked to him. "Let it go."

"What?" Hanford yelped. "*Shoot* it, man—*shoot* it!"

But Banyon lowered his hands.

The bird went. Not straight up into the sky, as Jonny would have thought most likely, but horizontally along the tops of the bushes. And . . . zigzagging. Zigzagging like. . . .

It disappeared beyond a gentle rise and Jonny turned to find Banyon's eyes on him. "Evasive maneuvers," the other almost whispered.

"Why didn't you shoot it?" Hanford barked, gripping Jonny's arm, his other hand clenched into a frustrated fist. "I gave you Cobras a direct order—"

"Doctor," Jonny interjected, "the bird didn't move *until* you suggested we try and capture it."

"I don't care. You should—" Hanford stopped abruptly as it suddenly seemed to penetrate. "You mean—? No. No. I don't believe it. How could it have known what we were saying? It *couldn't* have."

"Of course not." Banyon's voice was dark. "But it knew it had to leave; and it took a low, evasive route when it did. The sort of pattern you'd use against enemy fire."

"*And* it waited until you, Doctor, had your back turned," Chrys added, shuddering. "The one who gave the capture order. Jonny . . . this sounds too much to be coincidence."

"Maybe they've seen tool-makers before," Jonny said slowly. "Maybe the Trofts landed when they were surveying the area. That way they could know about weapons."

"They could all be part of a hive mind, perhaps," Porris suggested suddenly. "Each individual wouldn't have to be independently intelligent that way."

"The hive mind theory's been in disrepute for twenty

years," Hanford said. But he didn't sound all that confident. "And anyway, that doesn't explain how they knew our language well enough to realize I was sending you for a flash net."

Abruptly, Jonny realized he was still staring at the spot where the bird had vanished. He looked around quickly; but no vast clouds of attacking birds were sweeping down from the sky, as he'd half expected. Only occasional and far-distant specks marred the red-tinged blue. Still . . . "I think it might be a good idea to get everything packed up early," he said to the others. "Be ready to leave at a moment's notice if . . . it becomes necessary."

Hanford looked as if he would object, seemed to think better of it, and turned to Banyon instead. "Would it be possible to get a couple of Cobras to come on a hunting run with me? I want one of those birds—alive if possible, but I'm no longer that fussy."

"I'll see what I can do," Banyon said grimly. "I think finding out more about them would be an excellent idea."

In the end, Captain Shepherd accepted all the recommendations put before him. The quick-lift preparations were made, the perimeter Cobra guard was doubled, and the scientists shifted into an almost frantic high speed. Two separate hunting parties failed to make so much as visual contact with any of the mysterious birds. The facts, the speculations, and the rumors circulated widely . . . and the *Menssana* lifted a full twelve hours ahead of schedule. For once, there were no complaints.

Chapter 15

They spent a great deal of time wandering around the Huriseem marketplace—more time, York thought, than they'd spent at any other single place during their entire Qasaman tour—and he breathed a private sigh of relief when the end was finally in sight. The presence of so many mojos virtually eye to eye with him was something he found particularly unnerving, and Moff's continued absence wasn't helping a bit. He wondered how Mayor Ingliss would explain the latter, something he would have no choice but to do as soon as they left the marketplace mob. Alone with their escort, the team would *have* to "notice" that Moff was missing, and Ingliss would then have to spin some story.

York didn't want to hear it. It would be a packet of lies; worse yet, a packet of obvious lies. Moff's exit had been too smooth, the timing of it too well chosen, to have been accidental. Clearly, the team hadn't been intended to miss him at all. York's gut instincts told him that having to admit Moff had been away would be almost as bad in the Qasaman's minds as actually telling where and why he'd gone. The more York saw of the Qasamans—the more he listened to Moff's evasive answers to their questions, the more he saw of what they were and were not being shown—

through all of that the descriptions *overcautious* and *suspicious* were gradually giving way to the word *paranoid*. Whether their history had given them a right to be that way was irrelevant; what mattered at the moment was that York had seen paranoid minds at work before, and he knew how they worked. The simple fact of Moff's absence gave him not a single byte of useful information, but the Qasamans might not recognize that. They were just as likely to assume that their entire plot—or plan, or scheme, or damn surprise party, for all *he* knew—had been totally compromised, and that they would have to spring things prematurely.

York didn't want that. If Moff were planning something—*any*thing—it would be safer for all involved if it went off smoothly and on schedule. *Damn it, Moff, get back here*, he thought furiously into the air. *Get back here and keep your illusion that you're in control.*

So engrossed was he in watching surreptitiously for Moff that he completely missed whatever it was that started the fight.

His first rude notice, in fact, was a sudden grip on his shoulder by one of Moff's assistants, hauling him up short at the very edge of a ring of people that had formed just past the marketplace boundary. The open area so encircled was perhaps twenty meters wide; inside, barely five meters apart, two men without mojos faced each other. Their expressions were just short of murderous.

"What's going on?" York asked the Qasaman still holding his arm.

It was Ingliss, two people down the circle, who answered. "A duel," he said. "Insult has been made; challenge offered and accepted."

York's mouth went dry as his eyes found first the opponents' belted pistols and then the two hundred or more people gathered to watch. Surely they wouldn't start shooting *here*—

A man with a blue-and-silver headband appeared halfway around the circle and stepped to the two men. From a large shoulder pouch he took a thirty-centimeter rattan-like stick and a set of two small balls connected together by fifty centimeters of milky-white cord. Handing the stick and balls to one of the combatants, he went to the other man and gave him a second set from the bag. He stepped back to the edge of the circle, raised his right hand, and then brought it down in a chopping motion—

And the combatant to York's right, who'd been swinging the balls lazily over his head by their cord, abruptly hurled them at his opponent.

Hurled them well, too, with power and accuracy. But the other was ready. Holding his stick vertically in front of him, he deftly caught the spinning projectile on it, letting the balls wrap themselves up. An instant later his own set of balls were whirling back toward the first man, who similarly caught them on his stick. A momentary pause for each to disentangle his opponent's captured weapon and they were ready to begin again.

"What's going on?" York whispered again.

"A duel, as I said," Ingliss murmured back. "Each man takes turns casting his curse ball bola at the other until both weapons have been lost to the crowd or one opponent has conceded. The curse balls will leave impressive bruises, but seldom do more physical damage."

"Lost to the crowd?"

"If a throw goes wide or is otherwise not caught, the observers will not return it. Two such misses, clearly, and the duel must end."

"What keeps one of them from charging his opponent between throws and beating his brains out?"

"The same thing that keeps them from using their guns," Ingliss replied calmly. "Their mojos—there and there." He pointed to two of the spectators, each of whom had an extra bird on his shoulder.

York frowned. "You mean they guard against *all* attacks, even unarmed ones? I thought they only reacted to the drawing of guns."

"Oh, of course they can't defend against *all* attacks," the mayor shrugged. "You could hit me now, suddenly, before my mojo could stop you. Though it would keep you from continuing the attack." He nodded to the duelists, now beginning to show sweat sheens from their efforts. "But they are so obviously fighting that their mojos will keep them apart."

"I see." York thought about the implications of that for the Cobras, should they eventually need to go into action. Would the mojos recognize them as the source of the lethal laser flashes in a battle? There was no way to know. "At least," he commented out loud, "that explains why no one's tried to come up with a gun or weapon the mojos wouldn't recognize as such. You'd get one free shot at your target, but that's about all."

"You Aventinians seem to think a great deal in terms of interpersonal conflict," Ingliss said in a voice that seemed oddly tight. "Your planet must be a frightening one to live on. Perhaps if you had mojos of your own. . . . At any rate, you're correct about alternative weapons. In the early days of mojo domestication many people tried making them, with the result you've already deduced."

"Uh-huh," York nodded and settled down to watch.

It seemed to take a long time, but in actual fact the duel was over in just a few minutes. York couldn't tell offhand what it solved; but as the crowd closed in on the fighters, separating them as secondary masses of seemingly happy well-wishers and friends formed around each, he decided that *they* all considered it to have been worthwhile. Maybe Nnamdi could sort out the sociology and psychology of it aboard ship; for York, it was a low-priority worry indeed. Glancing around through the dispersing crowd, he located the islands of stability that were the rest of the contact team, Mayor Ingliss and the escorts—

And Moff.

York blinked, trying hard to keep any hint of surprise or chagrin out of his face. Despite his best efforts, the Qasaman had slipped back into the group unnoticed, just as he'd left it. It suddenly made the duel's timing suspicious . . . and if the duel was a fake it automatically raised the importance of Moff's secret errand; raised it uncomfortably high. Throwing together such a diversion required either a lot of people ready on a moment's notice, or else a smaller group capable of fooling the locals as well as the Aventinian visitors. Either one implied a great deal of effort and—perhaps—a fair amount of advance planning.

Were the Qasamans on to them? And if so, for how long?

"I'm sorry you had to see that," Moff said as the team and escort drew back together. "It's a form of aggression we've been unable to eliminate completely."

"It seems pretty mild compared to some I've seen," Cerenkov assured him. Neither he nor the others showed any reaction to Moff's reappearance, and York quietly let out the breath he'd been holding.

"It's still more than a truly civilized society should have," Moff said stiffly. "Our strength of will should be turned outward, toward the conquering of this world."

"And beyond?" Rynstadt murmured.

Moff looked at him, an intense look on his face. "The stars are mankind's future," he said. "We won't always be confined to this one world."

"Mankind will never be confined again," Cerenkov agreed solemnly. "Tell me, does this sort of duel happen very often? The whoever it was with the headband seemed to be right on top of things."

"Each village and city has one or more judges, depending on its population," Moff said. "They have many other duties besides overseeing duels. But come—we have a great many more places to visit here. Mayor Ingliss has yet to show you the local government center, and we should also have time to see a typical residential neighborhood before the krisjaw hunters return. At that point we'll be able to visit the farming areas."

Cerenkov smiled. "Point taken, Moff—we *do* have a busy schedule. Please, lead on."

They turned a corner and headed for the cars Ingliss's people had driven around the marketplace area for them, and York decided to be cautiously optimistic. Sticking to the tour at this point meant Moff believed his absence hadn't been noticed. Which meant whatever the Qasamans had planned would be going off on their original schedule.

Abruptly, he was aware of the gentle pressure of the calculator watch on his wrist, and of the similar feel of the star sapphire on his hand. Together with his pen, they were the sections of his palm-mate . . . a weapon neither the Qasamans nor the mojos had ever seen before. *One free shot*, the words echoed in his brain. *One free shot before the mojos can stop me. I'd damn well better make that shot count.*

It happened as they were driving back toward Sollas that evening, and their first warning was the sudden burst of static that replaced the hum of the *Dewdrop*'s radio link. At the front of the bus Moff stood up, steadying himself with his left hand. In his right hand was his pistol.

"You are under confinement," a voice boomed from the man sitting beside him—or, rather, from the phone-sized box in the Qasaman's hand. "You are suspected of spying on the people of Qasama. You will make no aggressive move until the final destination is reached. If you disobey your ship will be destroyed."

"What?" Cerenkov barked, his voice a blend of

shock, bewilderment, and outrage. "What's all this about?"

But there was no sound from his translator pendant and the words fell on effectively deaf ears. "Moff—" Cerenkov began, half rising.

"Don't bother," Rynstadt advised quietly. "That's just a recorder, not a translator. We'll have to wait until we get back to Sollas to clear this up."

Cerenkov opened his mouth, apparently thought better of it, and dropped back into his seat. Moff's gun hadn't so much as twitched, York noted uncomfortably. A steady man, with nerves not easily rattled—which severely limited the range of ploys that could be used against him. And his mojo . . .

His mojo hadn't so much as squawked at the sight of his owner with a gun drawn on another human being. None of the birds had. For whatever reason—appearance, odor, speech—the Aventinians apparently had been exempted from the automatic protection the mojos gave their Qasaman masters. York had almost dared to hope that any Qasaman action against the team would be at least hindered a bit by the mojos' presence. But that was obviously not going to happen.

Across the aisle, Joshua shifted in his seat. "They must have one gantua of a computer capability to get even that much of a translation this fast," he muttered.

"They presumably *have* been recording both our words and their translation, though," Rynstadt pointed out. He seemed relaxed, almost unconcerned, and for a moment York stared at him in utter incomprehension. Didn't the idiot *realize* just how much trouble they were in? *This isn't some game*, the snarl welled up in his throat. *These people are serious, and they're scared.*

He choked the words down unsaid. Of *course* Rynstadt wasn't worried—weren't there four Cobras aboard the *Dewdrop* ready to burst out and rescue them in a blaze of laser fire?

Except it wasn't going to be that easy; and if none of the others realized that York certainly did. Shifting his gaze to the window, he studied the darkening sky and the even darker forest flanking the road. *Moff's timed this well*, he thought, a touch of professional respect adding counterpoint to the pounding of his heart. Far from the *Dewdrop*, in dangerous and unfamiliar territory with night coming on, only a lunatic would attempt an escape. The sun glinted through a gap in the trees, and he realized suddenly that sometime in the past few minutes they'd turned to the southwest, off of the direct east-west route between Huriseem and Sollas. South, to the next city in the chain? Probably. Keep the hostages away from the temptation of a rescue, while to the potential rescuers themselves you did . . . what? What did the Qasamans intend to do to the *Dewdrop*?

He looked at Joshua, saw his own fears and uncertainties reflected in the younger man's taut face. Son of a Cobra, brother of a Cobra, he understood far better than Rynstadt the limits of the *Dewdrop*'s defenses.

A measure of fear prepares the body; panic paralyzes it, his old Marine instructor's favorite aphorism echoed through York's mind. Consciously slowing his breathing, he blocked the panic and let the fear remain. When the opportunity came, he would have to be ready.

The announcement that briefly penetrated the roar of static in the *Dewdrop*'s lounge was short and excruciatingly to the point: "You are suspected of spying on the people of Qasama. You will make no aggressive move or try to escape. If you disobey you will be destroyed."

The static resumed at full intensity, and Christopher spat something blasphemous. "How the *hell* did they figure it out—?"

"Shut up!" Telek snapped, her own heart a painful

thudding in her ears. It had happened—her worst nightmare—and she'd failed to get the team out before the hammer fell. She'd failed. *Oh, God. What am I going to do*—?

A voice from the intercom cut into her thoughts. "Governor, I'm picking up motion and hot-spots on top of the airfield tower," Captain F'ahl said. "No clear view of any weapons or people yet; they may have something like mortars or lob-rockets that'll avoid line-of-sight exposure."

With a wrench Telek shoved the rising panic out of her way. "I understand, Captain. Can our lasers take down the entire tower?"

"Probably not—and I wouldn't even want to try until we'd gotten everyone we could back on board."

"I wasn't suggesting we start now," she said icily. So F'ahl was already preparing himself to accept team casualties. Well, she was damned if *she* was going to give up that easily. "Anything on the computer screening? Joshua's split-frequency signal is supposed to be jam-proof by ordinary—"

Without warning, the field of snow on the displays abruptly cleared, and they were back in the Qasaman bus.

Telek leaned forward, hands tightening painfully . . . but the carnage she'd half expected wasn't there. The scene was almost exactly as it had been when the signal had been cut off a scant few minutes ago . . . except that Moff was sitting facing the Aventinians with his gun drawn.

Telek groped for the mike. "Joshua, let me see the rest of the team," she called.

The scene remained unchanged. "He can't hear you," Christopher murmured. "We can clean up the signal at this end, but there's no computer equipment out there to do the same."

"Great," Telek gritted. "Which means we can't contact Almo, either. Damn it all." She stared at the display another moment, then turned to the two men standing quietly just inside the lounge door. "Well, gentlemen, it looks very much like your paid vacation is over. Suggestions?"

Michael Winward gestured toward one of the displays showing the nearby forest. "The Qasamans presumably don't know Almo's out there, which is theoretically an advantage for our side. But if we can't tell him what's going on the advantage is pretty useless. Somehow, we've got to get his attention so that he'll set up the comm laser."

"In other words, you think you should try and sneak out to him." Telek hesitated, shook her head. "No. Too risky. Even if we could come up with a diversion for you you'd probably be spotted before you could get to cover. Let's see if we can wait until the usual check-in time."

The other Cobra, Dorjay Link, glanced at Winward and shook his head minutely. "The Qasamans may be moving people and weapons into the forest to cover the *Dewdrop* from that side," he told Telek. "Almo could come down from his nest right into the middle of them."

"He'd hear or see them, though, wouldn't he?" Nnamdi spoke up.

"Cobras are human, too," Winward said tartly. "And if he doesn't even wake up until they're in position they won't be making much noise."

Telek stared at the forest display. *I'm out of my depth*, she admitted to herself. *We've gone to a military situation without a scrap of warning—*

No. They *had* had their warning; and that was what really hurt. The purpose of Moff's mysterious disappearance a few hours ago was now clear: he'd been setting up this operation, coordinating things via the still unknown, triple-damned long-range communication system of theirs. In which case—"The soldiers and guns are probably already in place out there," she said out loud. "The only way to wake Almo up and simultaneously let him know there's trouble . . ." She stopped and looked back at the two Cobras.

Winward nodded—understanding or agreement, she didn't know which. "A quick sortie. Gunfire and all that. Let me get into my camouflage suit—be back in a minute. Dorjay, start looking for my best approach, will you?"

"Sure," Link said as Winward vanished out the lounge door. "Any chance, Governor, that we can wait until full dark?"

"No," Christopher spoke up before Telek could say anything. "Governor, we've got a new problem—the contact team's not being brought back to Sollas."

"Damn." Telek stepped to his side, looked at the display that was now showing an aerial photo of the area between Sollas and Huriseem. "How do you know?"

"Joshua's been looking around a little—I saw the sun out of the side window. Looks to me like they're taking this road—" he traced it with a finger—"down to the next city southwest of here."

Telek checked the scale. "Damn. Closest approach doesn't get them under twenty kilometers from the *Dewdrop*. Where's the next connecting road?—oh, there it is. Three kilometers past that point. Any idea where on the road they are?"

Christopher spread his hands helplessly. "The range finder doesn't seem to work when the computer's mucking with the signal like this. About all I can do is estimate their speed and extrapolate from Huriseem. Looks like they're about *here*, maybe fifteen or twenty minutes from that crossroads."

Telek looked over at Justin, immobile on his coach. If she'd just let him replace his brother as they'd planned . . . but, no, she'd wanted to have her damned window to the world. "We've got to intercept that car," she said to the room in general. "Either free the team outright or try to replace Joshua. Somehow."

"With Moff on the alert I somehow doubt the latter

option's open," Link said from in front of the display he'd appropriated from Nnamdi.

"I know." Telek gritted her teeth, then turned toward the intercom. "Captain, I want a pulse-laser message to the Troft backup ships right away. Tell them to get in here as fast as they can."

"Yes, Governor."

And it'll do no good at all. She knew it, and everyone aboard knew it. The Troft ships were too far away even to make orbit before dawn. The *Dewdrop* was on her own.

Which meant that Winward would have to make his suicide sortie in a few minutes . . . and Almo still had an even chance of getting caught before he knew what was happening . . . and it was all futility anyway, because there was no way a Cobra or even two could ambush that bus without killing or injuring everyone aboard in the ensuing firefight.

The inescapable conclusion was that it would be better to lift off now, hoping the *Dewdrop* would have the necessary speed to escape the Qasamans' shells or rockets.

To cut their losses. And if that was to be the decision, it had to be made before Winward went outside to sacrifice his life. Which meant within the next ninety seconds.

A no-win situation . . . and even as she wondered what she was going to do, there was a slight movement in the forest far to the south of them, and an invisible laser beam lanced out, catching the *Dewdrop* squarely in the nose.

Chapter 16

For a long moment Pyre lay quietly in his hammock bag, wondering what had awakened him. The level of sunlight filtering through the trees indicated sundown was approaching. He'd slept the whole day away, he realized, guilt twinging at him. Probably woke up simply because his body had had all the rest it needed; he must have been a lot more tired than he'd thought.

He was just starting to pull his arms out of the bag when he heard the muffled cough.

He froze, notching his auditory enhancers to full power. The normal rustlings of the forest roared in his ears ... the normal rustlings, and the fainter sound of quiet human voices. Ten or more of them, at the least.

Hunting party? was his first, hopeful thought. But he heard no footsteps accompanying the voices, just the occasional sounds of someone easing from one position to another. Even stalking hunters moved around more ... which implied that his unexpected guests were less akin to hunters than to fishermen.

And there were only two fish out here worth such a concerted effort, at least as far as he knew: the *Dewdrop* and himself.

Damn.

Slowly, moving with infinite care and silence, he began disentangling himself from the hammock bag and the defense cage. If they were looking for him the activity could well be a mistake; but whether it brought them down on him or not, he had no intention of getting caught wrapped up like yesterday's leftovers. The cage creaked like a tacnuke explosion as he opened it, but no one seemed to notice, and a minute later he was standing above the hammock bag with his back pressed against the tree trunk.

And the prey was now ready to become the hunter. The voices had come from the strip of forest between him and the *Dewdrop*; moving to the far side of the trunk he started down, pausing at each branch to look and listen.

He reached the ground without seeing any of the hidden Qasamans, but further noises had given him a better idea of their arrangement and he wasn't surprised to have avoided drawing fire. They seemed to be paralleling the edge of the forest nearest the *Dewdrop*, their attention and weaponry almost certainly focused on the ship. And to have been set up *now*, an entire week after the landing, implied something had gone wrong. Whether the contact team had gumfricked up or the exaggerated Qasaman paranoia had finally asserted itself hardly mattered at this point. What mattered—

What mattered was that Joshua Moreau was out there in the middle of it. And if he'd been killed while Pyre overslept—

The Cobra bit down hard on the inside of his cheek. *Stop it*! he snarled. *Settle down and* think *instead of panicking*. The fact that the Qasamans had not yet openly attacked the *Dewdrop* implied they were still in the planning stages here . . . and if so, then chances were Joshua and the others were still okay. Moving against the contact team would tip off the *Dewdrop*, and the Qasamans were surely smart enough to avoid doing that.

And with the ship and Cerenkov both unaware that anything was wrong, it was all up to Pyre now.

He didn't have a lot of options. His emergency earphone was a one-way device, with no provision for talking to the ship. His comm laser was well hidden and probably undiscovered, but if the Qasaman cordon line wasn't sitting on top of it they weren't far off. Take out the whole bunch of them? Risky, possibly suicidal, and almost certain to run the timer to zero right there and then.

But if the members of the cordon weren't in actual visual contact with each other, it might be possible to quietly take out the one or two closest to his laser without alerting all the others. Grab the laser, back off to somewhere safe—the top of a tree, if necessary— and call the ship. Together they might be able to figure out a way to snatch the contact team from under Moff's nose.

Mindful of the crunchy forest mat underfoot, Pyre set off cautiously toward the laser's hiding place, trying to watch all directions at once. He was, he estimated, only five meters from his goal when a sudden roar erupted from beside him.

He was halfway through his sideways leap before his brain caught up with his reflexes and identified the sound: his emergency earphone was screaming with static. He twisted it out and thumbed it off in a single motion, and as the echo of it bounced for another second around his head he realized with a sinking feeling that he was too late. Static at that intensity could mean only that the Qasamans were attempting to jam all radio communications in the area. They were making their move—

"*Gif!*" a voice hissed.

Pyre froze, his eyes shifting between the two Qasamans crouched facing him from half-concealed positions. The pistols pointed his way seemed larger than those he'd seen others wearing; the mojos with their wings poised for flight were certainly more alert.

One of the men muttered something to his companion and stepped toward Pyre, gun steady on the Cobra's chest.

There was no time to consider the full implications of his actions, no consideration beyond getting out of this without bringing the rest of the troops down on him. Clearly, his captors still hoped to keep their presence secret from the *Dewdrop*; just as clearly, they'd lose that preference once he made his own move. His first attack would have to be fast and clean.

Pyre had never killed a human being before. His closest brush with such a thing had been on that awful day long ago when Jonny Moreau and a man apparently returned from the dead shot down Challinor's fledgling Cobra warlords in two or three seconds of the most terrifying display of laser fire he'd ever seen, then or since. For a teenaged boy on a struggling colony world such a slaughter had been the stuff of nightmares—particularly as the knowledge of his own early support of Challinor carried with it a small but leaden piece of the responsibility for the deaths. The last thing he wanted to do was to add more deaths to that weight between his shoulders.

But he had no choice. None at all. His sonic weapons could stun men at this range, but not for long enough . . . and the necessary frequencies were unlikely to be effective on the two mojos. All of them had to be silenced before any of them—human or mojo—could screech out a warning.

The leading man was barely two meters away now, properly staying out of his partner's line of fire. Four instants of eye contact to give his nanocomputer its targets; the gentle pressure of tongue against the roof of his mouth to key automatic fire control . . . and as the Qasaman opened his mouth to speak Pyre fired.

His little fingers spat laser bursts, arms and wrists shifting in response to the computer-directed servos within them. Like all his Cobra reflexes, this one was incredibly fast, and it was all over almost before he had a chance to wince.

That wasn't so hard, he thought, dropping to a crouch as he waited to see if the quiet crash of falling bodies would draw attention. *Not too hard at all*. And his eyes strayed to the corpse which had landed almost beside him and the head where the laser burn would be, though the undergrowth was hiding it, and the mojo who had died so quickly its talons still gripped its epaulet perch, and he began to tremble violently and tried hard not to throw up.

He waited for nearly half a minute, until the worst of the muscle spasms had subsided and the taste of bile had left his mouth, before resuming his cautious move forward. With no buzzing earphone to startle him this time, he made it the rest of the way to his laser without attracting attention. Once, as he was pulling the device from concealment, he saw another Qasaman; but the other was looking another way and Pyre was able to complete his task without being spotted.

Moving deeper into the forest, he headed south, hoping the Qasamans hadn't lined the whole damned forest with soldiers. If they had, he might have to climb a tree to contact the ship, after all.

But their exaggerated caution hadn't carried them to quite that length. A hundred meters from his laser's hiding place the silent cordon line ended; Pyre went another fifty and then pushed his way cautiously to the edge. A convenient bush allowed him to get a clear shot at the *Dewdrop*'s nose without exposing himself to direct view of the airfield control tower. Flat on his stomach, he set up the laser as quickly as he could and aimed it toward where he thought the bow sensor cluster was located. Crossing his fingers, he flipped it on. "Pyre here," he murmured into the mike. "Come in, anyone."

There was no response. He waited a few seconds,

then shifted his aim fractionally and tried again. Still nothing. *My God—have they somehow taken everyone out already*? He searched the hull for signs of damage. Gas, perhaps, or sonics that could have penetrated without harming the ship itself? The taste of fear starting to well up into his throat, he again adjusted his aim—

"—*in*, Almo; are you there? *Almo*?"

Pyre's body sagged with relief. "I'm here, Governor. Phew. I thought something had happened to all of you."

"Yeah, well, it's about to," Telek said grimly. "Somehow they've tumbled to the fact that we're a spy mission, and it's probably a tossup as to whether they try and board us or take the safer way out and just blow us up."

"Any word from the contact team?" Pyre asked, forcing his voice to remain steady.

"Moff still has them on the bus, and so far they seem okay. They're being taken somewhere besides Sollas, though, probably the next city down. We were hoping you'd have a chance of intercepting them before they got too far away, assuming we could contact you in time."

"And?"

Telek hesitated. "Well . . . we estimate the bus will be passing the main road heading south from Sollas in ten or fifteen minutes. But that's twenty-plus kilometers from us—"

"How many Qasamans aboard?" he cut her off harshly.

"The usual six-man escort," she told him. "Plus their mojos. But even if you could get there in time I don't know how you'd get them out safely."

"I'll find a way. Just don't lift until I get back here with them . . . or until it's clear I'm not going to make it back at all."

He broke the connection without waiting to hear her reply and began crawling backwards from his concealing bush toward the protection of the forest, leaving the comm laser deployed for possible future use. Twenty kilometers in ten minutes. Hopeless even if he'd had clean ground to run on instead of a forest . . . but maybe the Qasamans would outsmart themselves on this one. Six guards in an ordinary bus was a fairly loose setup, even with the mojos and against four unarmed prisoners. In their place Pyre would transfer the Aventinians to a safer vehicle at the first opportunity . . . and to his way of thinking the crossroads to the south would be the ideal spot for such a switch.

And if his guess proved correct the whole party would be there for a few extra minutes. Long enough, perhaps, for Pyre to get there too.

At which point he'd have to face not only the busload of Qasamans but also whatever troops they'd assembled for the transfer. But there was nothing he could do about that. It was time for Almo Pyre, Cobra, to become what his implanted equipment had always intended him to be. Not a hunter, spy, nor even a killer of Aventinian spine leopards.

But a warrior.

Setting off at the fastest run the forest permitted, he headed south. It was all up to him now.

It was all up to him now.

York took a quiet breath, using his Marine biofeedback techniques to relax his muscles and nerves and to prepare him for action. To the right and slightly ahead he could see the buildings of Sollas silhouetted against the darkening sky, and if he remembered the aerial maps correctly they were now about as close to the city as this road got. It was time to make his attempt . . . and to find out just how deadly these mojos were.

His pen and ring were already resting casually in his left hand. Easing his calculator-watch off his left wrist, he fit the pen through its band, making sure the contacts were wedged solidly together. The ring slid onto the pen's clip to its own slot, and the palm-mate was ready. The arming sequence was three keystrokes on the calculator.

Wrapping the watchband into position around his right palm, he raised his hand over the back of the seat in front of him. Moff had given up his guard duty to one of the others a few kilometers back, but the Qasaman's attention was on Rynstadt and Joshua at the moment. *I get one free shot*, York reminded himself distantly; and bringing the pen to bear on the guard, he squeezed the trigger.

The Qasaman jerked as the tiny dart buried itself deep in his cheek, his gun swinging wildly in reflexive search for a target. Reflexive but useless; already his eyes were beginning to glaze as the potent mix of neurotoxins took effect. York shifted his aim to the mojo on the dying man's shoulder and a second dart found its target . . . but as he brought the palm-mate to bear on Moff's mojo all hell broke loose.

They were smart all right, those birds. The dead Qasaman hadn't even fallen to the floor before the remaining five mojos were in the air, sweeping toward him like silver-blue Furies. He got off two more shots, but neither connected—and then they were on him, talons digging into his face and gun arm and slamming him hard into the seat. Through the haze of agony he could dimly hear screams from Rynstadt and the incomprehensible shouts of the Qasamans. Mojo wings slapped at his eyes, blinding him, but he didn't need his sight to know that his right forearm was being flayed, his right hand torn by beaks and talons as the mojos fought single-mindedly to get the palm-mate away from him. But it was wrapped firmly around his open hand, caught there though the will to hold it had long since vanished. His arm was on fire—wave after wave of agony screaming into his brain—and then suddenly the birds were gone, fluttering away to squawk at him from seat backs and Qasaman shoulders, and he saw what they'd done to his arm—

And the emotional shock combined with the physical shock . . . and Decker York, who had seen men injured and killed on five other worlds, dropped like a stone into the temporary sanctuary of unconsciousness.

His last thought before the blackness took him was that he would never wake up.

"Oh, my God," Christopher whispered. "My *God*."

Telek bit hard into the knuckles of her right hand, curled into an impotent fist at her mouth. York's arm. . . . She willed her eyes to turn away, but they were as tightly frozen to the scene as Joshua's own eyes were. Like a violent, haphazard dissection of York's arm—except that York was still alive. For now.

Beside her, Nnamdi gagged and fled the room. She hardly noticed.

It seemed like forever, but it was probably only a few seconds before Rynstadt was at York's side, a small can of seal-spray from his landing kit clutched in his shaking hand. He sprayed it on York's arm, sloppily and with an amateur's lack of uniformity; but by the time the can hissed itself dry Cerenkov had broken his own paralysis and moved in with a fresh can. Together they managed to seal off the worst of the blood flow.

Through it all Joshua never budged. *Terrified out of his mind*, Telek thought. *What a thing for a kid to see!*

"Governor?" F'ahl's voice from the intercom made her jump. "Will he live?"

She hesitated. With the blood loss stopped and the seal-spray's anti-shock factors supporting York's system . . . but she knew better than to give even herself false hope. "Not a chance," she told F'ahl quietly.

"He needs the *Dewdrop*'s medical facilities within an hour or less."

"Almo—"

"Might be able to get him here in time. But he won't. If he tries he'll just get himself killed, too." The words burned in her mouth, but she knew they were true. With the Qasamans and their birds jarred out of any overconfidence they might have had, Pyre wouldn't get within ten meters of the bus. But he would try anyway. . . .

And now there *was* no other choice. "Captain, prepare the *Dewdrop* for lift," she said, her eyes straying at last from the display, only to stop on Justin lying in his couch. His fists, too, were clenched, but if he recognized she had just condemned his brother to death he didn't show it. "We'll try to take out as much of the tower and forest weaponry before we go and hope the ship can absorb whatever we don't destroy."

"Understood, Governor."

Telek turned to the lounge doorway, where Winward and Link were standing, their faces pale and grim. "We won't be able to get it all from here," she told them quietly.

"Already figured that out," Winward grunted. "When do you want us to head out?"

The pre-launch sequence would take at least ten minutes. "About fifteen minutes," she said.

Winward nodded. "We'll get geared up." Together the two Cobras turned and left.

"Full survival packs," Telek called after them.

"Sure," the reply drifted back along the corridor.

But she wasn't fooling anyone, and they all knew it. Even if the two Cobras lived through the coming battle, there was virtually no chance the *Dewdrop* would be able to come back and pick them up. Assuming the *Dewdrop* survived its own gauntlet.

Well, they'd find out about that in half an hour or less. Until then—

Until then, there'd be enough time to watch Pyre die in his rescue attempt.

Because it was her duty to do so, Telek turned her attention back to the displays. But the taste of defeat was bitter in her throat, and she felt very, very old.

Chapter 17

Joshua's heart was a painful thundering in his throat, his eyes blurred by tears of fear and sympathetic pain. Hidden from sight by the white crust of the seal-spray, York's terrible arm injuries were burned into Joshua's memory as if the vision would be there forever. *Oh, God, Decker,* he mouthed. *Decker!*

And he'd done nothing to help. Not during York's escape attempt nor even afterwards. Rynstadt and Cerenkov had jumped in with their medical kits; but Joshua, terrified of the Qasamans and mojos, hadn't twitched a muscle to assist them. If it'd been up to him, York would've quietly bled to death.

People expect great things from us. He felt like a child. A cowardly child.

"We've got to get him back to the ship," Cerenkov murmured, raising a blood-stained arm to wipe at his cheek. "He's going to need transfusions and God only knows what else."

Rynstadt muttered something in response, too low for Joshua to hear. Lifting his gaze finally from the carnage, Joshua looked up toward the front of the bus to see Moff watching them, his gun braced and ready on the nearest seat back. The bus had sped up, Joshua noted mechanically, and ahead in the gloom he could see a cluster of dim lights. An unwalled village or crossroads checkpoint? Joshua guessed the latter. A half dozen vehicles were faintly visible, as was a small shed-like building.

And milling among them a *lot* of Qasamans.

The bus came to a halt among the cluster of vehicles. It had barely stopped before a burly Qasaman had the door open and had bounded inside. He exchanged a half-dozen rapid-fire sentences with Moff, then looked at the Aventinians. "*Bachuts!*" he snapped, hand jabbing emphatically toward the door.

"Yuri?" Rynstadt murmured.

"Of course," Cerenkov said bitterly. "What choice do we have?"

Leaving York propped up against the seat, they stepped past the newcomer and out the door. Joshua followed, his stomach a churning cauldron of painful emotions.

Four more heavily armed men were waiting in a semicircle around the bus door. With them was a wizened old man with stooped shoulders and the last remnants of white hair plastered down over his balding head. But his eyes were bright—disturbingly bright—and it was he who addressed the three prisoners. "You are accused of spying on the world Qasama," he said, his words heavily accented but clear enough. "Your companion York is also accused of killing a Qasaman and a mojo. Any further attempts at violence will be punished by immediate death. You will now come with your escort to a place for questions."

"What about our friend?" Cerenkov nodded back toward the bus. "He needs medical attention immediately if he's to live."

The old man spoke to the apparent leader of the new escort, was answered in biting tones. "He will be treated here," the old man told Cerenkov. "If he dies, that is merely his just punishment for his crime. You will come now."

Joshua took a deep breath. "No," he said firmly.

"Our friend will be taken back to our ship. Now. Otherwise we will all die without answering a single question."

The old man translated, and the escort leader's brow darkened as he spat a reply. "You are not in a position to make any demands," the old man said.

"You are wrong," Joshua said as calmly as his tongue could manage, the vision of York's flaying superimposed on the scene around him. If his bluff was called . . . and even as he slowly raised his left fist he knew he was indeed a coward. The thought of such a fate made his stomach violently ill . . . but this had to be tried. "This device on my wrist is a self-destruct—a one-man bomb," he told the old man. "If I unclench my fist without turning it off I will be blown to dust. Along with all of you. I will give you the device only when I have personally escorted Decker into our ship."

A long, brittle silence followed the translation. "You continue to think us fools," the leader said at last through the old man. "You enter the ship and you will not return."

Joshua shook his head minutely. "No. I *will* return."

The leader spat; but before he could speak again Moff stepped to his side and whispered into his ear. The leader frowned at him for a moment; then, pursing his lips, he gave a brisk nod and spoke to one of his men. The other disappeared into the darkness, and Moff turned to the old man, again speaking too quietly for Joshua to hear. The other nodded. "Moff has agreed to your request, as a gesture of goodwill, on one condition: you will wear an explosive device around your neck until you emerge from the ship. Should you remain inside for more than three minutes it will be allowed to explode."

Joshua's throat tightened involuntarily, and for a handful of heartbeats thoughts of betrayal and treachery swirled like a dark liquid through the cautious hope rising in his brain. Surely there were simpler

ways of killing him if the Qasamans so chose ... but
if they wanted to make sure the *Dewdrop* never lifted
again, there would be no easier way to penetrate the
outer hull. But that might lose them the secret of the
stardrive—but they might not care—but if he didn't
take the risk York was dead—but why would they
have any interest in a good-faith gesture when they
held all the cards—

He focused at last on Cerenkov and Rynstadt, who
were watching him in turn. "What do I do?" he
whispered from amid the turmoil.

Cerenkov shrugged fractionally. "It's *your* life that's
at stake. You'll have to use your own best judgment."

His life ... except that it wasn't, Joshua suddenly
realized. Together, the three of them had no chance
at all of being rescued ... but Cerenkov and Rynstadt
plus Justin might just be able to break the odds.

It was *all* of their lives at stake here. Corwin's
plan—the reason the Moreaus were here at all—and
the whole thing was in Joshua's trembling hands.
"All right," he said to the old man. "It's a deal."

The old man translated; and the leader began to
give orders.

The next few minutes went quickly. Cerenkov and
Rynstadt were taken to another, obviously armored,
bus and were driven off into the darkness along their
original southwest road. York, still unconscious, was
transferred by hand stretcher to a second armored
vehicle. Joshua, Moff, and the translator joined him.
As they rumbled northward toward Sollas and the
Dewdrop one of the escort carefully fitted Joshua with
his explosive collar.

It was a simple device, consisting of two squat
cylinders at the sides of his neck fastened together by
a soft but tough-feeling plastic band about three centimeters wide and a couple of millimeters thick. It
seemed to make breathing difficult ... but perhaps
that was just his imagination. Licking his lips frequently, he tried not to swallow too often and forced

his mind to concentrate instead on York's condition and chances.

All too soon, they had arrived.

The bus coasted to a halt some fifty or sixty meters from the *Dewdrop*'s main hatch. Two Qasamans unloaded a rolling table and placed York's stretcher on top of it, returning then to the vehicle. Moff motioned Joshua to stand and held a small box up to each of the cylinders around the Aventinian's neck. Joshua heard two faint clicks; felt, rather than heard, the faint vibration from within. "Three minutes only—remember," Moff said in passable Anglic, looking the younger man in the eye.

Joshua licked his lips and nodded. "I'll be back."

The trip to the ship seemed to take a lifetime, torn as he was between the need for haste and the opposite need to give York as smooth a ride as possible. He settled for a slow jog, praying fervently that someone would be watching and be ready to pop the hatch for him . . . and that he could explain all of this fast enough . . . and that they'd be able to switch the collar in the time allotted. . . .

He was two steps from the hatch when it opened, one of F'ahl's crewers stepping out to grip the front stretcher handles. Seconds later they were inside, with Christopher, Winward, and Link waiting for them in the ready room.

"Sit down," Christopher snapped tightly as someone took Joshua's half of the stretcher.

Joshua's knees needed no urging, dropping him like a lump of clay into the indicated chair. "This thing on my neck—"

"Is a bomb," Christopher finished for him. Already the other was tracing the strap with a small sensor, his forehead shiny with perspiration. "We know—they weren't able to jam your signal. Now sit tight and we'll see if we can get the damn thing off without triggering it."

Joshua gritted his teeth and fell silent; and as he

did so Justin entered the room, clad only in his underwear. For a moment the twins gazed at each other . . . and the expression on Justin's face sent half the weight resting on Joshua's shoulders spinning away into oblivion. They weren't in the clear yet—not by a long shot—but there was a satisfaction in Justin's eyes that said Joshua had done his job well, had made the decisions that gave them all a chance.

Justin was proud of him . . . and, ultimately, that was what really mattered.

The moment passed; and, kneeling before his brother, Justin began to remove Joshua's boots. Joshua unfastened his own belt and slid off his pants, and he was beginning to work on his tunic when Christopher gave a little snort. "All right, here it is. Let's see . . . bypass *here* and *here*. Dorjay?"

Joshua felt something cool slide between the collar and his neck. "Hold still," Link muttered from behind him. There was the soft crackle of heat-stressed plastic . . . and suddenly the pressure on his throat eased, and Winward lifted the broken ring over his head. "Out of the chair," Link said tersely. "Justin?"

Joshua's place was taken by his brother, and the collar lowered carefully around Justin's neck. "Time?" Christopher asked as the Cobras eased the two broken ends back together and began the ticklish job of reconnecting them.

"Ninety seconds," F'ahl's voice came over the room intercom. "Plenty of time."

"Sure," Link growled under his breath. "Come down *here* and say that. *Easy*, Michael."

Joshua got his tunic and watch off and waited, heart thudding full blast again as he watched Christopher and the Cobras work. If they weren't able to do it in time—

"Okay," Christopher announced suddenly. "Looks good. Here go the bypasses. . . ."

The wires came off, and the cylinders remained solid. Cautiously, Justin stood up and reached for

Joshua's tunic, and by the time Christopher had eased the protective ring out from under the collar he was nearly dressed. "I don't know where Yuri and Marck were taken," Joshua told him as he fastened on the other's watch.

"I know that," Justin nodded. "I *was* you, remember."

"Yeah. I just meant—be careful, okay?"

Justin gave him a tight smile. "I'll be fine, Joshua—don't worry about me. The Moreau luck goes with me."

He slipped out the hatch, and Joshua collapsed back into the chair as the shock of all that had happened finally caught up with him and his legs turned to rubber. *The Moreau luck. Great. Just great.* And the worst part of it was that Justin really *believed* in his imaginary immunity. Believed in it, acted on it . . . and while Joshua sat idly by in the *Dewdrop's* relative safety, his brother's superstition could easily get him killed.

"Damn them," he hissed at the universe in general—at Moff and the Qasamans; the Cobra Worlds' Council, who'd sent them; even his own brother Corwin, whose idea this had ultimately been. "Damn all of them."

A hand fell on his shoulder. Looking up through eyes suddenly tear-blurred, he saw Link standing over him. "Come on," the Cobra said. "Captain F'ahl and Governor Telek are going to want to hear your analysis of the situation out there."

Sure they are, Joshua thought bitterly. The sole value such a report could have would be to keep his mind too busy to dwell on Justin. But he merely nodded and got to his feet. He was too tired to argue . . . and, actually, some distraction might not be a bad idea right now.

He took a moment to stop by his stateroom first and get dressed, letting Link go on ahead without him. York was nowhere in sight when he finally reached the lounge, but Telek allayed his worst fears before he was able to voice them. "Decker's stable, at least for now," she said, glancing up at him before returning her gaze to the outside monitor display. "Monitors and I.V.s are all hooked up; he'll be all right until we can figure out what to do about his arm."

Translation: where exactly it'll need to be amputated. Swallowing the thought, Joshua stepped behind Telek and looked over her shoulder. Moff and Justin were just getting back into the armored bus. The explosive collar, he noted with marginal easing of tension, had been removed, as had the "self-destruct" watch with which he'd bluffed the Qasamans. "What's he supposed to do now?" he asked Telek. "I mean, you *did* give him some sort of plan to follow, didn't you?"

"As much of a plan as we could come up with," Winward grunted from another display. "We're assuming he'll be taken to wherever they've got Yuri and Marck. Once he's inside—well, we're hoping Almo will have followed the other two when they headed south. With Cobras inside and outside, they should be able to break out of wherever the Qasamans put them."

"Almo was going to follow us?"

"He was going to try. If he didn't get down to the crossroads in time—" Winward shrugged fractionally. "We'll hope he'll follow the road and try to catch up. It's the only logical thing for him to do."

Follow the road . . . except that he wouldn't know Moff would be bringing a second vehicle up from behind. Joshua shivered at the vision of Pyre caught, alone, between two carloads of armed Qasamans and mojos. And with the radios still jammed there was no way to alert him to the potential pincer closing on him.

Telek leaned back in her seat, exhaling a hissing sigh. "Well, that's it, gentlemen," she said. "We've done everything we can for the moment for Yuri and

Marck. Next job, then, is to figure out how to deactivate the defenses around the *Dewdrop* so that they've got a ship to come back to. Let's get busy on that one, shall we?"

The armored bus sped past Pyre's place of concealment. Though the windows were small and dark his enhanced vision enabled him to identify two of its occupants: Moff, and the same driver who'd earlier taken the vehicle toward Sollas with Joshua and an apparently injured Decker York aboard. It was back now, following the same road Cerenkov and Rynstadt had taken a half hour or so ago. And the major question of the hour: who exactly was in there?

Pyre rubbed a hand across his forehead, smearing the sweat and dirt there as he tried to think. *York, Joshua*, and *Moff head toward Sollas; Moff, at least, heads away shortly thereafter*. Had they decided to split up the contact team, with Cerenkov and Rynstadt stashed away down south while York and Joshua were hidden in Sollas? Possible; but given the lengths the Qasamans had gone to to keep their prisoners as far away as possible from the *Dewdrop* it didn't seem likely. Had they taken York to the nearest hospital to treat what had looked to be one double hell of an arm injury? But then why take Joshua along?

The sounds of the bus were fading away down the road. If he was going to follow it, he had to make that decision fast.

When he'd first dashed off through the forest on this crazy rescue attempt the question hadn't even been a debatable one. But since then he'd had time to think it all through . . . and though it wrenched his soul to admit it, he knew he'd gotten his priorities scrambled.

The contact team was, at least from a purely military standpoint, expendable. The *Dewdrop*, with all the data they'd collected about Qasama, was not.

The *Dewdrop* had to be freed . . . and three-quarters of her Cobra fighting force was still trapped inside.

To the southwest, the sounds of the bus had vanished into the forest. Notching his optical sensors up against the darkness, Pyre began circling cautiously around the vehicles and men that still straddled the crossroads. He could stay within the relative cover of the forest for a few kilometers, but long before he got to the airfield area he would have to move into the city proper if he wanted any chance of approaching the Qasamans' tower defenses undetected. The contact team had spent little time on the streets of Sollas at night—and none of it near the edges of the city. Pyre had no idea what sort of crowd level he'd have to get through once he left the forest. If he could steal some Qasaman clothing . . . but he couldn't speak word one of their language; and he would at any rate be instantly conspicuous by his lack of a mojo companion.

The crossroads, he judged, were far enough behind him now to risk a little noise. Senses alert for forest predators as well as wandering Qasamans, he broke into a brisk jog. Whatever he came up with, the inspiration had better come fast. In five minutes, ten at the most, Sollas was going to play host to its first Cobra.

Chapter 18

Joshua's implanted sensors were reputed to be the best the Cobra Worlds had available; but sitting in a bouncing vehicle across from a man he'd seen almost constantly for a week, Justin recognized with an unpleasant shock just how limited his piggybacked experience of Qasama had really been. The texture of the seat where his hands rested on it—the odd paving of the road as transmitted by the bus's vibration—above all the tangy and exotic scents filling the air around him—it was as if he'd stepped into a painting and found that the world it depicted was real.

And the whole effect made him nervous. He was supposed to be an undetectable substitute for his brother, and instead was feeling like the new kid on the block. All he needed now was for Moff to pick up that something was off-color here and bury him a hundred kilometers from Cerenkov and Rynstadt while the Qasamans figured out what was going on.

When your defense stinks, attack. "I must say, Moff," he remarked, "that you people are nothing short of astonishing at learning new languages. How long have you been able to speak Anglic?"

Moff's eyes flicked to the old man two seats down, who let loose with a stream of Qasaman. Moff replied in kind, and the translator turned back to Justin.

"*We* will ask the questions today," he said. "It will be *your* position to answer them."

Justin snorted. "Come on, Moff—it's hardly a secret anymore. Not with your friend here speaking as well as I do. And you said something to me yourself, right after you switched on the little insurance policy you had around my neck. So come on—how did all of you learn it so fast?"

He kept a surreptitious eye on the old man as he spoke, watching for hesitations with words or grammar. But if the other had any trouble, it wasn't obvious. Moff eyed Justin for a moment after the translator finished, then said something in a thoughtful tone that the Cobra didn't care for even before he heard the old man's version: "You seem to have regained some of your courage. What did those aboard your ship say to strengthen you so?"

"They reminded me of what your planetary superiors will say when they're informed how you have threatened a peaceful diplomatic mission," Justin shot back.

"Oh?" Moff said through the translator. "Perhaps. We shall soon see if that, too, is one of your lies. By the time we have reached Purma, or perhaps even before."

"I resent the implication I would lie to you."

"Resent it if you wish. But the cylinders you wore into your ship will show the truth of the matter."

Justin felt his mouth go dry. "What do you mean?" he asked, hoping his sudden horrible suspicion was wrong.

It wasn't. "The cylinders contained cameras and sound recording devices," the translator said. "We hoped to get a first approximation of the situation and number of personnel aboard."

And smack dab in the middle of the tape would be that free and unexpected bonus, the Moreau twin switch. And when they saw *that*— "A fat lot of good it'll do you," he snorted, putting as much scorn into his voice as he could scrape together. "We told no lies about our ship or people. What are you expecting— hundreds of armored soldiers squeezed into that little thing?"

Moff waited for the translation and then shrugged. *Apparently really* doesn't *understand Anglic*, Justin decided as the two Qasamans held a brief discussion. *Just learned that one phrase to emphasize the three-minute limit, probably. And we fell for it like primitives. Stupid, stupid, stupid.*

"We shall see what is there," the old man said. "Perhaps it will help us decide what should be done with all of you."

I'll just bet it will, Justin thought, but remained silent. Moff settled back in his seat, indicating the conversation was over for the moment . . . and Justin tried to get his brain on-line.

All right. First off, the spy cameras probably weren't transmitting a live picture from the *Dewdrop*—the Qasamans would've had to open up part of their radio jamming, and an action of that sort might have been detected. So Moff and company didn't yet know about the Moreau switch, an ignorance they would keep until those back in Sollas found out themselves and were able to blow the whistle. The jamming meant Justin was safe enough while the bus was still on the road. If he made his move before they reached the next city—Purma, had Moff called it?—he'd take them totally by surprise . . .

And would then have to search the whole city for Cerenkov and Rynstadt.

Justin grimaced. He *could* afford not knowing where the others were being kept, but only if Pyre had followed their bus instead of waiting for Justin's. There was no way of knowing which option the other Cobra had taken, and Justin didn't dare gamble on it. He would just have to let them take him to the other prisoners, hope he could take out all the additional guards and mojos that would undoubtedly be present—

And pray the bus didn't stop outside of town at a checkpoint with long-range communications capability.

Damn. If they did *that* then all bets were instantly off. Moff was being pretty casual about his prisoner, but that was surely based on a week's worth of observation of Joshua's character and reactions. If he found out he had someone else he was bound to react with a tighter leash ... and there were ways to render even a Cobra helpless.

Through the window ahead the bus's headlights showed nothing but road and flanking forest. No city lights yet ... Carefully, methodically, Justin activated his multiple-targeting lock and sequentially locked onto all the mojos in the vehicle. Just in case.

Easing back into his seat, he watched the road ahead and kept his hands well clear of any possible obstructions. And tried to relax.

"What do you suppose is keeping them?" Rynstadt asked quietly from the lightweight table in the middle of their cell.

Standing at the barred window, Cerenkov automatically glanced at his bare wrist, dropping it back to his side with an embarrassed snort. All jewelry had been taken from them immediately after they left the Sollas crossroads—fallout, obviously, from York's gun and Joshua's "self-destruct" bluff. For Cerenkov, not knowing the time could be a major annoyance at the best of times; under the present circumstances, it was an excruciating form of subtle torture. "It may not mean anything yet," he told Rynstadt. "We haven't been here all that long ourselves, and if transferring Decker to the ship took longer than expected Moff and Joshua may still not be overdue."

"And if—" Rynstadt let the sentence die. "Yeah, maybe you're right," he said instead. "Moff would undoubtedly want to be here before they start this silly questioning."

Cerenkov nodded, feeling frustration welling up within him at having to stifle the thoughts clearly uppermost in both their minds. Such as whether York had really been allowed back into the *Dewdrop* . . . and whether it would be Joshua or Justin who would soon be joining them in their cell. But after the old man at the crossroads Cerenkov had no intention of assuming none of the guards lined up against the cell wall understood Anglic.

And so he kept his thoughts and speculations to himself. But time *was* dragging on . . . and as the minutes slowly added up he began to feel as if he and Rynstadt were standing on a sheet of rapidly thawing ice. If Justin had been forced to take premature action, that would also explain the delay . . . and it would leave the two of them in a dead-end position here.

Outside, a flicker of light caught Cerenkov's eye, off toward the right. Pressing the side of his face to the glass, he could just see what appeared to be another of the armored vehicles he and Rynstadt had arrived in. A handful of figures stepped to the door. "Looks like they're here," he announced over his shoulder, striving for calm. Now the *real* fun would begin . . . especially since they wouldn't know themselves which twin they had until he took some sort of action. That would be tricky; he didn't want to get caught flatfooted in a crossfire, but neither did he want to be poised on tiptoe waiting expectantly for the order to hit the floor. Moff or one of the guards might pick up on something like that—

The thought froze in place. The bus was pulling away from the building, its welcoming committee heading back inside . . . but no one else was with them.

An empty bus? was his first, hopeful guess . . . but he didn't believe it for even a moment. The vehicle

was speeding up now, heading further into the city
... and deep within him, Cerenkov knew Moff and
Justin were aboard it. Something had gone wrong.
Badly enough wrong that the prisoners were being
split up, apparently on the spur of the moment.

And Cerenkov and Rynstadt were in their own private hole. A very deep private hole.

Slowly, he turned away from the window. "Well?"
Rynstadt demanded.

"False alarm," Cerenkov murmured. "It wasn't
them."

Justin watched the tall building disappear from
view through the window as the bus picked up speed,
muscles tight with adrenaline and the sinking certainty that the game was, in one sense or another,
over. Moff could pretend all he liked that they'd
stopped only for information from Sollas; but Justin
had been watching the driver as Moff consulted with
the men from the building, and it was clear that he'd
been taken by surprise by the order to move on.
Almost certainly Cerenkov and Rynstadt were somewhere in that structure behind them. Moff's studied
casualness merely underscored the fact that they
wanted Justin to attach no special significance to the
place.

So they knew. The films had been seen, word had
been flashed south from Sollas, and Moff was taking
him somewhere high-security for a long talk and
probably some careful study as well. Justin had to
act fast, to kill or disable everyone aboard and escape before the Qasamans figured out exactly what
to do with him.

He had his omnidirectional sonic tuned to the opti-
mum human stun frequency and was on the verge of
triggering it when a sudden, sobering thought struck
him.

No matter how he did this, it was going to be
obvious to whoever examined the bus afterwards that

the attack had come from inside the vehicle. From *inside* ... from a man who'd already been searched and stripped of anything that could possibly be a weapon.

A cold sweat broke out on Justin's forehead. What would the Qasamans make of such a conclusion? Could they possibly deduce the truth?—or even get close enough as made no difference? The question had little relevance to the immediate situation, of course—the *Dewdrop* would hopefully be long gone by the time the local experts began sifting through the debris. But if the Council decided to take on the Trofts' mercenary job here, such forewarning could give Qasama an edge against the arriving Cobras.

But what were his options? Shoot up the bus thoroughly from the outside after escaping, hoping he could do a convincing enough job of it? Or wait until he was taken some place where the existence of an armed infiltrator would at least be possible? Or even probable—Pyre was out here somewhere, and he clearly hadn't taken out the other prison buiding. Perhaps he'd arrived late at the crossroads and was even now tailing Justin's bus.

Moff was saying something. Justin turned to look at him as the old man translated: "At least I now understand your changed attitude when you emerged from your ship."

For a second Justin considered playing dumb, decided it wasn't worth the effort. "That three-minute limit was the key," he said calmly. "Any longer than that and we might have picked up on what those cylinders really were."

Moff nodded at the translation. "Our experts felt two and a half minutes safer, but I didn't want to have to take you close enough for that limit to seem reasonable. I didn't know then that your people were still monitoring you and wouldn't misunderstand our approach." His eyes bored into Justin's face. "We are very interested in your conversation with your double."

"I'll just bet you are," Justin said.

"I should also tell you that some in authority feel you are an as-yet unknown danger and should be eliminated quickly."

Abruptly, Justin realized that half of the eight Qasaman guards had their pistols drawn, two of them going so far as to point them in the Cobra's direction. "And how do *you* feel?" he asked Moff carefully.

For a long moment the other studied him. The mojo on his shoulder, sensing perhaps the general tension level, twitched its wings nervously. "I agree that you are dangerous," Moff said at last through the old man. "It is perhaps foolish to keep you alive in hopes of learning your secrets. But unless we discover your intentions toward us we cannot know how to properly defend ourselves. You will therefore be taken to a place where you may be properly questioned."

"And *then* be eliminated?"

Moff didn't reply . . . but the conversation had already made up Justin's mind. Qasama was already tacitly assuming a war was likely, and to give them anything he didn't absolutely have to would be a betrayal of those who'd come after him. Besides which, it might be interesting to see what sort of place they'd consider safe enough to hold an unknown threat. And besides *that* . . .

He caught Moff's eye again. "Just out of curiosity, how did you come to the conclusion that we were spying on you?"

Moff pursed his lips thoughtfully. Then, with a slight shrug, he began to speak. "Your double correctly interpreted a sign in the village of Huriseem this morning," the translator said. "It showed that, despite our efforts, you still had a visual connection with your ship. A device you had not told us about, and which was clearly designed to be undetectable."

Justin frowned. "*That* was all you had?"

"It was enough to justify questioning you. York's

similarly undetectable weapon—and his use of it—
proved our guess was correct."

"You were the one who picked up on our hidden
camera, I suppose?"

Moff nodded once, a simple gesture that admitted
the fact without the trappings of pride or false mod-
esty. Justin nodded in return and settled down to
wait, the last piece of his rationalization complete.
He had no desire to kill any more people than absolutely necessary when he made his break, and leaving
someone with Moff's observational skills behind as
witness would be a poor idea. No, he would wait
until they reached their destination and Pyre had
made his appearance. Together, the two Cobras would
leave the Qasamans wondering for a long time just
how the escape had been managed.

So he settled back in his seat and tried to keep
track of the bus's path through the wide streets of
Purma. And thought about his father's stories of his
own war.

The strip of clear land that would, farther north,
open up to become the airfield was barely sixty meters wide here at Sollas's southwest edge; but Pyre
found little comfort in that fact as he raced across it
toward the darkened building that was his target.
None of the structures at the city's edge seemed to be
showing many lights—another concession to the wandering bololins, perhaps?—but he felt as if a thousand pairs of eyes were watching him the whole way.
Two thousand eyes, one thousand guns. . . .

But he reached the building without challenge, and
for a minute he stood in relative shadow considering
his next move. The four-story structure beside him
was made of brick, and in the weeks before the mission the First Cobras had taught him how to scale
such things. Once on top, he could theoretically leap
from rooftop to rooftop until he reached the more
open areas near the airfield.

Pyre looked up the flat side of the building, grimacing. *Theoretically.* Most of the streets in his path were the wider bololin-speedway type, and while jumping one of them would be reasonably within his servos' range, he wasn't at all sure he wanted to try it a dozen or more times.

Around the corner of the building, a faint scrape reached his ears. Notched up to full power, his audio enhancers pulled in the sound of several sets of footsteps.

Sidling to the corner, Pyre took a cautious look down the street. Barely two hundred meters away, at the next intersection, a group of six Qasamans were standing in a loose circle, conversing in low tones. As he watched, three of them split off and began striding purposefully down the street directly toward him.

Pyre eased back. Sealing the city's edge with a sentry net was a precaution he hadn't expected even the Qasamans to bother with, given they thought they had everyone under lock and key.

Unless . . .

Of course. They'd found the men he'd killed in the forest.

He mouthed a silent curse. With all that had happened he'd completely forgotten that glaring evidence of his presence. And with the sentry patrols alert and in visual contact with each other, he'd now run out of choices. Locking his fingers around the bricks facing him, he began to climb.

It was a long way to go, and Pyre had had very little practice in this sort of thing, but the Qasaman patrol was apparently in no special rush to take up its post and he was nearly to the top before they emerged from the street. He froze, holding his breath . . . but neither the men nor their mojos looked up, and after a few seconds he continued his climb, taking care not to make even the slightest sound.

Which probably saved his life. Reaching the low parapet surrounding the roof, he raised his head over

it—and found himself eye to eye with a kneeling
Qasaman not three meters away, his hands in a small
cloth bag in front of him.

The man's eyes and mouth went wide with surprise. But his hand was still scrambling for his gun
when Pyre's arm swung over the parapet and a flicker
of laser light caught his spread-winged mojo in the
breast. He was still trying to draw the weapon from
its holster when the second flicker caught him in the
same place and he fell gently to the side, his astonishment still unvoiced.

Pyre was over the parapet in a second, trembling
with the hair's-breadth closeness of the call and the
cold knowledge that he was by no means safe yet. If
the ground sentries had heard anything—or if an
observer on the next roof over had witnessed the
incident—

Activating his optical enhancers, he raised his head
cautiously and checked the nearest buildings. The
roof to the south was vacant. The one to the north
held another figure, some sort of light-amp binoculars at his eyes as he gazed out toward the forest. A
quick glance over the parapet showed the sentries
below were undisturbed. Crawling to the dead Qasaman, Pyre reached into the other's bag, found a set of
the same light-amp glasses and what looked like a
water container and some sort of vegetable cake.

So the rooftop guards, like those on the ground,
had apparently just now taken up their positions,
which explained how he'd made it safely from the
forest. So he was in, and behind their first lines, and
temporarily undetected. So . . . now what?

Pyre found himself gazing at the dead mojo. Whatever he did, he was going to need a certain amount of
camouflage. . . . Carefully, trying not to wince, he
rolled the dead man over and eased off his jacket.
Beneath it the man had worn a knitted sweater-like
garment; cutting and unraveling a piece of it, Pyre
used the yarn to tie the mojo's talons to the jacket's

epaulet. Smoothing the wings back in place, he tied them together with more yarn. The whole effect would never hold up even under moderately close scrutiny, but with luck it wouldn't have to. Keeping close to the roof, he struggled into the jacket which was, thankfully, too large rather than too small. The dead man's gun belt came next; and, almost as an afterthought, he scooped up the light-amp binoculars as well. Then, mentally crossing his fingers, he headed for the cityside edge of the roof.

He made it, again, without raising any obvious alarm. Below him was one of the narrower, northeast-southwest streets; across it, the building roof facing him appeared deserted. At both of the closest street intersections he could see triads of sentries, their attention apparently ground level and outward. Giving all the rooftops in the immediate area one last scan, he gathered his feet beneath him, got a good grip on his mojo, and jumped.

His leg servos were more than equal to the task. A second later he hit the far rooftop, rolling on his right shoulder to soften the sound of his impact. Coming up on one knee, he lifted the light amps to his eyes and, trying hard to look like a Qasaman sentry, waited for a reaction.

It didn't come, and a minute later he eased across the roof and repeated the procedure. One more building and he had left both the rooftop and the groundside sentries far behind him. Two more, and he began to breathe again.

And finally he had to make a decision. Each move in this direction angled him a little farther from the *Dewdrop*, and with the perimeter penetrated it was time to head north. But straight north now would take him near the center of the city, and while the streets immediately below were deserted, he had no real hope that things would be that easy for long. The city's center was where the mayor's office and, presumably, the rest of Sollas officialdom were located, and if the place wasn't crawling with people he would be very surprised. He would have to work his way around it, threading the region between that activity and the sentry line—

Or else run smack through the middle of it.

Pyre paused at roof's edge, rolling the sudden thought through his mind as if tasting it. Hitting the Qasamans' political stronghold would be a grand gesture, a message of Cobra courage and power the leaders here couldn't possibly miss. Tactically, it would serve to split the Qasamans' attention, drawing fire-power away from the *Dewdrop* and perhaps from Cerenkov and the other prisoners as well.

And speaking of them, if he could manage to take the mayor captive or hold some critical nerve center, he might even be able to wangle their freedom without the dangers a brute-force approach would entail.

All in all, he decided, it was worth trying.

Scanning the street one last time, he lowered himself quickly over the parapet and dropped to the ground, bouncing off a convenient window ledge halfway down to ease the final shock of landing. Checking the cross street, he started northeast toward the center of town at a deceptively easy-looking lope, enhanced vision and hearing alert for the Qasamans who would inevitably appear.

The static crackle of the Qasamans' radio jamming blanket dominated the *Dewdrop*'s lounge, its monotony matching perfectly the unchanging still-life on the ship's outside monitors. For all the evidence offered, the entire population of Qasama could have fallen off the planet immediately after Justin had been taken away nearly an hour ago. Telek glanced at her watch, sloshing the untasted cahve in her mug as she did so. Three minutes gone, and not even a hint the Qasamans intended to reply. "Try it again," she told Nnamdi.

He nodded and raised the mike to his lips. "This is

Dr. Hersh Nnamdi aboard the Aventinian ship *Dewdrop*," he said. "We urgently request communication with Mayor Kimmeron or other Qasaman leaders. Please respond."

He lowered the mike into his lap and Telek strained her ears, listening. The *Dewdrop*'s most powerful tight-beam transmitter was spitting Nnamdi's translated words directly at the nearby tower. Jamming or no jamming, *some* of that signal should be getting through. If the Qasamans were listening.

If they weren't, this was a complete waste of effort. If they were, even if they didn't care to reply, Winward might have a chance.

Might.

"Stage two," Telek said to Nnamdi. "Put some emotion into it."

The other's cheek twitched, but he lifted the mike. "This is Dr. Hersh Nnamdi aboard the *Dewdrop*. I would like to send an unarmed representative out to negotiate our companions' release with you. Will you grant him safe-conduct to someone in authority?"

Static. Beside Nnamdi, Christopher stirred and looked at Telek. "You realize, of course, that if Justin and Almo have made their move down south, Kimmeron will know we've got super-warriors aboard and will be waiting for Michael with all the guns they've got."

Telek nodded wordlessly. Winward knew it too, of course. She stole a glance at the Cobra as he sat in quiet conversation with Link at one of the other displays. They would be discussing tactics and strategy, she knew—and what good it would do she couldn't imagine. Shots or shells fired from a distance by an unseen gunner weren't something that could be fought. Not even by Cobras.

"Someone—*anyone*—answer me, *please*." Nnamdi's voice cracked a bit, and Telek shifted her attention back to him. The strain was beginning to get to him, she realized uneasily. A little of that would add be-

lievability to the whole scheme, but too much could
be trouble. "Look, I'm going to send out my second-
in-command, Mr. Michael Winward," Nnamdi continued. "*Please* talk to him, all right? There's no need
for any more bloodshed than we've all already suffered. I'm sure we can make a deal if you'll only
agree to negotiate."

Nnamdi paused, looking to Telek. Steeling herself,
she nodded. He licked his lips and turned back to the
mike. "I'm sending him out now. Okay?"

The static remained unbroken. Putting down the
mike, Nnamdi slumped in his seat and closed his
eyes. Across the room, Winward got easily to his feet.
"That's my cue, I believe," he remarked, picking up
his formal tunic from the back of a chair and slipping it on over his black nightfighter combat suit.

"Comm set," Link murmured,

"Got it," Winward nodded, scooping up the translator-link pendant/earphone set laying on the table in
front of Nnamdi. "Governor, I'll try to find and hit
the jammer first, but if I can't find it I'll go straight
for the tower's defenses. If you pick up gunfire and
explosions from back there, sweep the forest with
comm laser fire and send Dorjay out."

"Right," Telek said, trying to match his calm tone.
"Good luck, and don't take any stupid chances."

He twitched a smile at her and left. Sinking into
the seat next to Nnamdi, Telek watched the screen
. . . and a minute later the outside monitors showed
the Cobra walking slowly toward the tower, a half-
meter-square white flag held prominently in front of
him.

No shells arced out of the sky as he made his slow
way across the airfield. Telek's heart thudded painfully, her emotions flip-flopping between hope and
the fear that too much hope would automatically
bring about disaster. Link, who had moved to watch
over her shoulder, twice reached down to jump the
magnification. The second time he did so they saw

that a force of eight Qasamans had gathered at the
foot of the tower to await Winward's arrival. Eight
Qasamans, and of course eight mojos.

Two stepped forward as Winward neared the group,
their drawn guns glinting in the faint backwash of
Sollas's lights. They relieved him of his flag and
frisked him for weapons. The entire force then formed
a box around him and led him away, not into the
tower but around toward the building's side. *Taking
him to someone in authority?* Telek wondered. *Maybe
even to the officer in charge of their antiaircraft weapons?*

They all disappeared around the corner . . . and a
minute later the breeze carried with it the sound of a
single gunshot.

Chapter 19

The bus pulled finally to a stop beside a darkened building and Moff motioned toward the door with his pistol. "Out," the old man added unnecessarily. Keeping his movements smooth and nonthreatening, Justin stood up and let the Qasamans escort him outside.

The building was a shock of déjà vu, and it took Justin only a second to realize what it reminded him of. "Looks like a stunted version of the Sollas airfield tower," he remarked as Moff led him toward a guard-flanked door. "Oddly out of place here in the middle of a city."

Moff didn't answer. *Two separate doors at least,* Justin noted, scanning the structure casually, *and three floors with windows. Lots of ways in. Come on, Almo—hit these guys and let's see what's in there.*

But no flashes of laser light interrupted them as they walked to the building door. There Moff stopped and turned, leveling his gun at Justin's chest. "You will put your hands behind your back now," the old man said from behind the ring of Qasamans.

Justin complied, and cold metal bands clamped around his wrists. *Almo, where are you?* he thought fiercely, flicking glances at the surrounding buildings.

Moff led them between the guards and into the

building. The high-security building where the Qasamans felt it safe to bring an unknown danger.

The sweat was beginning to break out on Justin's
forehead. *It's all right,* he told himself. *It's all right. So
you're on your own; but you've been trained for this
sort of thing. Two doors, and three floors of windows,
remember? Getting away will be a snap.* Carefully he
let his fingers explore the cuffs holding him. The
wrist rings were dauntingly thick ... but it was a
short chain, not a solid bar, that connected them. A
moment's experimentation showed he could curl either of his fingertip lasers to rest against one of the
links. While he might get burned in the process, it
should only take a few seconds to cut himself free.
Though not if the targeting lock wanted to hit the
mojos first.... Shivering at what could have been a
nasty mistake, he canceled the lock. *Take it* easy,
Justin—you're letting yourself get flustered.

Moff led them down a hallway to an elevator. A car
was waiting for them. "Where are we going?" Justin
asked, just to break the silence.

But no one answered. Three of the guards herded
Justin into the car; Moff and the old man joined
them. *Steady, kid, steady.* Justin bit down on his rising fear. *Just see where they're taking you, then knock
'em against the walls and out a window.*

Moff pushed the bottom of a *long* row of buttons
... and the elevator started *down.*

Down. Into the ground—*deep* into the ground, if
the buttons were each a full floor—where there were
no doors or windows to escape through. And for perhaps the first time in his life Justin realized he was
terrified. The universe, which had always seemed to
protect him, was a long way up, far above his little
elevator car. He was surrounded by the armed guards
and hairtrigger killer birds of a frightened and angry
society ... and it dawned on him with a sharpness
like the smell of ozone that the men he would soon
be facing intended him to die in this deep hole. They

didn't know he was a Moreau, didn't care that he was a Cobra, and when they were through with him they would kill him.

And Justin panicked.

All thoughts of finding out what this place was, all considerations of not revealing his Cobra equipment, all thoughts even of mercy—all of it simply fled his mind before the bubbling wave of panic that welled suffocatingly up into his throat. The men, guns, and mojos surrounding him were a claustrophobic pillow across his face ... and without making a conscious decision to do so, he exploded into action.

His fingertip lasers and sonic fired first, the former at the chain binding his wrists, the latter in a stunning wavefront in all directions. An instant later his head slammed into an invisible wall and he recognized with a fresh surge of panic the folly of using a sonic in such an enclosed space. His arms tugged convulsively against the handcuffs as the lasers fired again, and abruptly the metal snapped and his arms swung free.

But the brief sonic blast and flash of light had alerted the Qasamans. Even as Justin's arms came loose they were grabbed by hard hands. Grabbed tightly—and the servos beneath the skin and muscle twisted the arms up and forward, slamming the two men head to head. Their grips slipped and he pulled free—and then there was no time for anything but terror as the five mojos screamed to the attack.

Justin's mind blanked completely then, and the only memory he had of what happened next was the sounds of the birds and the horrible thunderstorm dazzle of a hundred laser flashes. . . .

The stench brought him back to reality a few seconds later; the stench of burned meat and of his own vomit. Unsteadily, he got to his feet and looked around at the carnage. The mojos—all of them—were dead. The five Qasamans ... Justin couldn't tell. Two of them definitely were, with prominent laser burns over vital spots, but the others—Moff included—were less certain. But whether burn shock, the sonic, or his flailing arms had put them out of action wasn't important. They could not hurt him, and he had no desire to inquire further.

The elevator was still going down. The whole thing had clearly taken less time than it'd seemed to, and it penetrated dimly into Justin's rattled consciousness that unless the elevator contained monitors the Qasamans waiting below for him would be unaware of what had just happened. He might still be able to escape.

He jabbed at his best guess for the ground floor button . . . and then at a second and a third before he realized that, unlike those on Aventine, this elevator design didn't allow for cancellation. The car would keep going down until it reached the floor Moff had signaled. Where more Qasamans would be waiting for him.

He had flipped over on his back on the unmoving bodies and his antiarmor laser was already tracing an off-center square in the ceiling before he recognized on a conscious level that he would not, *could* not, face whatever awaited him at the bottom of the elevator shaft. The false ceiling and relatively thin metal behind it were no match for the laser, and as the charred square fell practically into his lap Justin scrambled to his feet. He took a bare second to gain his balance and jumped.

Never before, not even in training, had he pushed his leg servos to their limit, and he actually gasped in shock as he shot through the opening like a misshapen missile. All around him, only dimly visible even with the aid of his enhancers, were cables and guy lines. A flicker of light from a door crack washed over him—then another, and another—he was slowing down—stopping in midair—

Instinctively, he grabbed; and a second later he

was again moving downard, his arms wrapped solidly around the main elevator cable.

So he was out of the car, and out of the direct line
of fire from the Qasamans below . . . but he was still
deep within their stronghold and had left a trail a
child could follow. He had to figure out a way to
escape, and he had to do so fast.

Oddly enough, though—or so it seemed to him—
the suffocating panic had dissipated far enough for
him to be able to think again. His incredible jump
had been a sledge-hammer reminder both of the power
his Cobra equipment gave him and of the fact that
his father, too, had once been imprisoned like this
and had survived.

A sheet of light swept by: one of the landing doors
he'd jumped past seconds ago. On a hunch, he shoved
off the cable toward it, fingers and feet finding holds
on framework and opening-mechanism bars. He found
a narrow ledge to stand on and regained his balance
as, a meter away, the cable continued its way down.

Carefully, he took a shuddering breath. *I am Justin
Moreau*, he reminded himself firmly. *A Cobra, follow-
ing in my father's footsteps. I will—I will—survive this.
Fine. So how do I start?*

One thing was for sure: he had several floors to go
before he even got to the surface. Shifting his grip, he
leaned out as far as he safely could. The position of
the door directly above could be inferred from reflected light, but there were too many bars and other
metallic junk in the way for it to be visible. So jumping floor to floor was out; ditto for climbing through
stuff that questionable. A service ladder? But a quick
survey of the shaft showed nothing that would serve
such a function.

A meter away, the cable abruptly slowed and
stopped . . . and from below came the faint sound of
elevator doors opening.

Again Justin shifted position, swinging his left leg
to point directly toward the hole he'd cut in the car's

ceiling and simultaneously bringing up his optical
enhancers' magnification capabilities. The sight of
the bodies on the floor sent a fresh wave of revulsion
through him; but before he had time for more than a
quick shiver there was an explosion of Qasaman voices
from below, and someone stepped into the car.

Damn. Justin mouthed the word, caught once more
in indecision. Should he try and get out of the shaft
before the Qasamans below came to the obvious conclusion as to his whereabouts, or should he stay and
try to discourage pursuit?

The decision was made for him. Abruptly, the figure below became a face and a pistol, and the shaft
thundered with the echo of his shot.

A wild shot, of course; he couldn't have any idea
where Justin actually was. The Cobra's response was
considerably more accurate, and even at this range
the antiarmor laser was perfectly adequate for such a
purpose. The gunner fell in a heap onto the bodies
beneath him. A second face appeared, and Justin
shot that one, too—

And from below came the sound of the car's doors
closing. A second later, the cable beside him started
upwards.

Justin gaped for a couple of heartbeats before his
mental wheels caught and he jumped over to again
cling to the cable. What had happened was now obvious: having reached the floor Moff had sent it to, the
elevator was now responding to the buttons Justin
had pushed on the way down.

For the moment, at least, Justin seemed to be one
step ahead of them.

After the flurry of activity preceding it, the ride
toward ground level seemed to drag on and on, and
it gave him the chance to assess his own injuries.
Both hands, particularly the little fingers, were speck-
led with tiny molten-metal burns from his blasting of
the handcuff chain an eternity earlier. The rings themselves were biting hard into his wrists as he pressed

against the greasy cable. Something, presumably blood, was dripping slowly down his cheek from a cut over his left eye that hurt like blazes. He hadn't realized before that any of the mojos had gotten so close . . . and the thought of what might have happened—or could yet happen—

Reality broke into the uncomfortable speculation: the elevator was slowing down. The car, he estimated, was about three floors below him. When the doors opened he would begin sliding down the cable toward it, keeping his antiarmor laser aimed and ready. If the Qasamans still hadn't caught on he would drop through the ceiling hole, out the door, and make a mad dash for the exit, relying on his speed and computerized reflexes to get him through.

Below him the car doors opened—and as they did, the top of the car was abruptly flooded with light and the roar of sustained gunfire exploded into the shaft.

Justin jerked violently, nearly losing his grip. The car was already being obscured by a haze of smoke. Through it the staccato flashing of the guns lit up the shaft with an unearthly glow. Splinters of shattered steel scythed the air in counterpoint to the invisible battering of the bullets that were demolishing everything in range.

And Justin's brief respite from panic was over.

Across from him another of the landing doors was visible in the flickering light. As the barrage below reached its peak his leg swung convulsively around, the laser within it tracing a distorted ellipse across the doors. For that heart-rending second it didn't matter that the Qasamans might have a dozen gunmen ringing each elevator door; didn't even matter that a moment's study probably would have revealed an emergency mechanism that might have given them far less warning of his presence. All that mattered was that the guns below could be turned upwards at any second, and that he wanted out of the deathtrap *now*. Twisting his legs to the horizontal, he shoved hard against the cable with his hands. The charred ellipse broke like foil as he hit it, and he flew helplessly into the hallway beyond, slamming into the far wall and bouncing off into a barely balanced crouch.

The hallway was empty.

For a long moment he sat there trembling on his haunches, his brain struggling to pierce the unreality of the situation to figure out what had happened. They *knew* he was in the shaft—the roar of gunfire still coming from below more than proved that. So why weren't all the exits from the shaft being guarded?

Because they thought he was still on the elevator roof?

Probably. A concealed weapon would likely not have been powerful enough to kill the two men from any further away than the roof. And they wouldn't have any idea just how high his servos let him jump.

Getting to his feet, he gulped a ragged breath and took stock of the situation. The hallway stretched for thirty meters or so in both directions, its walls lined with incomprehensibly labeled doors. At the far ends small windows reflected his image.

Small, but probably large enough to get through. Picking the closest of the two ends, Justin headed for it at a dead run.

And he almost made it. But if guarding all exits from the elevator shaft hadn't been the Qasamans' first priority, neither had it been forgotten. His own footsteps masking the sound of their approach, Justin's first warning was the blood-chilling scream of a mojo directly behind him. He twisted around, getting just the briefest glimpse of talons arcing for his face before his nanocomputer took over.

The servos in his legs wrenched him to the side, out of the mojo's line of flight. Its wingtips brushed his face as it overshot him, screaming again in what sounded uncannily like rage. At the far end of the hall, five Qasamans had come from somewhere, their guns aimed and ready; and four more mojos were sweeping to the attack.

And for the second time that night the sight of the birds drove all reason and nerve from his mind. Falling backwards to slam against the wall, he snapped his burned hands up . . . and as his brain fogged over with terror, his nanocomputer turned them into fountains of laser fire.

He came to a few seconds later to find all five mojos dead. At the end of the hallway, he could see at least three Qasaman bodies, as well. The survivors—if there'd been any—had vanished.

Witnesses to his Cobra firepower; but that thought didn't occur to Justin until a long time afterwards. Back on his feet, he headed again for his target window, sonic disruptor focused on it. The weapon found and locked onto the window's primary resonance, increased its amplitude . . . and with Justin two steps from it, the glass shattered, taking much of the sash framework with it in its violent demise. Increasing his speed, Justin put down his head and dove through the hole.

Three floors below him, the edge of the tower was a blaze of floodlights and the crazy-quilt shadow pattern of running men. Justin saw just enough to realize he would most likely land outside the lit area before his nanocomputer pulled his arms and legs tightly in toward his torso. He tensed; but a second later when the limbs snapped out to normal position again he was relieved to find the computer's calculation had been correct. Properly vertical once more, he hit the ground on his feet, servos taking the impact as they fought against his forward momentum to regain his balance before he ran full tilt into the building immediately across from his former prison. The effort was a success; turning to run parallel to the building, he sprinted to the nearest corner and rounded it.

He'd not had a chance yet to really focus on his

surroundings, but as he picked up speed now he realized the universe had betrayed him one final time. Directly ahead the buildings and street abruptly gave way to the sort of open grassland that surrounded Sollas as well. The bus had taken him through several kilometers of city before reaching the tower; ergo, what he faced now was Purma's southwestern edge.

He was running directly *away* from Rynstadt and Cerenkov . . . directly away from the *Dewdrop*.

I should turn around, he thought. *Or at least circle around a block or two and head back along a different street*. But his feet kept running; and as he crossed the sharp line between city and grassland he finally recognized that no intentions in the world were going to make his body turn around. Behind him were the mojos, and the paralyzing fear their talons induced in him was far more terrifying than the talons themselves.

His father had faced the might of whole Troft armies and won through without flinching . . . and his only Cobra son had turned out to be a coward.

The city was far behind him now, but as Justin keyed in his optical enhancers he saw the forest that had flanked the road into Purma had receded sharply this far south. The nearest edge, his enhancers' range finder told him, was over a kilometer away— much too far to reach in time if the Qasamans had taken up the chase. Throwing a glance over his shoulder, Justin skidded to a halt and dropped down on his stomach in the knee-high grass, turning to face the city with all senses alert.

But so far there was no sign of pursuit. Did they think he'd headed north, as he should have? Or were they perhaps not even aware yet that he'd escaped from the building?

There was no way to tell . . . and with emotional fatigue washing over him, Justin almost didn't even care. Whatever he did now, Cerenkov and Rynstadt were as good as dead unless Pyre had already managed to free them. No matter how fast Justin got to their prison, he would find the place hip-deep in guards.

His burns and bruises throbbed with aches both sharp and dull, but they were no match for his fatigue. Slowly but inexorably his eyelids dragged themselves closed, his head sank down to rest pillowed on his arms, his shame found the only oblivion available.

He slept.

Chapter 20

For the third time in five minutes a vehicle approached from ahead, and for the third time Pyre tensed and forced himself to maintain a steady walk. The vehicle passed without slowing, and the Cobra sighed quietly with relief.

Momentary relief, at best. If his memory of Sollas's layout was correct, he was only two or three blocks from the building where Joshua and the others had been taken a week ago to meet Mayor Kimmeron. The trip so far had indicated that no one was considering the possibility that any of the Aventinians could have made it this deep into the city, but it was equally clear that the bubble could burst any time now. There were bound to be sentries surrounding the mayoral office, as well as various people scurrying around with errands as these supposedly peaceful people continued their war against the *Dewdrop*. A straight-in penetration, Cobra firepower or no, was likely to be pretty bloody. On both sides.

But so far he'd been unable to come up with anything better. He'd passed a handful of parked cars, but a quick check had showed their drive mechanisms were locked and he had no idea how to bypass the system. Rooftop jumping was possible, but its usefulness decreased in direct proportion to the number of nearby ears that might hear the thud of the landing and eyes that might see the leap itself. If he had some timed bombs he could set up a diversion a few blocks from his goal; but none of his meager supply of equipment could be adapted to such a purpose. The propellant in the bullets, perhaps? Surely there was a goodly amount of it—you didn't take down an animal the size of a bololin without a lot of punch behind the projectile.

Bololins. . . .

The ghost of an idea brushed his mind. Looking around quickly to make sure he was unobserved, Pyre found a dark section of wall and began to climb.

The rooftop, when he reached it, didn't have what he was looking for; but a careful study showed a likely candidate two buildings away. Two jumps later he was squatting next to a square yellow box mounted with a large-mouthed horn.

A bololin alarm.

Fingertip lasers made quick work of the box's access panel, and Pyre was soon poking gingerly around the wires and components inside. The reasonable way to set such a device up was to run it off the building's own power supply, with the on/off switch several floors down and inaccessible . . . but if the Qasamans had been as cautious here as they seemed to be everywhere else. . . .

And they had. The horn's emergency battery took up nearly a quarter of the box's volume.

A few minutes' work tracing wires and Pyre had the system figured out. Cutting the main power line *here* would allow the battery—and, more importantly, the emergency trigger switch—into the circuit. The battery's switch seemed to be designed for radio control, though. He would have to come up with some other way to trigger the thing.

By the time the preliminary cutting and adjustments were complete he'd thought of one. Maybe.

It took nearly fifteen minutes more to complete the

jury-rig trigger. Then, wiping the sweat off his fore-head, he took a moment to study the landscape. The mayor's office ... that one there, probably. Circle cautiously and find a roof past it to wait on ... that one.

Glancing at his watch, Pyre grimaced. Time was slipping away from him, and with each lost minute the chances increased that the Qasamans would kill one of their hostages or take some action against the *Dewdrop*. Dropping down the side of the building, he began to run silently through the deserted streets.

Luck was with him. Fifteen minutes later he was on his chosen rooftop, ready to go. Two buildings away, the mayoral building was, from the muted sounds reaching his ears, indeed surrounded by mill-ing groups of people. Four blocks beyond it Pyre's optical enhancers located the bololin alarm and the stolen light-amp binoculars resting atop the box there. Taking a deep breath, Pyre locked onto the binocu-lars, raised his left leg, and sent a low-power antiarmor shot toward it.

The light triggered a pulse through the light-amp's electronics, a pulse which Pyre's rewiring sent not to the lenses but around the alarm's emergency switch system—

And the hoot of the horn tore into the darkness.

Pyre was ready. Stray eyes were still a danger, but for the moment there was no way anyone in the street below was going to hear the impact of his landings. He reached the edge of his building and jumped, getting a glimpse of running people below. He hit the next roof, crossed it in a dead run, and with a quick prayer to the patron of fools, jumped again.

Not to the mayoral building roof, but to a spot midway down the side—and that only to provide a slight braking impact before he hit the street. The building was seven stories high, its lit windows testi-fying to activity inside, and Pyre knew he was taking a big gamble going in at ground level. But the mayor's office itself had been on the first floor, and the Cobra was betting that Qasaman paranoia would bury the most important facilities underground.

And then he hit the street and there was no time left for planning and thought. Most of the thirty or so people in sight were hurrying away from him in the direction of the hooting alarm, but the two who flanked the ornate door were standing fast . . . and their frozen astonishment didn't extend to their mojos.

But the birds saw no drawn weapon, and their movements were the slow ones of surprised study instead of the swifter ones of attack. Pyre targeted and shot both out of the air; and then, as the guards belatedly reacted, he shot them as well. He took the three outside steps in a single bound and slipped inside.

He hadn't been paying all that much attention to the route the one time Cerenkov's team had been in this place, but fortunately the layout seemed straightforward. Pyre followed the main corridor to the first junction and branched right. At the next cross corridor he turned left, aiming toward the center of the building—and there, barely ten meters away, were the two liveried guards he remembered seeing at the mayor's door.

They looked at him in frowning surprise, hands dropping to their guns. Pyre shot both of them out from under their mojos, then killed the birds as they tried to disengage their talons from their epaulet perches and become airborne. Mentally bracing himself, he shoved the doors open and stepped inside, hands held at the ready.

It was almost a repeat of the scene he'd seen through Joshua's sensors the last time, with two important exceptions. The fumes that both he and the contact team had missed out on before were an almost literal sledgehammer to the nose, bringing him to an abrupt halt and nearly gagging him. And this time the mayor's cushiony throne was vacant.

It took Pyre a handful of heartbeats to get his breath and voice back. For the people seated at the low tables around the throne, those few seconds turned out to be their salvation. Whether the fumes enhanced their mental processes or whether they were simply naturally observant he didn't know, but by the time he was able to function again all of them had apparently deduced who he was and were making mad dashes from the room. Within seconds the scene was deserted.

"Damn," Pyre murmured under his breath. The smoke, he discovered, tasted odd, too. Clicking up his audio enhancers, he held his breath ... and from somewhere out of sight among the free-hanging curtains he heard the faint sound of shallow breathing.

So they *hadn't* all made it out of boltholes. Was the straggler armed? Probably ... though none of the others had tried to use their guns, and that carried some interesting implications. But even if the skulker was afraid to shoot, Pyre had no desire to hunt him down in this maze, with only the diffuse sounds of breathing to guide him. But there might be another way. If the mojos were really as touchy about weapons as they'd seemed when the contact team first stepped outside the *Dewdrop*'s lock ...

Left hand ready for trouble, he reached down with his right and drew his stolen pistol.

The sound of steel on leather was loud in the silent room—and the single flap of bird wings that followed gave direction enough. Ahead and to the left ... he sprinted around the curtains there and came face to face with a crouching, terror-eyed man.

For a second they gazed at each other in silence. Pyre's main attention was on the Qasaman's mojo, but the bird seemed to realize that an attack would be suicide, and it stayed put on its shoulder perch. Shifting his full attention to the man, Pyre said the only Qasaman word he knew: "Kimmeron."

The other, apparently misunderstanding, shook his head wildly. "Sibbio," he choked, slapping his chest with an open palm, eyes dropping to the gun still in Pyre's hand. "*Sibbio*."

Pyre grimaced and tried again. "Kimmeron. Kimmeron?" He waved his free hand vaguely around the room.

The Qasaman got it then. Even through the haze of fumes Pyre saw his face visibly pale. *Doesn't know where the mayor is? Or* does *know and the place is top-secret?* The latter, he suspected; Sibbio's clothes seemed too ornate for a mere servitor. Taking a long step forward, the Cobra glared as hard as he could at the man. "Kimmeron," he bit out harshly.

The other gazed into Pyre's eyes and silently got to his feet.

The bolthole was right where, in retrospect, Pyre should have expected to find it: directly in front of the cushiony throne. Sibbio showed him the hidden lever that released the trap door; looking down the hole, Pyre saw the meter-square shaft change a few meters down into a curving ramp that presumably dumped the passengers into the safety of a heavily guarded room somewhere down the line.

Unfortunately, the trap's position implied it was also useful for getting undesirables out of the mayor's sight, which meant the guards below would be trained to handle potential nuisances. But there was nothing Pyre could do about that on his time budget ... and now that the trap was open, there was no point in further hesitation. Giving Sibbio's mojo one last glance, the Cobra stepped into the pit.

It was a smooth enough ride, the curved section of tunnel beginning early enough and gradually enough to ease him onto his back for the final thirty-degree slope. It was also a much shorter trip than he'd planned on, and he had barely registered the dim square outline rushing toward him when he shot through the light-blocking curtain and landed flat on his back on a giant foam pad, the gun slipping from his grip as he hit. His eyes adjusted—

To find a ring of guns surrounding him.

Five of them, he counted as he lay motionless. The guard nearest his fallen weapon scooped it up, jamming it into his own empty holster. "You will make no move," said a man standing at Pyre's feet in the middle of the semicircle, in harshly accented Anglic.

Pyre locked eyes with him, then sent his gaze leisurely around the ring of guards. "I want to talk to Mayor Kimmeron," he said to the spokesman.

"You will not move until you are judged to be weaponless," the Qasaman told him.

"*Is* Kimmeron here?"

The other ignored his question. He spoke instead to his men, two of whom handed their weapons to the others. They knelt down on either side of Pyre ... and the Cobra kicked his heels hard into the pad.

The pad was spongy, but the kick had servo strength behind it and an instant later Pyre was flipping rigidly around the pivot point of his head. One of the guns barked, too late—and then it was too late for any further response as Pyre triggered the laser salvo he'd set up while looking around the guard ring. For an instant the room blazed with laser fire ... and by the time Pyre's body had completed its flip the five Qasamans were kneeling or lying on the floor in various stages of shock, their flash-heated guns scattered among the dead mojos.

Pyre got to his feet, eyes seeking the spokesman. "I could as easily have killed all of you," he said calmly. "I'm not here to kill Mayor Kimmeron—"

Without warning, the other four Qasamans leaped to their feet and rushed him.

He let them come; and as the first one got within range, he snapped out his arm to catch the other in the chest with his palm. There was a *wumph* of expelled air, the sharper *crack* of snapped ribs, and the Qasaman flew two meters backwards to crash to the floor.

The other three skidded to a halt, and Pyre saw an abrupt swelling of fear and respect in their faces. It was one thing, he reflected, to be disarmed by effectively magical bursts of light; it was quite another to see brute physical force in action. Or to feel it, for that matter. The temporary numbness in his palm was wearing off and the skin there was aching like fury. The Qasaman would feel a lot worse when he woke up. If he ever did.

Pyre's eyes caught the spokesman's again. "I'm not here to kill Mayor Kimmeron, but merely to talk with him," he said as calmly as his tingling hand permitted. "Take me to him. Now."

The other licked his lips, glancing over to where one of his men was ministering to his injured colleague. Then, looking back at Pyre, he nodded. "Follow me this way." He said something else to his men, then turned and headed for a door in the far end of the room. Pyre followed, the two remaining Qasamans falling into step behind him.

They passed through the door, and Pyre felt a split second of déjà vu. The same cushiony throne and low tables as in the office upstairs were here as well. But this room was smaller, and the hanging curtains had been replaced by banks of visual displays.

And glaring darkly at one of the displays was Mayor Kimmeron.

He looked up as Pyre and his escort approached, and the Cobra waited for the inevitable reaction. Kimmeron's gaze swept Pyre's matted hair and growth of beard; his borrowed jacket over camouflage survival suit; the dead mojo now hanging over his shoulder by a single thread. But his expression didn't change, and when he looked up again at Pyre's face the Cobra was struck by the brightness of the other's eyes. "You are from the ship," Kimmeron said calmly. "You left it before our cordon was set up. How?"

"Magic," Pyre said shortly. He glanced around the room. Another fifteen or so Qasamans were present, nearly all of them staring in his direction. All had the usual sidearm and mojo, but no one looked like he was interested in making any move for his weapon. "Your underground command post?" he asked Kimmeron.

"One of them," the other nodded. "There are many more. You will gain little by destroying it."

"I'm not really interested in destroying anything," Pyre told him. "I'm here mainly to arrange our companions' release."

Kimmeron's lip curled. "You are remarkably slow to learn," he spat. "Didn't the death of your other messenger teach you a lesson?"

Pyre felt his mouth go dry. "What other messenger? You mean the contact team?"

For a moment the other frowned. Then his face cleared in understanding. "Ah. The jamming of your radio signals was effective against *you*, at least. I see. So you do not know the man Winward left your ship without permission and was shot."

Winward? Had Telek started her breakout attempt already? "Why did you shoot him?" he snapped. "You just said he was a messenger—"

"For the unprovoked deaths of eight men in Purma and six here you are *all* responsible. You have spied and you have murdered, and your punishment will be that of death."

Pyre stared at him, mental wheels unable to catch. Winward . . . shot down like a spine leopard, probably without so much as a warning. *Then why aren't they shooting at me?* Simple fear?—*he* wouldn't be taken by surprise, after all. Or was it something more practical? With Winward gone and whatever the hell had happened in Purma—whatever *that* was—all over, did they want a live Cobra to study?

His gaze drifted to the particular bank of displays Kimmeron had been studying. Rooms, corridors, outside views . . . three showed the *Dewdrop*. *Must be from the airfield tower*, he realized. *Live picture?* If so, there was still a chance for some of them to escape; the ship seemed undamaged.

"We would prefer to keep you alive at present," Kimmeron broke into his thoughts. "You, and the ones named Cerenkov and Rynstadt, have no possibility of escaping. I tell you this so that you will not try and thereby force us to kill you prematurely."

"Our ship might escape," Pyre pointed out. "And it will tell our people of our imprisonment."

"Your ship, too, cannot escape." Kimmeron was quietly certain. "The weapons set against it will destroy it before it reaches the end of the field."

But the Dewdrop *can lift straight up*. Would that make enough of a difference? There was no way to know . . . but given the national paranoia, Pyre tended to doubt it. "I'd still like to talk to you about release of our companions," he told the mayor, just for something to say.

Kimmeron arched his eyebrows. "You speak foolishness," he bit out. "We have you and the body of Winward, from which your so-named 'magic' powers can surely be learned."

"Our magic cannot be learned from a corpse," Pyre lied.

"*You* are still alive," the other said pointedly. "From Cerenkov and Rynstadt we will obtain information about your culture and technology which will prepare us for any attack your world launches against us in the future. And from your ship—intact or in pieces—we will learn even more, perhaps enough to finally regain star travel. All that is within our hands; what could you offer of greater value for allowing your departure?"

There was no answer Pyre could give to that . . . and it occurred to him that a method which allowed its users to learn Anglic in a week might indeed let them reconstruct the *Dewdrop* and its systems from whatever wreckage remained after its destruction.

Which meant that his gallant rescue attempt was

now, and always had been, doomed to failure. Cerenkov and Rynstadt were beyond help, and Pyre's own
last minutes would be spent right here in the mayor's
underground nerve center. If he could somehow find
the communications panel—and then find a way to
shut off or broadcast through the jamming—and then
figure out how to signal the *Dewdrop* to get the hell
away—and all before sheer weight of numbers overwhelmed him—

And as the impossibilities of each step lined up
before him like mountains the universe presented
him a gift. A small gift, hardly more than a sign . . .
but he saw it, and Kimmeron did not, and he had the
satisfaction of giving the mayor a genuine smile.
"What do I have to offer, Mr. Mayor?" he said calmly.
"A great deal, actually . . . because all that was in
your hands a moment ago is even now slipping
through your fingers."

Kimmeron frowned . . . and as he started to speak
Pyre heard a sharp intake of breath from the guard
spokesman beside him. Kimmeron twisted to look
behind him . . . and when he turned back his face
was pale. "How—?"

"How?" Pyre shifted his eyes over Kimmeron's
shoulder, to the displays that showed the airfield
tower and environs.

—Or that had done so a few minutes earlier. Now,
the entire bank showed a uniform gray.

How? "Very simple, Mr. Mayor," Pyre said . . . and
suppressed the shiver of that boyhood memory. Like
MacDonald before him on that awful day of vengeance against Challinor. . . . "Winward, it appears,
has returned from the dead."

Chapter 21

It was so unexpected—so totally unexpected—that Winward never even had a chance to react. One minute he was walking around the tower with his Qasaman escort, surreptitiously searching the building and immediate area for weapons and additional guards and trying to work out exactly what he would say when they reached whoever he was being taken to. Just walking peacefully . . . and then the leader muttered something and turned around . . . and before Winward could do more than focus on the other the night lit up with a thunderous flash and a sledgehammer slammed into the center of his chest, blowing him backwards into nothingness as the crack of the lethal shot echoed in his ears. . . .

The blackness in his brain faded slowly, and for what seemed like hours he drifted slowly toward the reality he could faintly sense above him. The pain came first—dull, throbbing pain in his chest; sharp, stinging pain in his eyes and face—and with that breakthrough the rest of his senses began to function again. Sounds filtered in: footsteps, doors opening and closing, occasional incomprehensible voices. He discovered he was on his back, bouncing rhythmically as if being carried, and every so often he felt a trickle of something run down his ribs under his tunic.

And slowly, he realized what had happened.

He'd been shot. Deliberately and maliciously shot. And was probably dying.

The only general rule he could recall from his first-aid training was that injury victims should not be unnecessarily moved. And so he remained still, eyes closed against the pain there, as he waited for loss of blood to dim his consciousness back into darkness.

But it wasn't happening. On the contrary, with each passing heartbeat he felt his mind sharpening, with strength and sensation rapidly returning to his limbs. Far from dying, he was actually coming back to life.

What the hell?

And it was only then, as his body and brain finally meshed enough to localize his wound, that he realized what had happened.

The Qasaman had shot him in the center of his chest. Directly over the breastbone. The breastbone which, coated with ceramic laminae, was functionally unbreakable.

The aftermath was less clear, but its main points weren't hard to figure out. The bullet's impact had knocked the air out of him, possibly even temporarily stopped his heart, and for the past few seconds or minutes he'd been fighting to get oxygen back into his system. His face and eyes must have taken the impact of burning propellant to sting as they did, and for a painful heartbeat he recognized that he might have been permanently blinded.

But somehow even that didn't seem important at the moment. He was alive, he was reasonably functional—

And the Qasamans thought he was dead.

They would pay for that mistake. Pay in blood.

Starting right now. Winward's eyes might be unusable, but the optical enhancers set into the skin around them were harder to damage and fed into the optic nerves further back inside the skull's protection. They weren't really designed to replace normal vision, but a minute's experimentation showed that a zero-magnification setting combined with the lowest light-amp level provided an adequate picture.

Between the four head-and-upper-torsos bobbing at the edges of the view, he could see a ceiling passing overhead. Carefully, keeping the motion slow, he eased his head a few degrees to the side. A couple of doors went by, the party turned a corner, and abruptly they were through open double doors and into a white-walled room with bright steel fixtures extending to the ceiling in various places. The four stretcher-bearers set him down on a hard table, and he let his head loll so to leave it turned to his right, toward the exit. The men left, closing the doors behind them, and he was alone.

Though probably not for long. The room he was in was very obviously a sick bay or surgery, and in the Qasamans' place Winward would want a preliminary dissection started on a dead Cobra as quickly as possible. The doctors were probably prepping in another room, and could arrive at any time.

Forcing himself to again move slowly, Winward eased his head up and down until he located the glassy eye of a fisheye monitor camera. It was in a back upper corner, out of direct line of any of his lasers or his sonic disruptor. He could lift his hands and fire, of course, but if someone was watching the monitor closely the alarm would be raised before he even got through the double doors into the hall. Using his omnidirectional sonic to shake up the picture before shooting wouldn't help appreciably, either. What he really needed was a diversion.

Behind him there was the sound of a door opening, and a second later four white-gowned people came around the maze of support equipment and into view.

And a diversion abruptly became vital. The soldiers and stretcher-carriers outside might miss his slow breathing or the fact that the skin of his chest was still bleeding, but the approaching doctors hadn't a chance in hell of doing so. He had to keep them away before they found out he was still alive.

The leader was within a meter of him now. Activating his omnidirectional, Winward ran it to its lowest frequency setting and held his breath.

Their reaction was all he could have hoped for. The leader jerked to a stop as the inaudible waves hit him, the second in line stumbling into him as she staggered slightly. For a minute they all stood together in a little knot just beyond the most uncomfortable zone, conversing in voices that sounded both concerned and irritated. Winward waited, gritting his teeth himself against the gut-rattling sound as he waited for their next move.

It came quickly, and was one more indication of how much the high command wanted the Cobra dissected *immediately*. Waving the others back, the leader picked up a sharp-looking instrument from a nearby tray and stepped to the table. He reached down to pull back Winward's tunic—

And jumped back with a strangled gasp as the Cobra's sonic disrupter flash-heated the skin of his hand. Followed by one of the others, he dashed around the table to the back door, shouting as he ran.

The door opened and closed, and for a moment the last two Qasamans huddled together, whispering in fear or awe or both to each other. Winward tried to guess what they'd try next, but the grinding of his sonic combined with the throbbing pain in his chest and face was fogging his mind too much for him to hold a coherent train of thought.

Again, he didn't have long to wait. One of the two disappeared toward the back of the room, returning a minute later with a coil of insulated electrical cable. Snaring a knife from the instrument tray, he began stripping the insulation from one end ... and as the other Qasaman plugged the wire's other end into what appeared to be a ground socket beneath a wall outlet, Winward realized with growing excitement that the break he'd hoped for was here.

Clearly, the Qasamans had jumped to the conclusion that their colleague had suffered an electrical burn from Winward's body and were preparing to try and drain the excess charge away.

Another minute and they were ready. The first Qasaman replaced the knife in the tray and swung the bare copper wire gently as he prepared to loft it over the Cobra's chest. Moving his right hand fractionally, Winward lined up his fingertip laser on the socket where the cable had been grounded. It was going to be a bit of a stretch, but he had no choice but to try it. The copper snake flew through the air, draped itself across his chest . . . and Winward fired his arcthrower.

A bit of a stretch indeed, and for a heart-stopping fraction of a second he watched the clean light of the laser burning its solitary way through the air without any response from the capacitors deep within his body cavity. Then the split second was past, and the ionized path reached the required conductance and a lightning bolt shattered the air. And even as the thunderclap seemed to split open Winward's head, the sudden current flow overloaded the circuit breakers—

And the room was plunged into darkness.

Winward was off the table before the echoes had faded away; was out through the double doors a second later. If the monitor camera hadn't been taken out with the room's lights, it was almost guaranteed that the afterimage of that flash would mask the brief flicker of hall light as the Cobra escaped.

For a wonder, the hall was deserted. Presumably the medical area had no command stations within it and, hence, little traffic under normal conditions. He headed down the hall to look for a stairway; and as he did so, he carefully pried open his eyelids.

Nothing. The Qasaman's gunshot had blinded him. Perhaps beyond even Aventine's surgical abilities.

The cold fury simmering within him began to heat up again. Along with York's arm, it was one more score to be settled with this world.

He changed hallways twice before spotting anyone; and when he finally did, he hit the entire jackpot at once. Rounding a corner, he was just in time to see the elevator he'd been seeking disgorge a half dozen Qasamans barely ten meters away from him. One of them was the man who'd shot him.

The whole group froze in shock, and even the limited quality of his enhancer image gave Winward the grim satisfaction of watching sheer unbelieving terror flood into his former assailant's face. Three seconds they all stood there; four seconds, five—and, abruptly, they all went madly for their weapons.

Winward pirouetted on his right foot and cut a blaze of death across them with his antiarmor laser.

The mojos escaped that first shot, but even as they swept toward him in impotent rage his fingertip lasers shot them to the floor. Winward didn't waste a backward glance as he jumped over the charred bodies and between the closing elevator doors. The selector panel gave him momentary pause—there were at least three times as many buttons as the tower ought to need. But he knew where he needed to go. Pushing the top button, he listened to the faint hum of the elevator's motor and prepared himself for combat.

The door opened, and he stepped out into a dimly-lit room to face a dozen drawn pistols.

They barked as one . . . but Winward was no longer in the line of fire. Leg servos snapped him upwards, flipped him over in time to hit the ceiling feet first, crashing shin-deep through the tiles there to bounce off the stronger ceiling above; pushed him back toward the floor behind the line of gunmen, again flipping him over in midflight. He hit the floor with fingertip lasers blazing . . . and it was doubtful that any of the Qasamans realized what had happened before they died.

Again the mojos outlived their masters, and again Winward made that escape momentary. But this time one of them got through before dying, its talons opening up a ten-centimeter gash in his left arm.

"Damn it all," Winward snarled aloud, tearing off the bloody tunic sleeve and wrapping it awkwardly around the wound. The ambush meant the alarm had gone out, though he hadn't heard any sirens . . . and as he focused for the first time on the room around him, he realized why they hadn't needed any such warning.

Ringing the room at eye level were large windows— presumably one-way since he hadn't noticed any windows this high from the outside—through which he could see the *Dewdrop* lying so painfully vulnerable out on the darkened landing field. Below the windows was a ring of monitor displays.

So he'd found the situation room, or at least an auxiliary one. On some of the displays armed men were rushing about madly, and Winward stepped back to the elevator doors to listen. The car was on its way up—filled, no doubt, with suicidal soldiers. Looking around the room, he found the three monitor cameras and put laser bolts into each. Blinder now than he was, they'd just have to guess what he was up to . . . and while they sweated that one, he had a couple more surprises in store for them.

Moving to the side away from the *Dewdrop*, he put his face to the windows there and looked down. He hadn't had much of a look out back before he was shot, but he'd seen *something* . . . and, sure enough, from above he could pick out the heavy guns waiting in the tower's shadow. Ready to be pushed from cover and throw explosives at the ship . . . but only if there was someone there to do the pushing.

The nearest monitor cabinet displayed duplicates of a dozen other screens around the room, as if it was the feeder nexus for another monitor station elsewhere in the building. Winward sent an arcthrower charge into the mechanism to trip out any power lines; then, gripping it firmly, he pulled it out of its wall fastenings and raised it to a precarious balance over his head. The glass—or whatever—of the window was tough: it took nearly fifteen seconds of the Cobra's sonic disruptor. Winward wondered what those below would make of the sudden rain of glass as he stepped to the opening and hurled the cabinet at one of the guns with all the accuracy and strength his Cobra gear could give him.

The startled yelps began the instant before the cabinet smashed into the gun crew; and, simultaneously, the elevator doors across the room slid open. But Winward didn't stay to count the reinforcements. Stepping into the shattered window frame, he turned and jumped in a single motion. His hands grabbed the window's upper edge as he flew past it, changing his direction and angular velocity just enough to pinwheel him neatly onto the tower roof.

And right into the middle of a small crowd who'd apparently rushed over to investigate the commotion below.

Winward didn't bother with lasers or sonics for this group, and they *still* didn't have a chance. Swinging his arms like a servo-powered threshing machine, he hurled them in all directions, bleeding or stunned. The mojos were a different story; but he was getting used to their arch-winged attack, and took a perverse pleasure in burning them out of the air.

And that flicker of overconfidence nearly killed him . . . because four of the Qasaman contingent had stayed by their weapons across the roof, and as Winward looked up from his latest carnage, he found their four mojos arrowing in bare meters away.

His computerized reflexes saved him in that first instant, recognizing the projectile threat and hurling him down and to the side in a flat dive and roll. It was a maneuver he'd experienced innumerable times while fighting spine leopards . . . but neither spine leopards nor the antipersonnel missiles the system had been designed for had the mojos' hairpin maneuverability. Winward had barely rolled back to his feet when the first two birds reached him ... and this time they got through his defenses.

He gasped with shock and pain as talons dug deep into his left forearm, a beak shredding at the makeshift bandage he'd wrapped around the gash there. He twisted his head aside barely in time to avoid the second mojo's slashing attack at his face, but even so its wing caught him full across the eyes, smashing the tip of his nose with stunning force. The last two mojos reached him then, one swooping down to a grip on his right forearm, the other landing on his right shoulder and digging its beak into his cheek.

And Winward went berserk.

He dropped onto his back and slammed both forearms hard onto the rooftop, feeling mojo bones crack under the crushing impact. He smashed them down again and again until the bloodied pulps loosened their grips and fell off. Reaching up with his right hand, he grabbed another mojo by the neck and twisted hard. He heard it snap; and then the last bird was back, diving toward his face. He grabbed for its feet, missed, caught the wings instead, and pulled sideways. One wing tore off, and Winward hurled both pieces from him. Across the roof there was the flash-boom of a gunshot and a bullet whistled past him. Winward swept his antiarmor laser across the crouching gunmen, then leaped to his feet and ran to them.

All four were dead. Winward glared down at them, gasping for air ... and as his rage subsided into the rivers of new pain coming from arms, cheek, and shoulder, his brain began to function again and his eyes searched out the weapons his enemies had been manning.

Mortars, or something very much like them. Simple tubes with a firing mechanism at the bottom, the shells stacked nearby. By inference, they were designed with an equally simple impact detonator. Scooping up an armful, he trotted back to the rear of the roof.

A couple of faces were peering upwards from the window he'd smashed, and his first shell therefore went in there. The explosion blew out a couple more windows, and Winward followed it with one aimed more toward the monitor room's center. Then he turned his attention to the guns and ground crews shooting uselessly at him from below. By the time his arms were empty it was abundantly clear that those cannons wouldn't be firing again for a long time.

Behind him, the roof stairway door slammed open. Winward didn't even bother to look, but grabbed the parapet edge and swung down into the room below. His nanocomputer compensated for a slight overbalance, and he landed among the glass shards on his feet.

The place was a mess. Where the two mortar shells had hit, floor and ceiling were torn and blackened. Dozens of the monitor screens had been smashed by flying debris; the rest were blank. At least six bodies were visible.

I did all this. The thought hit him with unexpected force, sending a queasy shiver through his body. For the first time in his life, he truly understood why the Dominion of Man had won its war against the Trofts . . . and why its citizens had rejected their returning protectors.

Gingerly, he picked his way through the rubble to the elevator and pushed the call button. Risky, perhaps, if the Qasamans hadn't learned yet not to send piles of people against him. But the emotional reaction combined with loss of blood was making him feel light-headed, and for the moment the elevator seemed safer than trying to handle stairs.

An instant later a flash of light from the side caught his eye, and he turned to find the woods beyond the *Dewdrop* on fire.

Involuntarily, he hissed with the fear that he'd been too late, that the ship was being attacked. But on the heels of that came the memory of his instructions to Telek before he left. F'ahl had heard the explosions and obediently swept the forest with laser fire. What it had done to the soldiers waiting there was uncertain; but it had sure as hell not done much for the foliage, and if any surviving Qasamans were still at their posts they were probably thinking more of escape than attack.

Speaking of which. . . .

The elevator car arrived—empty—and he punched the second button from the top. For a wonder, the elevator performed as directed—perhaps the override controls had been on the top floor?—and he bounded out into a small, deserted room.

Deserted, but not quiet. Like the floor above, this one was filled with electronic gear, and from a panel near the middle two voices were speaking.

Propping open the elevator doors, Winward stepped over to the talkative board. Communications, probably, left running when the people on duty heard the ruckus overhead and wisely cut out. He wondered whether the mike at this end was still open, decided there was a simple way to find out. "Can you hear me?" he called.

The voices stopped abruptly. "Who are you?" one of them asked a moment later in passable Anglic.

"Michael Winward, currently in charge of this tower," he said. If he was lucky, they'd tell him why he wasn't really in control yet, and he'd know where he needed to attack next. Link should already be on his way over from the *Dewdrop*; together the two of them should be able to make a respectable showing—

"Michael, this is Almo," Pyre's voice cut unexpectedly into the line. "What's your situation?"

Winward had to try twice to get any words out. "Almo! Where *are* you?"

"In the mayor's underground command center,"

Pyre replied. "Your return from the dead seems to have rattled him somewhat."

Despite his pain and weakness, Winward felt a grim smile spread across his face. Rattled, indeed. Out-and-out terrified, if the man had any sense at all.

Pyre was speaking again. "Now, Mr. Mayor, the situation seems to have changed. I have you, Winward has the tower—"

"He does not control the tower," Kimmeron put in. "I have been speaking to the tower commander—"

"I can take control whenever I wish," Winward interrupted harshly. Pyre was clearly attempting to negotiate with the Qasamans; the stronger the hand Winward could give him, the better the chances he could get back to the ship before he passed out from loss of blood. "And the weapons trained on the *Dewdrop* have been neutralized. F'ahl can lift any time he wants to."

Kimmeron's voice was low, but his words were precise. "You seek to trade your lives for more of ours. I have said that that is an unacceptable bargain. You know too much about us; at whatever additional cost, you must not be allowed to leave."

Winward didn't wait for Pyre's reply, but stepped quickly back into the elevator. In Kimmeron's place he would probably have made the same decision, and before Pyre's negotiations officially broke down he wanted to be on his way back to the *Dewdrop*. The long floor-selection panel gleamed at him as he reached toward it—

And paused.

All those those buttons . . . *far* more than a building this size needed. . . .

Blocking the doors open again, he stepped back into the communications room. Pyre was saying something about mass destruction; Winward didn't bother to let him finish. "Almo?" he called. "Listen—remember the idea someone had that a lot of the Qasaman industry was underground? I think this tower is an entrance to the place. Shall I go out and get Dorjay and head down to take a look?"

He waited, heart pounding, hoping Pyre would know how to use the opening he'd just given him. Winward had a dim idea, but his mind was beginning to fog over, and he knew instinctively he couldn't trust it to follow any straight logical lines. He hoped Pyre was in better shape.

"You seem upset, Mr. Mayor," Pyre's voice came through the fog. "May I assume your underground facilities are something you'd rather we not see?" There was no response, and after a moment Pyre went on, "We *can* get down there, you know. You've seen what we can do, and how little effect your guns have on us. With our ship free and clear, we can go down the tower, take a good look, and still get off Qasama alive."

"We will kill you all," Kimmeron said.

"You know better than that. So I'll offer you a deal: release all our people unharmed and we'll leave without seeing what you've got down there."

Kimmeron's laugh was a harsh bark. "You seek to trade something for a lack of something. Even if I wanted to agree, how could I persuade others to do so?"

"You explain that we take home details of city and village life, or we take home every secret you've got," Pyre told him coldly. "And your time is running out. Winward will start down the tower in three minutes, and I can't guarantee Link won't find his way underground even sooner."

It took the full three minutes and a little more, but in the end Kimmeron agreed.

Chapter 22

It took another fifteen minutes for Kimmeron to get the agreement of the Purma officials who were holding Cerenkov and Rynstadt. The radio jamming wasn't lifted for five minutes longer, but Pyre had already been allowed to send Link a message via the tower's outside speakers, warning the other Cobra to lie low and hold off on any attack. Telek, when Pyre was finally allowed through to her, agreed to the arrangement and directed Link to wait in the tower with Winward until Pyre made it back. Then, with Kimmeron his reluctant companion, Pyre got into a car and headed down the broad avenues toward the airfield . . . and waited with lasers ready for the inevitable ambush.

It didn't come. The car passed through several sets of sentries, none of whom even raised a weapon; passed beneath tall buildings without so much as a brick being thrown; passed even among the grim mass of Qasamans at the base of the airfield tower. Nothing. They pulled up to the *Dewdrop*'s main hatch, and Pyre waited with Kimmeron close beside him until Winward and Link returned.

The two Cobras entered the ship, and Pyre turned to Kimmeron. "We've completed our part of the deal," he said, putting as much quiet steel as he could into the words. "You've done half of yours. I trust you won't be tempted to back out."

"Your two companions will be waiting when you land at Purma," Kimmeron said coldly.

"Good. Now take the car and get clear before we lift." Pyre stepped into the hatchway, and the airlock door closed.

The inner door slid open, and in that same moment the *Dewdrop* lurched slightly and they were airborne.

Link was waiting as Pyre stepped into the ready room. "Looks like we might actually pull this off," the younger Cobra said quietly.

"Heavy emphasis on the *might*," Pyre nodded. "How's Michael? He looked in pretty bad shape when you passed me out there."

"I don't know—the governor's looking at him now. Probably in better shape than Decker."

"Yes, what happened to him? I saw him carried away from the bus on a stretcher, but I couldn't tell anything more."

Link's lip twitched in a grimace. "He tried to break the contact team out of the bus at the beginning of all this. The mojos flayed his arm, practically down to the bone."

Pyre felt his neck muscles tighten. "Oh, God. Is he—?"

"Too soon to tell anything, except that he'll probably live." Link licked his lips. "Listen . . . did Kimmeron say anything about Justin? He switched with Joshua when they brought Decker in and was taken off toward Purma."

For the unprovoked deaths in Purma, Kimmeron had said, sentencing the *Dewdrop* to death. Justin's work? Undoubtedly. But Kimmeron hadn't mentioned him in negotiating the other prisoners' release. Was he, then, free somewhere out in the Qasaman night?

Or was he dead?

"Kimmeron didn't say," he told Link slowly. It had

happened, his mind told him vaguely; the danger to Justin he'd worried about all the way back at the beginning of this mission. "Well. First things first, I suppose. We'll land at Purma, get Yuri and Marck safely aboard ... and then try to find out what we can about him."

"Yeah." Link searched his face another moment, then nodded. "Yeah. Come on, let's get back to the lounge, find out what's happening."

"Sure." Back to the lounge, where Joshua would be waiting. . . . But Pyre wouldn't have to tell him his brother might be dead. Not yet, anyway.

Strapped tightly into the highly uncomfortable interrogation chair, Rynstadt stared at the door through which his questioners had left, trying to keep his expression neutral for the cameras he could see focused on him.

It wasn't an easy task. The questioning had been loud and brutal, and it'd been a relief when the four Qasamans abruptly switched off the painful strobe lights and left the room. But as the minutes had dragged on and he'd had time to pull himself together, their continued absence began to seem increasingly ominous. What were they preparing for him that took a half hour to set up? Shock treatments? Sonics? Maybe even something as crude—and horrible—as slow dismemberment? His stomach churned at the thought. Death—fast death—he'd been willing to risk for the opportunity of coming to Qasama. Slow torture was something else entirely ... and he knew far more about Aventinian technology than he really wanted to tell them.

Without warning the door swung open, causing Rynstadt to jerk against his restraints. Two of the four interrogators entered and stepped over to him. For a moment they stared down at him, Rynstadt forcing himself to return their gaze. Then, still wordlessly, they bent down and began unstrapping him.

Here it comes, Rynstadt thought, steeling himself. The torture chamber had been readied, and he was about to find out what they'd come up with.

The Qasamans finished their task; but even as Rynstadt uncramped his legs and got them under him the men turned and left. The door banged shut, and he was left standing there, alone.

It made no sense to his befuddled mind, but they didn't give him time to wonder. "Rynstadt," a hidden speaker boomed, "your companions have bargained for your release. You will be allowed to eat and drink and then be taken to city's edge."

The speaker went off with a loud click, and simultaneously a slot in the base of the door opened and a steaming tray was pushed through.

None of this made any sense, either. What did the *Dewdrop* have to bargain with that the Qasamans would consider worth Rynstadt's life? But at the sight of the food, one clear thought cut through the confusion in his mind.

Poison.

The stew and hot berry juice were poisoned . . . and he would soon tell them anything they wanted to know in exchange for the antidote. Or else he really *was* being released, in which case he'd be dead before the *Dewdrop* cleared the system, in a final act of Qasaman vengeance.

His stomach rumbled, reminding him he hadn't eaten since lunch in Huriseem, a medium-sized eternity ago . . . and on closer examination, poisoning him *did* seem a little melodramatic.

Again his stomach growled. Suppose he simply refused to eat? If the food was indeed safe, probably nothing, except that he'd go hungry. If it was poisoned . . . presumably they'd come and hypospray the stuff into him.

Walking over to the tray, he picked it up and sniffed cautiously at the bowl and mug. He'd had the stew and juice several times before during the contact team's tour, and both smelled just the way he remembered. For a long moment he was tempted ... but if there was really a chance for freedom, he'd be foolish to take even slim risks. "Thanks," he called to the hidden mike as he set the tray back on the floor by the slot, "but I'm not hungry right now."

He held his breath. If the Qasaman voice sounded angry or annoyed ... "Very well," the other said simply. The slot opened again, and Rynstadt glanced down to see a hand snare the tray and pull it back out of sight.

A *shiny* hand.

A hand encased in a surgeon's glove.

The slot cover slid back in place, and Rynstadt walked back to the chair, feeling cold all over. Poison, for sure—but not in the food. On the tray. Mixed with a contact absorption enhancer and spread on the tray.

And now it was on his hands ... and in his blood.

He sat down, legs trembling with reaction. He *was*, then, being released—there was no need for such an elaborate subterfuge if the poison was just part of his interrogation. Released—and simultaneously murdered. Melodramatic or not—barbaric or not—they had opted for vengeance.

Was there any chance at all of coming through this alive? Perhaps, but only if the Qasamans had timed their dosage so as to let the *Dewdrop* get a good distance away before their treachery became known. How long? One hour? Two? Twelve?

There was no way to know. But the fact that he knew he'd been poisoned gave Telek and the medical analyzers aboard ship the maximum time to identify and counteract the specific toxin used on him.

Come on, he urged the Dewdrop silently. *Get me the hell out of here*. In the meantime ... letting his body slump in the chair, he consciously slowed his breathing. The slower the metabolism, in theory, the slower the poison would be absorbed into his tissues.

And he settled back to wait.

*   *   *

The distinctive whine of gravity lifts, faint even in his enhanced hearing, finally dragged Justin from his sleep. For a moment he lay quietly in the tall grass, reorienting himself, allowing the bitter memories to return. Then, carefully, he raised his head.

The motion drew an involuntary hiss between his teeth; he'd forgotten all the places his body ached. But the sight in the northern sky drove all such considerations into the background. Against the blazing stars of Qasama's night a hazy reddish oval was drifting.

The *Dewdrop* was making a break for it.

He watched the haze for a long minute, teeth clamped together as he tried not to cry. They were leaving. Without him. Without Cerenkov and Rynstadt, as well? Probably. There was no way to know for sure; but Telek had counted on him to rescue them, and his failure probably meant they were all marooned.

Marooned.

Automatically, as if trying to insulate itself from the emotional shock, his mind began tracing out his options. He could escape into the forest, living off the wild game there, and hope he could hold out until the military expedition that would surely follow. Or he could try to find a village that would trade his Cobra skills for sanctuary from the central authorities. Or—

Or he could just stay here in the grass until he died. It all amounted to that in the end.

It was only then that the realization broke through to him that the *Dewdrop* was moving too slowly.

Much too slowly. *They crippled it*, was his first, awful thought . . . but if the grav lifts had been damaged F'ahl should have kicked in the main drive by now to assist. No, something else was happening . . . and abruptly, he understood.

They were flying low and slow on purpose. Looking for *him*.

He'd rolled over on his back in an instant, glancing toward the city as he lifted his left leg, but not really caring if anyone there spotted his signal. In a few minutes the *Dewdrop* would be here . . . and after his moments of despair the promise of rescue was flooding his mind and body with adrenaline-fueled determination. Let the Qasamans come for him now—let the whole *city* get in his way if they wanted to.

Targeting the *Dewdrop*, he fired his antiarmor laser three times.

Thirty kilometers away, the ship's hull would barely register the heat of those shots; but for the watchers aboard, the flashes of light should be impossible to miss. Assuming someone *was* watching.

And apparently they were. From the front-inside of the red oval the *Dewdrop*'s landing lights flicked twice in acknowledgment. Shifting to a crouch, Justin got ready to move, keeping alert for trouble from the city.

It took the *Dewdrop* a few minutes to come to ground—and it did so, inexplicably, a good kilometer north. Justin briefly considered signaling again, decided it would be safer to just go to it, and set off in a crouching run.

No one opened fire before he reached the ship. Link was waiting by the open hatchway as he came up, and favored the younger man with a tight smile. "Welcome back," he said, gripping Justin's hand briefly. He gave the other a fast once-over before returning his eyes to the city. "You've never seen a group of people so happy as when we saw your signal."

"I was happy enough for all of you put together," Justin told him, following Link's gaze. A half-dozen cars and a bus could be seen approaching from city's edge. "Looks like a good time to get out of here."

Link shook his head. "They're bringing Yuri and Marck—Almo struck a deal for their release."

"What kind of deal?" Justin frowned.

"A sort of promise not to tear up their industrial base before we go." Link glanced at the other. "Why

don't you go inside, get any injuries seen to. I can
handle this."

"Well . . . all right." Something about this felt
wrong, but for the moment Justin couldn't figure out
what. Turning, he stepped into the hatch and sprung
the inner door—and walked straight into his brother's arms.

For a minute they just held each other—the man
who'd done his job, Justin thought bitterly, and the
man who hadn't.

But for the moment his shame was swallowed up
in the relief of being safe again.

Joshua released him and stepped back, still gripping his brother's shoulders. "You hurt anywhere?"

"I'm fine," Justin shook his head. "What's happened since I left?"

Joshua glanced toward the hatch. "Let's get to the
lounge where we can watch that convoy," he suggested. "I can give you a fast rundown on the way."

They reached the lounge a minute later to find
Nnamdi and Christopher gazing at the outside monitors, the scientists' greetings muted by their attention being elsewhere. That suited Justin; he'd already
had more of a hero's welcome than he properly de-
served. "Where's the governor?" he asked Joshua as
they took seats in front of another screen.

"Back in sick bay with Michael. She should be
back by the time the others get here. And Almo's
outside, behind the front landing spotlights, where
he can back up Dorjay if the Qasamans make any
trouble."

"But they won't," Nnamdi spoke up. "They've made
their deal, and it's a fair one. And we've already seen
they follow through on their promises."

Justin snorted. "Like with that fake explosive
collar?"

All eyes turned to him. "What do you mean, fake?"
Christopher asked.

"I mean they suckered us royally. Those cylinders

held cameras and recorders, not explosives. They let Joshua come in so that they could get a quick look inside the *Dewdrop*."

Christopher swore under his breath. "But then they must have seen you two switch places. My *God*—you're lucky you got out alive after that."

Some of the burden seemed to lift from Justin's conscience. Seen in *that* light, perhaps he hadn't done such a bad job, after all.

The convoy outside had halted a hundred meters from the *Dewdrop* and a crowd of Qasamans was forming around the vehicles when Telek reappeared in the lounge. "Justin; glad you made it," she said distractedly as she leaned over Christopher's shoulder. "Any sign of them yet?"

"I don't see them," he replied. "They're probably in the bus off to one side, there." He pointed; and as if on cue, two figures emerged from the vehicle, struggling a bit as they plowed through the knee-high grass.

Cerenkov and Rynstadt.

The edge of the crowd withdrew a bit as the two men passed on their way to the *Dewdrop*. "Watch for drawn weapons," Telek said to the room in general. "We don't want them pulling a last-minute suicide rush or some such trick."

"If they were going to pull something, wouldn't they have done it while they still had Almo, Michael, and Dorjay under the gun?" Nnamdi suggested.

"Maybe," Telek grunted. "But we were hair-trigger alert then. Maybe they expect us to be lulled now. Anyway, I don't trust them—they accepted this deal too easily for my taste."

"Like they accepted my ultimatum to bring Decker back," Joshua muttered. Justin looked at his brother, found him staring at the approaching men with a look of intense concentration on his face.

Telek glanced in the twins' direction. "Something?"

"Tell her, Justin," Joshua said, eyes and frown still on the display.

Justin explained again about the spy collar. "Um," Telek grunted when he'd finished. "You think they've planted a bomb or something on one of them, Joshua?"

"I don't know," Joshua said slowly. "But I suddenly don't like this."

"Me, neither." Telek hesitated, then picked up the mike and punched for the outside speakers. "Yuri, Marck? Hold it there a second, would you?"

The two men came to a hesitant looking halt about twenty meters from the hatch. "Governor? What's wrong?" Cerenkov called.

"I want you both to strip to your underwear," she told them. "Safety precaution."

Rynstadt glanced back over his shoulder at the silent Qasamans. "Can't we skip that?" he called, his voice almost breaking with strain. "They didn't put anything in our clothes—I'm sure of that. Please—let us get aboard."

"Something's wrong," Christopher muttered. Grabbing the mike from Telek, he punched a new button. "Dorjay, signal them to tell you—*quietly*—what's going on." Without waiting for an acknowledgment he switched back to the outside speaker. "Come on, guys—you heard the governor. Strip."

Flicking off the speaker, he handed the mike silently back to Telek, who accepted it the same way. On the screen, the two men were pulling off their tunics; and because he knew to watch for it, Justin could see Rynstadt's lips moving. They were working on their boots when Link's voice came quietly into the circuit. "Marck says they've both been poisoned— some sort of toxin on a meal tray that the server wore gloves to avoid touching."

"No wonder they were so willing to let them go," Nnamdi growled. "We've got to get them aboard right away and into the analyzer, Governor."

But Telek was staring through the screen, her face frozen into a mask of horror. "They're not poisoned," she whispered. "They're *infected*. They've dosed them with something to kill all of us."

For a long moment shock hung thickly in the air. Telek recovered first. "Almo, get back in here—use the cargo hatch you went out by. Dorjay . . . come inside and seal the outer door. Now."

"What?" Christopher and Joshua yelped in unison.

"No choice," Telek snapped back. Her hand was white-knuckled where she clutched the mike, and her face looked very old. "We haven't got isolation facilities aboard—you all know that."

"The medical analyzer—"

"Has an even chance of not even figuring out what they've been given," she cut Christopher off, "let alone knowing how to cure it."

Beneath his feet, Justin felt the deck vibrate slightly as Pyre closed the cargo hatch; an instant later it was echoed as Link sealed the main hatchway.

And on the outer display, Rynstadt and Cerenkov froze in horrified disbelief. "Hey!" Cerenkov yelled.

"I'm sorry," Telek said, the words almost a sigh. She seemed to remember the mike, lifted it to her lips. "I'm sorry," she repeated. "You've been infected. We can't risk taking you aboard."

"Guns being drawn!" Nnamdi said abruptly. "They know we've figured it out."

"Captain—comm laser on the Qasamans," Telek snapped toward the intercom. "Dazzle them. Then . . . then prepare to lift."

"You can't leave them here."

Justin hadn't even noticed Pyre's entry into the lounge, but his voice made it clear he'd been there long enough to know what was happening.

And that he wasn't going to accept it.

Telek turned to face him, but there was no fight in her eyes. "Give me an alternative," she said quietly. "Put them in spacesuits for two weeks?—and watch them die there because we can't get to them to even attempt treatment?"

"The rest of us could stay in suits," Pyre said.

"Oxygen wouldn't last long enough," F'ahl said from the bridge. "And recharging in a contaminated atmosphere would be damned risky."

The display screens lit up briefly as comm laser fire swept the Qasamans. Rynstadt and Cerenkov broke their paralysis as the sound of gunshots and mojo screams became audible, the two men dashing for the *Dewdrop*'s tail. Heading for what cover the ship would provide, Justin guessed . . . until it lifted into space away from them.

And suddenly he had it.

"Almo!" he shouted, interrupting Telek but not caring. "Two spacesuits—out the cargo hatch. Hurry."

"Justin, I just got done saying—" Telek began.

"We can lift with them in the hold," Justin continued, the words tripping over each other as he tried to get them out as fast as possible. "The hold's got an airseal—we can evacuate it and set up UVs to sterilize the outsides of the suits."

"And watch them die in there?" Telek snarled. "The hold hasn't even got a true airlock, and we haven't got the facilities—"

"*But the Troft ships out there do!*" Justin shouted back.

And the lounge was abruptly quiet, save for the deep hum of the idling gravity lifts and the fading sounds of Pyre's running footsteps down the hall.

Three minutes later, in a highly inaccurate rain of bullets from the Qasamans, the *Dewdrop* lifted and made for the starry sky. An hour after that, Cerenkov and Rynstadt were inside a Troft warship's isolation facility, prognosis uncertain.

An hour after that, the *Dewdrop* was in hyperspace, heading for home.

Chapter 23

The *Menssana* had returned from its survey mission to Aventine to the sort of welcome explorers throughout the ages must have received. Its personnel were received with an official vote of congratulations by the Council, its magdisks of data copied and disseminated to hundreds of eager scientists around the planet.

The *Dewdrop*'s reception, two days later, was considerably more subdued.

The last page of Telek's preliminary report vanished from the comboard screen, and Corwin put the instrument aside with a sigh.

"Reaction?"

Corwin looked up to meet his father's eyes. "They were lucky," he said bluntly. "They should all have been killed out there."

Jonny nodded. "Yes. The Qasamans' only error was that they wanted as much information as they could get before destroying the mission. If they hadn't cared they could have blown up the *Dewdrop* any of a dozen different times."

Corwin grimaced. York's arm gone, Winward's eyes only slowly coming back, Cerenkov and Rynstadt still in critical condition aboard an orbiting Troft ship—and with all of that, he could still consider the mission *lucky*. "What in heaven's name have we gotten ourselves into?" he muttered.

"A real mess." Jonny sighed. "How long before Sun and company finish with their debriefing? Any idea?"

"Uh . . ." Corwin retrieved his comboard, punched up a request. "Not before this evening. And they're not releasing anyone to the public until morning."

"That's okay; we're not public." The elder Moreau stared into space a moment. "I want you to call your mother and arrange with her to go to the Cobra Academy tonight—use my name to get in, and if they give you any interference quote 'em some next-of-kin perogatives—I'm sure you can find *something* applicable on the books. Don't talk politics with your brothers, and don't keep them up too late; life'll get hectic again for them when the Council gets its turn tomorrow."

Corwin nodded. "Will you be there, too?"

"Yes, but don't wait for me. I've got a couple of errands to do first."

"Alone?"

Jonny gave his eldest a lopsided smile. "My joints just had a nice vacation on sunny worlds. I can face Aventine's winter on my own for a few hours, thank you."

Corwin shrugged. "Just asking."

But he lingered in the outer office long enough to hear Yutu make arrangements with the starfield for a ground-to-orbit shuttle. His father, it appeared, would not have to worry much about Aventine's winter tonight.

Winter, as such, didn't exist aboard Troft warships.

For the fourth time in almost that many minutes the comboard screen seemed to blur in front of Telek's eyes; and for the fourth time she shook her head stubbornly and swallowed a mouthful of cahve. It was late, she was tired, and she would need to be at least marginally coherent for the Council meeting in the morning. But this was the first chance she'd had to see the *Menssana*'s report, and she was determined to have at least a passing acquaintance with what they'd found before she checked out for the night.

There was a light tap at the door. "Come," she called.

It wasn't, as she'd expected, one of the Academy medical staff. "The nurses at the monitor station are annoyed you haven't gone to sleep yet," Jonny commented as he walked into the room.

She blinked, then snorted. "They brought you all the way from Capitalia to tell me that?"

"Hardly. I was in the neighborhood and thought I'd drop in." Pulling up a chair, he sat down.

Telek nodded. "They did good. You can be damn proud of them."

"I know. Though Justin doesn't think so."

"Well, he's wrong," Telek growled. "If he'd tried to get to Purma's underground stuff, he wouldn't have made it out alive. Period. And if he hadn't made it out, we might have taken Yuri and Marck aboard before we knew how the Qasamans like to stack their deals."

"I understand that. He will too, eventually. I hope." Jonny waved toward her comboard. "The *Menssana*'s report?"

"Uh-huh. You people did pretty well yourselves."

Jonny nodded. "They all look promising," he agreed. "At least two are better even than that."

Telek looked him in the eye. "I want those worlds, Jonny."

He returned the gaze without flinching. "Badly enough to fight a war for?"

"Badly enough to do whatever we have to," she said bluntly.

He sighed. "I'd rather hoped that what happened on Qasama would have blunted your eagerness a bit."

"It's made me aware of what it'll cost. But the option is the loss of the last nineteen thousand people on Caelian."

"Or so goes the argument. They *can* always move back here, you know."

"But they won't. Anyone who was willing to lose that much face by admitting defeat has already done so. We can't move the rest of them back to civilization—their pride won't take it."

"Whereas *your* pride won't let you turn tail on the Qasamans?" he countered.

"Pride has nothing to do with it."

"Sure." Reaching into his tunic, Jonny produced a magdisk and handed it to her. "Well, whatever your motives, as long as you're solidly hell-bent on smashing Qasama, you might as well know as much about the place as possible."

Telek frowned at the disk. "What's this?"

"The official Baliu'ckha'spmi report on Qasama."

She looked up at him, feeling her mouth fall open. "It's *what*? Where did you get it?"

"From the Troft ship out there," he replied. "Clearly, any ship sent to back up our mission would have their own world's report aboard for emergency reference. So I went up this afternoon and got a copy."

"Just like that?"

"More or less. A combination of bluff, bluster, and legal footwork." He smiled faintly. "Plus a healthy new respect for us on their part."

"God knows we earned *that* much," she said quietly. York and Winward alone had earned them at least that much. . . . She shook off the sudden resurgence of guilt for her failures on the trip. "So why give it to me?"

"Oh, the whole Council will get copies in the morning," he shrugged. "As I said, I was in the neighborhood."

"Yeah. Well . . . thanks."

"No charge." Jonny got to his feet—wincing with

the effort, she noticed—and walked to the door. There he paused and looked back at her. "Lizabet ... I'm not going to let the Worlds go to war for your new planets," he told her quietly. "Not after what we've seen of Qasama. A surgical strike against their technological base, perhaps, if feasible; aerial bombings, probably, if it'll actually do any good. But no land war. Not even for Caelian."

She nodded slightly. "I understand. And I'm as willing to look for middle ground as you are."

"Let's hope we can find it. Good night."

He left, and Telek found herself staring at the Troft magdisk in her hand. Suddenly she was very, very tired. . . .

Ejecting the *Menssana*'s report, she inserted the Trofts' into her comboard, keying to run it through the Academy's central translator. Then, sighing wearily, she splashed more cahve into her mug and began to read.

Chapter 24

The Council meeting was postponed two days, to give the members a chance to read both the Qasama Mission debriefing and the Troft data package Jonny had obtained. But when the debate finally began it was quickly and abundantly clear that the cautious approval that had existed for the original mission had flipped solidly in the opposite direction.

And it wasn't hard to figure out why.

"If the damn planet wasn't a lost human colony no one would be nearly this emotional about the whole thing," Dylan Fairleigh growled afterward as the governors gathered for their own meeting.

"Neither of the Caelian syndics was complaining," Vartanson pointed out quietly. "We know what the trade-off is here."

"Us or them?" Jonny asked. "Is that it? Come on, now—we don't even know why the Trofts are so worried about Qasama."

"Don't we?" Roi shot back. "A thriving, highly cooperative, highly *paranoid* human culture? That's not something to be afraid of?"

"A culture without starflight, without even system space travel?" Hemner quavered.

"We don't *know* they don't have spaceflight capability," Fairleigh reminded him tartly. His eyes flicked to Jonny. "There's a *lot* we don't know about their industrial and technological base. That we *should* have found out."

Jonny bristled; but Telek got her word in first. "If that's a slur on my team in general and Justin Moreau in particular, you're invited to withdraw it," she said coldly.

"I only meant—"

"If you'd like, *you* can head the next trip to Qasama," she cut him off. "We'll see then how well *you* do."

Stiggur chose that moment to make his own belated entrance, his presence stifling the budding argument. "Good afternoon; sorry I'm late," he said with an air of harried distraction as he sat down at his place and pushed a pile of magdisks into the center of the table. "Preliminary biological data analysis—just came in. Summary in the front. Take a quick look and we'll discuss it."

It was, as Jonny had expected, an analysis of the *Dewdrop* and Troft data, concentrating on the mojos. He skimmed the summary and was halfway through a more careful study when Vartanson harrumphed. "Nasty. Reminds me of some of the feathered killing machines we have on Caelian."

"Aside from the weird reproductive setup, I presume," Roi said. "The whole arrangement looks pretty fragile to me. Kill off enough of their embryo-hosts— these whatyoucallem, these tarbines—and you could wipe out the species overnight."

"Most ecosystems look that unstable at first glance," Telek put in dryly. "In practice, you'd find you'd need to kill a *hell* of a lot of tarbines to make any real dent. I take it, though, that you feel the mojos to be the major threat to any Cobra forces we put down there?"

"No question," Roi said. "Look at the record. No one except Winward suffered any appreciable damage from the Qasamans' guns, and that single case was a surprise attack. But the mojos got him *and* York and came close with Pyre and Moreau."

"They really *are* the first line of defense," Fairleigh agreed. "And the Qasamans know it. Hell, they design their *cities* to keep the things happy."

"Makes sense, of course," Stiggur said with a shrug. "Why risk human deaths in a battle when you've got animals to take the brunt of the attack?"

"That's not how the arrangement began," said Telek. "It was originally for defense against predators and evolved into a personal bodyguard system."

"And now shows itself easily adapted to warfare," Stiggur said. "The history doesn't concern us as much as the current situation does." He turned to Jonny. "Is there any way you know of to make the Cobra equipment better able to deal with the mojos? Some change in the targeting mechanism, for instance?"

Jonny shrugged. "The targeting procedure is designed to allow fast target acquisition while minimizing accidental lock-ons. Make it any easier and faster and you'll automatically get more misfires."

"Then how about reprogramming the nanocomputer to identify mojos as hostile?" Fairleigh suggested. "That way at least the next generation of Cobras could handle them."

Vartanson snorted. "If that could be done, don't you think we'd already have something like that for the Caelian Cobras? Shape recognition just takes up too much computer memory."

"It's actually more basic than that," Jonny shook his head. "The minute you put some kind of automatic recognition targeting into the Cobras, you rob them of their versatility and, ultimately, their effectiveness. Once the Qasamans figured it out, they could throw birds by the hundreds at us, and while we're helplessly shooting down ones who couldn't even get near us for three minutes, the Qasaman gunners shoot us at their leisure. Automatic single-purpose weapons are fine in their place—and you're using them quite effectively on Caelian—but don't try to make them out of Cobras."

There was a moment's silence. "Sorry," Jonny muttered. "Didn't mean to lecture."

Stiggur waved the apology aside. "The point was reasonable and well taken. I don't think anyone wants to have specialized cadres of Cobras. So. Is there some other way to reduce the mojos' effectiveness?"

"Excuse me for changing the subject," Hemner spoke up hesitantly, "but there are still some points about Qasama generally that bother me. History, Brom, you implied wasn't important, but I'd like to know a little about the colony's background. Specifically, how and when it came to be."

"I didn't mean history wasn't *important*." Stiggur poked at his comboard. "Only that—oh, never mind. Let's see. The historians' report indicates the original Qasamans left the Dominion circa 2160, probably as colonists bound from Reginine for Rajput. The direction vector is about right, and the various historical references and language—not to mention the name Qasama itself—all point to one of Reginine's basic subcultures."

"The *name* Qasama?" Vartanson frowned.

"You've *got* this report yourselves," Stiggur said, a bit tartly. " 'Qasama' is an Old Arabic word meaning 'to divide.' It's come into Anglic through a couple of different languages and changes to become 'kismet,' meaning 'fate' or 'destiny.' "

"Divided by destiny," Roi murmured. "Some linguist aboard the original ship had a strange sense of humor."

"Or sense of manifest destiny," Telek said, half to herself. "I never saw a scrap of evidence the Qasamans had any humor whatsoever. They took themselves incredibly seriously."

"Fine," Hemner said. "So Qasama's been in existence for something under three hundred years, and in that time the mojos and humans have become symbiotically entwined. Correct?"

"Correct," Stiggur nodded. "Though 'symbiosis' might be too strong a word."

"Oh?" Hemner raised an eyebrow. "The people kill the tarbines' protector bololins so that the mojos can breed more easily; in turn the mojos protect their owners from attack. What's that if not symbiosis? But my real question is what did the mojos do before humans came along?"

All eyes shifted to Telek. "Lizabet?" Stiggur prompted. "Any ideas?"

"Not off hand," she answered slowly, a frown creasing her forehead. "Huh. Never even occurred to me to wonder about that. Have to be a predator, certainly—a *big* one, to deal with the bololins. I'll have to check the Troft records, see how many likely candidates there are."

"If you'll forgive me," Roi put in, "I don't see that this is a vital part of figuring out how to stop the mojos now that they *are* riding around on the Qasamans' shoulders."

"If you'll forgive *me*," Telek shot back, "one never knows in this business where a key fact will show up."

She launched into a mini-lecture abut the interdependence of biological structure and function with ecological position, but Jonny missed most of it. Skimming the Qasaman biological data, he hit a small sentence that brought his eyes and mind to a screeching halt. He backed up and read the section carefully . . . and a not-quite-understood shiver went up his spine.

Stiggur was saying something mollifying when Jonny's attention returned to the group. He waited until the governor-general was finished and then spoke up before anyone else could do so. "Lizabet, have you had time to study the fauna records the *Menssana* brought back? Specifically, the ones from the planet Chata?"

"I glanced through them." Her expression said *you know I did*, but the thought remained unsaid. "You driving at anything specific?"

"Yes." Jonny tapped keys to send the two pages he'd been looking at to the others' displays. "On the left is our profile of the flatfoot quadruped of Chata; on the right, yours of the Qasaman bololin. If you'd all take a moment to scan the two pages, I think you'll see what I mean."

"Interesting," Vartanson nodded a minute later. "A lot of similarity there."

"In particular the use of magnetic field lines for navigation," Telek agreed. "Highly unusual for large land animals. Probably a classic example of the Trofts' so-called common-stock theory—you know, the same argument as to why we get similar flora and fauna on Aventine, Palatine, and Caelian."

"Uh-huh," Jonny said. He'd found the other two pages he needed and now put them on the displays. "Okay, then, how about the mojo on the right and *this* bird on the left?"

Fairleigh snorted. "From a binocular photo and computer-generated views? Even *I* know you need more than that for a similarity study."

Jonny kept his eyes on Telek. "Lizabet?"

"Both predators," she said slowly. "Beaks and wing coverts very similar. Feet . . . not enough detail, but . . . interesting. Those short filaments coming off the crown and lore—here and here? The mojo's got some sort of vibrissae there, too; tied somehow into its auditory system, we think. Unless that's a false construct generated by the computer. Where did you spot this—oh, there it is. Tacta. The last planet on your survey, right?"

"Right," Jonny said absently. So the mojos were apparently close cousins to the strange bird whose behavior had spooked them off its world. Which meant . . . what?

"For the moment, at least," Stiggur said, "Lizabet

is right that the mojo data needs more detailed study before we can discuss a counter to them. So I'd like to move on to a strategic discussion of the society itself, particularly the structural aspects that we already know. Uh ... let's see ... right: page 162 is where it starts."

The discussion lasted nearly an hour, and despite the relatively raw state of the data a picture emerged which Jonny found as depressing from a military standpoint as it possibly could have been. "Let's see if I've got all this straight," he said at the end, trying to go as easy as he could on the heavy sarcasm. "We have a society whose members all regularly carry firearms, whose population is largely spread out in small villages, whose light industry is also solidly decentralized and whose heavy industry is buried deep underground, and whose exact technological level is still unknown. Does that pretty well cover it?"

"Don't forget their willingness to use brain-boosting drugs and to hell with the personal consequences," Roi growled. "And all of them hellbent paranoids on top of it. You know, Brom, the more we get into this, the less I like the idea of them sitting out there ready to explode across space as soon as they reinvent the stardrive."

"You sound as if they'll be orbiting us the next morning," Hemner said. He coughed, twice, the spasms shaking his thin shoulders, but when he continued his voice was firm enough. "Qasama is forty-five light-years away, remember—it'll take them *years* to find us, even if they're specifically looking. Long before that they'll run into the Trofts, and whether they begin trade or warfare they'll be tied up with them for generations. By then they'll have forgotten this little fiasco and we'll be able to start fresh with our brother humans as if this had never happened."

"A nice speech, Jor," Telek said tartly, "but you're missing a few rather vital points. One: What if they hit Chata and the other worlds out there *before* they find the Trofts?"

"What of it?" Hemner replied. "If we quit the job now our people won't be out there, anyway."

Telek's lip might have twitched, but her voice was even enough as she continued. "Second is your assumption the Qasamans will forget us. Wrong. They'll remember, all right, and whether it's a year or a century they'll brace for war the minute they run into us again. You may not believe that," she added, glancing around the table, "but it's true. *I* was there; *I* saw and heard the way they talk. You wait until Hersh Nnamdi's final report is in, see if he doesn't agree with me on that. And third: We let them get off Qasama and we're in for a long and very bloody war indeed. Our current technological edge is meaningless with brain-boosters in the picture—a few months or years of warfare and they'll be at our level, whatever it is at the time. And if you think they're decentralized *now* wait'll they're dug in on Kubha and Tacta and God knows where else."

"Your points are certainly valid," Stiggur said as Telek paused. "But all your tactical arguments miss the one big emotional stumbling block we're going to face here. Namely, are the Cobra Worlds *really* going to fight as Troft mercenaries against other human beings?"

"That's a rather inflammatory way of putting it," Vartanson accused.

"Of course it is. But it's the way that side of the issue is going to present their case. And in all honesty, I have to admit it's a valid point. We started this whole affair worrying about looking weak in the Trofts' eyes, if you'll recall, and a world's ethics are certainly part of its total strength. Besides, wouldn't we actually be adding to our position to have other human allies on the Troft border?"

"You're ignoring history, Brom," Jonny put in quietly. "Having two human groups on their borders is

precisely what got the Troft demesnes worried enough
to jointly prepare for war fourteen years ago."

Fairleigh snorted. "There's a good-sized difference
between the Dominion of Man and Qasama as far as
border threats go."

"Only in magnitude. And remember that Trofts
don't go in for mass destruction from starships. They
make war by going in and physically occupying territory . . . and Qasama would *not* be a fun place to go
in and occupy."

"Agreed," Telek murmured with a slight shudder.

"Or in other words," Hemner said, "the Trofts can't
bring themselves to slaughter, so they're hiring *us* to
do it for them."

Several voices tried to answer; Vartanson's was
the one that got through. "For*get* the Trofts for a
minute—just forget them. We're talking about a threat
to *us*, damn it. Lizabet is right—we've got to deal
with them, and we've got to deal with them *now*."

For a long moment the small room was quiet. Jonny
glanced at Hemner, but the old man was staring
down at his hands, clenched together on the table.
Stiggur eventually broke the silence. "I think we've
done about as much as we can with the data at
hand," he said, looking at each of the others in slow,
measured turn. "The final geological, biological, and
sociological studies are due in ten days; we'll meet
then—prior to a full Council meeting—and try to
come to a decision." Reaching to the side of his
display, he shut off the sealed recorder. "This meeting is adjourned."

Chapter 25

Stiggur's prediction of the opposition's tactical methods took only a few days to be borne out; and as he had when the Qasaman story first broke weeks earlier, Corwin abruptly found himself in the middle of the whole public debate.

But with a difference. Before, Qasama had been seen as little more than a mathematical equation: an abstract challenge on one hand, with the very concrete hope of more than doubling the Cobra Worlds' land holdings on the other. Now the comfortable fog was gone. As details of Qasama's people and dangers were released, a growing emotional fire began to simmer within even the most logical and rational arguments, both pro and anti. Most of the antis Corwin talked to were only marginally mollified by the assurance that Jonny was also against a massive war with other humans, their attitude usually being that he should be doing more to bring the Council over to that point of view. The pros tended simply to ignore such sticky ethical questions while claiming that the Cobra Worlds' own safety should be Jonny's first priority. It made for a verbal no-win situation, and within three days Corwin was heartily sick of it.

But it wasn't until he got a call from Joshua that

he realized just how much the phone and public information net had again taken over his life.

"Have you had a chance to see Justin lately?" Joshua asked after the amenities were out of the way.

"Not since the evening after your debriefing." Corwin winced at that sudden revelation. Four days, it had been now, without talking to *anyone* in his family except his father. He wasn't used to getting so far out of touch. "I haven't had much time lately."

"Well, I think you'd better find the time for this. Soon."

Corwin frowned. "Why? Something wrong?"

Joshua's phone screen image hesitated, shook its head minutely. "I don't know. It's nothing I can put my finger on, but . . . well, he hasn't come back from the Academy yet, you know."

Corwin didn't. "Medical observation?"

"No, but he's spending almost all his time alone in the room they've given him out there. And he's doing a lot of computer library searches."

Corwin thought back to Justin's report, which he'd hurriedly skimmed and filed away two days ago. His brother had gone through hell's own porch out there . . . "Maybe he's just killing time while the emotional wounds heal over a bit," he suggested. But even as he said them the words rang false in his ears. Justin simply wasn't the type to lick his wounds in private.

Joshua might have been reading his mind. "Then those wounds must be a lot deeper than he's letting on, because he's never holed up like this before. And the library search stuff bothers me, too. Any way for you to get a list of what he's been researching?"

"Possibly." Corwin scratched his cheek. "Well . . . did you remind him we're having a Moreau Family war council this evening?"

"Yes," the other nodded. "He said he'd try to make it."

"Okay," Corwin said slowly. "Okay. I haven't talked to you, so of course I don't know he's been reminded.

I'll call him up like a good big brother should, and while I'm at it I'll see what else I can get out of him. All right?"

"Fine. Thanks, Corwin—this has been driving me just barely south of frantic."

"No problem. See you tonight."

Joshua disappeared from the screen. Scowling, Corwin punched up the Cobra Academy and asked for Justin. A moment later his brother's face came on. "Hello?—oh, hi, Corwin. What can I do for you?"

It took Corwin a second to find his tongue. Seldom if ever had he known Justin to be so coolly polite, so—the term *businesslike* leapt to mind. "Uh, I was just calling to see if you'd be coming to the family round table tonight," he said at last. "I presume Dad told you about it?"

"Yes, a couple days ago, and Joshua again today. I understand Aunt Gwen's going to be there too."

Nuts, Corwin thought with a mental grimace. He'd been planning to drop that tidbit on Justin himself as a surprise bonus incentive to attend. Aunt Gwen— Jonny's younger sister—had been Justin's favorite relative since childhood, but her visits had been few and far between since her move to Palatine six years earlier. "That's right," he told Justin. "She's one of the geologists working on the Qasama data."

Justin's lip might have twitched at the name *Qasama*; Corwin wasn't sure. "Yes, Dad mentioned that. Well, as I told Joshua, I'll try to make it."

"What's to keep you away?" Corwin asked, studiously casual. "You're still off-duty, aren't you?"

"Officially, yes. But there's something I've been working on lately that I'm trying to finish up."

"What sort of something?"

Justin's face didn't change. "You'll find out when it's done. Until then I'd rather not say."

Corwin exhaled quietly and admitted defeat. "All right, *be* mysterious; see if I care. But let me know if you need transport and I'll send a car for you."

"Thanks. Talk to you later."

" 'Bye." The screen blanked, and Corwin leaned back in his seat. The trip to Qasama had definitely changed his younger brother—and not necessarily for the better. Still, as he'd told Joshua, some things simply took time to work out.

His intercom buzzed: Yutu with something new on the public net that needed an official response. Sighing, Corwin turned on the net and, pushing his worries about Justin into the background, got back to work.

For Pyre, it was just like old times. Almost.

An invitation to the Moreau family dinners had always ranked at the very top of his list, not only because he enjoyed their company but also because their tacit acceptance of him as part of the family was an honor bestowed on few other outsiders. Over the years he'd had the privilege of watching the three boys move from high chairs to boosters to full adult participation; had learned by osmosis some of the intricacies of Cobra World politics; had even gotten to know Gwen Moreau, barely three years his senior, well enough to seriously consider marriage to her. Tonight as he looked around the table, listening and contributing to the chitchat, he felt the memories of those happier times drifting like the scent of good cahve through his mind.

But tonight the warmth was chilled, and all their efforts could not dispel the cloud that Justin's empty chair cast over the proceedings. Jonny had assured them that Justin would be there in time for the discussion, but as dinner wore down to dessert and then cahve Pyre began to doubt it.

And worse than Justin's voluntary exile was the cold certainty in Pyre's gut that ultimately it was his fault.

Not just the fact that he'd been Justin's Cobra trainer, the one responsible for making sure the boy was ready for the mission. Pyre had trained Cobras before, and if Justin had failed to develop that touch of defensive paranoia a man in danger needed, that was simply the other's basic personality. Too, he *could* have forbidden Justin's participation on the mission; but the Council wanted the twins aboard and there was nothing Pyre could have pointed to to justify dropping them out.

But if he'd followed the armored bus when Moff had taken Justin from Sollas to Purma. . . .

It was a scenerio Pyre had played over and over in infinite variation on the trip back to Aventine, and it still haunted the quiet times of his day. If he'd followed the bus he could have broken Justin out at that first stop, the two of them then freeing Cerenkov and Rynstadt. Or even have waited until the high-security building and then backtracked to the others' rescue. Justin would never have had to face the situation of being deep in enemy territory, abandoned by the outside assistance he'd counted on.

And he wouldn't have had to learn quite so hard the fact that even Cobras were allowed to be afraid. Allowed to panic.

Allowed to remain human.

Dinner ended, and the group moved into the living room. But Jonny had barely begun when there was a quiet knock on the door and Justin let himself in.

There was a brief, awkward moment as everyone tried for the right balance of greeting, interest, casualness, and solicitude. But then Joshua managed to break the ice. "About time," he growled, mock-seriously. "*You* were supposed to be bringing the main course."

Justin smiled, and the tension eased. "Sorry I'm late," he apologized, also mock-seriously, to his brother. "The gantua steaks will be along in a minute—and as partial compensation for the delay, the meat is *exceptionally* fresh."

He sat down beside Joshua, nodded to the others,

and then turned his eyes expectantly to his father. "How much have I missed?"

"As a matter of fact, we were just starting." Jonny hesitated. "What I'm about to say—about to suggest—is going to sound pretty strange," he said, glancing around at the others. "What's worse is that I haven't got any solid evidence whatsoever for it. That's the main reason you're all here: to help me decide whether I'm actually on to something or just hallucinating." His eyes shifted to Chrys, seated on the couch between Corwin and Gwen, and stayed there as if seeking strength. "I asked you to read the report on the planet Tacta that the *Menssana* brought back, in particular the section on the bird we've nicknamed the *spookie*. What was in there wasn't much—mainly just a brief encounter we had with one near the ship's perimeter. What *wasn't* there was the strong suspicion I've had ever since then that the spookie is in some degree telepathic."

The word seemed to hang like smoke in the air. Pyre flicked his eyes around the room: at Chrys, who looked troubled; Corwin, Gwen, and Joshua, whose faces appeared to register astonished skepticism; at Justin, whose expression was closed but . . . interested.

"All my evidence is subjective," Jonny continued, "but let me describe exactly what happened and see what you think."

Carefully, almost as if giving evidence in court, he went on to tell of the spookie watching him from the low bushes; of its agitation when he called others over to see; of its deftly timed, deftly executed break for freedom; and of the mission's failure to locate any more of the species. When he finished there was a long silence.

"Anyone else come to this conclusion?" Gwen asked at last.

"Two or three others are wondering about it," Jonny told her. "Understandably, none of us put it in our official reports, but Chrys and I weren't imagining things out there."

"Um. Doesn't have to be a complete, mind-reading telepathy, does it?" Gwen mused. "With a spookie's brain capacity it shouldn't have the intelligence to handle input like that."

"Dr. Hanford made a similar comment at the time," Chrys said. "We've talked about the possibility the spookies might form some kind of group mind, or that the sense boils down more to a feeling for danger than actual mind-reading."

"I'd vote for the latter," Corwin put in. "A group mind, even if such a thing could exist, shouldn't worry too much about losing one of its cells. In fact, it might deliberately sacrifice a spookie or two to get a look at your weaponry in action."

"Good point," Jonny nodded. "I lean toward the danger-recognition theory myself, though it requires a pretty fine scale to have timed things that well."

"The fine-tuning, at least, could have been coincidental," Corwin suggested.

"Or the whole thing could have been coincidence," Joshua said hesitantly. "Sorry, Dad, but I don't see anything here that can't be explained away."

"Oh, I agree," Jonny said without rancor. "And if I hadn't been there I'd be treating it with the same healthy skepticism. As a matter of fact, I hope you're right. But one way or the other, we've got to pin this down, and we've got to pin it down fast."

"Why?" Pyre asked. "It seems to me Tacta's fauna is pretty far down the priority stack. What's the big rush for?"

Jonny opened his mouth—but it was Justin who spoke. "Because the Council's about to make a decision on war with Qasama," he said evenly, "and the mojos are related to these spookies. Aren't they."

Jonny nodded, and Pyre felt the blood draining out of his face. "You mean to say we were fighting *tele-pathic birds* down there?"

"I don't know," Jonny said. "You were there. You tell me."

Pyre licked his lips briefly, eyes shifting to Justin. The immediate shock was fading and he was able to think. . . . "No," he said after a minute. "No, they weren't strictly telepathic. They never recognized that we were Cobras, for one thing—never reacted as if I was armed until I started shooting."

"Did you ever *see* how they reacted to a conventional weapon, though?" Gwen asked.

Pyre nodded. "Outside the ship, the first contact. The team had to leave their lasers in the airlock."

"And Decker," Joshua murmured.

"And Decker," Pyre acknowledged, swallowing with the memory of York's sacrifice. "In fact, I'd go so far as to say the mojos don't even sense the presence of danger, at least not the way you claim your spookie does. When I climbed up a building at the edge of Sollas that last night I surprised both a Qasaman sentry *and* his mojo. The bird should at least have been in the air if it felt me coming." He cocked an eyebrow at Justin. "You notice anything, one way or the other?"

The young Cobra shrugged. "Only that the group mind thing goes out the window with at least the mojos—none of them learned anything about us no matter how many of their friends we slaughtered." He paused, and a haze of emotional pain seemed to settle over his face. "And . . . there may be one other thing."

The others sensed it as well, and a silence rich in sympathy descended on the room. It took Justin a couple of tries to get started, but when he finally spoke his voice was steady and flat with suppressed emotion. "You've all read my report, I expect. You know I—well, I panicked while I was being taken underground in Purma. I killed all the mojos and some of the Qasamans in the elevator, and a few minutes later I killed another group in the hallway upstairs. What ... what some of you don't know is that I didn't just panic. I literally lost my head when each set of mojos attacked. I don't even remember fighting them off, just sort of coming to with them dead around me."

He stopped, fighting for control ... and it was Joshua who spotted the key first. "It was *only* when the mojos were attacking you?" he asked. "The Qasamans themselves didn't bother you?"

Justin shook his head. "Not to the same extent. At least not those in the elevator. The others ... well, I don't remember killing them, either, I guess. I don't know—maybe I'm just rationalizing for my failure."

"Or maybe you're not," Jonny said grimly. "Almo, did *you* experience anything like that when you were fighting the mojos?"

Pyre hesitated, thinking back. He wished he could admit to such a thing, for the sake of Justin's self-esteem. If the mojos actually *had* been fueling the younger man's reaction. ...

But he had to shake his head. "Sorry, but I'm afraid not," he told Jonny. "On the other hand, I never faced mojos who'd already seen I was danger-ous, either. I was always in a position to target and eliminate them in the first salvo. Perhaps we could talk to Michael Winward, see what he went through."

Joshua was gazing into space. "The cities. They're *designed* for the mojos' benefit. You suppose there's more significance to that than we thought?"

Gwen stirred. "I have to admit I don't understand this 'designed city' bit, especially the lunacy of let-ting herds of bololins charge up your streets. Wouldn't it have been simpler to just go out on hunting trips when you wanted to let your mojo breed?"

"Or else set up tarbine aviaries in the cities," Chrys suggested. "I would think it harder to go out and trap wild mojos than to breed tame ones, anyway."

"That would certainly make the most sense," Pyre said.

"Assuming," Corwin said quietly, "that the Qasamans were the ones making those decisions."

And there it is, Pyre thought. *What all the rest of us are skating around, out in the open at last.* He looked around the circle, but superimposed on the view was an unsettling image: a Qasaman as marionette, its strings in the beak of its mojo. . . .

It was Justin who eventually broke the silence. "It's not as simple as the mojos being able to take control of people," he said. "We had mojos all around us that last night and still were able to escape."

Pyre thought back. "Yes," he agreed slowly. "Both outside of Purma and in Kimmeron's office in Sollas the mojos should have been able to influence me. If they could."

"Maybe they need a longer association with a person," Corwin said. "Or there's a distance or stress factor that inhibits them."

"You're talking degrees now," Chrys spoke up, her voice low. "Does that mean we're all agreed that somehow, on some level, the mojos are influencing events on Qasama?"

There was a brief silence; and, one by one, they nodded. "The cities," Joshua said. "That's the key indicator. They've gone to enormous trouble to duplicate the mojos' natural breeding patterns, even when simpler ways exist. Funny none of us picked up on that before."

"Maybe not," Pyre told him grimly. "Maybe the mojos were able to dampen our curiosity that much, at least."

"Or maybe not," Joshua retorted. "Let's not start giving these birds *too* many superhuman abilities, all right? They're not even intelligent, remember. I think we humans are all perfectly capable of missing the obvious without any outside help."

The discussion went back and forth for a while before turning to others matters . . . and so engrossed did they all become that Pyre alone noticed Justin's quiet departure.

The desk in his temporary Cobra Academy room was small and several centimeters shorter than he liked; but it was equipped with a computer terminal, and that was all Justin really cared about. He'd just punched in a new search command and was waiting for the results when there was a tap at the door. "Come in," he said absently. Probably someone here to complain about his late hours again—

"No one ever tell you it was impolite to leave without saying good-bye?"

Justin spun his chair around, surprise and chagrin flooding his face with heat. "Oh ... hi, Aunt Gwen," he managed to say without stuttering. "Uh—well, you were all busy discussing the mojos, and I had work to do here. . . ."

He trailed off under her steady, no-nonsense gaze, the look that since childhood had been more effective on him than any amount of brimstone or lecture. "Uh-*huh*," she said. "Well, it's too bad you took off when you did. You missed *my* report."

"The one on the Qasaman strategic material situation?"

"That's the one. *And* the surprise bonus: the Qasamans' long-range communication method."

Justin blinked, his heartbeat speeding up. "You've figured it out? Well, come on—how do they do it?"

"I'll trade you," she said, waving at the desk and its scattering of papers and maps. "You tell me *your* secret first."

He felt his mouth twist into a grimace ... but he'd have to tell someone soon, anyway. Aunt Gwen he could at least hope to be sympathetic. "All right," he sighed. "I'm trying to work up a tactical plan for the next intelligence raid on Qasama."

Gwen's eyes remained steady on his. "What makes you think there'll *be* another mission?"

"There *has* to be," he said. "The first mission ended with too many critical facts still unknown. Those underground manufacturing centers, at the very least, and if Dad's right the mojos as well."

"Uh-huh. I presume you plan on leading this expedition?"

Justin's lip quirked. "Of course not . . . but I *will* be one of the team."

"Um." Gwen glanced around the room, snared a chair from beside the door and pulled it over to face her nephew's. "You know, Justin," she said, sitting down, "if I didn't know better, I'd think you were running away from something."

He snorted. "Heading to Qasama hardly qualifies as running away, in my opinion."

"Depends on what you have here to face. Staying put when you feel real or imagined public animosity isn't easy. But sometimes any other option is the coward's way out."

Justin took a deep breath. "Aunt Gwen . . . you can't possibly know what this situation is like. I failed on Qasama—pure and simple—and it's my job now to make up for it if I can."

"You're not listening. Failure or not isn't the issue. Rushing ahead with a premature course of action qualifies as running away, period. And yes, I *do* know what you're facing. When your father came back from the war he—" She stopped, lips compressed, then quietly continued. "There was an accident in town one night, and he . . . killed a couple of teen-agers."

Justin felt his mouth go dry. "I've never heard this," he said carefully.

"It's nothing we're anxious to talk about," she sighed. "Basically, the kids pretended they were going to run him over with their car and his Cobra reflexes countered in a way that wound up indirectly killing them. But the details don't matter. He wanted to run away afterwards—had a whole bunch of off-world university applications filled out and ready to go.

But he stayed. He stayed, and along with helping the rest of us cope with the ostracism, he just happened incidentally to save a few men from a fire."

"So he stayed ... until he left for good and came here to Aventine?"

Gwen blinked. "Well ... yes, but that's not the same. The Dominion government wanted the Cobras to come help open up the colony—"

"Could he have refused?"

"I—can't say. But he wouldn't have, because his skills and abilities were needed out here."

Justin spread his hands. "But don't you see?—you're giving my own argument back at me. Dad's Cobra abilities were needed, so he came; my Cobra abilities are needed on Qasama, so I'm going. It's the exact same thing."

"But it's *not*," Gwen said, her voice and eyes almost pleading. "You don't have the training and experience to be a warrior. You're just trying to cleanse your conscience through an act of revenge."

Justin sighed and shook his head. "I'm not out for revenge, really I'm not. Between the ride back and my time here I've had two weeks to work through my emotions on the matter, and ... I think I understand myself and my motives. Qasama has to be stopped, we need more information to do that—" he took a deep breath— "and if I'm not a real warrior, I'm probably the closest thing to one left on Aventine."

"Jonny has worked hard to make the Cobras a force for peace and development in the Worlds."

"But he had to go through his war first," Justin told her quietly. "And I have to go through mine."

For a long minute the room was silent. Then Justin gave his aunt a passable attempt at a smile. "Your turn now. What's *your* secret?"

Gwen sighed, a long hissing sound of defeat. "If you look at a topographical map of Qasama, you'll see that all the cities and villages are scattered along a low, roughly boomerang-shaped ridge four thousand kilometers or so in total length and maybe six hundred at its largest diameter. There's evidence that it was caused by an upwelling of basaltic magma in the fairly recent geological past."

"That's a *lot* of magma," Justin murmured.

"Granted, though there are even larger examples of this sort of thing back on some of the Dominion worlds. Anyway, I've done some computer modeling, and it looks very possible that the basalt intruded into some highly metallic rock layers. If that's the case the Qasamans have a ready-made waveguide for low-frequency radio waves a hundred meters below them, ready to dig antennas into. That sort of system's been used before, but with the metallic ore around it the basalt would keep nearly all of the signal inside it, leaking very little of it out for anyone to pick up."

Justin whistled under his breath. "Cute. Very cute. A planet already wired for sound." And if true, it would eliminate the last lingering doubts he had about mojo long-distance telepathic abilities. That was worth a lot right there. "When will you know for sure if you're right?"

She sighed again. "I suppose it won't be certain until your intelligence raid finds the antennas." She gazed at him another moment, then got to her feet. "I'd better be going," she said, backing toward the door. "Almo's waiting to take me back to my hotel. I'll . . . talk to you later."

"Thanks for coming by," Justin said. "Don't worry—this'll be done in a day or two, and after it's submitted I'll have more time to spend with the family."

"Sure. Well . . . good night."

" 'Night, Aunt Gwen."

For a long minute after she left he stayed where he was, eyes on the closed door. A hundred meters down to the Qasamans' basaltic waveguide. Thirty stories, more or less . . . approximately the depth of the Purma building he'd escaped from. Had *that* been all the place was?—the local communications center, not the industrial complex that he'd thought? If so—

If so, he'd missed little of truly vital importance by his premature break for freedom.

He was, perhaps, not a failure, after all. Or at least not as much of one as he'd thought.

It was nice to know. But, ultimately, it made little practical difference. There was still the job on Qasama to do, and he and his fellow Cobras the only ones who could do it.

Turning to his desk once more, he got back to work.

Chapter 26

Stiggur was neither impressed nor convinced by Jonny's arguments. Neither, very obviously, were most of the others.

"A telepathic bird," Vartanson snorted. "Come *on*, now—don't you think you're reaching just a little too far for this one?"

Jonny kept his temper with an effort. "What about the design of the cities?" he asked.

"What about it?" Vartanson shot back. "There are any of a hundred explanations for that. Maybe the mojos get sick if they don't breed regularly and the city dwellers don't want to take trips into the woods for the purpose. Maybe they can't wall out the bololin herds and this was the best compromise available."

"Then why *build* cities?" Jonny said. "They like being decentralized—why not just stick with villages?"

"Because there are social and economic advantages to a certain amount of population concentration," Fairleigh spoke up. "Masking any trace of their underground industry would be a good reason all by itself."

"And before you bring up the Tactan spookies," Roi said, "your correlation between those and the mojos is tentative at best—and the conclusions you

274

come to about the spookies is ridiculous. I'm sorry, but it is."

"That's a rather blanket assessment for someone who doesn't know a thing about biology," Jonny told him tartly.

"Oh, is it? Well, perhaps we ought to ask our resident biologist, then." Roi turned to Telek. "Lizabet, what do *you* think?"

Telek favored him with a cool look, which she sent slowly around the table. "I think," she said at last, "that we'd damn well better find out for sure. And that we'd better do it fast."

There was a stunned silence. Jonny stared at Telek, her unexpected support throwing his brain off-line. "You agree the mojos are influencing the Qasamans' actions?" he asked.

"I agree they're more than they seem," she said. "How *much* more is what we've got to find out."

Stiggur cleared his throat. "Lizabet ... I understand that your professional interests here are naturally directed more toward the mojos than the Qasaman technological base. But—"

"Then let me put it another way," Telek interrupted him. "I've known about Jonny's theory since yesterday—never mind how—and I've used that time to do a couple of new studies on the visual record the team brought back." She looked at Roi. "Olor, I would say that the Palatinian glow-nose is probably the most popular pet anywhere in the Worlds—you agree? Good. How many people on Palatine own one?"

Roi blinked. "I don't know, off hand. Eighty percent, I'd guess."

"I looked up the numbers," Telek said. "Assuming only one per customer the figure is actually under sixty percent. If you include all other pets the number of owners is still only about eighty-seven percent."

"What's your point?" Stiggur asked.

Telek focused on him. "Thirteen percent of an admittedly pet-crazy people don't own pets. But *every single damn Qasaman has a mojo.*"

Jonny frowned into the thoughtful silence, trying to visualize the scenes he'd seen from the records. It *was* possible, he decided with some surprise. "No exceptions?" he asked Telek.

"Only three the computer scan came up with, and two don't really count: children under ten or so, and dancers and duelists. The duelists get their birds back after their curse ball game, though, and I suspect the dancers have them waiting backstage, too. At which point we're back to one hundred percent of the adult population with mojos. The floor is open for speculation."

"They're living in a dangerous environment," Vartanson shrugged.

"Not really," Telek shook her head. "The villages ought to be safe enough, with the walls and the scarcity of the krisjaw predators that were mentioned. And with the bololin alarms even Sollas and the other cities aren't all that hazardous any more. The big 'danger' argument strikes me as a convenient but flimsy rationale."

"What about all their fellow humans running around with guns?" Roi snorted.

"Yes, what *about* that?" Jonny put in. Across the table Hemner muttered something and began fiddling with his display. Jonny waited a second, but he didn't say anything, so Jonny turned to Vartanson. "Howie, do you allow your people to carry their weapons inside the fortified compounds?"

Vartanson shook his head slowly. "The Cobras are armed, of course, but all hand weapons are checked inside the inner doors."

"The Qasamans have grown up with a tradition of carrying their guns, though," Fairleigh argued. "You couldn't get them to just give them up overnight."

"Why not?" Telek asked. "They've also got a tradition of not attacking each other, remember."

"Besides which," Hemner added without looking up, "banning in-city weapons has been done successfully in dozens of places in the Dominion."

"The Qasamans wouldn't put up with that, in my opinion," Roi shook his head.

"Let's get back to the point, shall we?" Telek said. "The question is why the Qasamans are still bothering to carry these birds around with them when it's not necessary to do so."

"But we've answered that question," Stiggur said with a sigh. "As long as *any*one carries a gun and a mojo, *every*one has to do so. Otherwise they won't feel safe."

"The cultural conditioning—"

"Will be adequate for most of them," Stiggur said. "But not for all. And if I were a Qasaman, I'd want protection against even that small group of dangerous people."

Telek grimaced, clearly hunting for a new approach. "Brom—"

"All right, we've talked long enough," Hemner said firmly. "We're going to vote on Lizabet's proposal. Now."

All eyes shifted to the frail old man. "Jor, you're out of order," Stiggur said quietly. "I know emotions are running high on all this—"

"You do, do you?" Hemner smiled thinly. His hands, Jonny noted with a vague twinge of uneasiness, had left their usual place on top of the table and were hidden from view in his lap. "And you prefer words to actions, I suppose. It's so much easier to manipulate people's emotions. Well, the time has come for action. We're going to vote, and we're going to pass Lizabet's mojo study. Or else."

"Or else what?" Stiggur snapped, irritation finally breaking through.

"Or else the nay votes will be eliminated," Hemner said harshly. "Beginning with *him*."

And his right hand came up over the edge of the

table, the small flat handgun clutched in it swiveling to point at Roi.

Someone gasped in shock . . . but even before the pistol had steadied on its target, Jonny was in motion. Both fingertip lasers spat fire, one into the pistol, the other tracing a line directly in front of Hemner's eyes. The old man jerked back with a cry as the heat and light reached his hand and face, the pistol swinging away from the others. Gripping the table edge with both hands, Jonny kicked back and up with his feet, sending his chair spinning across the room and flipping his body to slam onto his back on the table. His legs caught Hemner's arm full force, eliciting a second yelp from the other and sending the gun sailing into the far wall.

"Get the gun!" Jonny snapped through the agony the sudden violence had ignited in his arthritic joints. He swung up to a sitting position, grabbed both of Hemner's wrists. "Jor, what the *hell* was *that* supposed to accomplish?"

"Just proving a point," Hemner said calmly, the harshness of a minute earlier gone without a trace. "My wrists—*easy*—"

"You were *what*?"

"I'll be damned." The voice was Roi's and Jonny turned to look.

Roi was standing by the far wall, holding Hemner's "gun."

Which was nothing more than a pen and an intricately folded magcard.

Jonny looked down at Hemner. "Jor . . . what's going on?"

"As I said, I was proving a point," the other said. "Uh—if you wouldn't mind . . . ?"

Releasing his grip, Jonny climbed carefully off the table and walked around back to his seat. Roi sat down, too, and Stiggur cleared his throat. "This had better be good," he warned Hemner.

The other nodded. "Olor, were you armed just now

when I pretended to pull a weapon on you?" he asked.

"Of course not," Roi snorted.

"Yet even with a real gun I wouldn't have been able to shoot you. True? Why not?"

"Because Jonny was here and he's faster than you are."

Hemner nodded and turned to Stiggur. "Security, Brom. You *don't* need everyone carrying mojos for your citizens to be protected. The mojos attack *anyone* drawing a gun, whether their own masters are specifically threatened or not." He waved at his display. "The records of the bus attack on York clearly show that—I've just checked. Even if everyone wants to carry a gun, you still don't need that many mojos. Twenty percent, or even less, combined with the cultural bias against fighting would be more than adequate."

"Assuming they're that peaceful without that taloned reminder on their shoulders," Fairleigh growled. "Maybe they're more violent without mojos nearby."

Vartanson laughed abruptly. "Dylan, did you hear what you just *said*? Almost exactly what Jonny's been suggesting." He nodded at Jonny. "All right; I'm convinced the mojos need more study. But we need to learn about the Qasaman technological base, too, and I'm not sure which is more important."

"Then let's do both," Telek spoke up. Reaching to the stack of magdisks in front of her, she selected one and slid it into her reader. "This is a complete tactical plan that was submitted to my office yesterday via Almo Pyre. I'd like us all to read it through and seriously consider it as a basis for the next mission to Qasama. Brom?"

"Any comments or objections?" Stiggur asked, his eyes sweeping the table. "All right, then. Let's take a look."

Telek sent the report to the other displays and they all settled down to read. Jonny felt memories of his own tactical training rising to the surface as he studied the plan ... memories, and a growing respect for Pyre's work. Granted that there *were* some military manuals and histories in the computer library, it still took a great deal of raw talent to put together a scheme this comprehensive, especially with only the limited training the First Cobras had been able to give Pyre and his team.

It wasn't until he reached the end that he found the author's name ... and he stared at it for nearly a minute before he finally could believe it.

Justin Moreau.

The wait in Telek's office had stretched into nearly two hours, but Pyre had been almost too busy to notice. Justin's plan was highly detailed, but the boy naturally had not done any actual personnel assignments, a task that would fall to Coordinator Sun and the Cobra upper echelon if the plan was accepted. Nothing said Pyre couldn't submit his own roster for their approval, though. He'd finished the main group and was working on the first of the three outrider teams when Telek returned.

"Well?" he asked as she closed the door and sank into her desk chair.

"They bought it," she said with tired satisfaction. "Brom wants to submit it to a review board of First Cobras, but I doubt they'll change it too much. You still hold with two weeks to equip and train the task force?"

Pyre nodded. "All they'll need is the multiple-targeting enhancers and some tactical training. For a change, all the experience we've logged hunting down spine leopards is going to do some of us some good."

"Um. You ... ah ... plan to be out in the forest, then?"

"I had, yes. Unless you wanted me on the village force."

Telek pursed her lips. "Might be better for you

to stay aboard the ship, actually. To coordinate things."

"Oh?" Pyre eyed her. "You'd rather I not be down on Qasama?"

"I'd rather you not risk your life, if you must know," she said grudgingly. "You've done your bit."

"Ah. You feel the same way about Justin, Michael, and Dorjay? Or is it different because you specifically asked that *I* be aboard the *Dewdrop* the last time around?"

Her lip curled. "So you *did* know. I'd hoped I'd hid my tracks a bit better than that."

"I have friends among the elite, too. Which is why I was surprised you'd requested me."

Telek exhaled loudly. "Well, it *wasn't* because you were a good friend of the Moreaus," she said. "Though that *was* why I asked you and Halloran for the initial cost study. But for the trip itself. . . ." She paused, eyes drifting to the window and the Capitalia city-scape beyond. "It bothered me all the way from the beginning why the Baliu demesne should think Cobras would have a better shot at the Qasamans then they did."

"They already knew the mojos attack drawn weapons," Pyre suggested.

"True. And there was the whole question of whether this was a test. But it occurred to me that there was one other possibility."

Pyre frowned in thought . . . and suddenly it hit him. "You think they *knew* we were the same species as the Qasamans?"

"I think it highly probable," Telek nodded. "Cobras *would* have an advantage in a war against other humans. And being the connivers they are, of course, they wouldn't want us to know who we were facing until we'd committed to some course of action."

"Yeah," Pyre said slowly. "We nearly got killed on Qasama and we're *still* barely holding our own with public opinion. Imagine the furor if we'd known in advance we were being asked to exterminate another human society." He cocked an eyebrow at her. "That doesn't explain my presence aboard, though."

She took a deep breath. "I didn't like the fact that I might be called upon to betray another human colony out there. You were there to make sure I kept my priorities straight. Did you know, Almo, that I was married once?"

He shook his head, taking the abrupt subject change in stride. "Divorced?"

"Widowed. Since before I became a governor. He was a Cobra . . . and he died on Caelian."

She paused, memories flicking visibly across her face. Pyre waited, sensing what would come next. "You remind me a great deal of him," she continued at last. "In appearance; even more in spirit. I wanted you there as a constant reminder that we *need* a new world for the Caelians to move to."

"Even if that world is bought with the Qasamans' lives?" he snarled.

The words came out harsher than he'd intended them to, but Telek never flinched. "Yes," she said quietly. "Even then. My duty is to the Cobra Worlds, first and foremost . . . and it's going to stay that way."

Pyre looked at her, a sudden chill sending a shiver up his back. All the time together on the *Dewdrop* . . . and he hadn't really known her at all.

"I'm sorry if that makes you hate me," she said after a moment. "But in my opinion I had no choice."

He nodded, though to which part of her statement he wasn't sure. "If you'll excuse me," he said, hearing the stiffness in his voice, "I need to get back to work. I have a roster to complete for the team I'll be taking to Qasama."

She nodded. "All right. I'll talk to you later."

He turned and left . . . and wondered that he didn't hate her for her ruthlessness.

*   *   *

The Cobra board took Justin's plan apart, examined it, debated it, and—in places—changed it; and then they put it together again and pronounced it sound. The forty-eight Cobras and fourteen scientists who would be landing on Qasama were chosen and trained. The Baliu demesne expressed their displeasure at funding a second mission on what still amounted to speculation, but well before the training period was over Jonny and Stiggur were able to change the aliens' minds.

And less than a month after the *Dewdrop* had returned from Qasama, both it and the *Menssana* lifted quietly from the Capitalia starport and headed back.

Chapter 27

Night on Qasama.

The villages along the eastern arm of what was now referred to as the Fertile Crescent were dark as the *Menssana* drifted down on its gravity lifts. Dark, but visible enough in infrared scanners. The roads connecting the towns were visible, too, the network narrowing like a filigree arrowhead to point at the most southerly village at the end of the crescent ... with but a single road northward connecting it to the rest of Qasaman civilization.

The *Menssana* stopped first along that road, some twenty kilometers north of town; and when it lifted again it had left twenty-two people and the two aircars behind. The aircars themselves lifted before the ship was out of sight, bound on missions of their own; and, almost lazily, the *Menssana* swung southward toward the sleeping target village, its sensors taking in great gulps of electromagnetic radiation, sound, and particulate matter and spitting out maps and lists in return. The ship circled the village once, maintaining a discreet distance to avoid detection. When it finally set down in the forest some fifty meters from the wall, the forty passengers who emerged had a fair idea what they were getting into.

Within half an hour, though no one else yet knew it, they had taken the town.

The mayor got a full two steps into his office before his face registered the fact that someone else was sitting on his cushions—and he managed another step and a half before he was able to stop. His eyes widened, then narrowed as surprise turned to anger. He snapped something; "Who are you"? the *Menssana's* computer translated it.

"Good morning, Mr. Mayor," Winward said gravely from the cushions, his newly reconstructed eyes steady on the other's mojo. "Forgive the intrusion, but we need some information from you and your people."

The mayor seemed to freeze at the first words from the pendant around Winward's neck ... and as his eyes searched the Cobra's face the blood abruptly drained from his cheeks. "You!" he whispered.

Winward nodded understanding. "Ah, so Kimmeron circulated our pictures, did he? Good. Then you know who I am ... and you know the foolishness of resistance."

The mayor's gun hand was trembling as if in indecision. "I wouldn't advise it," Winward told him. "I can kill both you and your mojo before you can draw. Besides, there are others with me—*lot*s of others—and if you start shooting the rest of your people probably will, too, and we'll just have to kill a bunch of you to prove we can do it." He cocked his head. "We *don't* have to prove that, do we?"

A muscle in the other's cheek twitched. "I've seen the reports of your carnage," he said grimly.

"Good," Winward said, matching the other's tone. "I hate having to cover the same ground twice. So. Are you going to cooperate?"

The mayor was silent for a moment. "What do you want from us?"

Quietly, Winward let out the breath he'd been holding. "We want only to ask your people some questions and do a few painless and harmless studies on them and their mojos."

He watched the mayor's face closely, but he could see no obvious reaction. "Very well," the Qasaman said. "Only to prevent unnecessary bloodshed, I will give in. But be warned: if your tests aren't as harmless as you claim you'll soon have more bloodshed than you have taste for."

"Agreed." Winward stood and gestured to the cushions and the low switch-covered console beside it. "Call your people and tell them to leave their homes and come into the streets. They may bring their mojos but must leave their guns inside."

"The women and children, too?"

"They must come out, and some will need to be tested. If it'll make you feel better, I can allow a close relative to be present while any woman or child is being questioned."

"That . . . would be appreciated." The mayor's eyes held Winward's for a moment. "To what demon have you sold your soul, that you are able to return from the dead?"

Winward shook his head minutely. "You wouldn't believe it if I told you," he said. "Now call your people."

The Qasaman pursed his lips and sat down. Flipping a handful of switches on the console, he began speaking, his voice echoing faintly from the streets. Winward listened for a moment, then reached to his pendant and covered the translator mike. "Dorjay: report."

"Situation quiet at the long-range transmitter," Link's voice came promptly through his earphone. "Uh . . . looks like the mayor's message is starting to stir up things out there now."

"Look sharp—we don't want anyone sneaking in there to send an SOS off to Sollas."

"Particularly as they'd catch us dismantling and studying all the nice equipment in here," Link added dryly. "We'll be careful. You want me to continue managing the gate and motor patrols, too?"

"Yes. It'll get pretty hectic here once the psych people get their business going."

"Okay. Keep me posted."

Winward tapped the mike once to break the private connection and then covered it again. "Governor Telek? How're the pickups coming over?"

"Perfectly," Telek's voice said in his ear. "Got some good baseline readings on the mayor while he was heading through the building, and the high-stress ones there in the office look even better."

"Good. We'll get things started here as soon as we can. Any word yet from the outrider teams?"

"Just routine check-ins. *Dewdrop*'s not reporting any obvious troop movements, either. Looks like we sneaked in undetected."

Which should mean they'd have a few hours or even a day or two before the rest of the planet realized they'd been invaded. After which things could get sticky. "Okay. Dorjay says the tech assessors are already pulling things apart, so you'll get some data coming in on that front soon. Out."

The mayor leaned back from his console to look up balefully at Winward. "They will comply with your demands," he said. "For now, at any rate."

Getting his courage back? That was fine with Winward—the more mood swings the Qasamans went through, the more useful the data the hidden sensors would get. Provided the mayor didn't get *too* courageous. "Fine," the Cobra nodded. "Then let's go out and join them while our people get things organized. After you give me your gun, of course."

The Qasaman hesitated a split second before sliding the weapon out of its holster and laying it atop the console. "Okay; let's go," Winward said, leaving the gun where it was. If Telek's theory was right, chances were he could pick up the weapon without drawing a mojo attack ... but he wasn't ready to make a test case out of it, not yet.

Silently the Qasaman rose to his feet, and together the two men left the office.

The section of forest the outrider-two team had put their aircar down into was reasonably sparse, as such things went, reminding Rey Banyon more of the woods they'd seen on Chata than the denser forests of Aventine's far west region where he'd grown up. The good news was that the openness aided visibility; the bad was that it allowed for larger animals to live here. By and large, a fairly even trade.

But for the moment the forest's denizens, large *and* small, were keeping their distance. Eyes sweeping the vicinity of the aircar, he listened with half an ear to the conversation between Dr. Hanford and the *Dewdrop* in orbit above them.

"Well, *we* didn't spot anything when we swept the area," Hanford was saying. "Are you still showing something nearby?"

"Negative," the voice came back. "I think it went back under the trees and we lost it."

Hanford exhaled loudly. Banyon understood his irritation perfectly: this was the third time in the six hours they'd been on Qasama that they'd made a mad dash to the possible location of a krisjaw, only to come up empty.

And to make it worse, they weren't even sure that a krisjaw was what they needed to find.

"Any idea even which way it *went?*" the zoologist asked at last.

"Dr. Hanford, you have to understand the *Dewdrop*'s infrareds weren't designed for such pin-point work, at least not from this distance. Let me see ... if I had to guess, I'd say to try northwest."

"Thanks," Hanford said dryly. "Call if you spot another target."

"Northwest," one of the other two zoologists muttered as Hanford broke the connection. "*I'd* guess northwest, too, if I had to. That's the direction animals run on this crazy planet."

"I doubt the predators do." Hanford sighed. "Well, Rey? On foot or by air?"

"By air, I suppose," Banyon said. "We'll try spotting on our own for awhile. See if we can do any better."

"Can't possibly do any worse. Well, let's go."

The three zoologists climbed back into the aircar, followed by Banyon and his three Cobra teammates. Rising to just over treetop level, they headed slowly northwest.

Christopher flipped off the mike with a snort and settled back to glaring at the infrared display, muttering under his breath. Eyeing him over his own screen, York chuckled. "Having trouble, Bil?"

"This isn't even my job," Christopher growled without looking up. "How am I supposed to find krisjaw hot spots when I don't even know what they're supposed to look like?"

"You find a large hot spot that's moving—"

"Yes, I know all that. Elsner just better hurry up and get back here, that's all I've got to say."

"He still at the main display looking for a bololin herd for outrider-three?"

"Yeah." Christopher visibly shivered. "Those guys must be nuts. You sure wouldn't catch *me* chasing bololins around."

"You wouldn't catch *me* down there at all," York murmured.

Christopher sent him a quick look. "Yeah. I, uh . . . I understand you were asked to be on the *Menssana* with Lizabet, Yuri, Marck, and the others."

"That's right," York told him evenly. "I refused."

"Oh." Christopher's eyes strayed to York's new right arm—his new *mechanical* right arm—then slipped guiltily away.

"You think it's because of this, don't you?" York asked, raising his arm and opening his hand. The fingers twitched once as he did so, mute reminder of the fact that his brain hadn't totally adapted to the neural/electronic interfaces yet. "You think I'm afraid to go down there again?"

"Of course not—"

"Then you're wrong," York told him flatly. "I'm afraid, all right, and for damn good reasons."

Christopher's face was taking on an increasingly uncomfortable expression, and it occurred to York that the other had probably never heard anyone speak quite this way before. "You want to know why Yuri and Marck and the others are down there and I'm up here?" he asked.

"Well . . . all right, why?"

"Because they're trying to prove they're brave," York said. "Partly to others, but mainly to themselves. They're demonstrating that they can stick their heads in the spine leopard's mouth a second time if they have to, without flinching."

"Whereas you feel no such need?"

"Exactly," York nodded. "I've had my courage tested many times. Both before I came to Aventine and since then. I *know* I'm brave, and I'm damn well not going to take unnecessary chances to prove it to the universe at large." He waved at his display. "If and when the Qasamans make their move I can assess their military level just as well from up here as I could on the surface. Ergo, here's where I stay."

"I see," Christopher nodded. But his eyes still looked troubled. "Makes sense, certainly. I'm—well, I'm glad that's cleared up."

He turned back to his display, and York suppressed a sigh. Christopher hadn't understood, any more than the rest of them had. They still thought it was all just a complicated way of not saying he was a coward.

The hell with all of them.

Turning back to his own screen, he resumed his

watch for military activity. In his lap his mechanical
hand curled into a fist.

It was shortly after noon when the *Dewdrop* finally
located a bololin herd within the specified distance
of the village, and it was another hour before outrider-
three's aircar reached it. The herd had paused among
the trees to graze, and as the aircar drifted by overhead Rem Parker whistled under his breath. "Nasty-
looking things," he commented.

One of the other three Cobras muttered an agreement. "I think I can see the tarbines—those tan spots
behind the heads, inside the quills."

"Yeah. Great place for a summer home." Parker
glanced at the tech huddled over his instruments in
the next seat. "Well, Dan? Possible?"

Dan Rostin shrugged. "Marginal. We're pretty far
south of the direct route here—it'll take a large devi-
ation to get them on track. But if they cooperate as
well as the flatfoots on Chata it ought to work okay.
Hang on a second and I'll have the details for you."

It turned out not to be quite as bad as Parker had
feared. Nowhere would the magnetic field they would
be superimposing change the overall field line direction by more than twenty degrees, and the ampli-
tudes necessary were well within their equipment's
capabilities.

Of course, they would occasionally need to get
within a hundred meters of the herd's center, with
the risk to the aircar from the flanks that such a close
approach would entail. But then, that was why the
Cobras were along in the first place.

"Well, let's get started," Parker told the others.
"And let's hope they're as much like their flatfoot
cousins as the bio people say they are." Otherwise—he
didn't add—the Cobras might just wind up herding
them, rancher style, all the way to the village.

And *that* was a trick he wasn't anxious to try.

*   *   *

It was almost sundown when Winward returned from a tour of his Cobras' positions to the mayoral office building, where Dr. McKinley and the rest of the psych people had set up shop. One of the Qasamans was being escorted out of McKinley's room as Winward arrived, and he took the opportunity to take a quick look inside. "Hello," he nodded to the two men as he poked his head around the door. "How's it going?"

McKinley looked about as tired as Winward had ever seen a man; but his voice was brisk enough. "Pretty good, overall. Even without the computer analysis I can see the stress levels changing pretty much as predicted."

"Good. You about to close down this phase for the evening?"

"Got one more to do. If you'd like, you could stay and watch."

Winward eyed the Cobra guard standing silently against the wall. He, too, looked tired, though just as far from admitting it as McKinley was. "Alek, why don't you go ahead and get some dinner," he told the other. "I'll stay here while Dr. McKinley finishes up."

"I'd appreciate that," Alek nodded, heading for the door. "Thanks."

McKinley waited until he was gone, then touched a button on his translator pendant. "Okay; send in number forty-two."

A moment later Winward's enhanced hearing picked up two sets of footsteps approaching; and the door opened to admit another Cobra and a tense-looking Qasaman male. The Cobra left, and McKinley gestured to the low chair facing his appropriated desk. "Sit down, please."

The Qasaman complied, throwing a suspicious glance at Winward. His mojo, Winward noted, was almost calm by comparison, although it seemed to be rippling its feathers rather frequently.

"Let's begin with your name and occupation," McKinley said. "Just speak clearly toward the recorder here," he added, waving at the rectangular box perched on a corner of the desk.

The man answered, and McKinley moved on to general questions concerning his interests and life in the village. Gradually the tone and direction of the questioning shifted, though, and within a few minutes McKinley was asking about the man's relationships with friends, his frequency of intercourse with his wife, and other highly personal matters. Winward watched the Qasaman closely, but to his untrained eye the other seemed to be taking McKinley's prying with reasonable grace. The stress indicators built into the recorder and the man's chair, of course, would deliver a more scientific assessment.

McKinley was halfway through a question about the man's childhood when he broke off and, as he'd done forty-one times already that day, pretended to listen with annoyance to something coming through his earphone. "I'm sorry," he told the Qasaman, "but apparently your mojo's flapping noises are interfering with the recording. Uh—" He glanced around the room, pointed to a large cushion in the far corner. "Would you mind putting him over there?"

The other grimaced, glancing again at Winward. Then, body language eloquent with protest, he complied. "Good," McKinley said briskly as the Qasaman seated himself again. "Let's see; I guess I should backtrack a bit."

He launched into a repeat of an earlier question, and Winward shifted his attention to the mojo sitting in its corner. Sitting; but clearly not happy with its banishment. The head movements and feather ruffling Winward had noted earlier had increased dramatically, both in frequency and magnitude. *Nervous at being separated from its protector?* the Cobra wondered. *Or upset because it can't influence things as well at this distance?* The whole idea of the mojos having some subliminal power over the Qasamans made Winward feel decidedly twitchy. Alone among all he'd talked to, he still hoped Jonny Moreau's theory was wrong.

"Damn."

Winward turned his attention back to the interrogation to find McKinley scowling into space. "I'm sorry, but the recorder's *still* picking up too much noise. I guess we're going to have to put your mojo out of the room entirely. Kreel?—would you come in here a minute. Bring something talon-proof with you."

"Wait," the Qasaman said, half rising from his seat. "You cannot take my mojo away from here."

"Why not?" McKinley asked. "We won't hurt it, and you'll have it back in a few minutes." The door opened and the Cobra who'd earlier escorted the Qasaman in stepped into the room, a thick cloth bunched in his hand.

"You must not take him," the Qasaman repeated, the first hint of anger beginning to show through his stoicism. "I have cooperated fully—you have no right to treat me this way."

"Seven more questions—that's all," McKinley said soothingly. "Five minutes or less, and you'll have it back. Look, there's an empty office across the hall; Kreel can just stand there in the middle of the room with your mojo on his arm, and when we're done you can open the door and get it back. No harm will come to it—I promise."

Provided it behaves itself, Winward added silently. Kreel would have another Cobra in the room with him, lasers targeted on the bird the whole time, but Winward didn't envy him the job of standing there with mojo talons less than half a meter from his face.

The Qasaman was still protesting, but it was clear from his voice that he knew it was futile. Kreel meanwhile had wrapped the cloth around his left forearm and stooped to present it to the mojo. With obvious hesitation the bird climbed aboard. Kreel left, closing the door behind them, and McKinley resumed his questioning.

It was all over, as he'd promised, in less than five minutes; but well before it ended Winward came to the conclusion that he was seeing just how angry a Qasaman could become without physically attacking something. The man's earlier grudging cooperation became an almost palpable bitterness as he spat his answers at the recorder. Twice he refused to answer at all. Winward found his own muscles tensing in anticipation of the moment when the Qasaman's control broke completely and sent him diving across the desk in a strangulation attempt.

That moment, fortunately, never came. McKinley finished his list, and thirty seconds later the man and mojo were reunited across the hall. "One more thing and you can go," McKinley told him as he stroked the bird's throat soothingly. "Kreel's going to put a numbered ribbon around your neck so we'll know we've already talked to you. I presume you won't want to go through this again."

The Qasaman snorted, but otherwise ignored everyone except his mojo as Kreel wrapped the red ribbon snugly around his neck and sealed the ends together. Then, still wordlessly, he stalked down the hall toward the exit, Kreel a step behind him.

McKinley took a deep breath, let it out in a long sigh. "And if you thought *that* was rough," he told Winward wryly, "wait'll you see what's on-line for tomorrow."

"I can hardly wait," Winward said as they walked back to the testing room. "You really getting anything worthwhile from all of this?"

"Oh, sure." Swiveling the recorder box around, McKinley opened a panel to reveal a compact display and keyboard. He busied himself with the latter and a set of curves appeared on the screen. "Composite of the three hundred sixty Qasamans we tested today," he told Winward. "Compared to a data base-

line we took on Aventine the week before we left. The
Qasamans maintain a much lower stress level, despite the obnoxious content of the questions, as long
as their mojos are on their shoulders. It rises some
when we put the birds across the room, but it doesn't
really shoot up until the birds are out of sight. Then
it actually goes *above* our baseline levels—right here—
and it drops off much faster when they get the mojos
back."

Winward pursed his lips. "Some of that could be
irritation from having to go over the same questions
twice," he suggested.

"And some of it could be differences between our
cultures, though we've tried to minimize both effects," McKinley nodded. "Sure. We haven't got any
proof yet, but the indications are certainly there."

"Yeah." Subliminal control . . . "So what are you
doing tomorrow that'll be worse?"

"We're going to let them keep their mojos throughout the questioning, but we're going to irritate the
birds with ultrasonics and see how much if any of the
tension transfers."

"Sounds like great fun. You know enough about
mojo senses to know what'll do the trick?"

"We think so. I guess we'll find out."

"Um. Then day three is when you try mixing the
mojos and owners up?"

"Right. And we'll also do the hunt-stress test some
time in there, whenever outrider-three is able to get
their bololin herd here. I only hope we'll have enough
people with sensor-ribbons on by then to get us some
good numbers—it's for sure we won't be able to repeat *that* experiment." McKinley cocked an eyebrow.
"You look pensive. Trouble?"

Winward pursed his lips. "You really think it'll take
the rest of the planet two more days to figure out
something's wrong and make some major response?"

"I thought we *wanted* them to react."

"We want them to react sufficiently for us to see

their heavy weaponry, if any," Winward said. "We *don't* want them to put together something powerful enough to roll over us."

"Ouch. Yes; I concede the difference. Well ... if they move faster, I guess we'll just have to speed things up. And you Cobras will have to start earning your room and board here the hard way."

Winward grimaced. Heavily armed Qasamans ... and clouds of mojos. "Yes. I guess we will."

Chapter 28

York had put in a long day aboard ship and had looked forward to at least one good night's sleep before things heated up below. But he'd been asleep barely four hours when the intercom's *ping*ing dragged him awake. "Yes—York," he mumbled. "What is it?"

"Something happening on Qasama," the duty officer's voice said. "I think you'll want to see this."

"On my way."

Robed and barefoot, he was seated before one of the big displays in two minutes flat ... and the image there was indeed worth waking him for.

"Helicopters," he identified them to the two spotters on duty. "Possibly with auxiliary thrusters—they're making pretty good speed. Where'd they come from?"

"We first picked them up a few kilometers east of Sollas," the duty officer told him. "Could have come a fair distance, though, if they'd been going slower; it was the movement we noticed first."

"Uh-huh." York tapped keys, watched the results appear at the bottom of the screen. Six units, flying just a bit subsonic—which didn't prove anything about their actual capabilities—heading southeast toward the *Menssana*'s village. ETA, roughly two hours. "Get me Governor Telek," he said over his shoulder.

Telek had also been asleep, and by the time the *Menssana*'s duty officer rousted her out of bed York had a bit more information. "Two of them are fairly big, possibly implying troop carriers," he told her. "The other four are smaller; I'd guess reconnaissance or attack. Odds are probably good that they're converted civilian craft, instead of specifically military ones, which should be to our advantage."

"Well, at least they don't have gravity lifts," Telek mused. "That's one technological edge we know we've got."

"Not necessarily." York shook his head. "*No* one puts grav lifts on attack helicopters, whether they've got 'em or not—the things are wildly inefficient for tight, high-speed maneuvering. Besides, for nighttime applications a grav lift's glow makes you a flying bull's-eye."

"So these *are* something we should worry about?"

York snorted. "Worry and a half. We used a lot of helicopters back in the Marines, and I've seen them chew up areas twice the size of your village."

Telek's intercom image went tight-lipped. "Except that they'd kill three thousand of their own people if they try that."

"Right, and I doubt they're quite that desperate yet," York agreed. "*And* they're unlikely to hang around overhead sniping at the Cobras until they have an idea of what *we've* got to shoot back with."

"So the gleaner-team stays put," Telek said. "But the outrider teams go to ground?"

"They certainly make themselves inconspicuous. *And* the *Menssana* gets the hell out of there."

"Damn." Telek bit at her lip. "Yeah, you're right. You think going to ground a hundred kilometers away will be safe enough?"

"The farther the better. But you've got to move fast, before they're close enough to spot your grav lifts. I don't want to find out the hard way what sort of air-to-air capability they have."

"Good point. Captain Shepherd?"

"Three minutes to lift," the other's voice came into the circuit. "We've picked a tentative hiding place three hundred kilometers northwest of here, subject to your approval."

"What, right in the path of the helicopters?" York frowned.

"No, several kilometers off their approach. There's a large section of good rock cover under a crevasse overhang there—and it's certainly the last direction the Qasamans would expect us to run."

"Fine," Telek put in impatiently. "Just get us moving; I'll look the maps over when I have time. Decker, keep an eye on those helicopters and let us know if anything else shows up."

"Will do," York said. "And *you* people sit on your screens, too—they could have sneaked antiaircraft or spotters out there under the trees earlier today."

"You're a comfort in my old age," Telek returned dryly. "I've got to go now, get Michael on the line. Talk to you later."

Telek's image vanished from the screen. "At least they can't block or trace our communications this time around," the duty officer said.

"Unless they've learned about split-frequency radio in the past six weeks," York told him heavily. "And I wouldn't put it past them." Taking a deep breath, he chased the last of the sleep from his mind. "All right, gentlemen, let's get busy. Complete sweep of the village and everything for a thousand kilometers around it. If anything's moving out there, I want to know about it."

The helicopter formation broke up about fifty kilometers west of the village, two of the smaller ones heading straight in while the others circled to the north and south. Winward's Cobras braced for an attack ... but the craft made only a single pass overhead before regrouping to the east and swinging

around to head north. For awhile they tracked along
the road, and Pyre and his outrider-one team braced
in turn. But if they were spotted there was no sign.
Continuing north, the helicopters faded into the background somewhere near the next village, disappear-
ing from the *Dewdrop*'s screens.

"You think they picked us up?" Justin asked Pyre
as the ten Cobras of outrider-one returned cautiously
to their roadside positions.

"Hard to tell," the other sighed, checking his watch.
About an hour and a half to local sunrise—plenty of
time for the craft to refuel, rearm, even sit around for
awhile and discuss strategy, and *still* get back in time
for a predawn attack if they wanted to. "Depends
really on how good their infrareds are. Radar and
motion sensors would have been pretty useless with
the tree canopy this thick."

"I would have thought they'd have attacked if they'd
spotted us," one of the others commented.

"Unless they still think we didn't notice them in the
darkness," Pyre pointed out. "In that case they might
prefer not to tip off the gleaner-team by incinerating
a section of forest twenty kilometers north."

"They'll leave *that* for the ground troops in the
morning, I suppose," someone else put in dryly.

Pyre grimaced; the news of the convoy moving
south along the roads had come from the *Dewdrop*
only fifteen minutes earlier. "Probably," he admitted. "Though if I were them I'd bring the helicopters
back for the party, too. Not much point in subtlety
by that time."

"What fun," Justin said. "Any other good news?"

Pyre shrugged. "Only that the convoy's not due for
a few more hours at the least—which means some of
us should get reasonably caught up on our sleep
before then."

"Only some of us?"

"We've got to have sentries," Pyre pointed out.
"Can't count on the Qasamans not to sneak some-

thing past the *Dewdrop*—and the helicopters *might* come back. Hey, get used to it, friends—this is what warfare is all about: worry and lack of sleep."

Plus, of course, a lot of dying. Pyre hoped they wouldn't have to find out too much about that part.

The helicopters' early morning flyby hadn't gone unnoticed by the gleaner-team, of course. But it wasn't until the day's testing began that they discovered the villagers, too, had heard the overhead activity.

"You can see it in their faces and body language as clearly as if they were wearing wraparound displays," McKinley told Winward tightly an hour into the interviews. "They know the government's on to us and they're fully expecting some kind of move soon, probably within a day."

Winward nodded; York and the others aboard the *Dewdrop* had come to the same conclusion. "Well, we certainly can't sit put for a full-scale military operation here. What's the earliest time you can be finished?"

"Depends on how much data you want to take back," the other shrugged. "We're already combining the original day two and day three schedules, taking half the data points we'd originally planned for each—"

From one of the rooms down the hall came a muffled shriek and the crash of a falling object. "What—?" McKinley snapped, spinning around.

Winward was already moving at a dead run, auditory enhancers keyed for follow-up noises. The sounds of a struggle . . . muffled curses . . . *that* door—

He slammed it open to see one of the Cobras pulling a struggling Qasaman from the desk he'd apparently thrown himself across. The experimenter, picking himself up shakily from the floor behind his overturned chair, was white-faced with shock, the pale skin in sharp contrast to the oozing blood on his cheek. Beside him on the floor lay a dead mojo.

The Cobra looked up as Winward strode in. "The mojo tried to attack, and I had to kill it. I was a little too slow to stop this one."

Winward nodded as McKinley skidded into the room behind him. "Get him out of here," he told the Cobra.

"Killers," the Qasaman spat toward Winward as the other Cobra hauled him toward the door. "Foulspring excrement vermin—"

The door slammed on his tirade. "Loses a lot in translation, I'll bet." Winward and McKinley moved to the tester's side. "You okay?"

"Yeah," the other nodded, dabbing with a handkerchief at his cheek. "Took me completely by surprise—his control just seemed to snap, and there he was on top of me."

Winward exchanged glances with McKinley. "When was that? When his mojo was killed?"

"Oddly enough, no. As a matter of fact, I think they both jumped me at the same time. Though I couldn't swear to that."

"Um," McKinley nodded. "Well, the tapes will show the details. You'd better go to HQ, get those scratches looked at. No point taking any chances."

"Yes, sir. Sorry."

"Not your fault. And don't come back until you're sure you feel ready to continue. We're not in *that* much of a hurry."

The tester nodded and left. "If he's too obviously nervous it could skew his results," McKinley explained.

Winward nodded. He had the recorder box back on the table now and popped the rear panel. "Let's see what really happened."

The tester, it turned out, had been correct. Bird and man had attacked at precisely the same moment.

"You can see signs of agitation in both of them," McKinley pointed out, running the tape again. "The rippling feathers and snapping motions of the beak here; the shifting muscle lines in his face, here, and the hand movements."

"This is all in response to ultrasonics that humans can't hear?" Something prickled on the back of Winward's neck.

"Right. Just look at the tester here—he's in the same ultrasonic beam and isn't so much as sweating hard." McKinley bit at his lip. "But I wasn't expecting this *much* of a common reaction."

"They're getting some of their courage back, maybe, knowing troops are on the way."

"But the birds aren't supposed to be intelligent enough to pick up on things like that," McKinley growled.

"Maybe they pick it up via body language from their humans. Maybe that's the way the mojos' agitation transmits in reverse, too."

"Possible." McKinley sighed. "Unfortunately, the body language and telepathic theories are going to be very hard to distinguish between without long-term studies."

"Which we don't have time for." Winward grimaced. "Well, do the best you can—maybe you and the bio people will be able to pull useful results out of the raw data. In the meantime, try to avoid pushing any more of your subjects over the brink."

"Yeah."

Banyon took a deep breath, exhaled it carefully. At long last, paydirt.

The three creatures eyeing the humans from the undergrowth were krisjaws, all right—surely no two creatures on Qasama could have those wavy, flame-shaped canine teeth. Nearly two meters long, with the lean musculature and stealth of predators, they eased toward the four humans, eyes fixed on their prey.

And Governor Telek's theory had been correct. On the shoulder of each sat an equally attentive mojo.

"Now what?" Hanford murmured, a bit nervously, at Banyon's side.

"You have the recorders running?" The Cobra sensed rather than saw Hanford's nod. "Everyone else in position?"

Three acknowledgments came through his earphone. The other Cobras had the krisjaws boxed up . . . and it was time to test the predators' reactions. "Get ready," he muttered to the zoologists grouped behind him. "Here goes." Raising his hands, he fired a salvo from fingertip lasers into the brush at either side of the stalking animals.

The krisjaws weren't stupid. All three froze in place for a long minute and then began backing away as cautiously as they'd been advancing. They got barely a meter, though, before a second burst of laser fire from one of Banyon's hidden flankers traced a line of smoldering vegetation behind them. Again they froze, heads turning slowly as if to seek out their hidden assailant. "Well," Banyon said after a few seconds, "it looks like they'll be staying put for a bit. How close did you want to examine them?"

"No closer than necessary," one of the zoologists muttered. "I don't trust a flash net to hold anything that size."

"Nonsense," Hanford said—though not all that confidently, Banyon thought. "Let me take a shot at the one on the right. Everyone watch for trouble."

There was a soft *chuff* of compressed air from behind Banyon's shoulder, a glimpse of a tiny cylinder arrowing toward the target krisjaw—and with an explosive crack the flash net blew out to tangle the krisjaw's head and forelegs. Screeching, the mojo on its back shot clear . . . and the krisjaw went berserk.

Banyon had used flash nets against spine leopards on Aventine on numerous occasion—had trapped bigger and meaner-looking animals on the *Menssana*'s five-world tour a couple of months ago—but never in all that had he seen such a violent reaction. The krisjaw screamed in rage, slashing as best it could with teeth and claws at the fine mesh clinging to its body, rolling around in the underbrush and occasionally even twisting itself entirely off the ground in its frenzy.

And within seconds it had opened up tears in the net.

Hanford stepped a pace forward, raising his air gun again, but Banyon had already made his decision. "Forget it," he called to the zoologist over the noise, pressing the gun barrel down. Targeting, he swung his leg up and fired his antiarmor laser.

The landscape lit up briefly, and with one final scream the krisjaw collapsed among the ruins of the net.

Someone swore feelingly under his breath. "No wonder the Qasamans organize hunts against these things."

"Yeah." Banyon shifted his attention to the other two krisjaws, still waiting quietly. Waiting, but several meters further to the side than they'd been a minute earlier. A new line of blackened vegetation smoldered beside them. "What happened?—they try to slip away in the confusion?"

"They thought about it," one of the Cobras replied dryly. "I think we've convinced them to cooperate for the moment."

"Cooperate," Hanford mused. "I seem to remember the mayor of Huriseem mentioning the krisjaws were pretty peaceful when the Qasamans first got here."

"He said it was a legend," one of the others reminded him. "I find it hard to swallow that an animal's behavior would change that drastically."

"What do you think we're looking at right now?" Hanford snorted. "Those two krisjaws are being about as peaceable as they come."

"Only because they see they'll be cut to ribbons if they try anything."

"Which in itself is highly suggestive," Banyon put in. "Remember the gleaner-team report this morning about the apparent transfer of aggression between mojos and humans?"

"You think the mojo made the krisjaw fight back against the net?" Hanford shaded his eyes as he searched the trees for the escaped bird.

"Just the opposite," Banyon told him. "I'm wondering if perhaps the mojo was sitting on the krisjaw's natural aggression, holding it in check until it was forced too far away."

"That's crazy," one of the Cobras scoffed. "The krisjaws are sitting targets out there—their best survival tactic right now is to run or attack."

"Except that we've demonstrated we can kill them if they try either," Hanford said thoughtfully. "Remember the spookies on Tacta? If the mojos have a similar sense for relative danger they may recognize that their best bet really *is* to sit and wait."

There was a long moment of silence as the others digested that. "I suppose it's reasonably self-consistent, as theories go," one of the zoologists said at last. "Hard to see how a system like that would get started, though. Not to mention how you'd prove it."

"Given a telepathic ability, it seems pretty straightforward to me," Banyon said. "The mojos need some predator strong enough to take on a bololin in order to get access to their embryo-hosts. Maybe the mojo acts as long-range spotter for the krisjaw in return or something."

"Though with the mojo's control the relationship doesn't have to be particularly mutual," Hanford murmured. "The birds may be out-and-out parasites."

"Yeah," Banyon said. "And as for proving it . . . Dale, target the mojo nearest you, all right? Head shot; fast and clean, without affecting the krisjaw directly."

"Okay," the voice came in his ear. "Ready."

Banyon targeted the appropriate krisjaw and eased his weight onto his right leg. If this worked he wanted his antiarmor laser ready to fire. "Okay: *now*."

A flicker of light from beside and behind the krisjaw caught the mojo—and an instant later the krisjaw screamed and charged. Banyon leaned back as he activated the automatic fire control, his leg swinging up to fire point blank at the creature's face. There was a blaze of reflected light, and the krisjaw's fur blackened as the laser flash-burned it. The animal slammed heavily to the ground—

And Banyon looked up just in time to see the remaining krisjaw's mojo streaking for his face.

The landscape tilted crazily as his nanocomputer threw him out of the way of the bird's attack—but not before he saw the the krisjaw, too, was in motion. He hit the ground, rolling awkwardly on his left shoulder as someone screamed . . . and he came up into a crouch to see the krisjaw spring toward Hanford.

Banyon snapped his hands up in a fast dual shot at the predator, but what saved the zoologist's life in that first half second was his own reflexive shot with his flash net gun. The krisjaw hit, slamming Hanford to the ground, but with claws and teeth temporarily blocked by the netting it could do little except gouge at its victim. Banyon scrambled to get his legs clear of the undergrowth . . . but before he could bring his antiarmor laser to bear two brilliant spears of light lit up the forest and the krisjaw collapsed in a charred heap.

Banyon got to his feet, looking quickly around. The mojo was still unaccounted for . . .

But not for long. The bird was perched atop one of the other zoologist's crossed forearms, wings beating at the man's head and shoulders as it tried to work its beak in to the face.

Banyon was on it in a second, grabbing its neck with both hands and squeezing. The mojo released its grip, fluttering wildly as it tried to get at its new attacker. But Banyon's grip had Cobra servos behind it . . . and within a few seconds the bird lay limp in his hands. "You okay?" he asked the zoologist, wincing at the blood oozing through the other's sleeves.

"Arms and head hurt like crazy," the other grunted, lowering his guard hesitantly. "Otherwise . . . okay, I think."

His face, at least, was unmarked. "We'll get you right back to the aircar," Banyon told him, turning back to Hanford. The other Cobras had the krisjaw carcass off him now, and Dale was kneeling beside him. "How is he?" Banyon asked.

"Might have a cracked rib or two," Dale said, getting to his feet. "Not a good idea to carry him far; I'll go bring the aircar here."

Banyon nodded and knelt beside Hanford as Dale set off at a fast trot. "How are you feeling?" he asked.

"Scientifically vindicated," Hanford murmured, managing a weak smile. "We've now proved that mojos in the wild serve the same role they do for the Qasamans. They help the krisjaws fight."

"And apparently help decide when fighting's the best approach," Banyon nodded.

"As opposed to simply getting out of the way?"

Banyon looked up to meet the angry glare of the team's uninjured zoologist. "I wasn't running out on you," he said quietly.

"Of course not," the other snorted. "Just getting to a place where you could line up a clear shot, right? While it was busy with the rest of us. Fine job—really fine." He turned his back.

Banyon sighed, closing his eyes briefly. They would never learn—neither the people who assigned Cobras as bodyguards, nor the bodyguarded people themselves. In a pinch a Cobra's computerized reflexes were designed to protect him and him alone. There was no provision for heroic self-sacrifice in the nanocomputer's programming . . . and the civilians would never understand that, no matter how many times they were told.

There was a quiet click in his earphone: a relay from

the split-freq equipment in their aircar. "Banyon? This is Telek; come in."

"Yes, Governor. What's up?"

"Any results on your hunt yet?"

"As a matter of fact, yes. We can send them to you as soon as we get the recorders tied into the transmitter."

"Don't bother," Telek said, and Banyon could hear a new undertone of tension in her voice. "Just get yourselves and the data back to the *Menssana*—you've got our current location?"

"If you haven't moved since last night, yes. What's gone wrong?"

"Nothing, really," she sighed. "At least nothing unexpected. But I want to be able to pull out quickly if we need to."

Banyon grimaced as something tight took hold of his stomach. "The Qasaman convoy has reached outrider-one?"

"Ten minutes ago. And the team's under attack."

Chapter 29

The forest was alive with the stutter of rapid-fire guns and the furious sleet of bullets tearing at leaves and undergrowth and blasting great sprays of splinters from tree trunks all around. Flat on his belly behind the largest tree he could find near his station, Justin hugged the ground and waited for the barrage to ease up or shift direction. It did, and he took a cautious peek around the bole. A hundred meters away six Qasamans were running back toward the convoy from the tree trunk the Cobras had felled across the road. They'd been placing explosives, Pyre had guessed ... and even as Justin watched, the barrier erupted with yellow fire. The smoke cleared to show a section of the trunk had disintegrated.

"Barrier down," one of the Cobras reported in Justin's ear. "Convoy starting up again."

The hail of lead intensified, almost covering the sound of car engines, but little of the fire was coming in Justin's direction. "I'm on it," he said into his mike. Twenty meters closer to him was the next of the trees along the road they'd prepared so carefully last night. Raising his hand out of the matted leaves, he targeted carefully and fired.

The rope holding the precut tree snapped; and with a crack of breaking wood audible even over the gunshots it toppled gracefully across the road. "Barrier replaced," he reported.

"Stand by to pull back," Pyre said tersely. "Smoke . . . ?"

In response, the forest on both sides of the road erupted with black smoke. "Lead team, pull back," Pyre ordered.

Justin began backing away from his tree, balancing the need for speed with the need to remain low. The smoke would block visual and infrared targeting, but there were always lucky shots to worry about. So far the Qasamans' lack of experience with warfare had showed up clearly in their unimaginative tactics; but they more than made up for that with enthusiasm.

He was midway to his new cover, smack in the middle of nowhere, when a new stutter opened up from above. He froze, muffling a curse.

The helicopters were back.

Or at least one of them was. It was off to the east a ways, he estimated from the sound, probably blowing up some of the hundred or so "warm-body" infrared decoys they'd spent the morning setting up. But the machine was drifting closer. Making a quick decision, Justin leaped to his feet and dashed for cover. The pitch of the helicopter's drone shifted as he did so, and a second later he got a glimpse of the craft through the trees . . . and a rain of bullets abruptly splattered at his heels.

He put on a burst of speed, and was behind his target tree before the Qasaman gunner could correct his aim. "I'm okay," he called into his mike before anyone had to ask. "But I'm pinned down."

"I'm on it," someone grunted. "Someone give me covering fire?"

"Got it," Pyre said. "On three. One, two, *three*."

The helicopter had swung around, trying for a clear shot at Justin, and was framed almost perfectly between tree branches as Pyre's antiarmor laser flashed squarely into the cockpit windows.

The craft jerked, nearly destabilizing enough to slide into the treetops bare meters below. But the pilot was good, and within seconds the craft was nearly steady again . . . and from directly beneath, a figure shot upward through the leafy canopy to grab the helicopter's side door handle. Twisting his legs upward, the Cobra turned himself around his precarious grip to what was in effect a one-armed handstand along the helicopter's side . . . and with his feet barely a meter from the main rotor hub, his antiarmor laser blazed forth.

The pilot did his best. Almost instantly the craft banked hard to the side, throwing the Cobra off in an action that should have killed him. But with the nanocomputer's cat-landing programming even that small satisfaction would be denied the Qasaman . . . and as he carefully righted the helicopter the stressed rotor metal gave way. Two seconds later the forest shook with the thunder of the crash.

"Report," Pyre snapped as the explosion died into the dull crackle of burning fuel.

"No problem," the Cobra assured them all. "Watch the branches if any of you have to try that—the damn things scratch like hell."

Justin let out a relieved sigh . . . and suddenly became aware of the relative silence. "They've stopped shooting—"

"Almo, we've got a Qasaman on the road," one of the others interrupted. "He's alone—well, with a mojo—and he's holding a white flag."

A white flag. Winward had gone out under a white flag the last trip here . . . and had been shot for his trouble. Justin's jaw tightened as he wondered if Pyre remembered that . . . wondered what the other's response would be.

"Okay," Pyre said after a moment. "Everyone keep looking sharp—they may be using him as a diversion

while they sneak around to encircle us on foot. I'm
going to call him over and see what he wants."

"Target the mojo right away," someone said dryly.

"No kidding. Here goes."

Pyre's voice continued normally in Justin's ear as,
bullhorn amplified, the Qasaman translation echoed
among the trees: "Continue forward. Keep your hands
visible and your mojo on your shoulder. I'll tell you
where to leave the road."

Quiet returned to the forest. Notching up his auditory enhancers, Justin settled down beside his tree to
wait.

Telek rubbed her eyes with the heels of both hands.
"The problem," she told Pyre wearily, "is the same
one we've had ever since the convoy first appeared:
namely, we simply don't have enough data yet to
pull out."

"What you mean is that you haven't proved yet
that the mojos are directly controlling the Qasamans,"
he retorted.

Probably true, she admitted to herself. "What I mean
is that the gleaner-team hasn't finished its agenda."

"It may not get the chance," Pyre growled. "I don't
think they're bluffing when they say this is our last
chance to pull out before they turn up the fire. And if
they don't mind how much it costs them we really
aren't going to be able to hold them very long."

And that short reprieve would cost them ten good
Cobras—*and* probably give the Qasamans reasonably
undamaged Cobra equipment to study. "The last thing
I want is a full battle with you on the losing end,"
Telek told him. "But I don't see the hook yet, and
past experience tells me there's one somewhere in
this offer."

"Maybe there isn't. Maybe Moff just wants to avoid
bloodshed."

Telek's lip twitched at the name. Moff. Escort for
off-world visitors, sharp-eyed observer who'd pulled

the whole thing down on them last time, and now one of the leaders of this thrown-together task force. A man of many talents . . . and a man of luck, too, to have survived Justin's Purma rampage. She wondered how Justin was feeling about Moff's presence out there, chased the thought irritably from her mind. Moff. What did she know about him that might give her a clue as to what he was up to with this? Did he want to chase the invaders away from the village into an ambush where the Qasamans wouldn't be risking civilian lives? Was there something in the village they didn't want found? *Could* it really be as simple as an attempt to drag the two cultures back from an otherwise almost inevitable war?

But the gleaner-team needed more *time*.

"Governor?"

"Still here, Almo," she sighed. "All right, let's try an experiment. Tell them we'll pull out as soon as we've shown a representative that we haven't hurt or killed anyone in the village."

"Will that give outrider-three enough time to bring their bololin herd by the village?"

Telek checked her projections. "It might, if we take things slow enough. But we probably wouldn't have time after the hunt-stress test to remove the neck sensors the gleaner-team's got on the subjects."

"The Council was pretty firm on the point of not leaving any electronics behind," Pyre reminded her.

"I know, I know. Well, if we have to scrap that test, we scrap it, that's all. Look, just see if they'll buy the idea of a tour. I'll talk to Michael and McKinley while you do that, see if they have any ideas."

"All right." Pyre hesitated. "If it'll really help . . . we *are* prepared to die out here."

Telek blinked away sudden moisture. "I appreciate that," she managed. "But you also qualify as electronics I'd rather not leave behind. Talk to the Qasamans and call me back."

*   *   *

"Yes, I *do* have an idea," Winward told Telek with grim satisfaction. "I've been thinking about it ever since the psych people first started complaining that we needed to do long-term studies."

"And?"

"*And* if you can't do the studies themselves, the next best thing is to get the results," he said. "And I think I know just where to find them."

"We want it to be someone in authority, whose word the Qasaman leadership trusts," Pyre warned the messenger, watching his words carefully. "We want to prove our people have acted humanely."

"You invade our world and terrorize an entire village and then expect to earn a reputation as gentlemen?" the Qasaman spat. "You're in no position to make demands of us; but as it happens Moff is willing to accompany your escort to the village. As a gesture of good faith only, of course."

"Of course," Pyre nodded. Winward had called it correctly . . . and whatever Moff's own reasons for accepting the offer, he would soon be in their hands.

And at that point it would be up to McKinley and Winward. Pyre hoped they could pull it off.

"Two . . . one . . . *mark*." Dan Rostin flipped the aircar's huge electromagnet off as, in perfect synch, Parker swung the little craft into the air. Just in time: the flankers of the bololin herd thundering by grazed the aircar's underside with their dorsal quills. Parker grabbed some more altitude and blew a drop of sweat from the tip of his nose. "Outrider-three to Telek," he called toward the long-range mike. "Last course change complete. Can you confirm the direction is right?"

"Telek here," the governor's voice came back promptly. "Just a second—we're getting a reading from the *Dewdrop*." There was a short pause. "Yes;

confirmed. Have they picked up speed for some reason?"

"They sure have," Parker told her. "I think all these direction changes and field strength fluctuations are starting to get to them. If they keep it up they'll pass the village in about fifty minutes."

"*Dewdrop* gives us essentially the same number. All right, I'll let gleaner-team know. I hope it doesn't ruin their schedule."

"So do I," Parker snorted. "There's no way we're going to slow them down, that's for sure."

Telek sighed. "Yeah. Well . . . get back here, preferably without drawing attention to yourselves. Don't worry about making good speed; it doesn't look like we'll be moving from here for quite some time."

Moff drove his car through the open village gate and then said his first words since leaving the Cobras' blockade: "Where now?"

"The mayoral building," Justin told him. "It's ahead down the street and to the left."

The other nodded, and Justin sent a sidelong look at the Qasaman's face. Moff hadn't seemed surprised to have Justin assigned as his escort; but then, little ever seemed to surprise him. Even now, entering an enemy-held village, his face was impassive, only his darting eyes giving any indication of concern or worry. "Where are all the villagers?"

Justin glanced around. Except for a Cobra at each end of the block they were approaching, the streets were indeed deserted. He put the question via communicator to Winward. "They're all outside in the north and central parts of town," he relayed the answer.

"I'd like to see them before I speak to your leaders."

Justin shrugged, striving for unconcern. They were on a tight schedule, but he couldn't tell Moff that. "Okay with me," he said. "Just don't take too long. I want the talks to get underway before anyone starts shooting out there again."

"Our people won't start more fighting if yours don't."

Justin shrugged again and settled back to endure the detour. He was supposed to try and get an inkling of what Moff was up to, but aside from spotting a likely recording device built into the Qasaman's mojo perch he hadn't seen any sort of equipment that could give him any hints. The thought of the bacteriological attack on Cerenkov and Rynstadt on the last trip made his skin creep, despite the assurances by Telek and Winward that Moff was unlikely to risk his own life with such stuff when safer delivery methods existed. The Aventinians' logic, he kept remembering, was required by no law of nature to be the same as the Qasamans'.

Moff drove them around a couple of corners—and there, indeed, were the villagers.

It looked like a giant in-town picnic, to Justin's eyes, with most of the adults sitting around in small groups while children played games around and among them. At the edges of the square Cobras stood on guard.

"The remainder are through the archway there?" Moff asked, pointing.

"I think so, yes."

Without asking permission the Qasaman turned a corner and headed that way. The rest of the villagers were in a smaller open area a couple of blocks further north, and Moff stopped as they came within sight of the crowd. For a moment he looked them over, as if searching for mistreatment, and Justin noticed his shoulders turning slowly as he gave the recorder in his epaulet a sweep of the area. Allowing the troops back at the blockade to see the villagers were all right, if the recorder was transmitting a live picture—

Justin felt his body stiffen. No, *not* the villagers. He

watched the other's eyes, noted where they paused. Moff was looking at the guards.

He was counting the Cobras.

Of course. It was the same trick, turned inside-out, that he'd used to view the *Dewdrop*'s interior when Joshua and York were allowed back inside. Of the thirty Cobras in the village, Justin guessed about twenty were guarding the two groups of civilians—an absurdly small number for three thousand people, even given Cobra abilities. Moff had surely noticed that, and would just as surely conclude that the total number of Cobras wasn't much higher than the number visible.

Or, in other words, that the gleaner-team was a sitting target. Which implied . . . what?

Justin didn't know; but the others needed this information right away. Pressing his mike surreptitiously against his lips, he began to whisper.

York shook his head, eyes hard on the display before him. "No helicopter movement I can see," he told Telek. "You sure Moff's gadget isn't just recording?"

"We've found the transmission band it's using," she said tightly. "What about other aircraft? You said some fixed-wing craft had appeared on the Sollas airfield."

"They're still there. Almo still says no trouble at outrider-one's blockade?"

"Not unless they're sneaking troops in a *wide* circle around the area to head south on foot." Telek's image shook its head. "You think they're just waiting until we're clear of the village?"

York opened his mouth . . . and paused as a new thought struck him. "Tell me, does Moff seem to know his way around the village?"

"I'm sure they've got maps of the place in Sollas, yes," she said dryly.

"Right. Now tell me where there's enough room in the village for a landing shuttle."

"Why—" Telek broke off. "The area by the gate, and the two areas where we've got the villagers."

"And Moff's seen all three," York nodded grimly. "So he's now just confirmed what the helicopters last night probably reported: the gleaner-team has no ship standing close enough for a quick escape."

Telek let out a long, shuddering breath. "Damn. Damn, and damn again. No wonder he's not in any hurry to attack. He wants another crack at a starship, and he wants his task force in reasonable combat shape when it shows up. Hence the cease-fire. Captain, what's our best possible time to the village?"

"From here, no less than thirty minutes," Shepherd's voice came on. "The ship's not designed for extended high-speed atmospheric flight."

"Half an hour," York snorted. "*We* could drop down and reach them faster than that."

"Except that there's no way you could stuff the fifty people from gleaner and outrider-one aboard and still lift," Telek growled. "Well, gentlemen, we'd better figure something out, and fast. Our best chance at a diversion's due to hit the village in just under forty minutes now. Gleaner-team *has* to get out then."

Or, York added silently, *they might not get out at all*. Gnawing at the inside of his cheek, he stared at the display and tried to think.

The Cobra at the mayoral building's entrance stepped aside as Moff and Justin came up. "They're waiting in the first office on your left," he said, pulling open the door for them. Out of Moff's sight as the Qasaman passed, his hand made a quick brushing motion: the code sign for *stay back*. Justin nodded and drifted an extra half step behind Moff as they went to the office the guard had indicated. The door was open, and as they walked in Justin saw there were two men waiting for them: Winward and gleaner-team's head psychologist, Dr. McKinley. Both were standing in front of the room's low desk, and both looked vaguely tense.

"Good day, Moff," Winward nodded. "We've never actually met, but I've heard a great deal about you."

"And I you," Moff replied coolly. "You're the demon warrior who couldn't be killed. Or so it's said."

"Not by treachery, at any rate," Winward said, his tone chilling to match Moff's. "You'll note we treated *your* flag of truce more honorably."

"You speak of honor—"

"I speak of many things," Winward cut him off. "But before I do, I'd like to ask you to put your mojo in the next room."

Moff's back stiffened visibly. "So that I'll be totally defenseless before you?"

"Don't be ridiculous. If I wanted to harm you, both you *and* your damned bird would be stretched out on the floor there. You know that as well as I do. I'll ask you only once more."

"My mojo stays with me."

Winward sighed. "All right, have it your way." Reaching to the desk behind him, he scooped up a short-barreled, stockless rifle lying there and brought it to bear. With a screech the mojo leaped—

And shrieked again as the flash net caught it square across the beak.

"Here, Justin, put these in the next office," Winward said tiredly, handing the younger Cobra the immobilized bird and the net gun. "They don't show much capacity for learning, do they?" he remarked to Moff.

Moff's reply was lost to Justin as he deposited his charges next door; but by the time he returned Winward was speaking again. "Well, no matter. We have a pretty good idea of what the mojos do for you, and it's clear enough that if it comes to a full-fledged war we'll win easily."

"Because you cannot die?" Moff snorted. "Some may believe that; I don't. No demon protects you—or splits one mind into two men—" he added, throwing a baleful glare at Justin. "Your magic is simply science we have forgotten, and it will work as well for us when we've learned how it's done."

"Possibly," Winward shrugged. "But it's rather academic, because to learn how our magic works you'll need to kill some of us . . . and I doubt very much that your mojos will let you fight us face to face anymore."

Moff's mouth opened, but whatever he'd been planning to say apparently died on his lips. "What do you mean, won't *let* us fight?" he asked cautiously.

McKinley shook his head. "It's no use pretending, Moff. We've been taking data for less than two days and we already know how the mojos dangle you around like puppets. You've had three hundred years to study them—surely you know at least as much as we do."

"Puppets, you say." Moff's lip curled. "You understand *nothing*."

"Oh?" Winward said. "Then enlighten us."

Moff glared at him but remained silent. "The details don't matter," McKinley shrugged. "What matters is that the mojos have a vested interest in keeping their hunters—that's you—alive, and that they possess enough telepathic ability to back up their wishes. If they think you don't have a chance against us, they won't let you fight." He waved a hand. "The reactions toward us here in the village are all the proof we need."

"Oh, are they?" Moff spat. He seemed to be rapidly losing control, Justin noted uneasily. Were McKinley's assertions really so hard for him to take? Or was this perhaps simply the first waking moment Moff had had in years without a mojo by his side? A mojo keeping his human aggression under control. . . . "Then what do you say about the fighters waiting to sweep down on you twenty kilometers north of here? Are *they* unable to fight?" He jabbed a finger at McKinley. "The villagers have a fear of you based on superstition—our fighters aren't so handicapped. And once we've proved you can be beaten—as we will within hours—the fear the mojos sense and are paralyzing them with will be gone. The next time you return, you'll find a world united to oppose you."

"You don't think the mojos will try and save your lives?" McKinley asked.

Moff smiled thinly. "They will protect us, certainly—by tearing the flesh from your bones in battle. This conversation is at an end."

Winward and McKinley exchanged glances, and the latter nodded fractionally. "All right, if that's the way you want it," Winward said. "We'll be out of your way within those few hours you mentioned; and if we're lucky, we won't have to come back."

"It doesn't matter if you do or not," Moff said quietly . . . and to Justin his voice had the feel of an open grave about it. "We *will* rediscover the secret of star travel someday. And *we* will then come and find *you*."

Winward's lips compressed and his eyes sought Justin's. "Return his mojo and escort him outside. He can stay with the rest of the villagers until we're ready to leave."

Justin nodded and indicated the door. Wordlessly, Moff strode past him and out into the hall, where he waited until Justin had brought him his mojo, still entangled in its net. "Just unwrap it carefully and the bird won't be hurt," he told the Qasaman, handing the creature into the other's arms.

Moff nodded, once, and stalked to the door. Justin watched him walk down the street toward the civilian holding area, then returned to the office. "He's on his way to the square," he told Winward.

The older Cobra nodded, his attention clearly elsewhere. ". . . All right. If you're ready, so are we," he said toward his pendant. "You'll get outrider-one moving? . . . Good. Justin's here; I'll just go ahead and take charge of him. ETAs? . . . Fifteen and twenty; got it. Good luck."

"Well?" McKinley asked.

"The *Dewdrop*'s on its way," Winward said tightly. "It'll drop into the central square in about fifteen minutes."

"The *Dewdrop*?" Justin frowned. "Why's *it* coming down?"

"Because the *Menssana* would take longer to get here and be subject to attack the whole way." Winward turned to McKinley. "All the sensor collars off?"

"And packed for loading, along with the rest of the gear." The other picked up a small box that had been resting on the low table. "This is the last of it right here."

"Okay. Get your people to the square." Winward tapped his pendant as McKinley headed for the door. "Dorjay? It's a go. . . . Right; fifteen minutes. Get the people out and set up a perimeter to protect it. Watch out for Moff particularly—he's not nearly as impressed as the rest of them, and there are guns lying around he might pick up. . . . Good. Diversion's due in just under twenty—we'll need to be ready to go then. . . . Okay. Out."

Dropping his hand, he looked at Justin. "Let's get moving—you and I are going to be part of the helicopter defense, and we need to be at the wall when they figure out what's going on."

"And then what?" Justin asked quietly. "The *Dewdrop* can't possibly carry all of us."

Winward gave him a tight smile. "That's sometimes what rearguards are for, you know: to stay behind. Come on, let's hit the wall and find some good positions to shoot from."

"Okay, start easing back," Pyre murmured into his mike. "No noise, and be sure you're out of sight of the Qasamans before hitting the road."

There were answering murmurs in his ear, and Pyre shifted his attention to the knot of troops facing him twenty meters away. He'd agreed to stay within sight as a sort of exchange hostage while Moff was in the village ... which meant that when the timer ran down on this one he would have to be gone before the Qasamans decided to start shooting. Activating his auditory enhancers, he tried to listen for the excited voices that would mean the *Dewdrop* had been spotted.

The shouts, centered on the Qasamans' lead car, erupted barely two minutes later; and Pyre was racing through the trees before anyone thought to take a shot at him. With the need for stealth gone, he made straight for the road, where better footing would let him use his leg servos to best advantage. From behind came an explosion as the Qasamans destroyed the tree that blocked their path. Slowing as he passed the last of their prepared trees, Pyre sent it crashing down behind him, a move that should put the ground troops out of the game for good. Pushing his pace to the limit, he watched the sky for both the descending *Dewdrop* and the Qasamans' inevitable aerial response.

From his vantage point the events occurred simultaneously. Far ahead the glittering shape of the small starship dropped rapidly against the blue sky as, overhead, three small helicopters screamed southward to the attack. A hard lump rose into Pyre's throat as he watched them disappear behind the treetops. They were, as York had predicted, modified civilian craft ... but the Cobras' brief tangle with them had showed them well worth taking seriously.

He kept running. Far ahead the roar of the helicopters' engines changed pitch as they reached the village. Small explosions came faintly over the wind in his ears and, once, the sort of blast he remembered from the helicopter they'd shot down over the barricade. He wondered who had pulled it off this time, and whether the Cobra had lived through it. Blinking

the tears from his eyes, he squinted against the wind
and kept going.

And suddenly it was all over. A great roiling pillar
of black smoke rose above the trees; and seconds
later the *Dewdrop* shot out of it like a missile from its
launcher. The two remaining helicopters climbed after it, but their weapons weren't designed to fire
straight up and the *Dewdrop*'s gravity lifts were more
than adequate to maintain the starship's lead. The
three craft became points of reflected light in the sky
. . . and then were just two spots.

The *Dewdrop*, gleaner-team's scientists aboard, had
escaped. Leaving the Cobras behind.

Ahead, someone stepped from the trees along the
road and gave Pyre a quick wave before retreating to
cover again. Pyre slowed and joined him. "Any trouble?" the other Cobra asked.

Pyre shook his head. "They're at least ten minutes
behind me. Any sign of our escort yet?"

The other grinned. "Sure. Just listen."

Pyre notched up his enhancers. In the distance he
could hear a low rumble, accompanied by a well-
remembered snuffling. "Right on schedule. Everyone
ready?"

"This end is, anyway. I presume gleaner-team's
Cobras made it out while everyone was blinded by
the smokescreen."

"And were all busy assuming the Cobras were going
*in*ward instead of *out*ward," Pyre nodded. This would
be a whole lot easier if the Qasamans thought *everyone*
had escaped in the *Dewdrop*.

The rumbling was getting closer. . . .

And then, across the road, they burst out of the
woods: a bololin herd, running for all it was worth. A
big herd, Pyre saw, the far end of its leading edge lost
beyond a curve in the road and the dust of its own
passage. Maybe a thousand animals in all . . . and
among all those warm bodies, hidden from sight by

all that dust, forty Cobras would hardly be noticeable. Even if someone thought to look.

The leading edge had passed, the herd's flanks perhaps twenty meters away. Turning, Pyre and the other Cobra began to pace them, drifting closer to the herd as they ran until they were perhaps four meters away. Glances ahead and behind showed the rest of outrider-one joining the flow. At the herd's opposite flank, if all had gone well, the gleaner-team Cobras were doing likewise.

And for the next few hours, they should all be reasonably safe. After that—

After that, the *Menssana* lay three hundred kilometers almost dead ahead, presumably still unnoticed by the planetary authorities. If it could stay that way for the next six hours, the Cobras would be aboard and the ship in orbit long before any aircraft could be scrambled to intercept it.

Theoretically, anyway. Pyre settled his legs into a rhythmic pace, letting his servos take as much of the load as possible. Personally, he would be happy if things even came close.

And in this case, they did.

Chapter 30

They listened in silence as McKinley went through his presentation, and when he was finished Stiggur sighed. "No chance of an error, I don't suppose."

McKinley shook his head. "Nothing significant, certainly. We had enough test subjects to get good statistics."

Across the table from him, Jonny pursed his lips, the bittersweet taste of Pyrrhic victory in his mouth. He'd been vindicated, his "crazy" theory about the mojos more or less confirmed.

But the price of that victory was going to be war.

He could see that in the faces around the table. The other governors were *scared*—more than they'd ever been after the *Dewdrop*'s first mission. And even though some of them might not know how they'd respond to that fear, he understood human nature enough to know which way most would eventually go. Fight and flight were the only basic options ... and the Cobra Worlds had no place to run.

Fairleigh cleared his throat. "I still don't understand how the mojos can be doing all this. I mean, you've established their brain capacity is too small for intelligence, haven't you?"

"There's no particular need for intelligence in this," McKinley said. "It's the mojo's symbiont—either human or krisjaw—who actually assess the situation. The mojo simply picks up that evaluation and pushes for the response that is in the mojo's best interests."

"But that takes judgment, and *that* implies intelligence," Fairleigh persisted.

"Not necessarily," Telek shook her head. "Straight extrapolative logic could simply be part of the mojo's instinct package. I've seen instincts in other animals that appear to take as much or more intelligence than that would require. You'll notice that the Chata spookie seems to manage the same trick with only a slightly larger cranial capacity."

"It could be even easier, at least for the mojo," McKinley added. "Presumably the human comes up with his own list of possible responses, including—on some level—how each response would affect the mojo. Choosing among those takes no more intelligence than *any* animal needs to survive in the wild."

"Could you be reading the data wrong, somehow, then?" Stiggur asked. "We need to be absolutely sure of what's going on."

"I don't think we are, sir," McKinley shook his head. "We didn't get as many details out of Moff as Winward was hoping we would, but I think what he *did* say pretty well confirms this interpretation."

"Not to mention the krisjaw incident," Roi murmured. "There's no rational explanation for their behavior if the mojos weren't in at least partial control."

The room fell silent. Stiggur glanced around the table, then nodded at McKinley. "Thank you, Doctor, for your time. We'll get in touch if we have any more questions. You'll be able to give this presentation to the full Council tomorrow?"

McKinley nodded. "Two o'clock, right?"

"Right. We'll see you then."

McKinley went out, and Stiggur turned back to the table. "Any discussion before we vote on our recommendation?"

"How could something like this have happened?"

Vartanson asked, his tone almost petulant. "Symbionts don't just swap partners whenever they feel like it."

"Why not?" Roi shrugged. "I'm sure Lizabet could come up with dozens of other examples."

"Nothing like that many, but there are some," Telek nodded. "In this case, I think, you just have to look at the krisjaw's characteristics to see why humans look so attractive as partners. First off, the mojos need good hunters to kill bololins for them; but the viciousness that makes krisjaws good hunters also means a returning mojo probably has half a chance of being eaten itself until it reestablishes control. You saw the films of the attack—the mojos were barely off their krisjaws' backs before the animals went berserk."

"And their range is longer with humans?" Hemner asked.

"It seems to be, yes, but that may be only incidental," Telek said. "The real point is that humans with guns are simultaneously safer hunters *and* better hunters. That also means the humans seldom if ever lose the fight and get killed, by the way, which saves the mojo the trouble of finding and getting used to someone new."

"The training period being especially dangerous if it's breaking in a new krisjaw instead," Vartanson said, nodding heavily. "Yeah, I see now. What you're saying is that the Qasamans have made the planet a little slice of mojo-heaven."

Telek snorted softly. "Hardly. It may have been so once, but the mojos are rapidly heading down a dead-end street." She keyed her display, and an aerial map of the Fertile Crescent region appeared. "Down here," she said, tapping white spots onto the image with a pointer. "Here, here, and here. The Qasamans are adding on to their chain of cities."

"So?" Vartanson frowned.

"Don't you see? Cities are lousy places for a predator bird to live. They've got to fly long distances to do their own hunting or accept the equivalent of pet food from their masters. But the human population is increasing, and their cute little underground communication system requires them to stay in the same reasonably limited area of the planet. And *that* means cities."

"But I thought the cities were laid out expressly for the mojos' benefit," Roi growled. "That was your whole argument for the second study trip, remember?"

"For their reproductive benefit, yes," Telek nodded. "But not for their feeding benefit. I don't think we ever actually got to see a mojo hunting, but their usual prey is probably small birds or large insects; and no matter what the bololins and tarbines do, small birds are *not* going to venture into the cities in great numbers. The city design is essentially a compromise, and if I were a mojo I think I'd be feeling definitely cheated by it."

"Then why don't they switch back?" Vartanson demanded. "They did so once—why not do it again?"

"Switch back to what? Practically since they landed the Qasamans have been shooting every krisjaw that poked its head out of the grass. They must have the entire Fertile Crescent nearly cleared out by now, and they *still* pull people off work to go hunt the things every month or so. It's crazy."

"Maybe not," Jonny put in. "As you said, the Qasaman leadership knows what's going on. What better way to insure their bodyguards' continued loyalty than to make sure there's nowhere else for them to go?"

Telek shrugged. "Could be. They're certainly devious enough to come up with something like that."

"Which would imply, in turn," Jonny continued, "that they recognize the benefits of having mojos around to keep down interpersonal friction. If they consider that factor to be *that* important, perhaps instead of considering war we should instead be concentrating on getting rid of the mojos."

"How?" Telek snorted. "Kill them all off?"

"Why not? Whole species have been exterminated before, back in the Dominion. Species-specific pesticides can be made for *any* animal, can't they?"

"Theoretically, once enough is known about the animal's hormone sequence during breeding. We haven't got anything like that much data on mojos."

"We've *got* the time, though," Jonny persisted. "The tech assessment puts them at least fifteen years away from a stardrive."

"Won't help," Roi murmured. "The cities, Jonny. Any animal that would prefer a good breeding setup to a good feeding setup is going to be incredibly hard to kill off."

"Especially when the Qasamans will be on their side," Telek said. "Remember, whatever input the mojos had on the design of the cities, it was the humans who put them up. Could be that they actually didn't need much prompting after all—this arrangement encourages a steady supply of mojos for their growing population while at the same time keeps them on a short enough food leash that they won't just give up and go look for a krisjaw to team up with."

"And unlike the aviary approach, this looks more natural to the mojos," Roi mused. "Suckers them into thinking things are going their way while the Qasamans kill off every krisjaw for a thousand kilometers around."

Stiggur tapped his fingers gently on the tabletop. "The ultimate, crowning irony: the puppets conspire to keep the puppeteers with them."

"The crowning irony?" Hemner shook his head. "No. The crowning irony is Moff's last warning ... and the fact that, given their cultural paranoia, they might very well have cowered there on their one little world forever, afraid to venture into space where they might run into something they didn't like. If the Trofts hadn't poked at them, and persuaded us to do likewise, they might never have become even the smallest threat to either of us. Consider that when you're tempted to congratulate yourselves on how well we've handled this."

A long, painful silence settled on the table. Jonny shifted quietly in his chair, the dull ache in his joints echoed by the bitterness in his mind. Hemner was right; had been right, in fact, all the way from the beginning. And now the threat they'd worried and argued about was on its way to becoming a self-fulfilling prophesy.

And it was far too late to go back.

Stiggur broke the silence first, and with the words Jonny knew he would use. "Does anyone have a recommendation to make?"

Vartanson looked around the table, compressed his lips, and nodded heavily. "I do, Brom." He took a deep breath. "I recommend we accept the Baliu demesne's offer of five new worlds in exchange for eliminating the Qasaman threat."

Stiggur nodded. "Anyone else?"

Jonny licked his lips . . . but in his mind's eye he saw the Qasamans and their mojos moving on Chata, Kubha, and Tacta . . . and from there to the Cobra Worlds themselves. *We will come and find you*, Moff had said, and Jonny knew he'd meant it . . . and the objection he'd been about to raise died in his throat.

The others may have seen similar visions. Certainly, none of them spoke.

Three minutes later, Vartanson's recommendation became official.

It had been a long time since Justin had been in his Capitalia apartment. Standing at the living room window, gazing out at the city lights, he tried to count how many times he'd been back here since beginning his Cobra training . . . four months ago? Five?

The train of thought petered out from lack of interest. Sighing, he stepped back to his desk and sat down. The clean paper and magdisks he'd put there an hour ago were still untouched, and down deep he knew they were going to remain that way for a while longer. Tonight he could see nothing but the faces of the three men who'd been buried this morning, the Cobras who'd died getting the *Dewdrop* off Qasama. He hadn't even known there'd been casualties in the confusion of that time; hadn't known until they all arrived at the *Menssana* and he saw the bodies being carried by their friends.

Tonight was not the night to begin preparations for war.

The doorbell twittered. Governor Telek, most likely, come to check on his progress. "Come in," he called.

The door unlocked and opened. "Hello, Justin," Jonny said.

Justin felt his stomach tighten. "Hi, Dad. What're you doing out this late?"

"In the cold rain?" Jonny added with a half smile, shaking the last few drops off his coat before stepping into the apartment and letting the door close behind him. "I wanted you to come by the house tonight and your phone was off. This seemed the logical alternative."

Justin dropped his eyes to his desk. "I'm sorry, but I'm supposed to be working on . . . something."

"A battle plan?" Jonny asked gently.

Justin grimaced. "Governor Telek told you?"

"Not in so many words, but it wasn't hard to figure out. You've already shown yourself to have a surprisingly good tactical ability, and she was bound to want something to show the full Council tomorrow."

"Tactical ability," Justin said bitterly. "Oh, sure. A great plan, wasn't it?—except for the minor fact that Decker and Michael had to improvise an ending just to get us out. And even at that we lost three men."

Jonny was silent for a moment. "Most military plans wind up being changed somewhere along the line," he said at last. "I wish I could offer some words of comfort about the casualties, too, but only the inadequate line about them sacrificing themselves to save everyone else comes to mind. That one never satisfied me, either."

"So they sacrifice themselves for the mission, and the next thousand sacrifice *them*selves for the Worlds. Is that how it goes?" Justin shook his head. "Where do you draw the line?"

"Anywhere you can," Jonny said. "And the sooner the better. Which is why I want you to come back to the house tonight."

"A family round table?"

"You got it. We have until the Council meeting to come up with an alternative to war."

"Like a blockade or something?" Justin sighed. "It's no good, Dad—I've tried already to come up with a way to do that. But a planet's just too *big* to surround." He stared down at his hands. His Cobra-strong, Cobra-deadly hands. "We just don't have any other choice."

"We don't, huh?" Jonny said, and Justin looked up at the unexpected fire in his father's voice. "People have been saying that ever since the Trofts first suggested this mess. As a matter of fact, people have been telling me that for most of my life."

Carefully, Jonny got to his feet and walked to the window. "They told me the Trofts *had* to be thrown bodily off Adirondack and Silvern. Maybe they were right that time, I don't know. Then they said we Cobras *had* to stay in the Army because we wouldn't fit into Dominion society. Instead, we came to Aventine and built a society that could live with us. *Then* they said we had to fight the Trofts again or Aventine would be destroyed . . . and with a little work we proved them wrong *that* time, too. Don't ever accept that something bad *has* to be done, Justin; not until you've explored all the possibilities yourself." He coughed, twice, and seemed to slump as he turned back to face his son. "That's what I want you to help me do tonight."

Justin exhaled quietly. "What about Mom?"

"What about her? She doesn't want war, either."

"You know what I mean." Justin tried to get the words out, but his tongue seemed unwilling to move.

"You mean volunteering for the second mission without consulting with the family?" Jonny walked back to his chair and sank into it. "She was hurt by that, yes. We all were, though I think I understand why you did it. But watching her children go their own way has been one of the silent aches of being a mother since the beginning of time." He sighed. "If it helps any, I can tell you her fears and worries about you aren't entirely based on what you yourself have done. She's been ... well, *haunted*, I guess, by the memories and bitterness of the path *I* took after I'd done my service as a Cobra."

Justin frowned. "You mean politics? I know Mom doesn't care that much for politics, but—"

"You understate the case badly." Jonny shook his head. "She hates politics. Hates the time it's taken from us these past couple of decades. Hates what she sees as a wastefully high work-to-result ratio."

"But you were needed. She's told me herself you helped integrate the Cobras into the political system."

"Maybe I was needed once, but not any more. And with you seemingly determined sometimes to be a replay of me—well, it's brought things to a head."

"Well, she doesn't have to worry about me in *that* area," Justin said emphatically. "Corwin can *have* Aventinian politics, as far as I'm concerned. I'd rather hunt spine leopards any day."

Jonny smiled slightly. "Good. Why don't you come with me and tell her that yourself?"

"And while I'm there, come up with a way to stop a war?"

"As long as you're there anyway, why not?"

Justin shook his head in mock exasperation and

got to his feet. "Dad, you have *definitely* been in politics too long."

"So I've been told. Let's go; it's likely to be a long night."

The transfer module beeped its indication that the magdisk copying was complete. Stifling a yawn, Telek turned back to the phone and Jonny's waiting image. "Okay, I've got it," she told him. "Now you want to tell me why you had to wake me at—uh—"

"Four-forty," Jonny supplied.

"—at four-forty in the morning to receive a magdisk you could have sent to my office four hours from now?"

"Certainly. I wanted you to have those four extra hours to see if we've come up with an alternative to war."

Telek's eyes focused hard on his. "You've got a viable counterproposal?"

"That's what you're going to tell me. And the Council, if the answer is yes."

She licked her lips. "Jonny . . ."

"If it works, we *will* get the new worlds," he added quietly. "Corwin and I have already worked out how to sell the whole thing to the Baliu demesne as a reasonable fulfillment of their contract."

"I see. Thank you, Jonny. I'll get on it right away."

The Moreau Proposal, as the plan came to be called, eventually was given an eighty percent chance of success by the experts who studied it. Lower by several points than a properly managed war . . . but with vast savings in human and economic costs. After two weeks of public and private debate, it was accepted.

And two months later, the *Menssana* and *Dewdrop*, accompanied by two Troft troop carriers, once again headed for Qasama.

Chapter 31

Night on Qasama.

Again they dropped down silently, with only gravity lifts visible; but this time there were three ships instead of just one. The Troft transports set down in two widely separated wilderness areas along the inner curve of the Fertile Crescent, while the *Menssana* landed near the top of the Crescent's arc. For York, aboard the latter ship, it was a significant location: barely ten kilometers from the road connecting Sollas and Huriseem. A suitable place indeed for him to repay the Qasamans for his lost arm.

There was a crackle of split-frequency static from the bridge speaker. "*Dewdrop* to *Menssana*; hurry it up. We've got some very nasty-looking supersonic aircraft coming your way. ETA no more than fifteen minutes."

"Acknowledged," Captain Shepherd said calmly. "The Trofts drawing similar attention?"

"Not specifically, but we've got other aircraft scrambling in what looks like a search pattern toward their general location. They've been alerted."

"Better anti-radar equipment," York grunted.

"There they go," someone said from the bridge's left viewport.

York stepped to his side. The *Menssana*'s outer

floods had been dimmed to a soft glow, but there was enough light for him to see the silent exodus from the ship's cargo holds.

The mass exodus of spine leopards.

Most of the animals paused a moment as they stepped out onto the unfamiliar soil, looking around or visibly fighting for balance as the effects of their long sleep dissipated. But none lingered long by the ship. They loped off into the darkness of the forest, the mass already beginning to spread out as they vanished from view, and York could almost sense the eagerness with which they set out to study their new home. However they knew such things, they must surely know this was a world literally *full* of unclaimed territory. How large would their first litters here be, he wondered. Fifteen cubs? Twenty? No matter. An ecological niche existed, and the spine leopards would do what was necessary to fill the gap.

And with luck, the mojos would soon find they again had a choice of partners. York hoped to hell Telek was right about the birds' distaste for cities.

"All out," a voice came from the intercom. "Hatches sealed, Captain."

"Prepare to lift," Shepherd said. "Let's head home."

A moment later the ship was floating toward the stars. Peering out into the darkness, York sought one final glimpse of the almost literal seeds of discord they'd just sown on an unsuspecting world. *Be fruitful and multiply*, he thought the ancient command toward the spine leopards below, *and replenish the land. And subdue it.*

Chapter 32

"I understand," Joshua remarked, "that the Baliu Trofts weren't exactly overwhelmed by our solution to the Qasaman problem."

Corwin shrugged, his eyes lingering on the starfield for another second before turning to face his brothers. The *Menssana* was due to load at any minute and he didn't want to miss seeing that. "They weren't at all sure it was going to work, if that's what you mean," he told Joshua. "We had to pull out disks and disks of data that showed how really uncooperative humans normally were and how any progress toward space would be dramatically slowed or even halted altogether once the mojos deserted them."

"If they do," Justin murmured, his own attention still directed out the window.

"There *is* that," Corwin admitted. "Actually, the Trofts were more convinced that would happen than we were—it was the *results* of the change they weren't sure of. I get the feeling their biopredictor methods are a bit ahead of ours."

"Like everything else," Joshua agreed wryly. "Hey— here come Almo and Aunt Gwen."

"*There* you are," Gwen said as they came up through the milling crowd to the others. "I thought you'd be watching from around the other corridor."

340

"You get a better view of the passengers here," Corwin explained. "I was starting to think you were going to miss the event entirely."

Pyre shook his head. "We just came from saying goodbye. Everyone else had been shooed out already, but they made an exception for us. Amazing what being a hero will do for you."

The others chuckled—all except Justin, Corwin noted, who merely smiled slightly. Still, that was progress of a sort. The scars of his failings—real or perceived—were still visible, but at least they weren't bleeding any more. For his brother's sake alone Corwin could hope the Moreau Proposal succeeded.

"Jonny tells me you persuaded the Trofts to lend some troop carriers for the Caelian evacuation," Pyre continued. "How'd you sell them *that* one?"

Corwin shrugged. "Wasn't really hard. If the Qasamans *do* manage to get into space the Baliuies would just as soon they were as immediate a threat to us as to them. It's to their advantage to let us have the new worlds and help us a bit in settling them. Especially considering they've just saved themselves the cost of financing a war."

"There they go," Justin said suddenly.

Everyone turned to look. The line of passengers for the trip to Kubha—or Esquiline, as it'd now been officially renamed—were crossing the short distance from the old entrypoint building to the waiting ship. Near the front of the column Corwin spotted his parents, Chrys supporting Jonny with an arm around his waist but both walking with a firm tread. Bound for a new world. . . .

Behind him, Gwen sighed. "This really *is* crazy, you know," she said to no one in particular. "Emigrating in his condition—and to an untested world, yet."

"Not *entirely* untested," Pyre reminded her. "Besides, the hot climate there will be better for him than anything the civilized areas of Aventine have to offer."

"And there're no politics there, either," Justin murmured.

Corwin looked at the other, wondering how much he knew of that old parental sore spot. But Justin's face was giving nothing away. *Doesn't really matter*, Corwin thought with a mental shrug. What mattered was that his parents would have their last two or three years together away from the worst of Aventine's memories. Away from Aventine—and in precisely the same sort of culturally uncluttered world in which they'd first fallen in love. It was, Corwin thought, perhaps their best shot at happiness. He hoped it worked.

Together, the five of them watched Chrys and Jonny board the *Menssana*. Then Joshua let out a quiet breath and craned his neck to look down the hall. "I think we'll get a better view of the launch path from the gallery over there," he said, pointing. "Anyone want to come?"

"Sure," Gwen said. "Come on, Almo."

"I've seen enough lifting ships to last me both this life and the next," Pyre grumbled. But he nevertheless allowed her to steer him away.

Justin remained gazing out the window as the three left, and for a few heartbeats Corwin wondered if the other hadn't realized that he, too, had stayed behind. Then Justin stirred and glanced down the hallway. "You think they'll ever get together?" he asked.

"Who—Almo and Aunt Gwen?" Corwin shrugged. "Don't know. I guess it depends on whether Almo ever allows himself to give up the responsibilities of being a Cobra long enough to accept someone else into his life. You know better than I do how seriously he takes his job."

"Yeah." Justin was silent a long moment. "You realize if it doesn't work . . . well, Dad will be dead before the Qasamans can find the new worlds, but Mom might not be."

Corwin understood. "I don't know, Justin. But if the mojos really *do* leave them there'll be nothing in particular to unite them into a common front, warlike or otherwise. Especially since they'll probably flounder around for a while just getting used to the new competition. And if they're broken up into smaller states or factions they're as likely to open trade as to take shots at us."

Justin shook his head. "You're forgetting what they're like. I've seen them, Corwin, and I know they'll hold the grudge they have against us until their sun burns out. That kind of hate and fear will keep them working together against us, no matter what other competition arises."

"Perhaps," Corwin nodded. "But only if their paranoia level stays as high as it is now."

"Why would it change—?" Justin broke off as a look of disbelief crossed his face. "You mean . . . the *mojos* might have been behind that?"

"Why not? We know they can amplify human emotions when they want to."

"But what does it gain them to have their hunters jumping at shadows?"

"Well . . ." Corwin's lips twitched in a secret smile. "If *you* were convinced the universe was out to get you, where would you rather live? A city on a plain, or a village in the middle of a forest?"

Justin opened his mouth, blinked . . . and abruptly laughed. "I don't *believe* it."

"Well, maybe I'm wrong," Corwin shrugged. "But maybe in a couple of generations we'll find the Qasamans have become a perfectly reasonable society, ripe for trade and diplomacy."

"We can hope so, anyway." Justin sobered and turned again to the window. "It's so hard when the old folks leave the nest."

Corwin laid a hand on his brother's shoulder. "We'll

all miss them," he said quietly. "But . . . well, they're old enough to make these decisions for themselves. Come on, let's get over to the others. Traumatic times like this are what families were made for."

Together, they headed down the hallway.

ROBERT A. HEINLEIN

"Heinlein knows more about blending provocative scientific thinking with strong human stories than any dozen other contemporary science fiction writers."
—*Chicago Sun-Times*

"Robert A. Heinlein wears imagination as though it were his private suit of clothes. What makes his work so rich is that he combines his lively, creative sense with an approach that is at once literate, informed, and exciting."
—*New York Times*

Seven of Robert A. Heinlein's best-loved titles are now available in superbly packaged new Baen editions, with embossed series-look covers by artist John Melo. Collect them all by sending in the order form below:

TRAVIS SHELTON
LIKES BAEN BOOKS
BECAUSE THEY TASTE GOOD

Recently we received this letter from Travis Shelton of Dayton, Texas:

> *I have come to associate Baen Books with Del Monte. Now what is that supposed to mean? Well, if you're in a strange store with a lot of different labels, you pick Del Monte because the product will be consistent and will not disappoint.*
>
> *Something I have noticed about Baen Books is that the stories are always fast-paced, exciting, action-filled and seem to be published because of content instead of who wrote the book. I now find myself glancing to see who published the book instead of reading the back or intro. If it's a Baen Book it's going to be good and exciting and will capture your spare reading moments.*
>
> *Another discovery I have recently made is that I don't have any Baen Books in my unread stacks—and I read four to seven books a week, so that in itself is a meaningful statistic.*